The Dreadful Call and Other Stories of the Supernatural and Suspense

Written By Jon Ring

Illustrated by Vinessa Sanford

ISBN: 978-1-59152-280-5
Published by Jon Ring
Copyright 2021 by Jon Ring

For more information or to order extra copies of this book call Farcountry Press toll free at (800) 821-3874.

Produced by Sweetgrass Books
PO Box 5630, Helena, MT 59604; (800) 821-3874;
www.sweetgrassbooks.com
Sweetgrass Books is not responsible for the content of the author/publisher's work.
Produced and printed in the United States of America.
24 23 22 21 1 2 3 4 5

Table of Contents

A lot of people gave me their time, effort, suggestions and support during this endeavor. I would like to recognize their contributions, for without them this volume in your hands would not have been possible:

Kenny Ketner
Jodi Ring
Gil Silva
Jill Wofford
Marisa Mailand
Charles "Chuck" Buck
Jaesen Sheppard
Honey Ring
Ryan McDuffie
Lizbeth Potter
Joel Ring
Sean Brown
David Poelman
Terry Bieber
Mark Prichard
Draven Burfiend-Zyliak
Kim Barry
Ross Rinabarger
Will Condon
Ean Berg
Andrea Wilson
Kathy Springmeyer

Thank you all from the bottom of my heart,
Jon Ring

"You see me standing here beside you, and hear my voice; but I tell you that all these things—yes, from that star that has just shone out in the sky to the solid ground beneath our feet—I say that all these are but dreams and shadows; the shadows that hide the real world from our eyes. There *is* a real world, but it is beyond this glamour and this vision, beyond these 'chases in Arras, dreams in a career,' beyond them all as beyond a veil." - Arthur Machen, *The Great God Pan*

Tin Soldiers

The old man was having trouble with the door, struggling with the heavy oaken entrance, its weight ponderous with the solid construction and reinforcing iron bars on the portal's exterior. Mitch Connelly watched with a detached interest, born more of boredom than any real desire or care to see the fulfillment of the visitor's entry, but the incident had made him forgo his newspaper. The news had been decidedly uninteresting anyhow, mostly about the state funeral of Queen Victoria's youngest son Leopold and more talk of the United States' annexation of the Alaskan province from the Russian empire. He made no effort to help the elderly caller himself, preferring to stay behind his glass counter that housed various wares he had acquired in his dealings from previous guests.

Mr. Connelly was a pawnbroker, and typical of his breed, a cutthroat businessman that brooked no nonsense in his trade, looking for any edge, any angle, any trick that would put him ahead in his negotiations and trades. He had built his empire on the backs of the destitute souls that entered his shady domain, paying pittances for family heirlooms and valuable commodities from those unfortunate enough or foolish enough to request his nefarious services. A poor man, down on his luck, could bring in his deceased mother's china that she had scrimped and saved for years to finally obtain, looking to get just enough money to put food in his starving children's bellies while he was trying to find steady work. With a friendly smile, the glint of a few coins, and a false promise to let him "get it back when things turn up for ya" Connelly would gain possession of the items. The deal would be struck, and the contract would be signed, with all the hidden clauses agreed to with an unknowing signature. A month later the victim perhaps would return, finally able to put enough currency together to regain possession of his brokered items, only to hear "Sorry, the fees and maintenance aren't free you know. How much do you have? Not quite enough, but you can put some down towards it, and I'll keep it another month for you. Oh sure, anything for a friend and neighbor." And so on and so forth, until the hapless mark finally wises up and realizes that his treasure is hopelessly and entirely lost to him forever. Watching the old man now, with his cumbersome package so carefully tied in old twine, crushed to his chest with a protective embrace as he struggled with his free hand to pull the unwieldy door open, Connelly knew he would soon have another notch in his legion of monetary conquests.

Wearily the old man finally entered, and Mitch Connelly took stock of this latest sucker to walk through his doors. The man's garments were old and well-worn, but great care had been taken to patch the inevitable holes that had appeared from overuse. This generally meant a woman's touch at home Mitch knew, and he filed this tidbit away to use in the impending negotiations that would soon follow. His white hair was neatly cropped, and his horn-rimmed glasses bespoke a learned mind, so to Connelly that was a sign that if he was coming in the pawnshop that indeed the man's fortunes must have recently changed. He was quite different from Connelly's usual clientele, which generally were of the poorer class of London's dirty streets, uncouth and uneducated. The old adage he who speaks first in the deal loses was a favorite of Mitch's, so he waited patiently for the rube to state his purpose in the unexpected visit. He did not have to wait long for the sad story he knew was coming.

"Sir, my wife's sick, and I need money for her medicine," the old man began, his voice quiet and unobtrusive. "My tenure teaching history at the university was not as assured as I had thought, and I'm afraid the dean never did care for me, preferring the sycophants that crowd his halls to my more honest diatribes. When the opportunity arose, he did not hesitate to use it to his benefit and it cost me my position. We were able to scrape by awhile with myself doing tutoring work, and my wife doing some washing and darning, but once she took ill, more of my time was required to see to her various comforts. I took care of her the best I could, hoping she could pull out of it, but she only seemed to become more ill as time went by. Finally, as the situation became more dire I was forced to call on the doctor for aid, and he took what little monies we had remaining for the visit. He has diagnosed her condition, and I am hoping to secure enough with this," he patted the package softly, "to provide the cure for her future well-being."

Connelly had only half-heartedly listened to the man's story, not particularly caring for the reasons of why he was selling off his treasures, only listening and making perfunctory head shakes of agreement and noises of dismay at the appropriate times in order to gain the man's trust. A dastardly charade he was a master of, he spoke with well-practiced false empathy, "Sorry to hear that friend, perhaps I can help. Please show me what you brought so we can get the missus what she needs." The old man shook his head in agreement and obliged, placing the package on the counter-top with care, and slowly untied the brown string, removing it and folding back the cloth, revealing the hidden objects within. The contents both surprised and shocked the conniving pawnbroker, and he could not restrain his response.

"Toy soldiers?" His expression darkened, anger hinting in his voice at this obvious waste of his time.

"Yes, I obtained them years ago." The old man did not seem to notice the ire in Connelly's tone. "These are the pride of my collection. They were owned by Goethe himself!" Seeing the blank look on the pawnbroker's face, he explained further. "Johann Wolfgang Van Goethe, the famous German writer, scientist, and statesman. The father of the Romanticism

Movement. The great works *The Sorrows of Young Werther,* the *Roman Elegies...Faust?*" he asked, an incredulous tone in his voice. Connelly did not care for the perceived condescending attitude of the out of work professor, making a note to bilk him a few extra coins for the insult. However, the last entry did ring a faint bell in Connelly's memory and not one to let pride come before profit, he said, "Isn't that the story of the magician that makes a deal with the devil?"

"Indeed, indeed. *Faust* is one of his best known works. Exquisite detail in both script and direction. A veritable epic of man's eternal struggle of his strivings for power versus his wishes for atonement. Why, even Wagner made an opera of it, but typically romantic as it is..." Connelly let the old man continue with his tirade, while he examined the small metal men. They were in full military regalia, with tiny muskets held at attention in their minuscule hands. The detail was quite exquisite, and the painting from the little face down to the small buttons had been laboriously done true to both color and shade. Hefting one carefully to not alarm the still verbose learned man, he could tell the material used for the manufacture was solid, but probably made of tin instead of another more valuable, heavier metal. Three of the soldiers had a different look to them, and he realized that there was a sergeant, a lieutenant, and a captain, all correct in both insignia and uniform. The rest were privates, and he counted them, fifteen in total, making a contingent of eighteen that made a nicely even set. The soldiers were an upscale product, not his usual trade of more mundane items, but he did have his contacts within the more prestigious circles, and was fairly certain he could find a wealthy buyer for the tin soldiers fairly easily. The fact that a famous personage had owned them as well did not hurt his chances of extremely valuable payoff.

Connelly waited for the old man to finish his ongoing harangue on whether Goethe's statesmanship, literary skill, or scientific endeavors would be his greatest accomplishment. Before the aged educator could draw a breath to launch into another lecture, he said quickly, "I'll give you ten shillings for the lot. It's the best I can do in these trying times." The crestfallen look on his mark's face at the low number was priceless to Connelly's glee, and he felt he had repaid the old man for the boring prattle he had been forced to listen to unceasingly for the last few minutes.

"That's barely enough to cover her medicine, and I paid much more than that for them originally. Can't you do any more, please sir?" His begging tone made Connelly sick to his stomach, having no respect for any man in such a fool's predicament. His hardened heart knew no sympathy for those who required his services, no matter their reason. He was, however, adept at hiding his true feelings, and did so now as the time required it.

"I'm sorry, but the clientele that desire this sort of thing are lacking as of late. Everyday more factories are shutting down, jobs are lost, times are hard everywhere. In fact I'm giving more than I would usually for this sort of thing, on account of what's going on with your missus. I'm sorry I just can't do any more." He continued on, citing reasons from the mundane to the very acts of heaven itself of why no more could be paid for the items in question. Finally, at the end of his song and dance, he artfully pretended a feigned weariness of the situation and offered a couple more shillings, "just because he felt so bad for him and his wife". The poor man bought the act, hook, line, and sinker, and took the paltry sum, even thanking him profusely for the favor of having done so before he left the confines of the pawnshop. Connelly watched him leave, a cynical sneer on his face that changed to wide-split grin as soon as the old man had vanished.

"The old fool, what an idiot." Laughing at the ease of his new-found wealth and the naivety of the down-trodden professor, he went to pick up the parcel of toy soldiers and felt an excruciating pinprick on his thumb as he did so. Pulling his wounded hand back in amazement at the pain, he saw a tiny drop of blood welling up on the end of his finger. Looking down at the package he saw a sharp little bayonet sticking through the cloth, the obvious source of the assault. Placing his injured finger in his mouth to soak the wound, he used his free hand to carefully grasp the edges of the makeshift package, then carried the offending parcel into the storeroom behind his counter. Finding a free alcove on the wooden shelf, he deposited the package within to deal with later, and returned to the business of the front. He spent the remainder of the day in his usual manner, organizing and setting up items to sell, and of course bilking anyone unfortunate enough to enter his lair of ill-intent.

When the evening came Connelly shuttered the downstairs windows and locked the heavy front door, as was his normal routine, before retiring to his apartment upstairs. He lived alone in the small abode above the pawn shop. No wife for Mitch Connelly, his only love was that of the silver and gold variety. He made himself a hearty but plain supper in his tiny kitchen, and then afterwards retired to the den, and engaged in his favorite past time, counting his money. Pulling the worn oriental rug out of the way, he loosened the plank that hid the recessed access to his fortune. Taking the large bag from his hiding spot, he then took it to the telescoping table and horsehair armchair in front of the fireplace and after adding the day's profits to the store, counted it slowly and lovingly. He took his time, letting the feel of sovereigns, crowns, and guineas play through his hands as he caressingly tallied the coins. Once he had finished sorting he carefully stowed the treasures away again in their hidden cache, and then taking the lamp to his bedroom prepared for bed. He was sleeping a short time later, in a deep slumber that can only be enjoyed by the truly innocent saints and the most unrepentant sinners.

Connelly was awakened several hours later by a furtive scratching at his bedchamber door. Wiping the sleep from his eyes wearily, he noted that the offending noise was slight in volume, but significant enough to warrant an investigation on his part. It was most likely one of the countless rats that infested the city, but one could never be too sure about such things. He lit the lamp on his nightstand and once the light provided the needed illumination, reached for the drawer that held the flintlock pistol he kept at his bedside just for such emergencies. While he fumbled with the drawer to retrieve the weapon, he noticed that the scraping and scratching at the bedroom door had mysteriously ceased. Now properly armed, he approached the quiet door with great caution, seemingly more alarming now in its newfound silence than with the aforementioned clawing. He aimed the gun at chest height and with his other hand grasped the knob firmly, and in one fluid motion flung the door open to reveal the source of the unknown disturbance.

There was no sign of an intruder in the deserted hallway, but still holding the pistol at ready, he leaned forward and shined the lamp to the left and right of the entrance, peering into the darkness, trying to ascertain any sort of danger in the shadowy confines. Confidant that there was none, he stepped into the vacant hall, and was greeted by an extreme sharp pain in the bottom of his bare left foot as he walked forward. The pain was excruciating, and he madly hopped on his good foot, staggering back into the bed chamber until he reached the bed. Sitting down at the end of it, he placed the pistol next to him and brought his wounded extremity up with his free hand to examine the damage to his person. Bringing the light closer, he saw that a sharp nail had penetrated the flesh, and due to his unwittingly heavy step forward, was a good half inch inside of him. He pulled the offending piece of metal out, dark red blood pouring from the wound as he did so. Half hopping, half dragging the injured foot, Connelly made his way to the dresser, and opening one of the drawers, retrieved a pair of socks, and then returning to the bed, created a makeshift bandage from the items.

Rearming himself with the pistol again, and holding the lamp high, he gingerly stepped forward, testing the impromptu dressing. The pain from the puncture was acute, but bearable. The knowledge that someone must have placed the injurious nail in its detrimental position was not lost on him, and as he made his way back to the hallway, the disturbing thought that there must be an intruder in the building was foremost in his mind. He shined the light to and fro as before, but also thoroughly scanned the floor as well for further traps. Connelly was rewarded for his diligence, discovering several more nails arranged in neatly spaced rows. Any lingering doubts of the nature of his predicament vanished in that instant of discovery, and while he did not know what sort of strange game the interloper was playing, he planned on making him regret his unwanted trespass into Connelly's domain.

Making his way to the den at the end of the hall to check on the status of his concealed fortune, he entered the room and locked the door firmly behind him. He gave a momentary sigh of relief after finding no sign of the intruder's handiwork or personage after thoroughly checking the contents of the room. He saw that the position of the antique rug was blissfully untouched as well.

Still wanting to be sure of complete security of his fortune, he placed the pistol on the floor and opened the hidden compartment. Reaching inside the recess with his right hand, he felt a sharp slash across his fingers and he jerked his hand back in alarm and pain. Crimson blood welled across the lacerated digits, but concern for the well-being of his fingers was a distant consideration for him compared to the thought that someone had absconded with his wealth. Recklessly he shoved his hand back into the hole, and was savagely attacked again and again as he felt around blindly for his bag of money. His hand finally closed on the missing treasure, and he yanked the bag out quickly, taking even more stabs and cuts as he did so. He dropped the sack beside him, and cradling his hurt hand in his lap, he grabbed the pistol awkwardly with his left and pointed it at the dark hole in the floor. This was madness, he knew, that there was no way a man could have fit into the secret compartment, but his damaged phalanges told a very different story. Something was in that hole, and it had viciously attacked him. He retreated a distance away from the dark recess, taking the pistol and bag of money with him. Painfully ripping a irregular strip of cloth off his nightwear, he wrapped it around his bleeding hand while still keeping a vigilant watch on the cavity. He neither saw nor heard anything coming from the niche as he worked, and after his new wound was dressed, he picked up the lamp and carefully shined it above the compartment, trying to spy any movement within the opening. He even tried to illuminate further within the depths, but for safety's sake he could not peer in as far as he would have liked with his flammable light source. It would not do to add a fire to his list of troubles. For a brief moment he thought he saw a gleam in the darkness, like something metallic had reflected the light back, but it was so fleeting he was not sure if he had imagined it or not. His inspection complete, he considered the possibilities. A human being would have stolen the money, and could not have possibly fit in the hole. Could someone have cut an entrance from below the hidden cache and waited patiently to attack him? That possibility seemed extremely far fetched, especially considering the random nature of his choice to check his stash at that particular moment. Could it have actually have been a rat then, lurking inside the hidden recess and choosing that exact unfortunate time to strike? He disliked the option considering the previous event with the nail trap, but the two events could have been unrelated from one another.

The entire situation was quickly becoming thoroughly insane and untenable in his disbelieving mind. He had been a victim of a booby trap, then savagely attacked. Logic dictated that the happenings were separate, lacking any correlation, but the odds that two strange happenings in one hellish night would unfold simultaneously seemed to be well nigh astronomical in probability. Connelly decided to deal with one implausible problem at a time, choosing to the more pressing concern of the mysterious intruder that was probably still within his residence at this moment, doing God knows what to his inventory and property. Convincing himself at last that indeed an unwelcome rodent must have been the cause of the latest traumas to his person, but still uncertain of the safety of his treasure, he quickly stashed the bag under the cushion of his armchair for safekeeping while he attended to the matter of the trespasser. Strangely, he felt unseen eyes watching him behind his back as he did so, causing him to whirl around to see the source of the intuitive feeling, but he was forced to dismiss the instinctual notion as simple nerves after yet another thorough inspection of the room. He replaced the wooden board on top of the secret niche, but watching carefully for any sign or disturbance as he did so, and satisfied that none was forthcoming, recovered the hiding spot with the rug. Steeling himself for the inevitable showdown that would occur as soon as he found the culprit, he reluctantly unlocked the door and reentered the hallway, moving as quietly as his wounded state would allow. Carefully checking the bedroom first to see if his undesired guest had doubled back on him while he had been indisposed with the activities in the den, he headed next to the kitchen for investigation. The kitchen was deserted as well, with no suggestion of out of place happenings.

The upstairs now completely secured to his satisfaction, he turned his attention the door to the staircase that led down the pawnshop. It looked as though it was still shut as he had left it when he had retired to the upstairs apartment earlier, but upon closer inspection he saw that the door was open a barely noticeable hairsbreadth. As before he covered the area with the flintlock while grabbing the handle and flinging the door open violently, in order to hopefully shock the assailant into paralyzation and thus gain the upper hand in their exchange. Almost disappointingly there was no one there to receive his wrath, but to his surprise he saw several of the little tin soldiers arrayed on either side of the steps heading down. They were standing at attention, with their exquisite muskets held at shoulder level and miniature hands uniformly positioned at their sides, their tiny eyes staring unwaveringly forward almost as if they were participating in a military drill. Connelly wondered to himself whether the phantom intruder either had a very curious sense of humor or some baffling predilections. The silent honor guard inertly assembled on both sides was uncanny, almost surrealistic in nature as he began his descent past them to the shop floor. He conscientiously avoided stepping on the figures as he went, not wanting to destroy any of the valuable merchandise by careless footwork on his part. Hearing a clattering noise down below in the darkened pawnshop, he shifted his light and attention to spy further down the stairwell, attempting to find the source of the disruption. As he did so he suddenly felt minute stabs on his legs and feet as well as pulling on his lower night clothes, causing him to trip and lose his footing on the stairs from the vicious assault. He tried to recover, desperately attempting to regain his balance, but gravity had its uncompromising way. The accidental stumble turned to a full-fledged tumble down the stairs, his body going painfully end over end down the wooden stairs until he struck the hard stone floor headfirst with a loud crack. His mind, dazed from the shock, refused to function in its traumatic condition, and his vision swam alarmingly, with variations between pinpricks of light and empty blackness permeating his sight, rendering it useless. He blindly and groggily tried to rise in his disorientation, but the effort was too much for him and he sank into a black, dreamless sleep.

Connelly awoke later, unsure of how much time had elapsed or even that of his surroundings. His head throbbed mercilessly, and the rest of him was painfully bruised and battered as well. He could tell that he was standing, and his left arm and right leg were almost unbearable in their agony, pain shooting through his limbs like a torrent. That he may have broken them was an even more sobering prospect, but suddenly he smelled the acrid scent of smoke, and he forced his eyes to open despite his intense pain. After a moment to clear his still swimming vision, he saw light coming from his left. He realized the stairwell was on fire, flames licking up the sides and slowly spreading out to the walls. His lamp must have shattered after his fall, but how had he ended up right? Alarmed, he tried to move, but was hindered by an unknown source, not allowing him to walk forward or even bring his arms up. It dawned on him that he had been tied to one of the shelves out on his merchandise floor, and his struggles became more frantic but to no avail; he was unable to escape his bonds. Looking around for any help or solution to his new troubles, he saw strangely that tin soldiers were now arranged on the top of the counter. At first his mind refused to comprehend what his disbelieving eyes perceived, but then after staring at the unbelievable sight for several, heart-stopping moments he had to acquiesce to the validity of his vision.

The soldiers were moving, moving under seemingly their own volition! He saw that the little men were being led by the captain, who was solemnly watching them perform their duty as the lieutenant silently harangued his men to accomplish their task, dashing this way and that, exhorting them to move. The miniature privates themselves were wrestling with something larger than their diminutive forms, and he wondered what on earth they could be doing that so occupied them. Then the intent of their work became known, and he recoiled at the implication of their strenuous duty. They had his pistol, and were struggling to bring it to bear upon him! The shock of what was transpiring before his very eyes was difficult enough, but the realization that his unknown assailant and intruder had been of such an improbable nature shattered the last of his self-control. He yelled profanities at the tiny metal soldiers, screaming at them vile curses as he struggled ineffectually to extricate himself out of his fastenings. Horrified, he could only watch as they managed at last to right the flintlock, balancing it between them, and then aimed the squat barrel at him with deadly accuracy, awaiting the final order. The captain pulled his miniature sword out and pointed it at him, an act that seemed to prophesize Connelly's impeding doom to him even further.

He could feel tiny hands grasp him on the sides of his head and face, and he shrieked in dismay and terror at their cold, inhuman touch, shaking his head vigorously back and forth to dislodge them. A rough cloth began working its way down over his head, and realizing that the sergeant and some of the privates were attempting to blindfold him with one of the burlap bags from his storage room. He tried to thwart their progress, but they were diligent in their duty and succeeded in their appointed task in spite of his frantic twisting and turning to the contrary. The darkness and isolation inside the sack was maddening in its totality, with only his own heightened breathing and the increasing sounds of the expanding fire in abundance to his diminished hearing, with the occasional sharp patters of tiny feet receding from behind him. A lone tin bugle sounded out a few solemn notes, followed by the roar of the pistol, and then he heard no more.

****

The old man heard the slight scratching at the door despite the noise of the passing traffic and his advanced age, supposing that the rasping sound was the cat interested in returning indoors from his nightly dalliances and explorations. The ex-professor had been lost in thought, sitting in the small kitchen while his wife laid in their small bed. The terrible coughing spells that had so troubled her as of late were thankfully absent. He had been wondering what they would do next, the little money he had received for the last few valuable items they had owned was now gone, and their predicament was growing increasingly calamitous. The small amount of income he still received from the occasional tutoring he performed did not even cover the rent on the squalid apartment, let alone food or any of the other needs for their continued survival. It would not be long until the landlord was coming around to collect the payment again, and the red-headed giant did not seem to be the type of person who cared for his renter's trials and tribulations in the least. Fortunately the money he had received from that nice pawnbroker Mitch Connelly had afforded them the medicine his wife had so desperately needed, and it seemed to be working to restore her condition, if the current improvement in her situation was any hopeful indication. But the fact remained that even if she made a full recovery they would both soon be facing homelessness and possibly even starvation in the coming month, and that stark truth was the constant fear crowding into his thoughts this morning.

Shaking his head to clear the dark ruminations from his mind and rising to attend to the matter of the cat, he walked slowly to the door. Opening it, he was surprised to see that instead of the feline he had expected there was a large burlap sack, obviously full and sitting boldly on his front entrance. He looked both ways down the deserted hallway, but saw no sign of the benefactor of the item. His curiosity peaked, he bent down and retrieved it, taking it inside with him and shutting the door behind him. The sack was heavier than it had appeared, and as he deposited it on the kitchen table it made a clinking sound. Perturbed by the odd sound and the strange appearance of the gift, he was preparing to open the bag when he heard a soft, familiar voice behind him.

"What's that you have there, Edmund?" He wife was standing in the hallway, looking in on him from the entryway to the kitchen. Her forehead was damp from perspiration, and her hair was disheveled from her nap.

Fearing for her safety, he rushed over to her, crying out, "Eleanor, you shouldn't be up, you need to rest my love, remember what the doctor said."

She waved him off, sitting down in the rocking chair she was so fond of. "I'm fine, really. I just can't lay in bed any more. I'll go back in a while. I just need to sit out here with you for a bit." He argued with her, only staying his dissent once she had agreed to let him fetch a blanket for her to cover with while she sat. Returning to the table with the inexplicable sack, he opened the end and peered inside, giving a loud exclaim that gave his wife a start.

"What's the matter, Edmund?" He turned towards her, ashen faced, and slowly emptied the bag onto the table before her. The contents within spilled out with abandon, coins rattling as they fell, a hoard of them, a momentous pile of money, sovereigns, crowns, and guineas amassing before him even as he added to it. She let the blanket fall to the floor heedlessly and rushed over to him, awestruck by the gigantic fortune. He continued to pour, and as the last coins emerged a familiar package fell from the bottom of the burlap sack. Hands shaking, he placed the sack down and slowly unwrapped the package, knowing what was within even before he set his eyes on the contents. It was the tin soldiers he had pawned, each one laying down side by side next to their brethren. He could only stare, until his wife interrupted his reverie.

"Didn't you say you had to sell these for the medicine, Edmund? What are they doing here?"

"I don't know Eleanor. That nice pawnbroker must have returned them. But all this money! I can't believe it. He must have had a change of heart, I knew he was a good man. But this is too much, we can't possibly keep this." His wife agreed with him, and he resolved to go see their deliverer in person, and at the very least insist on returning some of the money. There was enough here for them to be comfortable a very long time, if not the rest of their lives. It must have been some kind of mistake, a little generosity was one thing but this! Fetching his hat and coat, he kissed his wife goodbye and left on his errand.

He made his way down the street where the pawnshop lay, but upon arriving he was horrified to see the shop was gutted by fire, burnt down to the very stones. Several men were shoveling the ashes and debris into a nearby wagon, and he hurried over to them to ask what had happened. One of the men stopped his labor long enough to answer his query.

"The whole thing burned to ground last night, sir. The pawnbroker, they found his skeleton inside. Poor bastard must have accidentally set it, and then must have not been able to get out. Terrible way to go, burning." Turning back to his compatriots, he resumed his work. The old man stared for a few minutes at the destroyed structure, trying to comprehend the turn of events, then shook his head and headed back home. Sometimes, he thought, perhaps it is better not knowing.

The Open Door

The door was open again. He knew he had shut it just this morning, and in fact had checked it twice just to ensure that he had done so. But there it was gaping widely, maddeningly halfway open just like the last time he had discovered it ajar. The disorganized shelves inside were filled with the odds and ends from a lifetime not his own, barely visible in the poor lighting from the storage room's curtained window. He went over to the offending portal, looking inside tentatively. What he expected to see within the storeroom's gloomy interior he did not know, it wasn't like someone would jump out from the shadowy confines to scare him on a lark, he thought wryly. He closed the door, just like he had done the day earlier, and like each time in the preceding few weeks he had found it in that particular state. The door and its accompanying room had been a mystery to him from the start, ever since he had first inherited the house after his great uncle had passed away unexpectedly.

He had barely known the estranged man, his relative not the sort of person to involve himself in family affairs. What little he knew of him had come from his mother's sketchy knowledge on the topic; that he was his grandmother's older brother, his name was Thomas Graham, and he had lived to the ripe old age of ninety-six. He had left home at an early age, joining the Navy and serving with distinction before settling down with his new wife. He had met her while on holiday in Scotland, and after a brief but torrid courtship, they married. Shortly thereafter he was reposted to Mississippi, where the happy couple had moved into an antique manor in the countryside there. When it came time for his reassignment he had retired his post instead, choosing to stay in the southern state. The rustic mansion was his home for the remainder of his life, even after his wife and what was to be his first of his progeny both tragically died during the childbirth.

The very same house that now he, his estranged relative Liam Hastane, had taken up temporary residence in. It was a glorious relic from the 1850s, done in the exceptional eclectic style of architecture made from blending both the Greek Revival method with the Gothic and Italianate styles into a seamlessly innovative structure, with spacious consideration inside with its two cavernous main floors and thirteen luxurious bedrooms. His great uncle had left the ostentatious house to him, though he had never met the man, not even once in his thirty-three years. He had not even presumed that his great uncle had known of his existence, let alone that he would have been gracious enough to include Liam in his will so lavishly.

The mansion had been a fortunate gift, and his wife had

used the opportunity to try to rekindle their failing relationship, insisting on a three-month vacation to the Mississippi property. Their marriage had been rocky at best the last few years, ever since her doctor had delivered the devastating news of their infertility. The information had struck her hard, and she had become distant, wallowing in her self-pity. She had needed his support more than anything, but he had been unavailable, the demands of his job making him blind to her suffering. He had been constantly working in that period, one project after another, a ghost in their house showing up at meals and bedtimes, with little to say to his wife before sleeping or returning to his labors. She had been very insistent on the idea of spending time together, but he wasn't sure that it was the idea of vacationing in a southern manor that had appealed to her so much, or the simple reasoning that he would be home for three months, unable to avoid his various husbandly duties. His boss had not been pleased of the idea of an extended sabbatical, but since he had not taken a vacation in years his boss had capitulated at last, granting the surcease after realizing that Liam, or more accurately his wife, was not willing to kowtow on the subject.

The trip down from their home had been uneventful, just endless driving for miles and miles until they had reached the Mississippi line. There the placid weather had turned suddenly sour, the wind picking up tremendously, ripping leaves and small branches off trees and blowing dirt and debris freely over the roadway. Driving rain ensued as well, making the road difficult to see, and the accompanying lightning and thunder came a tad too close for comfort in steady intervals, further complicating the matter. Normally driving was something Liam enjoyed, but in this case he had never been happier to see his destination, even looking unkempt and dismal as it did in the inclement conditions. The very first time he had visited the house he had explored the place from the yawning attic all the way down to the catacomb-like basement with its unfinished dirt floor. At that bottom level he had found a small room tucked away in the very back, its door halfway open in an inviting way. It was an unassuming room, filled with things his great uncle had not needed but had considered too valuable to throw away, neatly stacked on rough cut lumber shelves, dusty from disuse and lack of cleaning.

This was the exception to the rest of the house, which had been kept immaculately scrubbed and polished by the cleaning women who came every Thursday at ten like clockwork. The ladies were a team of mother and daughter housekeepers. When he questioned them on why they were still doing the work in spite of their employer having passed on, the elder woman said simply that he had paid them through the rest of the year before he died, and they were not ones to take advantage of someone just because he had "crossed over" as she put it. It went against what the good book said, and that was the end of that. When Liam asked her specifically about why that particular room did not receive the same treatment as the other ones, she had almost seemed afraid, and had hurriedly stated that his forbearer had insisted that they never enter that room, not to clean it or for any other reason, ever. Their strange behavior had seemed odd to him, but not wanting to alienate the free help he let the affair go, not deeming it worthy of pursuing, and simply closed the door. All had seemed well in the beginning, until he had gone downstairs again, and had noticed the door open again.

He closed it, and had gone upstairs afterward, asking his wife whether she had been in storage room to get anything out of it, or if she had opened the door for any other reason. He was greeted with a blank stare, and he had not pressed the matter further, knowing from her facial expression that she was thinking perhaps he was becoming a doddering old fool. The lack of interest from her concerning Liam's investigation into the unexplainable phenomenon was frustrating, and he found her condescending tones perhaps even more irritating than her lackadaisical attitude, saying that he must have left it open and forgotten about it.

"After all," she had said sardonically, "You have so much trouble remembering important things like my birthday and our anniversary, so perhaps your memory is slipping in your approaching old age."

"Ha ha, very funny," he had replied in mock banter, but inside he had seethed at her words. He knew he shouldn't feel that way, but the constant proximity to his wife was wearing on his nerves, like a wound festering and itching madly. They say absence makes the heart fonder, and before his work provided a welcome distancing between them, a bubble to recharge his store of affection and attachment to the woman he had married. Even if she had not always felt the same. Maybe he was turning into a crotchety old man, he mused, especially if he couldn't even handle a few months of uninterrupted couple time. Anyway, as certain as he was that he had closed it, perhaps he had just thought he had done so.

His wife had gone into town that morning, for provisions she deemed indispensable to their new abode, in spite of the overcast skies that warned of an impeding storm. So it was that he was currently alone in the big house, left to his own devices to amuse himself for the day. The day earlier he had double-checked the offending doorway before returning to the airy upstairs, finding it closed and shut just like it should be. But today he could not get the thought of its mysterious opening out of his mind, and soon he found himself back in the rear of the cellar before long. Confoundedly the door was open again, almost defiantly berating him with its silent insistence. It was beginning to drive him mad with its perpetual breaching, and he meant to solve the confounding mystery. Another man might have simply not cared, and just would have no longer visited that particular, entirely unnecessary section of the cellar, but Liam was as stubborn and fiery sometimes as his Celtic ancestors, and once he had made up his mind about something there was no convincing him otherwise.

He resolved to prevent the door's aberrant conduct, by replacing the simple knobs on its frame with more sturdy ones equipped with locks. Never one to spend money frivolously, he first attempted to search in the storage room, to see if in the mounds of junk the item he was looking for was there by some chance fortune. He discovered the room did not even possess any sort of electric lighting, probably having never been wired for it at all. He opened the rough fabric curtains, but the small amount of light coming through the only tiny cellar window would have been minuscule even on a day even more sunny than the current one, so he went back upstairs to retrieve the flashlight. He blessed his wife's foresight in packing what he had not even remotely considered important for their stay, and was able to resume his investigation. It was strange, but as he searched he was forced to periodically stop and raise his head to look about the room, even at one point asking if someone was there, thinking that his wife had returned from her excursion early and had entered the small area unbeknownst to him. No one was there, but slight, seemingly disquieting noises broke the tranquil silence infrequently, startling him ever so often, as well as the unexplainable feeling of unseen eyes watching him while he rummaged around the cluttered shelves. He tried laughing it off as his own wild imagination, a simple reaction to his non-comfiture of being alone in the darkened cellar room, but the uncomfortable feeling remained.

The random possessions of his grand uncle he found interesting, finding amongst other things, a lantern possibly of pre-Civil War origin, various old traps and snares, and even a brown bottle with a faded label proclaiming its contents, "Dr. Calatin's Wonderous Life-Changing Elixir." The boisterous explanation claimed to not only extend the lifespan of an average man by twenty years, cure baldness, and increase the sexual drive of the imbiber, but was a refreshing, great-tasting beverage as well. While wonderfully distracting, the items he found were completely unsuitable for the purpose he had set his mind upon pursuing. He was about to quit his poking around, when at the very bottom of one of the shelves, he found a large steamer trunk lying under some dirty muslin curtains. Pulling it from its dusty hiding spot, he noticed while it was heavy, it was not unduly so, and he wondered what strange things were being held within its secretive confines. It was tightly shut, and when he tried the heavy padlock keeping it closed it was unfortunately locked, resisting his attempt to open it. Not to be deterred, he hunted around in the storage room, hoping to find the key simply lying around in the odds and ends littered on the shelves, but after a few moments he gave up, realizing that the object must be kept somewhere else in the house, if indeed it was still around. The unnerving feelings from before were still plaguing him anyway, so he decided that after his wife came back with their car he would go into town himself. There had to be some kind of hardware store that had the door knobs he desired. He retreated back upstairs, after of course closing the door to the storage room firmly behind him.

The Open Door

When he reemerged from the darkened basement, he noticed immediately that the weather had indeed taken a turn for the worse, the crashes of thunder intermixed with the patter of heavy rain on the rooftop. He searched the upstairs for the lost key, first checking the drawers in the kitchen, then the multitude of bedrooms, parlor, and various closets. It was nowhere to be found, so he moved next to the master bedroom that he and his wife had claimed for the duration of their stay. After checking the filigreed night stands, ornate dressers, and grand closet, he began to doubt the very existence of the missing key, and decided to sit down on the bed to contemplate his next course of action. Directly across from him hanging on the wall was an oil painting, one he had seen nightly since sleeping in the chamber. He had not truly looked at it after his wife's exclamations of amazement had forced him to do so, art not being a particular interest of his, but he did so now, noticing for the first time the exquisite detail in the lines and the brazen, vibrant colors splashed across its surface.

It was a massive affair that seemed much too large for the room to be honest, featuring a woodland scene of an overgrown mound in the backdrop, with a tall, regal raven-haired woman standing in the foreground, surrounded at all sides by the thick wilderness of plants. He had not noticed it before but he could make out small humanoid shapes in the background now that it had captured his attention, little men and women peeping curiously from the green tangles of brush and trees. They were exceedingly difficult to see, but he found more and more of the tiny figures the longer he gazed at the remarkable painting, crawling under a limb in one area, or a petite face peering through the leaves in another location. It was bizarre, but he actually did not like the look of the miniature people, some seeming crafty in their disguised countenances and others downright malevolent in their evil-looking dispositions. It was an engrossing activity, however, trying to spot all the little denizens of the forest mound despite their grotesque appearance, and directly he stood and went over to the artwork to spy closer, as to not miss any of them hiding in their veiled kingdom.

He noticed that the bottom corner of the scenery seemed obscured somehow, and reaching up he brushed it with his hand, thinking it was some sort of blemish or perhaps debris that had collected over the years in that particular location. It felt cold and bumpy, and something small fell from the painting to the carpeted floor below. He stooped over and picked it up, and his heart beat surged a pace, realizing just what he held within his hand. It was a dark green key, and he saw that different colors had been painted across its surface, vibrant shades that been carefully matched to the painting. He took the item and compared it carefully to the corner it had fallen from, turning it around and around until it almost magically vanished from his view, a clever trick of camouflaging the object from vision while hiding it in plain sight. Almost joyous he headed back downstairs, an innate part of him absolutely certain of the key's ability to unlock the puzzling steamer trunk.

That was, until he saw the door, halfway open again in the dim lighting coming from the cellar windows. He walked carefully towards the opening, trying to move as quietly as possible in case there really was someone hiding inside the room. He had brought the flashlight again with him, and while it was a simple hard plastic spotlight lantern he had bought years earlier, the heft from its four D batteries felt vaguely reassuring in his hand, and he flicked it on, shining the light into the darkened storage room. He saw a pale, white face in between the door and its frame, and he nearly dropped the flashlight in terror. Liam backpedaled furiously and yelled, or more honestly screamed, at the top of his lungs from the shock of the unexpected sight of someone who should not have been there.

He stopped his retreat and shined the light again on the gap, wanting to keep the intruder in sight at all times. There was no one there now, but he had seen that face, thin and wasted, a moment earlier, and he strained his hearing while he stared, trying to use his ears as well as his eyes to locate the trespasser. As he shined he heard nothing, so fixing his eyes firmly on the open door he began to slowly back up again, not wanting to take the light off and turn around for fear of being attacked as he left the vicinity. He heard a voice upstairs calling out to him, filtering down the staircase along with the stomping of feet on the upper floor, and he realized his wife had returned from her outing in town, and he screamed her name to get her attention.

"SHARON! SHARON!"

His wife came to the top of the stairs, and returned his response crossly. "What is it Liam? What are you-"

"SHARON! THERE'S SOMEONE ELSE DOWN HERE CALL THE POLICE!"

"What, what do you mean someone's down there?"

"THERE'S SOMEONE DOWN HERE, FOR GOD'S SAKE WOMAN CALL THE COPS!" He heard her run to get her phone, and then could hear her frantic voice on the line as she finally did as he had instructed. He kept the light trained on the door the entire time, not willing to let whoever it was back in that room out of his sight for one second, to possibly murder him and then his wife upstairs. He heard footsteps retreating upstairs, and for a moment he thought she had deserted him to his fate. However, soon he heard light footsteps coming back towards him and down the stairway, and then he saw his wife descending, a long poker from the fireplace in her slim hands.

"Who is it, do you know? Is it some kind of homeless person, or a prowler, or what?" she whispered a tad too loudly to him, and he winced at the sound, even though earlier he had been screaming at the top of his lungs without any inhibition. She motioned to the staircase. "We should go upstairs and bolt the door to the cellar, so they're trapped and can't get out." It was sound advice, so they crept up the old stairs, wincing at every creak and shudder on the ancient wood steps. He kept the light marked on the open doorway, until he could do so no further, then urged his wife upstairs quickly so he could follow suit. They ran the last few steps with the enthusiasm only rampant fear can muster, slamming the door shut behind them and bolting the simple latch in place.

He seized the poker from his wife, and watched the closed cellar door anxiously, guarding the exit until the police came. They promptly arrived thirty minutes later, two cars from the Ulster County sheriff's department. Liam brought them up to speed on the current situation, telling them quickly of the entire ordeal from the beginning. They listened to his story closely, then had him wait outside on the lawn with his wife. He noticed that the weather had resumed its normal tranquil aspect, the rain glistening on the grass the only sign of the tempestuous passing from earlier. The officers returned several minutes later, and informed Liam and his wife that whoever he had seen was no longer there, and after inspecting the perimeter of the building reported no signs of forced entry on any of the tiny basement windows. One of the policemen, an Officer Baruch, asked him if the intruder could have fled past him, or at any point if he had quit his continuous watching of the exits, of either the cellar's downstairs entrance or the partially open storage room's doorway. He again said no, stating that the literal only time that either area had not been watched by him was the brief seconds in which he and wife had bolted for the upstairs, and at no time could have anyone slipped past them. Officer Baruch took his wife to the side, speaking softly to her in tones Liam could not hear while the other officer completed taking his statement, before the former parties rejoined the latter. The policemen left their card, explaining to call if they had anything further to report. Liam, watched them pull out of the driveway, his wife beside him, waiting for the officers to finish leaving before addressing her.

"What did Officer Baruch say to you? You looked anxious."

She laughed and replied back sassily, "He had wanted to know if you had any history of mental problems or substance abuse. Don't worry, I kept your stay at the ward in Warm Springs safe as well as your continuous cocaine use secret." She laughed again, making light of the situation, but he was in no mood for such antics.

"That's not funny. So he really thinks I imagined the whole thing."

"Well, look at it from his point, Liam. You tell him you watched the doors the entire time, and he saw no signs that someone broke in, so what is he supposed to think?"

"Oh, so you're taking his side? Now you think I imagined it."

"You've been crazy about this door for how many days now?" she spitefully retorted. "You've been obsessing over it since we got here. Maybe you just did imagine it Liam. God forbid you show an interest in this marriage, you choose to fixate over a damn door instead-"

"I saw it, Sharon, that face in the doorway was real."

"Fine Liam, let's go down there then." Her voice was rising in pitch now, the octaves grating harshly in his ears the way it always did when she took that particular tone. "The cop said no one was there, let's go."

Irritated at her refusal to believe him, he roared back, "Fine, let's go then." They both went downstairs, him leading the way, and soon they were standing in front of the doorway. It was wide open now he could see, the police leaving it that way after completing their search of the basement's confines. He stepped into the small room warily, his wife following closely behind. It was empty, save for the dirty items and shelves that should be inside, but there were definitely no signs of any intruder or hostile intent, or any sort of change at all. Everything was exactly as he had left it before, down to the last detail, including the locked trunk where he had pulled it from its hiding spot. His senses had said someone was there, but had someone truly been there? Had it merely been a trick of the light, or a mind so drawn into an idea that it had fabricated what it needed to justify its existence? He had been so certain of the pale face's reality earlier, but now in the light of the police officers' and his wife's disbelief, and with all the evidence pointing contrarily averse to his explanation of the event, he was not so sure as before, and his resolve in proving he was right wavered.

"You're right," he said wearily, "No one's been down here."

Her expression softened as he finally gave in to the overwhelming logic, and she said supportively, "I know you think you saw something, and I really think you did. But it wasn't what you thought it was, the police checked and no one's here. We don't see anyone here. Maybe it was a reflection from the light or something else, I don' t know." She placed her hand encouragingly on his arm, her eyes reflecting the genuine concern for his well-being. He clasped her hand gratefully, appreciating the gesture and fervently needing the emotional reinforcement that her look and touch entailed with their clearcut meaning. He reached out to her, needing more, and she came to his warm embrace eagerly, holding him as tightly as he held her. They stayed there a moment, each simply enjoying the basic pleasure of each other's contact and caring, something they had not done in a long time.

They left the room and went back upstairs, not before he carefully closed the door again. He helped her prepare dinner, slicing and chopping what she asked of him while she readied the meal. They made small talk while they worked, her telling him of the day in town while he listened and asked her questions periodically to clarify her details. Once the meal was ready they sat down together to share it, and afterwards they played a game of checkers in the parlor. They retired to their bedroom later, full of ardor for one another that the touches earlier had not assuaged. Afterwards both fell asleep entangled together in a close embrace, content and filled with love and devotion for each other.

However, sleep for him was fitful and plagued with disturbing imagery, and he dreamt of raging storms and secretive people watching him from unseen directions, hidden from his view but the sensation of their malice stabbing him like icy daggers. Dread coursed through his veins, and finally he saw the wasted, pale face loom before him, pleading to him in a language he could not understand, before he woke drenched in sweat, less from the humid Mississippi air than from the unknown terror caused by the reverie. He looked over at his peacefully slumbering wife, her chest rising and falling in a perfect state of euphoria in contrast to his still rapidly beating heart. The dream had thoroughly roused him, and while he sat pondering its disturbing quality his eyes roved the room languorously, more of inclination than any real need or purpose. The thin lace curtains did little to shut out the light of the nearly full moon, and his eyes easily picked up the shrouded details in the dark room, such as the embossed vanity strewn with his wife's belongings, and the spinning blades on the ceiling fan. The humming from the appliance was the only sound he heard, the white noise from its electric engine satisfyingly droning in continual vibration. He looked at the large hanging wall clock, making out the present time, a quarter past three o'clock.

He turned his attention to the over-sized painting on the wall nearest to the foot of the bed, the moonlight giving it a ghostly, ethereal quality not seen in the light of day. The woman seemed paler, her features pinched and withered, and instead of striding confidently forward she seemed like she was running away to him now, afraid of the secreted folk of the green mound. He tried to catch a glimpse of the tiny observers, but even with the bright moonbeams to illuminate the artwork they were hidden from his view. Still he endeavored to do so, but the more he stared at the enigmatic picture, the more uncomfortable *he felt,* like the wee people were staring back at him from their concealed settings, watching him for their own nefarious, inscrutable purposes. It finally grew so intense he was forced look away from the painting, and when even that did not abate the aggravating sensation, he decided to rise and fetch a glass of water, thinking the physical activity might clear his head. There was no reason why he should feel that way he knew, it was just an old artwork, another relic from his great uncle's past life that had no bearing on his own. He tried to be careful as he left the bed, not wanting to disturb his wife as he rose. She shifted from her back to her side in a seeming response to his movement, but whether she did so unconsciously or simply did not care what he was doing he did not know.

He passed his discarded pants lying on the floor and scooped them up, before exiting the bedroom and softly closing the door behind him. He walked down the hall a short ways before struggling his jeans back on, and while he did he felt a sharp pinch on his upper thigh. Reaching into his right pocket to discover the culprit, his hand closed on the green key he had found earlier, forgotten by him after the excitement involving the mysterious face and the police. He pulled it out and walked into the kitchen, studying it in the bright moonlight. He felt compelled to use it, to go downstairs and unlock the antique chest and see what it contained. It felt very natural to do so, in spite of the late hour. Recovering the flashlight from its resting place, he opened the cellar door and after carefully shining the flashlight down the stairs, proceeded to walk quietly down them, not wishing to wake his wife with undue noise on his part. The cellar itself was surprisingly well lit, the moonlight streaming in through the small windows at a prodigious amount he would not have thought possible. He made his way to the back of the room, and was relieved that when he ultimately shined the flashlight on the fickle doorway the entrance was still mercifully closed, just as he had left it.

He opened the door, the storage room's interior black as pitch in comparison to the illuminated main cellar, the dirt on the window blocking the majority of the moon's rays. He cast the light about the floor, not wanting to trip in the darkness, and presently saw the steamer trunk. Crouching down, he retrieved the key from his pocket, and slid it into the waiting padlock. He twisted, and at first it resisted, his hopes sinking as it did so, but then it clicked audibly, and he was able to remove the restraining device from the chest. He raised the lid, then shined his flashlight into the yawning opening, peering into it excitedly, anxious to catch his first glimpse of the secretive innards within. There was something white on top, and he pulled it forth, realizing quickly that it was an old-fashioned wedding dress, covered in frilly lace and small pearls.

He put it carefully to the side, and looked back in the chest, seeing three objects lying in its bottom. One was a small, oval stone, and it had evidently been carved by an unknown sculptor, its surface covered in intersecting lines, with runic letters and symbols neatly shaped within the criss-crossing outlines. It looked old, a bygone relic that looked out of place even in these austere surroundings. The second object was a heavy steel-encased barometer, its metal shell worn and shiny from use and age, but the glass face still intact, and the miniature hands still undamaged. It seemed to be functional as well, and remembering his lessons of long ago, he knew that the small black hand meant the current pressure, and it was pointing at 29.9. The gold hand, which could be adjusted, was set at 29.2, and he understood that to be a low pressure, usually equated with rain or bad weather. It seemed strange to him that someone would have set the device to that particular configuration, but he placed the barometer to the side for now, leaving that specific detail for later analysis.

Instead he lifted the final object out, a small parcel painstakingly wrapped in oilcloth to prevent moisture seepage, tied with brown string in a simple shopkeeper bow. The knot easily parted with a tug, and he folded back the package's casing to reveal its contents, a leathery, thin book, with the word "Memories" embossed on the front cover, in neat, engraved lettering. He opened the volume, and saw the name inscribed inside was his great uncle's, along with a cryptic remark, "Of the events following the solstice of June 21, 1967". Flipping quickly but gently through the slender work, he was able to surmise in a short span that it was a sort of diary, kept by his relative over the course of many years. He resolved to review the journal at a later time, and after replacing the ornate wedding dress back in the steamer trunk he gathered the stone, book, and barometer up, taking them with him as he departed the storage room. He shut the door behind him, firmly but not with such force to disturb his resting wife in the upper room. Ascending the stairs, he placed the newly acquired items inside the open-faced curio cabinet in the parlor, then returned to bed beside his still slumbering wife, finally exhausted.

The next day he was up early despite his nighttime excursion, waking his wife with a kiss before starting his day. She made it clear that she was not ready to leave the snug comfort of the bed quite yet, so he let her be and got ready himself, then went into the kitchen to prepare breakfast for the two of them. The smell of frying bacon and sizzling sausage managed to rouse her, and she joined him in her bathrobe for the repast. They chatted about minor things, such as the small greenhouse she had found out in the back of the house, just past the stone wall that formed the yard's boundaries. While she talked about the fascinating things she had found inside the edifice, his mind wandered, turning unexpectedly to the strange missive he had found last night, and the urge to read its timeworn pages grew exponentially within him. When she mentioned returning to the structure and perhaps exploring the surrounding modest tract of woods nearby he pounced on the idea, saying it would do her some good to take in the fresh air. She asked if he would care to accompany her, but he deflected, telling her of the old diary of his deceased relative's and his wish to read it, and that he still wanted to head into town afterward to run some errands. He could tell she was not altogether pleased with his response, but she held her tongue, merely telling him to pick up the tomatoes she had forgotten to get at the store yesterday and that she would see him when he returned. She went to get ready, and he retired to the parlor, eager to bury himself in the mysterious chronicle.

He barely heard the back door's harsh slam as she left, so engrossed in the slim diary that outside concerns seemed like the barest of distractions in comparison. The book itself was written in an elaborate cursive script he found mercifully undemanding to read, his great uncle's elegant pen strokes neat and concise, the product of countless years of practical use of the outdated form. While it was indeed a record of events from his relative's life, it was more of a retrospective report of several happenings that had so influenced the man he had thought to record them in literary form for his own inscrutable purposes. He found the account to be both astounding and poignant, and utterly absorbing in its detailed recitation. Liam was not normally a voracious reader, but he devoured several pages of the volume in a relatively short span, turning page after page in astonishing disbelief, the captivating tale ensnaring him completely.

His great uncle had met his wife under extremely strange

circumstances, while he had been hiking in the Scottish highlands, in the Knoydart peninsula. He had found her near one of the many moraines in those steep hills, shivering in the cool air, completely unequipped for the harsh climate, clad only in a simple homespun shift. She was near death, but he managed to save her life, carrying her over miles of rough terrain in order to get to the medical assistance she urgently required. She convalesced in a local hospital and while she was being treated for her infirmity he visited her daily, and a strong rapport was struck between the two. He had reported to the authorities she had kept deliriously repeating the same words as he took her to the nearest shelter, "No, no, I must get back, he will be angry." He took that to be her father, but no one had any knowledge of missing persons among the locals living in the wilderness area, or anyone else for that matter, visiting or otherwise. The doctors said she had amnesia, and after she recovered she could not even recall what she had meant by the cryptic comment, or even something as simple as her own name at all. She had to be called something, and everyone at the hospital came up with names until she found one she liked, Maev. He was at a loss to help her find who she was or where she had came from, but his continued presence seemed to bring her pleasure, and for himself as well. Eventually she was considered well enough to leave the hospital, but they stayed in close contact even after her departure. Their friendship quickly blossomed into something more, and it was not long before he asked her to marry him, which she eagerly accepted, seeming to be happily willing to leave her unremembered past forgotten and ready to start a new life with him.

Their love, a furious, powerful thing, proved to have longevity as well, and they were looking to forward the next step in their relationship, starting a family and raising children together. After the move to Mississippi they had found the magnificent manor to raise their aspired offspring, and all had been well at first, even with his early retirement from the service. But little by little she began to remember forgotten bits and pieces from her past, and what the both of them began to discover about her traumatic history was both strange and disquieting. She started having dreams, vivid illustrations of a tall, grey castle, faraway in a land that was not connected to any earthly realm, but mirrored it in shape and form. It felt similar to the way that shadows mimic the images they spring forth from, or that still lakes reflect their surrounding mountains and trees, real to the eye but not truly having any substance or form. There in the castle merry and riotous banqueting went on throughout its cavernous hall. She saw the celebrations teemed with unabashed ladies and frolicsome courtiers feasting and drinking to lively music, but their jubilation was a mask she unerringly knew, hiding their true colors and unnatural appetites. She herself was present at the great feasts, made to entertain the guests, dancing for their pleasure while they cavorted and dined shamelessly, forced to serve whether or not she wanted to. Presiding over the whole spectacle was a somber, golden-haired man in an iron crown, the lord of the castle. While she could not say why he filled her with an unholy dread as he turned her direction at the end of each of the dreams, it seemed like he could see her through her incorporeal self to her real body lying in bed next to her husband. She could feel his rage radiating furiously in response to her exodus from his realm, but something else was evident behind that raw emotion as well, that of venomous jealous. Although the sinister king had never spoken to her, she knew he considered her to be his property, and the loss of her was a vicious affront to his person. After several of the horrific nighttime visitations, she came to the conclusion that they were more than simple tricks of her subconscious mind, and she became convinced that they were truly repressed memories from her earlier life. She began to paint the images she saw, trying to recall as much detail as possible from the queer recollections as she could, including the one now hanging in the bedroom.

His grand uncle had laughed off such notions as foolishness at first, the idea of otherworldly monarchs taking an interest in his normal, albeit mysterious wife an utter preposterous suggestion. This only served to alienate his wife from him, and he was soon sorry that he had done so in such a careless and thoughtless manner.

****

The deep, metallic chiming of the grandfather clock in the room finally broke the serene silence of Liam's engrossed concentration, warning him of the late morning's hour. He had been reading nonstop for an inordinate amount of time, the several hours passing like minutes to his single-minded absorption of the intriguing literature. He placed the book back on the shelf next to the other items, pondering its extraordinary meaning for a moment as he did so, before grabbing the keys and heading into town as per his aforementioned plan. The drive to the nearby small town of Cuchlain wasn't a long one, taking only about twenty minutes, several of that on a dirt track before turning into proper blacktop. All the major businesses seemed located off on the principal thoroughfare, appropriately named Main Street by the unoriginal founder. He found the hardware shop quickly enough, purchasing the parts he required from the sallow-faced clerk who seemed more preoccupied with watching pretty passersby than any real interest in performing his duties. Stopping next at the local super market, he found the tomatoes his wife wanted in addition to a few other items for his own needs. The cashier was an elderly lady, performing her duties adequately as well as keeping up a constant rate of inquisitive chatter. She was easy enough to talk to with her characteristic Southern accent, and having no customers other than himself, regaled him with the local gossip as well as asking him about his personal interest in the area. When he mentioned where he was staying, her face clouded a moment before asking for clarification.

"You're staying at Thomas Graham's old place then?"

"Yes, he was my great uncle. I inherited his house, my

wife and myself thought it would be a good vacation for the two of us."

"It doesn't bother you then, what happened there?"

His blank stare was all the answer she required, more than happy to inform him of the small-town rumor he had not been privy to beforehand.

"Pardon me saying, but your great uncle Thomas was not particularly well thought of around here. He was curt and dismissive with most people, quite brusque, and not at all involved in the local community or even the Baptist church like other folks normally do here. Now, we could forgive all that, takes all kinds to make the world turn as Gramma used to say, but that business with his pregnant wife, he was lucky he didn't end up in the penitentiary over that. I still remember even though I was just a girl then, sixteen years old. It was right after the biggest storm we ever had, in '67. It blew down telephone poles, wrecked barns and fences, broke almost all the windows in town, even ripped the roof completely off the Polson house. They said it wasn't a hurricane or a tornado, just a powerful tempest, but I remember hunkering down with my family in the cellar, praying our souls out and hearing that awful racket above us, and I didn't know how we were going to make it, even with Jesus's help. And the flooding, it was just as bad, places that hadn't flooded in a hundred years went underwater, and a lot of people lost their homes then, the swollen rivers taking what the storm couldn't manage to destroy. Then your uncle came into town early the next morning, waking the sheriff up out of bed and getting him to help him find his wife. She had gone out in the storm the previous night and he'd lost her in the heavy rains and turbulent weather, finally realizing he needed help after hunting for her to no avail. The sheriff quickly formed a search party of willing neighbors, and those men and others beat the bushes for her for days, dredged the rivers and streams, walked the swamps and the fields, doing everything they could do to find her. My daddy went out with them, only to come back at night tired and worn out from searching high and low for any kind of sign. But they never found her, not one shred of evidence. She was gone, pure and simple. Some folks said she must have sank down in one of those bogs, down deep in the mud without a trace, or got swept out in one of the creeks around the Graham house, that eventually link up to the Mississippi and then out into the Gulf. But other people talked of other ideas, and what they talked about was that it wasn't no accident what happened to her, that her husband, your great uncle, might have had something to do with it, men like him having done worse things before, even to their own kind and others. My mama had known Maev Graham, and while she was as standoffish as her husband, she had a sweet, gentle disposition that everyone had respected and liked. Mama said one time that she had gone out to the Graham place to check up on Maev, being first time pregnant and all with no help from kin, and when she went to the door she heard arguing inside, a man's and a woman's voice raised in anger. Other people reported other things they had seen, about him wandering around at strange times of night, up to no good back in those woods and tributaries. Nothing but hearsay and gossip for the most part, and I'll be honest, people in a small town like to talk, and the truth gets stretched out from its original shape sometimes, but where there's smoke there's fire, and little sins add up to big ones most of the time. There never was any kind of inquest into the affair, especially since there was no body and no evidence to support one. No one but God will ever truly know what happened back then to Mrs. Graham and her baby way back then I suppose, but there isn't anyone here in town that shed any tears when your great uncle passed away, that's for sure. I just wanted you to know, you have the right to hear about it the way I see it."

The story was shocking to Liam, and went against what his own mother had said about the events that had transpired. But that version of the facts came from Thomas Graham himself, and it wasn't like a man would admit to murder even to his own family, especially an estranged one like his own. Liam thanked the gray-haired lady for her time and insight into his family's history, and then he took his groceries out to his waiting car. During the return trip back to the manor house, he thought deeply of what the woman had said, and he was more interested now than ever in finishing the delicate volume he left in the parlor, written by the only person who might really know what had happened on that fateful night of June 21st, 1967.

He was startled to discover, however, that when he returned his wife was sitting in one of the broad parlor chairs, the slim missive in her hands, thoroughly immersed into his great uncle's memoir. She was so caught up in the volume's captivating tale she had not even heard his entry into the home, and looked up in surprise, completely taken aback by his unnoticed presence.

"You scared me Liam, I didn't even hear you come in. This is crazy, what your relative wrote. It's almost like a fairy tale, finding your future wife out in the wilderness all alone and hurt, nursing her back to health and then getting married. It's a shame especially when you know it won't end happily ever after for them, so romantic but so sad."

"How far have you gotten?" he asked nonchalantly, more interested in her response than his casual demeanor implied. He had not expected this development, and was not sure exactly how he felt about her intruding encroachment into the strange mystery he had uncovered, having almost felt that it was his own private possession, his and his alone to explore. On the flip-side *she had said* she wanted to spend more time with him, and while it may not have been what either of them would have thought that doing so would have entailed, perhaps the shared experience could strengthen their marital bond.

"Not very far, only until they had moved here to this house," she said, breaking his erstwhile thoughts. "It's very strange, I almost feel as though there's something more to it than just him writing for himself, almost as if he knew some-one would be reading it later." It was an interesting thought, and not one that he himself had picked up on, and he decided then and there to bring her wholly into his examination into his great aunt's disappearance. He shared with her his fears and beliefs into what may have transpired, enlightening her of all the facts and specifics he had discovered thus far, includ-ing the discovery of the steamer trunk in the storage room and the fantastically disguised key found hidden in the paint-ing from their room. He showed her the strange objects he found within the chest during his late night jaunt, and shared the maligned gossip from the old woman in town concerning his relative's supposed guilt in the subject. He even spoke of the strange feelings and happenings in the house he felt were inexplicably interwoven into the fabric of the conspiracy, the strange sense of being watched by unknown and unseen voy-eurs, and the malevolent emotions that struck like diminutive pinpricks of abhorrence and resentment. She listened with rapt interest, and he hoped she would not be too upset about his initial concealment of what he had uncovered in the histo-ry of the abode they were sharing. When he finished he asked her what she thought of his conjectures and dealings into his great uncle's proceedings, fearing the worst, but he was re-lieved to see instead that she was uncommonly open-minded and accepting of his secretive behavior. The indifferent re-sponse received by him from herself and the police during the intruder incident made her overlook any of the minor indiscretions he had made, and was feeling somewhat ashamed herself for not believing him during those occasions.

They resolved to finish interpreting the small book together, and they took turns reading aloud to each other, supper forgotten in their hunger for the truth hopefully contained therein the record. The weather began to turn disagreeable and unpleasant as they read, the pealing sounds of thunder evident in the far-off distance rolling though the countryside. Soon the view of the formerly blue sky outside the large picture window turned grey and ominous, with the gentle patter of rain falling outside like a faint harbinger of the approaching storm yet to come. The dead man's written words spoken aloud in the parlor seemed even more eerie with the application of audible medium, almost as if they were reciting ancient passages to a forbidden tome, or reciting a supplicant's prayers to dark forces too terrible and obscene for ordinary man in his sunlit world of logic and reason.

His great uncle had noticed a slow but undeniable change in his young wife after the discordant dreams began, a more tightened reservation to her previously caring and open character, and he fought against it, even to the point of vehement argument between the two. He felt she was bit by bit pushing him away, like she no longer cared or needed him, while to him she was still the absolute center of his world. He began to observe a strange peculiarity as well, that her terrible nightmares seemed to coincide with violent and inhospitable weather patterns. He bought a barometer, and soon was able to position it to the exact setting to prophesize the coming severe weather conditions and their subsequent disturbing dreams. After one particularly terrible storm he was finally able to reconfirm their fractured relationship, breaking down her defenses with simple love and affection, in that act overcoming what his shouting and bluster could not. The event itself, in its horrific revelation, firmly made him realize as well that his wife was not imagining the uncanny circumstances plaguing her.

He had awoken one night in their bedroom from the crashing sounds of thunder, coming from a violent squall that had unexpectedly appeared, interrupting the peaceful ambiance of the formerly tranquil night. Turning over to check on his young wife, he saw ghostly apparitions, clothed in garments from a bygone era, perhaps from the early Middle Ages, surrounding her side of the bed. Arms outstretched, they were struggling to come near her, fighting laboriously forward as if against an underwater current, the air between her and their talon-like fingers acting like a thick barrier or curtain that was too dense for them pass through. Horrified at the ethereal visitors and alarmed at their proximity, he seized her shoulders and shook her awake, meaning to take her away from her wraith-like attackers. But he saw even as he did so the indistinct phantoms were retreating away, gnashing their teeth and howling in silent protest until they disappeared from view. She wept, clinging to him desperately as she told him she knew the nameless king wanted her back, and would not stop until he had her again under his thrall, as well as the unborn child she was carrying.

They resolved to protect themselves against the malicious specters, inviting one of the local pastors to bless the house and exorcise the demons that haunted their sleep. The preacher did agree in spite of obvious reservations in doing so, but his ministrations seemed to have no effect, and they were loathe to bring him further into their confidences, fearing recriminations from the superstitious parish where he was the shepherd. Witch hunts and their accompanying burnings may have ended in the previous centuries, but Thomas was not willing to test the acuteness of that verity with the lives of his family at stake, especially given his precarious standing in the community. Seeking to banish the unwelcome invaders themselves instead, they traveled to the new Gulfport-Harrison library almost daily to research the phenomenon for any insight into how to prevent the nightly visitations from occurring. They stayed in a hotel near the archive on especially long outings, but the change in venue did not halt the nightly hauntings, the different locale of their habitation seeming to have no bearing on the frightening phantoms' appearances.

However, the journey was not completely fruitless. After much delving in Celtic and Scottish lore, Thomas and Maev came to believe that her unknown origin and strange circumstances surrounding her amnesia may be related to what is known as the Otherworld, a place rumored to exist as parallel to our own dimension. More aptly it is a shadow of our world, where time and other physical laws of nature do not apply or even exist. The two planes are separated from each other by a veil, thinner in some places than others, that can permit movement from one world to the other. Legends abounded of people passing through these thin spots in the veil to the other plane, finding a faerie realm populated by a cruel and haughty people who harmed and manipulated the travelers for their own impenetrable intentions. They found additional stories too, about beings of the faerie realm traveling through the corridors and folds between worlds, wishing to leave and start a new life in the ordinary existence, forsaking their place in the Otherworld. He and his wife became convinced that she was such an individual, escaping the shadow dimension but now pursued by the denizens of that mystical realm. The concept seemed insane in its very theory, especially to Thomas, but the incredible actuality of what he had seen, and had continued to see, could not be denied.

But nowhere could they find an apparent solution to their supernatural dilemma. The practitioners of the long vanished Celtic ways had never recorded their magical rites and sacred rituals, being an oral tradition that was completely obliterated with the mass murder of the Druidic sect by the Romans under Claudius and Tiberius's empirical reigns in the early first century. The knowledge they needed to prevent the psychic onslaughts appeared to be unequivocally lost for all time, gone with the extinct druids and priestesses of a dead religion, if the information had ever existed at all. Working tire-lessly, together they searched countless paranormal works, from such mystical grimoires as *The Book of Abramelin* and the *Key of Solomon*, to the ancient cuneiform clay tablets of Mesopotamia and the obscure Zoroastrian incantations against demons. No stone was left unturned by the two, and Thomas and his wife, while willing to delve into the dark arts almost as deeply as it could be required, drew the line just short of ritual sacrifice and calling upon other darker, twisted entities for their preternatural assistance. The price, they felt, would be too high if they lost their souls or humanity in the process of trying to exorcise the eldritch presence from their lives.

However, when every avenue seemed blocked against them, a tendril of salvation came thrusting forth like a fortunate piece of driftwood to the clutch of a drowning man, banishing the bleakness of their overwhelming despair. They learned of a little known farmer living in Wales during the late seventeenth century, Arthur Blackwood, whose life and family were plagued by "demonic visitations from Lucifer himself". He was haunted by ghosts and "devil spawn" for several months during the wee hours of three to four, commonly known then as the witching hour. His wife purportedly defended him stoically during his rest, waking him as the satanic creatures came nightly to seize the man and drag him screaming to the abyss. Their unholy arrival was heralded by "storms of considerable power and consternation." All attempts by holy clergy and faithful servants of God were met with abject failure, and soon talk surfaced that Arthur himself was cursed. Many were certain it was no doubt due to his disreputable abandonment by unknown sinners when he was a babe, having being found orphaned near a reported faerie wood, squalling alone in the bitter cold of January. Only the intervention by a chance traveler had saved him from horrific death by exposure at such a tender age.

Seeking relief from his preternatural condition as well as genuinely concerned for his family's safety from the increasingly hostile neighbors, Arthur and his relations sailed to the New World and settled in Darien, Georgia to build a new life. The change was rife with hardship, not the least of which that the demonic visitors had followed him to the new continent as well, continuing to cause disturbances in both the surrounding weather and his nighttime slumber. However, an old woman descended from the original Highlander colonists heard of his constant ordeals and was willing to help the tormented man. She was what the locals called a *"ban-fhiosaiche,"* or "wise woman." Scottish lore purported them to be powerful seeresses thought to have been given powers by the Sidhe, the faerie beings from the Otherworld. Talking with Arthur, she ascertained from his mysterious origins that he was a changeling, a faerie child left behind in the real world, and now for unknown reasons the shadow world wanted him back, and had been sending its diabolical minions to reclaim him. The *Tuatha De Danaam*, the old gods of Scotland and Ireland, were fickle and impetuous lords, constantly fighting against one another, and if one of them sought Arthur's return perhaps another could be persuaded to assist against it. Using her mystical abilities, she was able to craft a special stone, engraved with powerful runes and symbols, that when activated at the proper moment could sever the thread connecting him to the otherworldly realm. The magical ritual was performed with Arthur's insistence, and the chronicle reported that he was never beleaguered again by the apparitions. The enchanted stone and accompanying spell itself the family saved, kept in the ancestral home of the Blackwood family in thankful remembrance of the wise woman's selfless deed.

Thomas Graham, excited at the possibility of quelling the spiritual intrusion at long last, made preparations to travel to Darien and obtain the runic stone and its incantation from the modern day Blackwood heirs. Maev was eight months pregnant at this time, and fearing for her and the baby's safety, he chose to have her remain at the mansion in Mississippi while he made the trip alone. She kissed him passionately before he left, and told him to mind his temper in his dealings, no matter the outcome. He drove without stopping to the township, only pausing for refueling until he reached his final destination. There he was met by solid resistance by Finn Blackwood, the last living descendant of the original Arthur Blackwood. Thomas had counted on the family's preassociation with the supernatural phenomenon to be instrumental in affording their help in his dire situation. However, the obstinate man refused to believe any part of Thomas's story, and in fact denying any element of his heritage's role in what he called "fanciful libel designed to have him part with a priceless family heirloom."

Angered by the other man's utter rejection to aid him in his terrible plight, Thomas reported the two came to blows in the course of their discussion, neither side willing to back down over the issue. In a fit of towering fury and desperate for his wife's sole deliverance, the outraged Thomas seized a brass vase from a nearby table, bludgeoning the obstinate man to unconsciousness, leaving him bleeding on his floor and absconding with the needed relic. Upon returning to his home in Mississippi, he was relieved to find his spouse in good health and unmolested by the eternal attackers. He said nothing of the recent altercation to his wife, choosing to not inform her of his heinous crime. The barometer showed the portentous reading of 29.4, foreshadowing that another manifestation would soon be eminent sometime in the next passing hours. Armed with the newly acquired arsenal against such excursions however, Thomas felt confident that they could banish the unwanted materializations from their lives permanently, and begin to resume their carefree, normal lives. He had his wife lie down in their bedroom, and he himself kept close watch over her slumbering form, alertly awaiting the otherworldly arrival. He was not to be disappointed. The weather outside escalated to a fevering crescendo, lightning and thunder booming in an almost repetitious pattern as buckets of rain poured from the heavens, the disastrous conditions more in common with the biblical deluge of Noah's era than any typical southern storm. At a quarter past three the apparitions emerged from the walls in their ghostly forms, lurching for the sleeping Maev with disembodied menace. He began to vocalize the wise woman's archaic spell, chanting in primeval Gaelic the magical words of severance, seeing the ancient carved runes glow with a brilliant blue light as he did so. The haunting specters came closer and closer, while he feverishly spoke the words of power, trying to finish the spell before they could conclude their dark abduction.

He had nearly finished the last line from the ancient enchantment when a stunning bolt of electricity blasted forth from the glowing stone, zapping him forcefully, stinging his arm, and causing him to drop the artifact and halt his zealous reading of the charmed script. Trying anxiously to take hold of the talisman and finish the disrupted spell, he saw the ghostly beings grasp his wife, making contact with her exposed flesh. Her eyes shot open, and she tried to scream, but only a hollow, distant sound emanated from her throat, like she was far away. Her body spasmed uncontrollably, contorting in twisting, painful shapes, then she began to shimmer and acquire an ethereal consistency. The malignant spirits started to sink slowly, dragging her downwards as well, and Thomas was horrified to see her passing through the bed underneath as if she too was incorporeal. Dropping to the floor, he searched under the bed, seeing the mass of intangible bodies disappear through the floor, leaving no trace of their transit through the wood. Fighting through the numbing pain in his wounded extremity, he quickly snatched up the discarded stone and ran for the cellar, making his way with extreme haste to storage room lying directly beneath their bedroom. Flinging the door open, he was just in time to see Maev being dragged through the room's only window, her pale white face twisted in pain and sorrow at the ghosts' insistence in pulling her immaterial form through the shuttered frame. Then she was gone, and Thomas ran outside to follow, frantically searching in the hammering rain and dangerous strikes of lightning for his precious loved one. He blindly hunted for her until dawn, finding no sign anywhere of her trail, exhaustion and sustained exposure to the rough elements wearing him down, even with his powerful need. He realized finally that he required outside help, driving at breakneck speed to Cuchlain and waking the sheriff with his panicked cries. They formed a search party, but Maev was never found, alive or otherwise. He was forced to accept that the shadow king had won, taking her back to the Otherworld along with his unborn baby.

He never stopped waiting for her however, even after many years elapsed. On stormy days he would search for her, calling her name over and over, hoping that she could make her way back to him from the prison of the parallel dimension. Despair reigned in his desolate reality, and he was unable to take any enjoyment from life's pleasures, saddled with the horrific knowledge that she may never return to his side. Years passed and little by little he lost what little hope he had left, becoming increasing bitter and frustrated, and while he was never a popular man in the area to begin with, he became hated by the local populace due to his callous and insensitive demeanor. He knew it was wrong to become what he had transformed into, but his grief was like a cloak that covered him at all times, oppressing him with its constant embrace. He at last shut himself away in the ornate manor, not wanting to inflict the harmful version of himself on anyone with its leprous vulgarity. He only let one local cleaning woman, renowned in Cuchlain for her thick skin, and her equally endowed daughter visit his abode, spurning all others. He became the surly hermit that no one called on or even cared about anymore.

But after thirty years of solitude one has time to become aware of things, and he began to notice a peculiar fact, one that breathed new promise into his famished soul. On days with inclement climate similar to the night of the tempest she had disappeared on the door to the cellar storage room would open ever so slightly, even from a closed state. He stringently tested the theory, spending countless hours watching the entryway when the barometer read the magical number of 29.2. The remarkable door would open by its own accord at the appointed impression on the device, and a strange feeling of not being alone would prickle his skin with gooseflesh at the same moment. He wondered if indeed it was Maev, trying to make her way back from the Otherworld to this plane of existence, attempting to travel through the veil but hampered in some way. Excited by the possibility of his wife's return, he gave the servant women orders to never go into that room, declaring it off limits in hopes of not jeopardizing the fragile metamorphosis that was taking place in the secluded area. More years passed, and the miraculous door opened further and further, and the voyeuristic feelings intensified with their escalation.

But Thomas Graham grew older and older, until finally he knew he was not long for this world. But he knew Maev may still return, even after he had perished and was gone from the face of the earth. He locked the wise woman's magical stone, the faithful barometer, and this account of his actions, good and bad, away in a sturdy trunk and hid the key in such a way that only a very special person would notice, the kind of person who noticed doors that open by themselves. To anyone reading his confession, if by any chance Maev returned from the Otherworld, he only asks that they tell her he loved her more than anything any world has to offer, and his only wish would have been to grow old with her and to raise the child he had never known together with her.

****

Liam finished reading the harrowing account to his wife, and looked up to see her reaction to its conclusion. Her eyes were wet with tears, and she looked sorrowfully at him.

"That poor man, to spend all that time and she never returned....."

"It is a terrible thought, a lifetime spent waiting for something that never happens. I feel for the man, I really do. But this is an insane story, how could it be possible? Faerie beings? Changelings? Druidic gods? *Other dimensions*? This could be a figment of a deranged mind, the creation of a fantasy explanation caused by either a man shattered by the tragedy of losing his wife in a much more plausible fashion or," and he grimaced sharply as he uttered the next words, "someone who did something so unspeakable that even he recoils from the horrific actions he has done."

His wife stared at him, aghast at the terrifying vision his application of logic had implied. "Not your own flesh and blood! Surely you don't think he would have killed his own pregnant wife!"

"I don't know what I believe, Sharon. He's a stranger to me, and everything I've heard does not paint him as a kind or caring individual. Quite the opposite actually." The lightning outside flashed with a brilliant luminous explosion as if to give reverence to his words, and was quickly followed by the sharp crack of dangerously close thunder.

"The storm Liam, check the barometer!" Not waiting for him to follow her command, she ran to the curio cabinet herself, pulling the instrument from the shelf. "29.2 Liam! 29.2! If he is telling the truth the door will open!" She ran to kitchen, and he followed her, nearly tripping over the ottoman in his need to keep up with her. He didn't want her going down there alone, not after what had happened to him. He had almost convinced himself that he had hallucinated the entire incident before, but the reality of the devastating tempest outside coupled with the strange account they had just read tore at his skeptical psyche. *But it couldn't be possible! Faeries don't exist! People don't vanish into thin air!* His own logic shouted at him as he ran downstairs after her, until they both stood trembling before the closed doorway. Breathless, their eyes locked in the handle, daring it to move. The storm outside raged violently, and they heard the tinker of glass upstairs as a window shattered from the furious assault.

They watched for several tense moments, seeing nothing happen, the door stubbornly remaining secured. Then, the knob slowly, almost imperceptibly shifted, turning around before their disbelieving eyes. The door itself opened ever so slightly, then wider and wider. The expanding space between the door and its jamb was midnight black, a growing darkness that was intimidating in its total absence of color. It exposed more and more of the enveloping gloom, swinging wider than ever before, until it was fully wide open. His back trickled with cold sweat, his heart racing alarmingly, and he dimly heard his wife whisper to him.

"Liam, it's opening! It's true! It's all true!"

Then a familiar pale white face appeared within the shadow of the opening doorway, and his wife screamed, the sound ringing in his ears even as he felt the blood leave his features from the terrifying sight. The horrifying visage loomed closer and closer, and his wife buried her face into his chest, clutching him tightly, the frightening suspense too much for her. Then the pale face fully emerged from the entryway, along with the rest of the owner's figure. It was a raven-haired, beautiful woman, clothed in garments more suitable for another time in history, and she clutched a small, oval bundle to her chest.

"I am Maev, daughter of the Dagda Mor." Her eyes flashed in merriment. "I believe I am your great aunt." His wife turned her head from its hiding place at the feminine tones, and still holding him stared with disbelief at the extraordinary visitor. Looking closer at her now, he could see she was the same woman as in the painting hanging on the bedroom wall. She began to speak again, and they listened closely to her extraordinary tale.

"Time passes differently in the Otherworld. To me only a few months have passed since I was taken from my love, your great uncle, by Taranis the storm god who wanted me for himself. He had captured me originally from my father's household and gave me a terrible choice, to serve him as a slave for all eternity or marry him, becoming his wife. I escaped to your world to avoid either of these fates, for I did not love him, knowing of his violent ways and terrible jealousy of the Dagda, nor would I acquiesce to his demands of servitude." Her eyes flashed angrily, "The daughter of the Dagda is no man's slave, not even a god's."

"Your great uncle found me after I had traveled the corridors between worlds. The Veil is a hard journey, even to one of our kind, and I had never trod its myriad of paths before, and I did so hastily, without preparation. It hurt me, and I lost my sense of identity in the ripples of multiple existences that the Veil links. I forgot who I was, or where I was from. But Thomas loved me for my essence, not for who I was, and I loved him back for the same reason." Her blue eyes briefly moistened, but she continued on. "Our love was the happiest moment of my life, but it was not meant to be. As pieces of my memories returned Taranis used them to find me, trying to steal me back to his palace from this world using the departed spirits of the Firebolgs, striking an unholy bargain with them for my recapture. My father, the Dagda wanted to help me but he could not take direct action, that being forbidden to the Tuatha De Danaam. Instead he helped guide Thomas to the information he needed, the description of Arthur Blackwood's liberation from his persecutors."

Her eyes closed briefly, as if recalling something painful. "I loved Thomas, but he was not without his faults. He could be shortsighted and vicious when the mood struck him." She looked poignantly at Sharon. "But we still love our men, do we not, in spite of their flaws?" His wife nodded ever so slightly in affirmation, and tightened her death grip on him.

Maev continued, "In killing Finn Blackwood, he destroyed any chance of help from my father by that evil act, rendering the spell he later recited impotent. Taranis's minions were able to fulfill their task for him, pulling me back through the folds of the Veil. But my father was waiting with his warriors when we reappeared in the Otherworld, and after a ferocious battle, destroyed the spirits, ended Taranis's evil influence.

But I was still weak, and the child was coming, so they took me to the Dagda's palace, where I recuperated and waited for the child to come. Soon I had Thomas's son in my arms, bold and handsome like his father. I wanted to return to this world, to raise the boy with Thomas, but by then my memories had returned in their entirety, and with them the bitter knowledge of what had befallen. The time distortion had already occurred, and Thomas was dead." Her voice quivered at the dolorous pronouncement, but she resolutely persisted in her story. "The Tuatha De Danaam have many powers, but we cannot restore a mortal who dies by old age, nor can we travel into the past."

She brought the bundle from her chest, revealing a tiny black-haired babe, the union of her and his great uncle's joyous love. "This is Arthur. I named him for the man whose story's ending I wished could have been our own, myself and your great uncle's. He is mortal like Thomas was, and cannot stay in the Otherworld. It would harm him over time, even with the Dagda and myself to help him. Nor can I stay anymore in this mortal realm. The Tuatha De Danaam lost that privilege a long time ago, and it was just the foolish dream of a girl that led me here in the first place." Her eyes flashed again, and she said determinedly, "Not that I would not do it again if I could."

"My son needs a home, and if Thomas and I cannot raise him, I would rather his own kin would do so." She looked softly at Sharon. "I know of your barren circumstance. I also know of the love in your heart for a child. You will make a fine mother." She looked at Liam more forcefully. "I know of the restless drive in your heart to succeed. I also know of the burning passion you still feel for your wife. Tempering the two is not always easy, but you need her as much as she needs you." Her expression softened. "My father is the Dagda. He knows the hearts of man like his own. He says you are ready to be a father, even though you may not think it is what you want." She hugged the precious bundle one last time, and kissed him lightly on the forehead. The baby cooed joyfully at the affectionate handling, and then she held the child out to his wife in offering, tears falling unashamedly down her cheeks at the terrible choice she was forced to make. His wife looked up at his face for confirmation, her eyes crying as well from the empathy she felt for the other woman. He nodded, unable to speak with the lump of sadness in his own throat from the unfairness of what was happening to Maev. His wife accepted the precious bundle from the other woman's shaking arms, drawing the boy close to her breast. Outside the storm seemed to lessen, and Maev seemed to take notice of the dwindling squall, and stood sadly empty-handed now. She closed her eyes and folded her hands in a strange pattern, seeming in intense concentration before reopening them.

"Treat my son as your own, Liam and Sharon Hastane. I have placed a geis on the child to make everyone think it is your natural son, born tonight during the tempest. He can never know who his mother is, but you can tell him that someone will always be watching out for him who loves him very much." She began to fade away slowly, her body turning to ethereal mist, but she looked directly at Liam as she did, speaking one last final time. Her words seemed distant and far away in his ears, but their meaning was crystal clear.

"But do not lose your temper!"

The Hitman's Altar

"We have him dead to rights," said Coleman. His partner was correct of course, Detective Alan Cramb knew. It was literally the definition of an open and shut case. They had been involved in a long investigation involving Marc Guiseppe, a junior lieutenant to the local crime boss of the Romano family, the notorious Luca Romano. After chasing several avenues of examination into the case there had finally yielded the possibility of several convictions in both the family and their unwholesome compatriots. Mr. Guiseppe himself had been very cooperative since his inopportune arrest involving several kilos of certain illegal substances, staying true to the old adage of there being no honor among thieves. The man residing currently in the interrogation room was one of the families' more disreputable associates, a man by the name of Nash Marsh. He was a freelance contract killer that Luca Romano had hired from time to time. Generally he had been reserved for sanitizing associates and family members whose double-crossing activities had made them become liabilities to the family, thus requiring a more discreet, distanced touch from Romano's normal blood-soaked hands. Mr. Marsh had acquired a well-earned reputation for himself, through these atrocious acts for the Romanos and similar activities for various other gangs and families, of being particularly meticulous and utterly dependable in his ghastly work.

In fact, if Marc Guiseppe was to be believed, he was possibly one of the most prolific and extraordinary murderers in the area of all time, citing various examples of well nigh impossible executions and contacts fulfilled despite insurmountable odds. Amazingly not one of the hundreds of hits which he is infamously credited with has yielded even one body, his unknown disposal methods being the stuff of legends by his peers as well. That is, until this fateful night when the detectives had burst in on him literally red-handed, attempting to wrap the body of the newly deceased John Jameson Briars of the notorious Irish gang the Smilers in plastic sheeting, after following a lead provided by the newly cooperative Mr. Guiseppe. After taking him into custody Detectives Coleman and Cramb were hoping to discover the whereabouts of some of his other luckless victims, but Cramb thought that may prove difficult especially given that that the man had not uttered more than a few monosyllable, terse sentences since his arrest.

The man in the interrogation room was fairly nondescript in both form and character, with a slight build, average features you wouldn't look twice at in a crowded room, and simple brown hair with green eyes in a clean but plain gray suit. A perfect set of attributes for a mob enforcer. He was sitting at the large stainless steel table with all the air of a man waiting patiently for the bus, arms placed neatly in front of him, posture aligned but not greatly attentive. His eyes looked carelessly at the two way mirror, and a sardonic smile played ghostly across his lips. In fact, if it wasn't for handcuffs tethering him to the table, someone might think that he was the one about to begin the questioning, given his lackadaisical appearance.

"Let's get this over with," said Coleman tartly. "He'll probably be calling for his lawyer within seconds anyhow."

The two men entered the room together, Cramb taking his accustomed place sitting opposite the perpetrator on one of the metal chairs, Coleman standing to the right, hovering in and out of sight slightly behind Marsh. Cramb began the questioning in the usual manner, asking questions to which they already knew the answers and recording his responses, such as his name, place of birth, time in the city, and occupation. To the last he seemed to contemplate the inquiry, and then gave a short, barking laugh and replied, "Priest." Cramb looked questioningly at him, then sighed and wrote down the seemingly flippant remark. Coleman began to add some statements and inquiries of his own in his normal agitated style, pressing home on the recent murder of Mr. Briars and the consequences of that action.

They questioned him about several murders they knew

from Guiseppe's testimony in which he had acted as the principal offender, seeing if he would mention some of the sordid details the police had not mentioned to the media outlets. He deftly avoided such blatant pitfalls, coming out ahead in every exchange with the determined officers. They turned the conversation to his unexplained modus operandi in body disposal, trying to ascertain just where his victims' remains were interred. Coleman began to lose his temper as Cramb had fully expected, finally storming out hotly to one carefully formulated reply from the nonplussed hitman. The cool-headed culprit watched him go dispassionately, and then looked levelly at the remaining detective.

"Do you enjoy your work Detective?" he asked Cramb in a quiet, even tone. The question caught Cramb unguarded with its seemingly unrelated quality, but he quickly recovered.

"Yes, I suppose so."

"No... for you it is something more it seems to me. This is more than a job to you. So, do you enjoy your work?"

Cramb saw no reason not to be candid in his reply. "I do as much as any man who does something he is enthusiastic about, whether it is his job, family, or hobby. Mine just happens to coincide with what I do for a living. Learning the truth and bringing the guilty to justice is my greatest joy, seeing men like you pay for their crimes." He had not meant to divulge quite so much personal information. His honest response had literally surprised himself with its audacity. The man had a dark charisma to him, drawing forth responses from him that he would not normally relinquish so easily. It was unnerving, and more than a little disconcerting to the normally stoic detective. He tried to formulate an articulate reply to regain control of the exchange, but his deliberation was interrupted by the poised criminal.

"I can tell that by the way you ask your questions, the way you formulate your next incursion into the realms of the mind, your willingness to do what is necessary to accomplish your goal. Your friend does not have that same strenuous ethic, I can tell by his ineffectual and impatient demeanor. No, you are cut of a different cloth than your poor, indolent friend. You are more like myself, not in vocation of course but in that unequivocal diligence we both feel in our line of business. As one assiduous individual to another I will tell you a small bit of what you seek, whether or not you choose believe me I will leave entirely up to your discretion. That is, as long as you are willing to put your childish lawman tricks to the side for now."

Detective Cramb did not bother to waste a single moment in debate, willing to let the man speak with freedom to hopefully ascertain some further informative illuminations of his criminal activities. "Certainly, please go on."

"Most stories start in the beginning. I am not telling you everything. Understand that you are only receiving a piece, a minor excerpt from my heretofore unmentioned existence. We will not be starting from the onset of my illicit life then, or even some other important juncture in my timeline. No, instead a point much more recent, perhaps even an average depiction of one of my days. The fact being is normalcy for one such as I is as removed from the everyday man matters little in this instance. You must understand, *I love my work*, just as much as you do, every second, every aspect......"

****

"I love my work. I love the solitude of working by myself, the sweet seclusion an anchor of self reliance in an increasingly dependent world. Naturally I love the handsome pay I receive for my unique skills. With it I can afford my luxurious lifestyle of fast cars, graceful women, and other lavish trappings, but that is more like icing on the proverbial cake than any real reasoning behind what I do and enjoy. I delight in the thrill of hunting down my hapless prey when the call comes through from my various nefarious employers that yet another quarry needed my special attentions. I cherish seeing the pleading in my victim's eyes before I murder them, and to see their life leave those same eyes as I finish the deed. I passionately feel the resistance of the soft flesh when I shove the knife in, the slackness of the mortal shell as it sags in defeat, and then the uncontrollable ecstasy caused by the fear of discovery while I carefully prepare the victim for transport. I relish the weight of the dead cadaver on my shoulder, the satisfying thump of heaving that dead weight into the trunk, and the sound of the lid slamming down with finality on a generally withered and wasted lifetime. On the long drive out of the city I listen to the radio, not too loud, not to quiet, tuned to the golden oldies of yester-year from the local broadcasting station. It serenades me on my nighttime journey down to the lonely stretch of road that leads to the marina and my conveniently situated boat, the music a constant source of simplistic pleasure. I savor creeping slowly into the sparse parking lot, leaving the car in an unobtrusive fashion away from the prying eyes of unwanted attention. I bide my time in sweet anticipation for the opportune moment when the careless guard will be out of my way to deliver my burden to the waiting boat, and then silently escaping to the tranquil sea under the shining moon. I love the feel of the powerful ocean waves rolling beneath my feet, slowly rocking back and forth in endless repetition. The salty, moist breeze coming off the cool water upon my face is a sensual delight, refreshing me as I navigate the treacherous waters leading to my favorite place in this world. The welcoming natural harbor always brings a smile to my face as soon as I sail in, seeing the large white cliff walls rising from all sides like towering temple walls. The seaside haven and its winding currents are well known to me, but other sailors tend to not my share my fascination and fondness of its delights, disliking the odd echoing sounds and treacherous waters, and tend to give the area a wide berth.

Slowing the boat down to a languorous pace now, I will carefully head towards the dark, rocky outcropping rising in the center of the prodigious grotto lying underneath the colossal cliffs. Here I can finally admire the ancient petroglyphs decorating the cliffs, whereas before they casually blended into the landscape as a natural occurrence. Illuminated in the bright moonlight, the pictures are of misshapen, hideous fish-men carrying tridents of unusually wicked shape, cavorting in the rolling waves, spearing with their armament a variety of sea life such as sharks, eels, and whales. A humongous sea serpent, an amazingly evil countenance drawn on its cold, piscine features, watches hungrily as I float by serenely. Another painting shows a sixteenth century Spanish galleon being boarded by the creatures, impaling sailors and then throwing the dead men to their waiting comrades below a raging sea. A vivid depiction of an early nineteenth century ocean liner crashing into an iceberg can be viewed, with the survivors being snatched off their lifeboats by grotesque, now familiar arms. As I sail into the enormous cave a chilling masterpiece adorns the ceiling, an almost reverent scene of the revolting creatures lying in prostration and homage to the massive sea serpent. A panorama of a wild, repulsive feast wraps around the inner walls of the cave, showing the abominable fish folk devouring various human flesh with primal, terrifying abandon. The art is primeval in its terrible accuracy and design, a wild thing that that stirs my blood, a rarer and finer thing to myself than any Rembrandt or Da Vinci creation could ever aspire to be.

With a practiced hand I cut the idling throttle and lash the anchoring ropes to a jutting rock rising feebly from the stony island. I will then retrieve my loathsome cargo and carry the wretched deceased off the boat and up onto the stony shore.

Carefully following the timeless steps carved in the rocky ground that seem just a little too long for human feet, I make my way toward the center of the island by the more than adequate moonlight softly seeping in. The terrain is bereft of anything but the blackish rock and is constantly soaked, making for slick footing, but I soldier on with a profane eagerness that is abnormal even for these preternatural surroundings. Reaching my destination, I lay my burden down on the only feature to break the monotone scenery, a large raised table made of the same black basalt. Carefully I remove the bloody clothing from the slaughtered corpse, tossing it to the side as so much discarded trash, and then stand back to await my nocturnal company. I do not have to wait long, hearing them before I can see them. At first the sound of the surface of the dark water breaking disturbs the silence in the echoing chamber, as unseen multitudes rise from the depths to pay homage to my infernal tribute. Next is the slow, nonrhythmic plodding of inhuman feet, obviously unaccustomed to walking upon the dry surface world. The sound of droplets fall from the unseen marchers in their discordant step, and then a chorus of croaks and groans that would horrify any normal man with its abominable noise reverberates in an unnerving crescendo in the gargantuan sea cave. One by one they appear finally, blinking in the moonbeams, arms up before them with their hideous clawed hands pointing downwards in an alien poise. The repulsive fish heads as seen in the petroglyphs are even more unnatural when seen in actuality, bathed in the luminous radiance, making thoughts wonder to what horrifying acts could lead to such an unsightly union of beast and man.

The crowd of piscine denizens slow upon reaching their destination, the black table waiting and laden with its newly acquired macabre trappings of human remains. The smell of rotting fish permeates the air as their pungent musk diffuses throughout the cave, too strong to swept away even by the gentle breezes that frequent the area. The foul throng parts to allow a great, striped brute to pass through their ranks, perhaps their leader or a shaman, either way a well respected member of their loathsome tribe. Its sex is indeterminable to human beings, much like the rest of its ilk with no formally displayed designs of gender. It shambles forth with determined fixation on the waiting corpse, then attentively inspects it before turning towards myself. Blinking and croaking, it bows in thanks for the well received offering. I genuflect as well, returning the gesture of courteous regard, and then I retreat a few steps further from the stygian slab to make room for the impeding rush I know will soon follow. The sea people do not make me wait long once again, each crowding one another in their obscene hunger as their leader begins systematically butchering the cadaver, tearing great red chunks of flesh with his keen talons and tossing them to the ravenous horde. If it was not for its horrifying nature the feast would be a fascinating study in tribal hierarchy as scientists love to show in nature documentaries, with the choicer bits fed to those of obvious higher standing and the tougher sections and bones reserved for the more common or lower caste of the amassed horrors, known by their less imposing bodies and twisted structures. Soon the body is reduced to an unrecognizable mass of raw, bleeding meat and gleaming bone before even that too is devoured in the orgy of salivating voracity. Finally all that is left is the alabaster skull, which the chieftain ceremoniously dashes upon the now blood slick table, cracking it open much in the way a man would crack a nut. It rips the shattered skull in half, flinging the pieces to the hooting, frightful mob, but leaving the exposed brain for itself. Cupping the pink organ almost tenderly, it reverently raises its share of the horrifying oblation high above its head. Then closing its eyes as if in some obscene prayer to its dark, depraved god, the leader lowers the sickening delicacy to its waiting hateful jaws. The indescribable sound of the horrendous chewing is unto the sweetest music to my ears, and the disgusting scene of the lustful mastication is of the most tantalizing loveliness to my eyes. All too soon for my perverted liking the feast is finished and the horrifying fish people begin to retreat back to their sunken lairs, leaving finally only the chieftain and myself alone on the island. The chief stares disquietly at me, slowly licking the final remnants of the gory meal from his bloodied lips with his black, scaled tongue, and then in broken, gurgling tones speaks in halting English.

"Our god Lir thanks you, human!"

Then he too vanishes, returning beneath the dark waves to his underwater kingdom, where the laws of man and the niceties of civilization hold no sway."

****

The silence from Detective Cramb is long and constrained, with the horrific account fairly draining him of physical action or thought. The unusual silence is further compounded by the unnatural stare of the newly loquacious killer, seemingly piercing his very soul with his preternatural gaze, watching his uncomfortable reactions to the appalling revelations. His partner Coleman returns suddenly, slamming the door open with a banging that causes Cramb to fairly jump in his heightened state of entrancement. The change in Nash Marsh's demeanor is immediately evident, returning to his cool aloofness with the former detective's advent. Coleman looks questioningly at the two men, perhaps realizing on a subliminal level some of the newly formed linkage between the two. Marsh, nonplussed as before however, merely looks at the hot-tempered detective and addresses him simply as one would a servant or other inferior personage.

"I would like to see my lawyer now. I have no further wish to talk with you or your associate."

Cramb leaves the details of that arrangement to Coleman, quietly withdrawing to his desk to ponder what he had recently ascertained in the interrogation room. Cramb, having heard many admissions and confessions from suspects in the past, is well acquainted with their petty falsehoods and concealing or omitted memories of recollected events. Listening to Marsh he knows that either the man had been telling him the truth or at least what the man believes to be genuine testimony. When Coleman returns he repeats the man's sickening recital to him, but Coleman laughs off the unsettling tale.

"An ancient race of fish men? Satanic cannibalistic rites in long forgotten caves? Oh, he's a sick one, ain't he? I bet he got you really going, huh? He is trying to play the insanity angle, no one is going to believe such outrageous lies. I wish I had been there for his cockamamie story." Coleman derisively snorts. Cramb, thinking of Marsh's description of the hot-tempered detective, is inwardly amused by the scornful comments. Putting aside the unsettling notions pervading his thoughts for now, he begins making plans with Coleman for their next order of business. Without warning a red-faced officer storms into their office in a high state of agitation.

"He's dead!" he exclaims to the mystified detectives.

"Who's dead?" Coleman loudly questions the distressed policeman.

"Your suspect! Come quickly!" He leads them back to the interrogation room. They are both in amazement at the sight within. Nash Marsh is sitting in the chair as before, but with his head thrown back, arms hanging limply at his sides. His eyes stare sightlessly at the ceiling of the room with the fixation only the dead can intently provide. A small rivulet is trickling from his mouth, and drops fall from his body into a large puddle of wetness underneath the chair. The smell of rotting fish permeates the room, adding further mystery to the site of the unthinkable crime.

"What happened here?" Coleman thunders, whirling on the hapless officer. Cramb slowly steps toward the dripping body of the deceased hitman, surreally noticing that he is completely soaked. There are no marks of foul play anywhere he can see, no any other sort of damage or distress to the lifeless corpse.

"I was arranging to take him back to his holding cell as you had requested, when I heard the sound of voices arguing inside the interrogation room. I thought at first perhaps you two had returned to question him further, but then I heard pleading and shrieking from within. I immediately rushed to the door to see what was the matter, but it was like it was locked on the inside, which is impossible as you both know, being how there is no lock on that door. I tell you I could not turn the handle, it was just like it was fused in place. As I tugged and fought with the door the sounds ceased within and then it was like whatever was holding the door had vanished. I opened it up and saw him sitting there like that, all wet. Seeing no assailant anywhere in sight, I rushed over and checked him for a pulse, then not finding one I scrambled to find you. It's the strangest thing, I swear no one could have left the room before I got there." The officer looked puzzled at the strange occurrence of events that had unfolded before him. Coleman joined Cramb in inspecting the departed contract killer's body, confirming Cramb's preliminary observations.

After conferring with the policeman for further, unfruitful details they reported what they knew to their captain, who had by this time been alerted to the baffling situation. After meeting their formal requirements to the internal affairs investigation that followed the strange death of the contract killer, the two detectives and the attending officer were able to clear their names of any mistreatment of the suspect under their care. Interestingly the cameras in the interrogation room had inexplicably ceased recording shortly after Coleman had left the room during Marsh's questioning, so no identification of the perpetrator was ever recovered. The most perplexing piece of the entire mystery was actually after the autopsy had been performed on the deceased man. Nash Marsh's cause of death had been drowning, somehow in a room bereft of water.

Red Scalp Woods

Clayton was sweating profusely from the exertion of the merciless chase and the heat of the day. Despite the late evening, the sun beat down like a blazing fire, cooking him just like the eggs on Marie's stove she used for preparing the morning victuals. His horse was tired, but he knew if he stopped his hectic pace they would catch up to him in no time at all. He could see the posse off in the distance from his vantage point on the hillside, following his trail in a deliberate but determined fashion. The men and horses were laboriously coming up through the north side of the coulee he had crossed a couple hours earlier. The riders were still too far off to spot individual men, but he could see a large black equine shape and he knew without a doubt the identity of that particular mount's rider. Big Jake Sanders was the only man in these parts to ride such a gigantic black roan, and he had done gotten on Big Jake's bad side long before his current predicament.

As he watched the men hunting him wind their way though the ravine, he thought of the series of occurrences that had led to this harrowing end result. Clayton Pellard was not a violent man. In fact around town he had been known as a quiet, hardworking ranch hand, helping tend Ma Jenkins's herd out at her property since she had hired him after Karl Jenkins had lit off for parts unknown. At least, that was the story everyone knew and shared out in the open about Karl in the small, isolated town of Ashcroft in the Montana territory. Behind closed doors some said Ma Jenkins had a little too much of Karl's whoring ways and had decided to finally settle up accounts between the two of them. Ma was a big woman, with a strength rivaling most men, but definitely that of her scrawny absent husband. If she had taken it in her head to do him wrong, there wouldn't have been much he could have done about it in a fair fight, or in an unfair one for that matter either. Ma Jenkins was a strong, tough woman, with more than her share of devilry and craftiness to boot, more than enough to even up the odds in the male dominated world of the western frontier.

Marie Jenkins, Ma's only offspring, was as sweet in disposition as she was in her gracious looks, of an even temperament and stunning grace to rival any fancy lady from back East. Clayton had fallen in love with her the very first time he had spotted her in her floral bonnet and calico dress, stepping outside the general store with the ranch's supplies. She had been struggling with a ten pound bag of flour when he had gentlemanly intervened, lifting the sack onto the wagon's bed proudly under her admiring looks. He had helped her load the rest of the provisions, chatting with her about anything and everything to keep those beautiful baby blues centered on him.

He discovered, quite by accident, that her mama was looking for a hand to hire on for helping with the spring's calving. Having no current prospects as a newcomer to town, he asked if he could escort her home, to which she ebulliently agreed. He offered to take the reins, and she demurely acquiesced as well. His heart was racing from the nearness of her voluptuous form and exquisite scent of her scant perfume. Most of the girls back home had paid little attention to Clayton, especially on account of his poor sharecropper parentage and slight build. His introversive, quiet demeanor did nothing to help dissuade this lackluster opinion in the slightest either. He had left the small, insignificant village in the Georgia back-country to make his fortune in the expansive west, where a man's progress was set in motion by his own two hands, not by his family's name or the wealth of his pappy.

Or so he had thought. Within five minutes of newly arriving in Ashcroft, while asking about job opportunities in the area, he made the mistake of bumping into two inebriated young men exiting the local saloon, a place named the Windbag. When he had attempted to apologize for the faux pas, one of the men, a tall, skinny man dressed in fine clothes had spat venomously at his boots, and berated him severely.

"Don't you just hate the way these dirty Southerners talk, Bill? No sense to their womanly speak, not like a man would talk at all." He smiled while he seemed to savor the discomfort of the words' effect on Clayton. "Always apologizing', those stinkin' Rebs done lost their manhood when the North beat it out them in the war."

"Yep, you right Nate, just look at his yellar ass turning red." The other man, a paunchy, slovenly cretin joined in the conversation, toadying up to the other man with vile sycophancy.

Clayton was incensed by the disrespectful comments, and was about ready to do something about the matter. But then he noticed the glint of steel hanging from their belts, versus his empty hip, causing him to angrily bite back his rage, and stalk away from the two. He knew they were looking for a fight and just goading him to get an unfair one going, typical of big mouthed cowards of their ilk.

"Yep, no backbone to those lily-livered Dixie scum. Why don't you run home to your mama, back where you came from!" he hollered at the retreating Clayton. Clayton's fists were balled-up spheres of pure fury, clenched together so tightly the nails were digging into his palms, hard enough to almost draw blood. It wasn't the first time since coming west that he had trouble with biased cretins, but sure didn't make it any easier for him. The men called out a few more curses, then saddled up and rode off eastward. A man who had witnessed the exchange sitting in front the blacksmith shop called Clayton over after they had left.

"Don't you worry none about that young fella, they're all

talk." His eyes were sympathetic and devoid of sarcasm.

"Hard not to worry about someone who hates you without even knowing you," he said, trying to keep the still ample anger he felt burning inside him out of his voice.

"Well, I can't blame ya to much for being mad, I'd feel the same way," the man said. Clayton looked over at the speaker, taking stock of him. He was probably in his early sixties, and wore an old faded work shirt and plain light brown buckskin breeches. The man went on. "It's a good thing you used yer head though. They've started fights with all the new faces around here. Killed a feller in fact just like yerself, provoked him, then murdered him, said it was 'self defense.' That mean one, the one you met, the one that started it, that's Big Jake Sanders boy, Little Jake. At least that's what he's called behind his back, don't seem to care for being called little, always figuring he's got something to prove on account of his daddy's reputation. Now his daddy, that's a cold son of a bitch if you ever met one. Little Jake may be mean, but Big Jake, now he's mean, smart, and rich, the worst combination of bastard you could ever have the misfortune to cross out here or anywhere."

The man was a talker, and Clayton soon learned more than he had cared almost to know about the town of Ashcroft and its denizens. His name was Shamus O'Rourke, and he worked odd jobs for the blacksmith (who had the shingles something fierce, he divulged conspiratorially), and acted as a farrier of sorts for the town. Clayton soon ascertained from him that the sheriff was a one Brady Sampson, and that he probably took payoffs from the whorehouse in the form of personal services from the working girls therein. He learned that minister was a redeemed ex-explorer who had been involved in the Sutter Buttes massacre before seeing the light and changing his killer ways. The saloon owner had a habit of ransacking some of his guests rooms when they weren't present to prevent it, and blamed it on the his hired help. He discovered that the widow Peterson had been taking men to her bed ever since the death of her late husband, evidently Shamus had noticed her making eyes at him and would be taking his turn shortly. When the rapturous Marie Jenkins had left the general store with her packages he had hurriedly said his goodbyes to garrulous Mr. O'Rourke and his never-ending stream of gossip, partly to study the enchanting creature further, and partly to recover the hearing in his ears.

Remembering the aforementioned events as he drove Ms. Jenkins back to her mother's ranch, he hoped he had seen the last of the Sanders and that the future did not hold many more run-ins with those of their nature. The ride to the property was a long one, long enough to get to know Marie much better. She said she liked his accent, said it was so smooth and wonderful to her ears. He let her know he was in need of work, and wondered if her mother would care to have him in her employ? Marie just knew her mama would take to him, he didn't have nothing to fret about. She confided in him that not many men were willing to work for her mother on account of her being a woman and the fact that Big Jake Sanders was mighty interested in her land, and not known for taking no for an answer. But Ma Jenkins was stubborn, and not interested in having any man tell her what do, especially a man with no claim on her. Clayton knew that this seemed like trouble, but looking at the buxom young lady beside him made such thoughts appear as far away as the wisp-like clouds hiding behind the tall mountains in the bright daylight.

They pulled up to the yellow farmhouse in early evening, and he was helping her unload the parcels when he first caught sight of Ma Jenkins. She was about eight inches taller than him, with massive arms as big as his thighs. She had matted, shoulder length hair unbefitting of a lady, worn with a simple ponytail, and thick, heavy mannish garments. Her eyes were set too close together, and where her face wasn't freckled it was scarred with large craters. Her nose was porcine in appearance, and she must have weighed over three hundred pounds. She was possibly the ugliest woman Clayton had ever seen, and he wondered how on God's green earth could such a creature have spawned the angelic Marie.

She spoke, with a voice reminiscent of grain being ground in a mill. "That you Marie? Who's that with you there?" She closed the distance between them quickly with monstrous strides more suitable to a draft horse than a woman.

Marie responded with her honeyed tones of ever cheerfulness. "This here's Clayton Pellard, he's new to town and he gave me a hand with the supplies at the general store and then escorted me back home safe and sound. He's such a Southern gentleman."

Ma Jenkins looked him up and down with obvious and intense scrutiny. He felt like a woman might have if a lewd man had sized her up with no shame in his lecherous nature. He could see the wheels turning within the big woman's head, and he was not sure if he entirely liked it.

She relaxed her obtuse inspection and seemingly satisfied, said, "Well, looks like you should stay out for supper at the least for your trouble. We don't eat fancy round here, but we do got plenty. Marie, you get started on them victuals," barking at her daughter. Marie curtsied to Clayton and departed for her chore, as Ma Jenkins just rolled her eyes. "I love my daughter, but she is full of all these fool notions she heard from her father on how a lady is to act. Now, I can see you are interested in my daughter. You can just put that idea out of your head right now. She's too young for that sort of thing."

"Ma'am, I would never---"

She cut him off with the sharpness of a Bowie knife. "Oh you would, all you boys would like to with my little Marie. Now you're new to this area, and obviously must not have kin round here. Are you looking for work?"

The ease of how she switched subjects threw him in disarray, but he managed to stammer out a reply. "Yes, ma'am I'm looking for work. I'm from Georgia and don't know anyone here, but I'm a hard worker and aim to make my fortune out here in the West."

She threw back her head and guffawed at his little speech. Wiping her eyes, she smiled at him with affection. "I'm sorry to laugh at you, but that was the most hilarious little piece of idiocy I've heard all year. So you left the South because of some pie in sky dreams about the great fortunes to be made out West eh? Well, I'll try you out, little Southerner. I work hard and I'll expect you to work just as hard. I am just a woman after all, so you should find it easy." The sarcasm in her tone did not go unnoticed by Clayton. They haggled on the price, less than he was hoping for, but catching sight of the heavenly Marie again made such inconveniences seem less burdensome. Seeing the gaze not go unnoticed by the matronly Ma Jenkins, he was fairly certain that the crafty woman had used her only daughter as a bargaining chip in their negotiations as well.

He found working for Ma to be just as hard as he had expected, but rewarding overall. She had an unnatural strength and relentless endurance that most men would envy, and she made sure that everyone on the place followed her example. He learned much about the workings of a ranch from the big lady, and she took him under her wing, teaching him her considerable skills in branding and caring for the livestock, how to properly herd and corral the animals, calving, and fencing. He was a good pupil, listening to her advice and applying it with foresight and diligence on his appointed tasks around the property. The spring days seemed to fly by in a veritable hive of activity to him, but not without its stolen moments of joy and pleasure. Marie was as innocent as the day was long, but her furtive glimpses at him while he worked belied an interest that was more than just idle curiosity. She would bring him little treats like blackberries she had picked along the crick, or a little bits of honeyed cornbread she had baked into little heart shapes. He accompanied her to town on the visits to Ashcroft for supplies, where he helped her with the affairs she attended to there if she needed him, or visited with Shamus and some of the other more friendly townsfolk if his services were not required by the pretty girl.

On one such occasion, he had been discussing some of the local history with Shamus after tidying up the errands with Marie in town. Discussing being an arbitrary term when dealing with Shamus, more like listening to his incessant rambling. He had decided to ask Shamus about the great woods that lay northward out past the rolling hills near the Jenkins' ranch. He had questioned Marie about them in the past, and she had instantly looked frightened and whispered they shouldn't talk about the woods. She had looked so panicked and petrified that he had immediately ended his queries as to not frighten to poor girl further. He later had asked Ma Jenkins about the woods, but all she said was, "You stay out of them woods, Clayton Pellard. No one in their right mind goes in there, and nobody sure as heck comes out again. You'll stay out of them Red Scalp Woods if you know what's good for you." And that was it, her tone and posture he had come to know so well meant nothing more would be coming forth from this line of conversation. But his curiosity had been peaked by their evasive silence on the subject, and now that he was speaking with probably the most winded conversationalist in seven counties, he felt sure he could discover the root of the enigma.

But even the loquacious Shamus was frustratingly taciturn of the subject. "Clayton, there are some things people ought not know in this world, and some things they should avoid. Red Scalp Woods is one of those things. Just steer clear of those woods. Don't think about them, don't talk about them, and what ever you do, don't you ever go into them." Clayton tried to reason with the newly retractable old timer, but he would not elucidate further on his cryptic remarks. Finally, after much badgering by the inquisitive cowboy, Shamus added some further clarification, but his normally boisterous tones were reluctant at best.

"The ancient Balori Indian tribe used those woods for their worship. I don't know what they did in there and how much of what's said is true, but the early mountain men and Spaniards said they used to practice dark magic there, performing human sacrifices including the women and children they kidnapped from their enemies. They had a strange power in the nighttime it was said, but I don't know exactly what that meant. The other tribes I guess finally got tired of their devilish practices and they all banded together to wipe them out. Murdered the whole lot of 'em by all accounts. Later on when Red Cloud went on his warpath some of the Army got it in their head he might be hiding out in those woods with his people. They sent this big-headed fool, a certain Lieutenant Conroy Matheson, and he went up there with a small squad to check and see if Red Cloud was really there. The Indian scouts he had wouldn't go in there, and they warned Matheson against it, but he wasn't listening to no native mumbo jumbo. He took his men in there, and they all went crazy, starting killing each other, including Matheson. A few made it back out, said they weren't no Indians in there, but something else was in there, but it weren't man nor beast, weren't nothing a man could fight. By the time word got back to the Bozeman fort about what had happened in the woods, Red Cloud had done quieted down again, so they decided to leave it alone, so the Army never went back."

"Later on after people started settling in these parts, folks who went in the woods would come back addled in the head, or just vanished entirely. Everybody started giving it a wide berth, and that seemed to be alright for a time. That is, till this German entrepreneur named Heinrich Krause gets this idea to harvest the forest for lumber. He had to hire lumbermen from out of town, seeing how all the locals won't have nothing to do with the woods. So Krause sends in his crews, and they all start going crazy, just like them soldiers all them years before, hacking on each other with their axes, murdering each other fit for the devil. Now, most man having seen something like that would know it might be better off to leave them woods be, but no, not our German friend Heinrich. Old Heinrich, he's takes it real personally like, and you know how them Germans are when they get something in their heads, so he goes off into those woods with kerosene and fire to get revenge for his men."

"Now, a few of the folks in town followed him out there to see if he really was going to go through with it, and they saw him go in those woods, but they all waited a respectful distance from the wood's edge. They all said you could see a little plume of black smoke that day, but it got snuffed out real quick by something in that woods so the blaze didn't spread and burn down the forest like Heinrich planned. Then the screaming started, and everyone knew that whatever was in there had a hold of poor Heinrich now. You could hear that German screaming for miles, screaming and shrieking in such a way that his very soul must have been being tortured by whatever hellish thing lives in those woods. Everybody watching lit out when this happened, seeing how no one's too sure about the reach of that demonic grove, and none of them were that close of friends with Heinrich anyway."

"They found him the next day on the very edge of that damned wood, naked, spread-eagled, chunks of skin and muscle cut off of him in sacrilegious patterns, the devil himself couldn't have done worse to him. But that's not all. Whatever did it scalped him too, red blood and white bone showing where his hair used to be. They found his scalp a little bit later, they say you could see it nailed up some forty feet off the ground on this old tree. Problem was, it was thirty yards into those terrible woods to retrieve it and there weren't nobody willing to go in there after it, not after all that had happened and seeing how that German had brought it on himself by messing with things best left alone by good Christian folk. So they left it up there, hanging in the breeze, and it would still be there if the buzzards hadn't got to it. That's why they call it Red Scalp Woods and that's why no one talks about it. We stay out of the woods, and the woods leaves us be out here. Now don't you ask me about this ever again, because I won't speak of it anymore." He left in a hurry, without even so much as a goodbye to Clayton in his haste.

The old man was clearly frightened just talking about the woods, and Clayton couldn't blame him after hearing the hauntingly surreptitious tale. However, he had heard some tall ghost tales as well in the back-country he had grown up in, but that's all they were, stories. Clayton was not a superstitious man, so the idea that a simple woods could turn men into killers and take a hand itself from time to time was ridiculous. Strangely here everyone seemed to believe that the twaddle was true, and walked on eggshells around a bunch of trees. Preposterous! Shaking his head at the utter nonsense of it, he hoisted the seed bag he had been toting back on his shoulder and went to see if Marie was ready to head back.

He found her with one of her friends, Emma Thompson. That would have been bad enough, seeing how Emma was an empty headed, classist witch he had no use for, but the two of them were in the company of two men he recognized quite well. It was Little Jake Sanders and Will Mayberry, the two disagreeable ruffians who had met him the day he had arrived. Jake had a riding crop and was slapping it unconsciously against his leg as he chatted with the two girls, while Will had his usual slothful appearance, a stupid grin on his dull face. Jake spotted Clayton with his heavy load, and turning to Marie, said in an overtly disrespectful voice, "Oh, its your hired boy, Walk-Away Clay. Good to see one of those yellow crackers learning their place. Has he finished all the little chores you need him to do?"

Emma and Will seemed to find that funny, laughing hysterically as if he had told the most amusing joke in the history of Ashcroft. Clayton's eyes narrowed, and looking over at Marie he checked to see if she was laughing as well. She was not, he was relieved to see, but neither was the offending man either. He was watching Clayton, like a cat watches a mouse, waiting to see if he would do anything in his irritation. Clayton noticed that he still had the pistol on his hip, but he was not about to take this kind of treatment in front of Marie, no sir, not a second time from this spoiled brat. He walked over to the wagon, dropping his load into the bed before heading over to the quartet, where the riotous laughter had quieted. He pretended to ignore the comment like he hadn't heard it at all, and quietly said, "Marie, we need to head back to your ma's, it'll be dark soon."

Jake spoke before she could reply, directing his disparaging comments to the Southern man. "Now Marie knows when it time to go, Walk-Away Clay. A hireling such as yourself shouldn't be so familiar with your betters. She'll leave when she's good and ready to."

"No, Clayton's right. We should be heading back." Marie started to walk towards Clayton, but Jake lightly but firmly restrained her with his free hand by grasping her arm. This was too much for Clayton. He strode towards Jake with a vehement start, intent on finishing what the insulting bully had repeatedly instigated. Jake saw the indignant southern man's movement towards him and its intent, and releasing Marie, darted forward to intercept his charge, crop raised high above his head. As the two neared Jake brought the wicked lash down with all his force on the man's unprotected face, but before he could connect, Clayton, seeing his intent, snatched the crop from Jake's grasp with his superior work hardened strength.

Now armed with the lash, he intended to do unto Jake as he was going to do unto him, but as he brought the implement back for the mighty blow to follow, he felt an iron hand clutch at his forearm from behind, preventing his strike, squeezing like a vise on his extremity. Adrenaline coursing through his veins, he whirled on this new opponent, and was greeted by the sight of Big Jake Sanders. This was the first time he had laid eyes on the infamous cattle baron, and he could see now how he received his ominous appellation. The man stood well over six foot, and must have weighed over two hundred and fifty pounds, none which seemed to be fat. He had a stern, unforgiving look to him more reminiscent of a carved stone statue than mortal flesh.

"Now see here boy," he said, taking the crop in his free hand from Clayton's suddenly limp fingers, "Now you don't want to do something that you're going to regret later." He changed the target of his ire. "Jake, now these nice folks need to get back home. Why don't you and your friend give them a hand loading their wagon?" His voice was not angry or vexed, but the tone brooked no nonsense. He was instantly obeyed by his son and Will, who quickly loaded the provisions from Marie's visit in the back of the wagon. He released Clayton's arm, and gestured towards the waiting buckboard, watching him as he climbed into it. Big Jake helped Marie to follow suit, cordially telling her to give his greetings to her ma. Clayton slapped the reins, giving the horse notice to begin the journey back home. He looked back over his shoulder as they left, seeing with some relish Big Jake curtly dressing down Little Jake. The words were not clear above the noise of the wagon's progress, but the look on Little Jake's face was telling of the reprimand.

The ride home was mostly spent in uncomfortable silence, with Marie attempting to break it with her frivolous chatter, and he responding to her with monosyllable responses. He was foolishly angry with her for associating with Little Jake and Will, and had realized it was probably more her friend Emma's doing than any action on her part, but the pervasive emotion remained nonetheless. He was actually relieved when they finally arrived at the ranch so he could part ways with her; he was finding her company that vexing for the time being.

The next day he had gotten over the suppressive exasperation, and while Marie made the morning's meal he attempted to banter with her playfully, but received a cold welcome from the young woman. Evidently even the softhearted Marie was true to the old saying of hell and scorn, but gradually he broke down her frigid defenses, and by the time her mother came down for breakfast they had made up nicely and were back on friendly terms. As they enjoyed their repast together, a knock at the front door suddenly interrupted their morning refreshment.

Clayton answered the door, surprised to see it was Big Jake Sanders again.

"Who is it Clayton?" Ma shouted from the kitchen.

"It's Big Jake."

Ma moved to the door quicker than an angry rattlesnake caught outside in a rainstorm, literally shoving Clayton out of her way in her haste. "What brings you down here on this fine Sunday, Jake?" she asked with a guarded but polite inflection in her voice.

Big Jake smiled with a wolf's intent, saying, "Well now, Lucille I think you know why I'm here. I've given you a few months to think about my offer, and I've been plenty patient with you. Now the bank is set to foreclose come December on account of your late husband's debts he ran up over at the saloon. Now, I told you I can pay that off and give you plenty besides for this here property. All you have to do is come down off your high horse a little and sign-"

Ma Jenkins cut him off in mid-sentence. "And I told you, Jake, that I don't intend to sell it, not for you, not for the bank, not for nobody. This here is my land, my fool husband may have threatened that with his penchant for fine drink and cheap harlots, but I'll be damned if it'll ever go to likes of you. Clayton, see that *Big Jake* as he likes to be called finds the front gate!" She whirled from the front door in a red-faced huff, just in time to see the look of stunned pain on her daughter's face before Marie fled the room. Clayton knew why Marie was upset. Ma Jenkins was always careful not to talk poorly about Marie's daddy in front of her, so the disparaging words about him must have been quite a shock to the girl.

He returned to his appointed task, but Big Jake was already heading back to his horse, the massive black roan. Clayton watched him saddle up, intent on performing his duties to the letter if necessary. But Big Jake left placidly, just stopping once on his way out and turning to the young man.

"It's about to get a little heated around here. I really wish she would just take the money. But then again, I never really thought she would. Stubborn, just like her daddy was. Never knew what she saw in Paul Jenkins. Too soft and oily for a woman like her. Just goes to show, they all go weak-kneed when a man says a few nice words to them and gets them to believe it." He snorted with derision, then focused sharply on

Clayton. "You're not from here, this ain't your fight. You're better off just moving along."

"I'm not interested in your opinion of what I should be doing either, Mr. Sanders." His audacity shocked himself a little, but it definitely raised the ire in Big Jake. He took a long, hard last look at Clayton, then spurred the roan back towards town. Clayton watched him ride off, knowing that trouble would be brewing soon. He headed back into the house, intent on sharing his newfound information from Big Jake with Ma. He found her inside with her back turned to him, body shaking with tears. Knowing she must not have heard his approach, he retraced his steps then loudly entered to give the big woman time to compose herself. He waited until she was sufficiently recovered before relaying what Big Jake had said outside, pretending not to notice the tear-streaked cheeks. She thanked him, and asked him point blank if he planned to stay.

"My mama died when I was almost too young to remember her, and my daddy was a poor sharecropper that looked at us kids more like slaves than his own offspring. My older brothers and sisters all left home as soon as they could, can't blame them much for that seeing how Daddy was. You and Marie have treated me more like family than my own. I ain't going nowhere."

His strong words seem to bolster the big woman, and she seemed to regain some of her enduring spirit. "Well, if you're in for the long haul, we better see about outfitting you." She left the room and returned with an old cap and ball Colt Walker, a Smith & Wesson Model 1, and ammunition and powder for both. She looked at him solemnly. "You take one of these you're in it now for sure. I can't promise you this will turn out alright." He nodded, and took the Walker. She strapped on the Smith & Wesson, and they went out back behind the barn. She had him help her set up some hay bale targets, then showed him how to load and aim the handgun. He was a quick study, with a natural skill that soon had him sending tufts of blasted hay skyward in no time. They practiced for a spell, and then Ma went off to take care of some pressing work. He kept the big gun strapped on, liking the weight of the weapon. He headed to the barn to return the bales, finding that in the loft Marie had been watching the two of them practice. He can see that she had been crying earlier as well, the tell-tale signs evident on her fair features. Unlike with her strong mother he asked her about it, looking to ease the young woman's heartache.

"I never knew that about my pa. Mama never really spoke good about him, but she never said anything ill either. I knew they used to fight after I'd go to bed, and my father would storm out of the house and head to town, but I never knew it was so bad, or what he was doing there. I just figured he was drinking. When I was younger they seemed to be so happy, I don't know what caused them to drift so far apart. I know my mama's not a good looking woman but he was married to her. Why would a man cheat on his own wife who borne him a child like that?"

"I don't know Marie. I wouldn't do that, not never."

"Would you? Or are you just like every other man in town and just say that because you think I'm pretty for right now? All you men seem pretty similar when it comes to that." With that she flounced out of the barn before he could say anything further. He considered pursuing her and continuing the unwelcome argument, but he decided some time to cool off might be more advantageous for the time being. He went about his daily labor instead, and by the time he had a spare moment to talk with Marie, she had shut herself in her room with no intention of coming out. Later at supper she was cordial to him, but with an aloofness that was perturbing to the young man. Truly, he thought, the ways of women are a mystery.

The first few days passed without event, similar to the carefree times before Big Jake's visit. Except for the continued coldness of Marie, that was. He didn't know why, but it seemed she was blaming him for her own father's perfidious deviance. He tried to engage her in idle conversation or a passing jest, but she resolutely held him at arms length. In fact, the next time she went to town she purposely did not even tell him, he had only discovered that she had gone by the missing horses and wagon. He tried to speak with Ma Jenkins about the sudden change in her daughter, but she refused to take sides in the matter.

"A woman has the right to her own mind when it concerns affairs of the heart. While I think she could do much worse than you Clayton, it is not my place to make her choose you or any other man. This is your affair, and you must be one to win her over if she is to have you." The admonishing words did not bring Clayton much comfort, but it did give him something to mull over.

Soon, however, events were unfolding that made Clayton's lovelorn complications seem trivial in comparison. A section of fence in the north eastern pasture that was in no way shape or form dilapidated or damaged beforehand suddenly was completely fallen in at a twenty foot section. Clayton had noticed its conspicuous absence fortunately before any livestock managed to utilize the lately created egress. Upon inspection he saw the posts had been sawn at the bases and the barb wire cut in deliberate fashion. He managed to fix the compromised section, but its root cause was highly suspect.

A few nights later, while they were seated at dinner, the abrupt sound of gunshots and then agitated lowing from the cattle pens disturbed the tranquil peace and shattering any misconceptions about the nature of any further misfortunes. He and Ma rushed out to protect the frantic livestock, but only saw unrecognizable shapes riding off in the late evening darkness. The cows were mercifully unharmed, but the message was clear: they could not protect the herd everywhere at all times. They started night watches nevertheless, trying to catch one of the culprits hopefully red-handed in an unlawful act. The next week went by thankfully without further mishap, but the illusion of complacency was shattered when after midnight, a large rock with the words "Git Out or Die!" crudely painted on it smashed through the kitchen window, scattering shards of glass throughout the entire room. Ma Jenkins was incensed by the sheriff's callous attitude to the reported incident after she returned from town, calling him numerous names and insults, including "gutless" and "lick-spittle" to name some of the more pleasant appellations. She was becoming increasingly short tempered in addition to being keenly on edge like the rest of them from the ever increasing attacks.

When they found the first slain cow is when her stolid composure truly and inevitably cracked. Its throat had been slashed at some time quietly during the night, and she had been the one on watch and had never seen or heard anything. She just sat next to slaughtered animal, sobs of futility wracking through the big woman's body as tears of guilt rolled down her cheeks. Clayton, not knowing quite what to do, let her be in her remorse and shame. Ma's breakdown bothered him more than a little, and in seeing Marie trying to console her mother he knew something needed to be done, and soon. The two people he cared about most were in pain, and he felt helpless against the overwhelming forces that seemed arrayed against them.

He had resolved to do something about it in the morning, but the disappearance of Marie when he and Ma awoke disrupted his plans. She had left a note, simply saying that she was going into town and they needn't fret over her outing. Ma read the paper twice in her deliberation, finally decided to have Clayton watch over the ranch while she went into town to retrieve her missing daughter. He busied himself with the normal day to day jobs that needed to be done despite the current situation, and waited for her and Marie's return. The morning passed in a tedious and protracted fashion, with his mind giving him no respite from the worries of their present predicament.

Ma returned with Marie that afternoon, but the shared looks of displeasure on the two women's faces brooked no questioning from the young man. They both spoke little thereon, and Clayton wisely stayed out of their way while performing his duties, in spite of his overwhelming curiosity. A short while later Ma took him to the side and informed him to continue watching over the livestock while she was going to see the marshal in Virginia City, to find out if he would be of more help than the sheriff with the current troubles they were facing. She went into the house to speak with her daughter as well, which due the loud volume of their ensuing argument Clayton was able to catch the words "shameful," "town," and "stay." He also caught his name as well as Little Jake's in the heated conversation, and wondered to the meaning of the references.

Then Ma jerked the front door open with such force it caused a banging sound as it ricocheted off the wall, and Clayton pretended to be busy inspecting her horse's shoes for the journey to give the illusion he had not been eavesdropping.

She seemed not to notice fortunately, and parted ways with him with little fanfare. Ma told him to look after Marie while she was gone, and to take care of himself. He promised solemnly that he would, then watched her ride off into the distance. He entered the house to speak with Marie, but the girl was in no mood for chatter, closing herself off into her bedroom again. No amount of coaxing would get her to abandon her haven, so eventually he gave up and went about the further business of the ranch, heading up to the north forty acres plot so the cattle could graze freely. By the time he had returned to the house to grab a bite to eat before setting back out it was much later, the trip and resettlement of the cattle having taken the majority of the day.

The evening was soon in coming, and the farmhouse and barn was bathed in a red glow from the impending setting sun. The normal chatter of the farmyard was abnormally silent, with not even the sound of the wind to break the monotonous quiet. Clayton set out for the barn to unsaddle and water his horse, but then a low groaning sound became apparent to his ears, making him stop dead in his tracks. The sound seemed to be coming from the barn, so he relinquished his firm hold on the reins, leaving the animal behind, and stealthily crept towards the source of the disturbance. The sounds were not harmonic, instead with a discordant satisfaction that grew louder the closer he came to the building, until he reached the barn entrance.

The noises were distinct now, with heavy breathing and

soft moans coming from the interior. As he silently made his way into the barn, he could see a man's shirt carelessly discarded on to the dirt floor. Further in he saw a sight that literally left him too astonished in disbelief to even contemplate its terrible meaning as he watched. He saw Little Jake, shirtless, pants pulled down to his ankles, pumping furiously on top of a female form, the source of the guttural noises of pleasures. If that was not shock enough, he saw Marie under him, dress hiked halfway up to her waist, legs spread, eyes closed in pleasure. Finally understanding the horrible image searing into his mind, he became dizzy, causing him drop to his knees and reach forward to steady himself.

His hand touched the handle of the old pitchfork, and as the full realism of what was transpiring before him sank in, his emotions turned to anger and betrayal. His touch on the implement turned to a solid grip as the pain and rage coursed through his veins, giving him a matchless strength and vigor. Coming to his feet once more and grabbing the tool with both hands, he stared at the deplorable surrealism of the scene before him. Clayton's face was red and hate-twisted, the fury in his thoughts becoming almost molten in its intensity to which there lay only one outlet: murder. The writhing couple did not hear him in their frantic embrace, as he advanced on them in a red haze of self righteous anger until he stood over the fornicating pair, all sane control lost to him as the circling madness of hatred and unfaithfulness took over in his recently unbalanced mind.

As if somehow suspecting the danger hovering above him, Little Jake twisted his sweaty neck and face upwards, half realizing his doom even as the killing blow streaked towards him in a powerful thrust by Clayton. The pitchfork impaled him through his chest and into the female form below, the force of the blow so severe that the tines sank a full two inches under her. She never opened her eyes again, the strike mercifully killing her instantly and relatively painlessly. Little Jake was not so lucky, letting loose with a dying wail that reverberated throughout the barn. His dire rage unsatiated, Clayton slowly drew his gun, firing a single shot into Jake's face, turning it into a bloody red mass instantly before the now lifeless body fell, slumping over the dead girl's form. The heinous deed now finished, Clayton's mind began to retreat even farther from its previous unsettled state, horror and shock over his own actions reeling in his brain as the stress of action receded along with its adrenalized excitement. The distinct sounds of a person running outside brought his lapsing attention back to the present from its interlude however, and gun in hand he left the scene of carnage to investigate the footsteps.

It was Will, dashing pell-mell away from the barn's large entrance with a quickness that seemed impossible for the portly man. He must have been outside out of eyesight or in the house when Clayton first arrived in the farmyard, and Clayton's intensity in discovering the source of the perplexing moans coming from the barn must have led to his overlooking of the boot-licking lackey's presence. Will must have come out of concealment and either heard Clayton's dolorous actions or possibly even witnessed his monstrous handiwork firsthand; consequently he decided to run away hastily to avoid becoming the next target of the other man's wrath. Clayton aimed dead center at his cowardly retreating backside and pulled the trigger, fully expecting the plump interloper to pitch face first in the waiting dust of the yard. Unfortunately, the load must have been bad, because instead of a resounding roar there was only a pitiful click as the Walker misfired. Will continued his desperate run to the side of the house, as Clayton frantically cocked the single action revolver again then brought the pistol to bear on his target just as the fat man disappeared behind the structure. Seconds later he heard agitated neighing and then rhythmic hoof-beats receding in the distance. As he raced forward around the building to send another shot in the direction of the unwanted trespasser, he finally caught sight of him.

But it was too late, it was plain to see the intruder was firmly out of the pistol's short range, firing would just be a foolish waste of ammunition. Clayton speedily headed back to his horse to chase after him, but by the time he was able to saddle up he could see that pursuit was no longer an option. Will was a mere speck now, headed back in the direction of the town. He knew he would not have long before the sheriff would be giving chase, and Big Jake would hardly set idle with his son's murderer free and abroad. He set his mount to the water and feed troughs, and then packed up further provisions for the horse and himself for the journey ahead. He thought about leaving a consolatory note to Ma Jenkins, but he knew no words could ever make right the wrong he had inflicted on the poor woman. He took one long last look at the ranch he had considered home for the last few months, and slowly rode away northward, figuring the inevitable pursuit would not think to head that direction.

This last act, unfortunately, had led to the current predicament he was facing. The posse had caught up to him more quickly than he had imagined, bringing him to the conclusion that whoever was doing the tracking must be highly skilled indeed. The sun had set, and the dying light would soon be extinguished, both helping him avoid the pursuers and hindering his progress with the lack of illumination. Looking again down into the coulee nervously and seeing with alarm the significant progress the mounted group was making, he flicked the reins to signal his tired mount to renew their ascent up the hill. Ponderously they climbed the rising ground, bypassing the abundant sagebrush and solitary firs in the best possible route.

Finally cresting the hilltop, he looked out over the landscape spread before him. To his right it led down to the plains below, where he knew there was no place to hide in the open ground and the posse would easily catch up to him. The way to his left consisted of hills like the one he was on, that later gave way to even more mountainous terrain. This could be an advantage if he could hide among the valleys and their passages, but the fatigued horse versus the constant elevation could prove to be his undoing. Directly ahead of him, the hill sloped down to a short plains bisected by a small stream. Across from that stream was a bristling, large woods, so thick that the light itself seemed disappear into its murky gloom. He recognized the imposing forest, which was none other than the object of the townspeople's incredible fear and horror, the Red Scalp Woods. Weighing his options, he knew he would have little choice but to enter the forbidden region if he was to escape from the posse's wrath, and he was hoping that the superstitious townsfolk would be unwilling to cross into its dark, shadowy interior.

He began to make his way down the hillside, reaching the bottom and letting his weary horse drink from the cold, clear water before crossing the small creek and proceeding on to the dark woods. The wind, which had been lifeless before, was a chilling force that blew at divergent intervals, unusually inclement for what had been such a warm day before. As he came closer to the edge of the woods a foreboding sense of dread seemed to well up within him, and the stubborn memory of his talk with Shamus O'Rourke of the insanity and deaths spawned by the forest did little to placate the incessant feelings of trepidation. His horse began to balk at the continued course of action, and he was finally unable to get the animal to move at all; it stood stock still and refused any commands forward from him contrarily. Dismounting from the intractable beast, he attempted to pull it forward by the reins to the forest, but it stubbornly persisted in its defiant behavior. Finally reduced to strikes and curses in spite of the fact he was loathe to use them on the poor equine, he soon found that even those desperate measures would not incite any movement on the part of his unreasonable animal. He resolved to remove the saddle bags of supplies from the horse, and continue on foot into the woods. As he finished with the task, he saw on the top of the hill the riders had ascended and would soon be quickly approaching, and he knew he could not waste any further time. He slapped his horse on the hindquarters, hoping it would lead the pursuers away as it galloped off. He plunged ahead to the blackness awaiting him below the thick pines, stumbling over thick grass tufts and gnarled, exposed roots in his haste.

Inside the forest it was as dark as it had appeared, and his eyes slowly accustomed themselves to gloomy interior. The pine trees were large and thickly proportioned, their long and abundant needles effectively blocking the sunlight from reaching the forest floor. Knowing he could easily lose his sense of direction with the lack of any kind of landmarks, he sought to walk as straight as humanly possible. The quiet in the woods was disconcerting at best, with the normal sounds of insects and birds strangely absent. Even the chill wind that perturbed him earlier was missing now, so deadened and becalmed that even the soft, natural undertones of breezes traveling through branches and of the slight movement of pines swaying were not heard in the slightest. All sound was notoriously missing, as if the very land itself was holding its breath. It was the quietest place he had ever been in his lifetime, and he doubted that he ever could find anywhere as silent this side of the grave. In fact, if it had not been for the sound of his own progress, he could have thought he had been struck deaf in its completeness.

As he walked, thoughts in his head seemed to be occupied with the atrocious deed he had done. He regretted what his brash action had resulted in, at least in the subsequent death of Marie. With Little Jake's demise he had felt firmly justified, his personal dislike powering his overwhelming hatred of the young man. But he had loved Marie, or so he had thought. He recalled the time they had spent together on the ranch, the sweet little tokens of affection and the earnest familiarity when they had talked about the future. True, she had turned cold in the last few days, but how does a person change themselves and their heart so completely in such a short span of time? He saw again her lying under Jake, eyes closed in wanton lust, and his jilted anger returned to the forefront, seeing the pitchfork stab through the disrespectful antagonist and into her lying, *betraying* form, and he soon felt an abnormal satisfaction at the heinous accomplishment of murdering the two lovers. The sensation was anathema to him, and he felt it did not come from within him but from some outside unseen presence, like some exterior force was causing the feelings of pleasure over the despicable act. He tried to shake off the sentiment, but it persisted in its vile assault upon him, returning to his mind with thoughts of the terrible happening repetitiously, no matter how many times he attempted to dismiss it.

Straining his vision in the twilight conditions, he spotted a flash of white ahead and made his way towards the bright break in black monotony ahead. He soon discovered its source, large white rocks arranged in strange patterns, looking extremely random in some placements but eerily familiar in others. He had seen Indian markings and decorations from various tribes in his travels westward, and these looked nothing like the pictures and writings he had seen, so he was uncertain to why some seemed so natural to him. He knew he was no expert by any means, but they did not seem to conform to any rudimentary people he knew of. The familiarity was like the sensation of pleasure from before, unbidden in his mind, so alien from his own thoughts that it seemed separate, *outside*.

He continued his path through the rocks, but the further he ventured into the stone arrangements the more they seemed sacrilegious in their conception, like their very creators were idolaters of some blasphemous religion of gods that should have been shunned by all men. His innate observations proved to be horrifically true to his chagrin, upon finding a large circular pit with moss-covered bones of antiquity in the center of the formations. Viewing the smashed and broken skeletons, he could tell two important details, one of which the remains were not just animal, seeing human skulls present in the skeletal mix. Secondly, that they did not die naturally, with the holes and fractures of long ago wounds callously distributed in abundance on the derelict frames. The massive carnage was chilling to behold, despite its age, more so when he saw the smaller skulls and bones of obviously human children mixed among the remnants.

Resuming his pace, wishing to leave the site of such desecration, he redoubled his efforts to cross the woods. The strange, alien thoughts in his head had withdrawn after leaving the white rocks, leaving him to believe that he had imagined the sensations, perhaps created by his repeated thoughts of the old man Shamus's tall tales of the forest, the desolate and disturbing landscape, and the unconscionable acts of violence he had perpetrated. The deafening silence continued however, and when it was finally broken he did not notice it at first, thinking it was a fiction his sensory-starved mind had created in the absence of stimulation. It was a low humming sound, deep and rhythmic, almost a buzzing with its consistency. It started almost inaudibly, but the further he progressed the louder it became until he could no longer ignore it, or pretend it was a hallucination.

He stopped for a moment, but the humming soon became an irresistible call, making him continue towards its unseen source. He tried to resist, but the siren sound ground down his resolve, attacking his fears with its sweet cadence until he no longer had the will to fight it, instead willingly giving in. The rough terrain no longer hindered him, as his feet with predetermined surefootedness found the best possible route through the thick foliage in spite of never having walked in these ancient woods before.

The ground soon began to rise, gradually at first, and then more steeply. In spite of the ascending countryside, he felt refreshed and boundlessly full of energy, able to continue his amazing pace unhindered. The problems and worries he was currently facing seemed to melt away with the prodigious exertion he was performing, and he felt fundamentally changed by the throbbing and humming, now not only hearing the phenomenon but feeling it as well, rising up from the ground into his extremities, propelling him forward. At last he came within view of a large cave entrance, and he knew despite his unfamiliarity with the scene that this was the source of the strange resonances.

He slackened his pace, and after taking a long swallow of tepid water from his canteen, rummaged for his flint and steel. He found a suitable branch and mosses and duly created an impromptu torch for light. He left his pack and supplies at the cave entrance, not wishing to be hindered by their bulk in his exploration. He proceeded into the preternatural gloom of the cave, seeing parietal art carved and painted on the high walls as his torch lit scenes that had not most likely seen by man for hundreds of years. The cave paintings were infinitesimally accurate in the minutest of details, showing that the painters were possessing of the highest degree of aptitude despite their inherent age. He studied the scenes closely, thoughts of pursuit from the posse seemingly vanished from his newly freed mind.

Some of the scenes were familiar, proving Shamus O'Rourke's yarns more correct than even he had probably suspected. Drawings of the theft of native men, women, and children by assailants from their primitive shelters, of attacks and murders on unsuspecting victims by dark shapes on starless nights, and of bloodthirsty sacrifices and terrible slaughter of the innocent. But there were unfamiliar scenes as well, of a colossal god blinded in one eye rejoicing in the dark sacrilege and worship, of his defeat and subsequent wounding by a warrior of light, and then a great migration of him and his followers from a far away land across vast bodies of water, momentous plains, rolling hills, and massive mountains. The detail was exquisite in every picture, and left little to the imagination except in its unknown references. Passing by the momentous drawings, he came to a crudely carved stair, and began to descend it, down to the yawning darkness below. It seemed to go on infinitely, to the very core of the earth itself, winding in convoluted shapes downward, bereft of normal human design.

He eventually reached the bottom, finding his torch sputtering and gasping from the lack of normal breathable air. He himself did not feel any ill effects, the strange humming still calling to him and giving him singular strength. It was more pronounced down here, and using the last of his torchlight he could make out an iron door, much too large for human dimensions and rusted from disuse, across from the staircase. The call seemed to be coming from behind the door, and he stepped up to the entrance, grasping an over-sized iron ring bolted on the structure, and pulled with all his strength. The door opened slowly, much easier than he had imagined from such neglect, but still with some difficulty due to the great size. A dull red glow peaked from around it, so he swung the massive portal open the rest of the way, throwing it back to display the source of illumination.

He dropped his makeshift torch, the remnants providing little illumination anyway for guiding his way. Letting his eyes grow accustomed to the muted crimson light, after a short time he found he could see almost as well as before. He studied the interior of the room, noting that a small pathway, only a few feet wide led from the door to the center of the chamber, a circular island. Everywhere else was engulfed by a large chasm, so deep he could not see the bottom. The top of the room was equally impressive, leading off into unknown and unseen heights as well. The light bathed everything visible in the crimson glow, and he saw it came from a large jewel, ruby-like, in the center of the chamber, possibly the largest he had ever heard of, let alone seen. It was shaped like a massive heart, complete with valves and chambers, and he could hear now that the hum-like throbbing was coming from it, gigantic beats so slow and intertwined that it produced the continuous vibrations to the human ear.

Even now it called him further to it with its desirable

song, spurring him to travel down the narrow pathway across the black abyss, until he stood face to face with the pulsating organ, feeling as well as seeing the deliberate rhythmic beat. He stared deeply into it, and without registering it to his conscious mind, placed his hands on the ruddy surface. The touch seared into his mind and soul, surprising him with the now apparent action he had taken, and with its glacially cold feeling, not at all as he had expected from something glowing with such warm fervor. He stared into the lustrous gemstone, amazed by its sanguine fluorescence, feeling it draw him deeper and deeper within it. He could see now past its crimson superficial layer, until he could see its black core, so dark that light itself could not escape its clutches. He could feel the external thoughts again, more deeply now with the close contact, and his mind was forced open to examination by the strange, alien manifestation.

He saw his painful life with his abusive father, altercations he had as a child with other children, fights as a young man, and the dark events that had transpired so recently. He saw the memories not as an outsider would have, with an impartial vantage point, but from his singular point of view at the time, complete with the feelings and emotions that had accompanied the recollections. He stood for an indeterminate period of time, countless hours or simply passing moments, lost in remembrance of tragic days. He felt each occurrence as it felt for the first time, pain, anger, and suffering welling up in his overloaded senses. Finally the assault of traumatic reminiscences receded, and then he felt the presence's sentience, deep and cruel, coil inside his mind, filling him with its thoughts as it sought to communicate its purpose with him. It spoke through a combination of emotions and images, telling him of its capacity for destruction and willingness to share it with him. Depictions of power and sights of glory appeared in his mind from the unknown source, filling his head with dreams of him destroying the men following him, of killing them, of luxuriating in their slaughter.

He felt the pleasure of murdering them as well, of the death of all those who opposed him. He wanted that power, the primal urge of the kill, the capacity for violence, the bestial feeling of the conqueror for himself. Drunk on the blood crazed thoughts and longing for the malicious abilities, he shouted to the vibrating, scarlet heart, "Give it to me! Give me the power!" He was answered by the omnipotent voice, and he felt massive stores of energy pouring into him through his tightly gripped hands on the exterior of the gem, strengthening him, *changing him*, into something more than human but less as well. He no longer cared, however, as he beheld with his newly assisted body, feeling stronger and more vigorous than ever before in his lifetime, far beyond mortal strain. The generous entity urged him to wield his power against those that followed him, to enjoy the inevitable massacre and then to return and share the images and emotions with it.

Elated and filled with zeal, he rushed from the room, flying up the stairs in moments, bursting from the cave's dark womb like a reborn soul. The night was in full effect now, the black, moonless sky lit only by the gleaming stars. He felt exuberant in the nighttime air, unstoppable, more akin to a force of nature than mere man. He leapt from the cave edge down the steep hillside, finding he could easily bound from place to place, jumping on all fours like a great cat would do in its hot pursuit of prey. Seeing just as well with his new night vision as he could previously in the daytime, perhaps even better, he could navigate the dense forest with ease and accuracy. The sounds he made were minimal, with nary a cracked twig or misstep on loose shale. Running through the forest at incredible speed, he soon find himself at its edge. He began to search the plains adjacent to the great woods, careful to stay within the dark fringe. While he was supernaturally strong and quick now, he knew he was by no means invincible, a stray bullet could easily strike him as dead as a normal man.

He spotted the campfire of the stationary posse after relentless searching, and he found they had camped for the night, miles from where he first entered the forest, at a respectful distance from the feared trees. He watched with his nocturnal sight, seeing that most were seated around their fire, backs to the dark, enjoying a late meal after the day's riding. They had set up tents, and had their horses picketed close by. He could plainly see a lone lookout with a rifle posted, who was watching the forest from his not so hidden vantage point about twenty paces from the closest person arrayed around the fire. Clayton recognized him as Will, and his anger flared like a torch within, the savage urge to kill the portly man almost overriding his sense of caution. Quieting his bestial fury, he chose to study him instead. After several moments of scrutiny he noticed the man was expectantly lackadaisical in his duty, turning back in the direction of the fire whenever someone laughed or spoke loudly, his rifle held loosely in his hands.

Clayton crept unseen towards the sentry, using the darkness of the night and the tall grass and brush along with his new sense of preternatural stealth to mask his approach. The fleshy man remained blissfully unaware of the horrendous doom until it was too late. Waiting until Will stared back at the campfire at a boisterous guffaw, he ran forward silently at him, pouncing savagely and bearing him to the ground. He felt the large intake of air precipitating the fat man's scream and quickly took action, wrapping his hands around his throat and crushing his larynx with a powerful squeeze. Wanting to enjoy the sensation in spite of the danger, he easily held Will down, pinning his arms at his sides. With his free hand, he covered his mouth and nose with tight pressure, cutting off his air supply. The impotent thrashes brought a smile to lips, and he savored the dying man's fearful look in his eyes with an inhumane relish. Waiting to remove his suffocating lock for a suitable length of time to insure that he was unequivocally deceased, he then checked the campsite, making sure no one had noticed the struggle.

They all were still unaware of what had transpired, so taking the dead man's rifle he carefully checked to see if it had been chambered properly, especially given the weapon's previous owner. It was a Winchester 30-30, and Will had loaded five cartridges in satisfactorily, to his good fortune. Taking stock of the sitting targets he saw seven men, but none were Big Jake. He did recognize the ineffectual sheriff Brady Sampson, and resolved to send his corrupt soul to hell next. He fired three shots with unerring accuracy before any of the men were able to so much as move a muscle due to his abnormal speed and heightened skill. The first shot turned the lawman's face to a satisfying red mush, the second finding its mark easily in the chest of another man with a silver badge, probably one of his deputies. The third struck the neck of a large man with a duster, spraying blood in an obscene spray on the others who were finally reacting to the startling assault.

Time was moving in a slowed fashion for Clayton compared to the almost sleepily-appearing group, and as one man went for his pistol he blasted him to oblivion as well, and then switching targets, sent another to his maker when he attempted to dive for cover. The last two went separate ways, one dropping down and the other running madly in the opposite direction. Grasping the still warm barrel in two hands, he sprang forward, closing the distance in seconds on the cowering form. Using the gun as a club, he struck in a tremendous downswing, smashing the butt on the man's unprotected head with such force he shattered both his skull and the wooden stock. Men were coming out of the tents now, and he let the fleeing coward escape to deal with the new threats. He threw the useless rifle like a javelin at closest target, impaling him in the guts with supernatural strength behind the toss. Pulling his pistol, he dispatched three more foes quickly, leaving just one figure left, a hulking brute he easily recognized as Big Jake Sanders. Big Jake spotted him and fired shots wildly at him, missing with the first two but striking his right arm on the third. He attempted to dodge as he had before, but the large rancher was a better shot than his fellows, and landed a hit in his side with another well-aimed bullet.

By that time however, Clayton had closed the distance on the big man, and seizing the initiative, batted the pistol out of his hand with a well-aimed strike. Big Jake clenched his teeth at the pain, but immediately tried to grab the young man with what he thought would be superior strength. He was however, woefully wrong, incredulously staring with disbelief as Clayton grabbed his hands as a man would a child and applied pressure back. Clayton saw the astonishing look, and threw back his head and laughed maniacally under the black sky. The things he did to Big Jake afterwards were not things any man should ever do to another, the stuff of the most sickening nightmares, and he did not do them hesitantly or quickly.

After finishing his debased labors the dawn was beginning to break, so he began making his way back to the cryptic cave and his otherworldly benefactor. The feeble dawn's light hurt his eyes, even under the cover of the thick forest, and his newfound strength seemed to ebb away as well, leaving him feeling sapless and void. The climb up to the entrance to the cave was laborious in the extreme, forcing him to stop and catch his breath multiple times as he ascended. He finally reached the cavern, spent from the exertion. The dark interior of the stairwell helped a little with the strange listlessness, making him feel slightly more rejuvenated, but not to the level of power he had held before the dawn. He stumbled down the darkened stairs, dragging his feet down the ancient stone stairs until he reached the bottom. His side ached from the wound he had taken from Big Jake, and his arm throbbed from the errant graze it had received as well. Crossing the rock-hewn room, he could feel the unseen presence once more, calling to him in the crimson abyss past the iron door. He crossed the narrow pathway to the now sluggishly beating heart, and raising his hands, placed them on the ruddy surface. The mind connection made, he relayed the images and emotions of the previous night's depraved actions with the alien mind, feeling its sadistic pleasure while it devoured the reprehensible thoughts.

Time once again seemed to have no meaning as they shared the appalling introspection, the being showing Clayton its mystical origins after absorbing the memories from him. He saw the presence in its original corporeal form, a large giant god known as Balor, thrice as big as a mortal man, formidably formed with a one piercing green eye, covered by a rough patch of translucent marred skin. He saw the giant slaughter many noble heroes and fellow gods, warriors from a distant age, decimating his foes with his massive spear and poisons from his malefic eye, always laughing manically as he murdered and slew. He could feel the satisfying pleasure in the kills like a fiery wave wash over him as he witnessed the destruction, cascades of vicious gratification pouring into him. He learned that the night gave the giant his formidable power, while the sun sapped his strength, forcing him to hide away from the light in caves and the dark spaces between worlds. He saw the great fight between Balor and an imposing warrior, their furious clash, and the eventual downfall of Balor.

His worshipers bore his body across a great ocean, finding a new land to hide their god and themselves from their vengeful enemies. Grievously wounded past redemption, the dying god used the rest of his power to transfer his essence within the jeweled heart his followers created at his behest. No longer a being with any sense of form or commonality with mankind anymore, it was radically and drastically changed by the metamorphose. Cheating death to reside forever with its cult of followers in the forest, it sent its minions to murder, kidnap, and sacrifice in its name, vicariously living through their terrible deeds as they returned. But this reign too came to an end, the local tribes banding together and attacking its people in the daytime as they slept, slaughtering all of them to extinction to banish Balor to oblivion. But the now immortal god lived on, a prisoner in the solitary confines of its own making.

It learned to feel through the trees that grew around the

cave, their roots acting as conduits for its malevolent thoughts. But the tribes around the forest remembered the dark deeds of yore, and shunned the woods of their hated former enemies, never coming near enough for Balor's influence to take hold within their consciousness. Later a new race of men came and entered the wood, men from across the sea as his original followers had been, but they had forgotten about Balor, and its tainted touch caused them madness and death. Only Clayton had been strong enough to survive its terrible proximity in his mind, and Balor needed him to restore its former glory by bringing other worshipers to the divinity, to restart the kidnappings and the sacrifices in its honor. It showed Clayton that he could be the most powerful man in the world, leader of millions, with treasures beyond his wildest imaginations, and women in throngs for his pleasure.

But that was the god's mistake, for Clayton thought again of Marie, for no other woman had touched his heart like she had done. The monstrous deity latched onto to her thought within the young man's mind, unable to help itself from bringing up the remembrance of her death at the young cowboy's hands, drinking the recollection from him like a delectable wine. Clayton saw the detestable memory as well, psychically linked with the insane god's sight, and witnessed the hateful scene again and again, rewinding it over and over like broken phonograph cylinder. He enters the barn, sees Jake on top of Marie, he grabs the pitchfork, and kills the two lovers. He enters the barn, he sees Jake on top of Marie, he grabs the pitchfork, and kills the two lovers.

The terrible scene slows in his mind, the god enjoying the respite from its years of starvation and savoring every second of the crime, every blood-soaked image. Clayton is able to see everything now, every minute detail there to be examined and reviewed. He walks in the barn. Jake is on top of Marie, pumping away *while her eyes are closed and tears are on her cheeks, crying, not moans of pleasure from her lips but moans of pain and anguish.* Clayton finally sees the scene as it really was in reality, not what his anxiety and madness had told him it was in his broken, severed mind. Jake had been raping the poor girl, and instead of saving her from Jake's cruel attack Clayton had viciously murdered her along with her tormentor.

The shock and horror of what he has done breaks the mesmeric spell of the baleful entity, disconnecting him from the parallel communication. The god, realizing something is amiss, attempts to discover the reason for the disturbance, but it is already too late. Unable to live with the ramifications of the vile deeds he had done, and knowing that the demonic deity will continue to seduce and corrupt mankind for all eternity if he continues to serve as its vessel, he has but one final recourse left to him. Summoning the last vestiges of his ebbing strength, Clayton tackles the jeweled crimson heart, and clutching it tightly to his chest, launches himself with it off the narrow island into the vast empty abyss below. His lasts thoughts are of Marie, and he hopes that she can find a place

where she can be at peace, a place where men like him cannot
go.

Old Soul

They say an old soul is someone who is wise beyond their years, and generally has an appreciation for the creations of man produced well before their short lifespan. It is said as well that old souls are the most traveled and reincarnated of all spirits, returning to the mortal form again and again in well worn, accustomed patterns in the endless cycles of life and death. Matthew Somersworth is one such soul. He collects antiques and fossils in a picturesque collection of his own choosing and predilections, and has always loved old things from before his time his entire life, drawn to them like a moth to a flame. Hearing a melody from a hundred years in the past will bring him exquisite pleasure, and viewing a painting from the Baroque or Classical period fills him with a melancholy tranquility that is undue for one such as himself living in these modern times. Myths and stories from history books of the Celts, Franks, and Norsemen, describing their customs and practices, swell him with an earnestness and desire for such simpler times, when men and women lived in harmony with the land instead of bending it to their arbitrary will. He even unknowingly has adapted a physical look that suits him created from the fashions of the past, with a goatee more common to a medieval courtier, sideburns strangely reminiscent of the Victorian era, and a gait more common to Tudor sailors.

Nor are all his familiarities pleasant remembrances of cheerful times and charming nostalgias painted with rose tinted glasses. The first time he had ever laid eyes upon a Roman soldier's heavy scale armor, pilum, and gladius on display in one of London's museums filled him with a strange sense of deep dread. It was as if he had beheld it somewhere before in harsher times, but he could not remember the source of the horrific acquaintance or the context it seemed to carry to him. Even more peculiarly never before seen places he would visit on occasion would bring a queer sense of knowledge of what lay behind an undiscovered corner, like when he visited the Queen Mary, the decks and halls of the luxurious liner feeling as natural as his own childhood home as he strode its majestic opulence.

Mr. Somersworth's nightly dreams are filled with varied and wondrous scenes and images of long vanished civilizations, glorious battles, and lore of past ages. One night he could be a postal clerk of olden London, going about the daily business of letters and parcels. On another twilight encounter he could be a farmer in an ancient Sumerian village, scraping a living from the meager soil, and praying to forgotten gods of unknown patronage in vain attempts for rain and surcease from hostile forces. The nighttime reveries were vividly life-like as well, and also have a familiarity that is as natural as his own current time and place. Sailing the vast and broad Pacific waters in a tiny whaling vessel in what surely must be the early 1800s, riding horses across the Pontic steppe with his fellow Cossacks, the wind whistling in his ears, the thunder of the charge roaring in his veins, or the quiet solitude of a Hindu yogi, seeking enlightenment in renouncement from the worldly pleasures and extravagances, these became as real to him as his normal day to day life.

The amazing and varied landscapes of his subconscious imagination are as apt descriptions of the lives and times of characters within them as those told painstakingly in books of history, the small details of his nighttime hallucinations fitting perfectly with such treatises and memoirs scholars had described on the subjects. The fascinating aspect to the entire circumstances is that he would have the dream, utterly lifelike and memorable, and then upon recalling it after waking, he would research the subject in a textbook of human history and find that his experiences in his sleep to be as exact and precise as the information recently ascertained. It was uncanny in the extreme, and the thought that he was a conduit for such mysterious and undisclosed details and particulars was as exhilarating as it was unfathomable. He became obsessed with the idea of discovering the source of the mystical comprehension and unconscious thoughts, poring over tomes of the metaphysical as well as contemporary psychologists and scientists on the subject. After considerable time spent on the quandary, he became enamored to the idea of reincarnation, of souls that have lived countless lives before and will again. It explained the subconscious impart of knowledge he never possessed, as well as the déjà vu that accompanied his perception of items and places he had never seen or walked upon. In his pursuit of determining the origin of the dreams and undisclosed acquaintanceship with antiquity, he began seeing a psychologist of some renown in the field of dream interpretation, a certain Dr. Robertson, who struck an enduring friendship with Mr. Somersworth as well as lending his medical expertise to his cause.

However, upon disclosing his theories of reincarnation to the good doctor, he was met with resistance and contempt for such ill-conceived forays into self diagnosis, even to the point of ridicule by his friend. How could any sane modern man believe such foolishness, Dr. Robertson exclaimed, pointing to many explanations for the baffling osmosis of thought as well as the strange familiarity, including memory consolidation and emotional regulation. He even invoked the nowadays oft-shunned views of Sigmund Freud and Karl Jung on the subject, stopping short only of unwarranted explorations of the Oedipus complex variety. Finally, the two men, both becoming equally taciturn and reticent on the subject, unwilling to see the other's point of view, Mr. Somersworth hit upon a solution to their impasse. He would undergo hypnosis by the psychologist, and try bring forth equivocal and undeniable evidence to his hypothesis of reincarnation. Dr. Robertson agreed wholeheartedly to the experiment, if only in order to placate his stubborn friend's insistence upon proving his insane theory. The next Thursday at ten o'clock in the evening was chosen to recreate the approximate time to Mr. Somersworth's normal bedtime customs for maximum effect. Over the course of the next week Dr. Robertson began to grow more or more eager for the approaching experiment, firmly believing that at the testing's end his friend would finally kowtow to science's overwhelming superiority in such matters.

On the appointed date Mr. Somersworth arrived ten minutes early as was his custom, tardiness never being one of his vices, and was greeted by the doctor at the door. After exchanging their friendly greetings and sharing some good humor together, the doctor showed him to his office with the leather couch that Mr. Somersworth was to recline upon in the course of the experiment. Dr. Robertson provided him with a small pillow for comfort's sake, and Mr. Somersworth took his place lying on the sofa, hands clasped at his chest, face turned towards the doctor. The doctor positioned a well furnished desk chair across from his patient, and after seating himself, removed a large silver pocket watch from the recesses of his jacket. Clasping the top of the metal chain, he instructed Mr. Somersworth to watch the oscillating instrument closely and to let its rhythm lull him to a state of complacency. Making a continuous back and forth motions with the timepiece in front of the reclining man, he spoke in low, soothing tones, encouraging the reception of the hypnotic state.

"Look at the watch, Matthew. Watch its pendulous movements, back forth, to and fro, so natural, so perfect. As you watch you can imagine you drifting, quietly, serenely, down a placid creek on a languid afternoon, so calm, so relaxing. You need to close your eyes; just drifting in the warm sun. Your entire body is so relaxed, so peaceful, nothing but my voice calmly telling you the wondrous truth, to sleep, to dream, to voyage into the times of past lives."

Mr. Somersworth did not resist the mesmeric trance he was being induced into, and Dr. Robertson found him a willing and highly susceptible subject to the hypnosis. He soon had his patient lightly breathing in even unison, with the telltale rapid eye movements beneath his eyelids showing that he was firmly in the dream state they had sought.

"Where are you now Matthew?"

"I am in a fortified settlement named Alesia. There are many people here. They are starving. The Romans have encircled the fort with trenches filled with water and battlements manned with many legionnaires. In the beginning we sent sorties out to disrupt their building and break through the defenses, but all attempts have been unsuccessful. Our people are diseased, and many are becoming unfit to fight, too weary to continue. We sent the old and sick as well as many men's wives and children out of the fort to surrender to the Romans, but Caesar has refused, leaving them to starve and die as well."

"Who are you Matthew? Why do you identity with these people?"

"I am Gevein, warrior of the Pictones, and currently serving under Vercingetorix's combined force of Gauls. We no longer wished to be under the harsh Roman rule, and many of the Pictones rebelled when Vercingetorix gave the call to arms, believing him that we could beat the Romans once and for all, to leave us in peace and master of our own destinies. But Caesar heard of our alliance, and quickly moved to crush our rebellion. Surrounded now here in this desolate city, there is but one hope left to us now. Vercingetorix has received word that our allies have amassed for an attack against the Roman outer lines, and we go soon to coordinate our assault with theirs to break free." Here Mr. Somersworth gave fascinating details of the sights, smells, and sounds of the devastated fort, the excitement of the coming sortie, and the fear and adrenaline of those assembling under the tall walls to face the hated enemy.

"We are marching across the fields now, it is slow going, the trenches must be back-filled as we go, and we are taking heavy casualties as the Romans pick us off with javelins, ballista, and other ranged weapons. I am in the midst of the contingent, I can see my comrades falling ahead, but finally the trenches are filled, and we run, running at the Roman legion with their square shields and cruel spears, long pilum in their hands. We dash against the wall of men and push, trying to gain entry, but they are too strong, they are pushing us back."

Mr. Somersworth has become violently agitated, and shaking uncontrollably, his pupils darting madly back and forth under his eyelids in a frenzy.

The doctor, concerned over seeing the strenuous spasms of his patient, intervened. "Matthew, you are not Gevein, you are Matthew Somersworth, not a Gaul warrior, but a modern man living in the twentieth century. You need to remember that." This seemed to quiet the fearful quaking in the man, and he relaxes visibly with the soothing words.

"Yes, I am Matthew Somersworth. I need to provide evidence that I am here. I can see the battle, I can see the dying. The Romans are killing the Gauls, they are breaking their formations in their zeal to destroy us. The Gauls are retreating, running from the slaughter. I can see one of Romans is apart from the rest, he is wielding his gladius on a fallen Gaul. I recognize the weapon, I have seen it in a museum. It is so familiar, is it the exact one I recall seeing? I believe it is, no, I am certain. I can take it from him, *can I bring it back with me?* It may be possible, *I must try.*"

Visible sweat is glistening on Mr. Somersworth's forehead, and he is thrashing in his strange awakened yet still asleep state. "I have surprised him, I have a grip on the gladius. We are fighting over it, he is so strong, he has shoved me down......" A loud scream rips from Mr. Somersworth's throat, a loud death knell, and his eyes fly open and he writhes in obvious pain and terror. Dr. Robertson is frozen into inaction by the sudden change of events, his normal reserved demeanor shattered. He looks at his patient's writhing form, and is horrified to discover that a dark stain has appeared on Mr. Somersworth's chest, and an ancient sword protrudes from his body, his blood-slick hands grasping the hilt in a futile clutch.

"I brought it back, Doctor, but now I know it was that which killed me, in two lifetimes now, and I know why I was right to fear it in the first place as well." His twitching and labored breathing suddenly stops, and his death grip loosens on the antique blade as his head hangs to the side, his life gone from his body. His normally orderly mind reeling from this unexpected turn in their experiments, Dr. Robertson looks down with unbelieving eyes on his dead patient, his logical mind unable to accept this contradiction in the laws of nature. Thoughts and rationalizations spin through his mind, the knowledge that the human brain can create hysterias and delusions that even reason cannot overcome, but *the sword is still there*, taunting him, refusing to obey the principles of physics itself. Only two possibilities can explain its unexplainable presence, that either Mr. Somersworth could travel through his lifetimes, and had literally visited past eras and the lost places he had spoke of, or the doctor has joined the madness that ailed the now deceased man's mind. For him and his unchallengeable scientific views, however there is only one of the possibilities he can accept as true, and its meaning quickly dawns on him. He too is now delusional, part of the madness his patient believed in so fervently. The doctor's perfect, treasured mind has now been tainted by the hysterias of a dead man, and that is not something that the rational doctor can abide. His unbelief has now become his funeral dirge, and there is only one answer to that fate in his own, locked brain. The window of his office shatters more easily than he had envisioned it would, but the fall to hard, unyielding street below takes infinitely longer.

DVLHSPD

The Apparition of Midir Road

His cell phone had clearly said the winding network of back-country lanes and old logging roads was not the quickest route to get to his destination. However, the short description in the online guide he had checked stated that the drive was full of appealing scenery not usually seen on the more direct thoroughfares. Intrigued and knowing he had plenty of time to spare, he decided to give the alternate route a chance. But then his cell service vanished, leaving him unable to validate the direction of the ambiguous program's choice, and he began to wonder if perhaps he had indeed taken a mistaken route to his destination. He had been driving for countless miles on the dirt track through the picturesque settings, with only the occasional dwelling to be seen, while the mid June foliage of the trees still showed the brilliant green of life. Bountiful, thick bushes and clusters of emerald grass intermixed with white flower blossoms and light blue bonnets, multiplying with abandon due to the spring's frequent rains. They reveled in their exuberant growth before the searing flame of summer would come to wilt and scorch the woodland finery with its typical blazing temperatures and droughts. The soaring mountains of the Castle range look down mightily on the meandering roadway, like solemn giants watching his miniature progress through their dignified domains. Old cabins and dilapidated barns, dot the fascinating landscape infrequently, relics from past pioneering lives completely forgotten by their modern successors. They fall quietly into ruin from lack of maintenance and disuse as well the extreme swings of Montana's temperamental climate from the blistering summers and freezing winters. Here and there he saw wildlife as well, whitetail deer and the sporadic muley, rabbits and their hunters, the great eagles, hawks, and osprey. Once he even spotted a black bear strolling easily along a high trail on one of the peaks he traversed. The animal raised up on its hind legs as he passed, seeming to want a better view of the trespasser to his domain. It studied him briefly, then returned to its unknown purposes, satisfied apparently with the car's continuing progress.

The road itself was rough and filled with potholes, its slightly muddy terrain in bad need of grading after winter's terrible toll. When he saw the coarse track reconnecting to blacktop ahead he was glad to be soon traveling on the familiar frictionless level surface. While the previous route had been interesting enough to warrant the unplanned side trip, he had found the perpetual need of caution and restraint in his speed much less invigorating. Turning onto the aged pavement, he saw a peeling wooden sign, simply labeled Midir Road. The road's condition was not as nice as most of the asphalt roads he had experienced in the state, with the occasional crater-like pothole and uneven, chipped edges from lack of maintenance. However, it was still a far cry from the bumpiness of mud holes and ruts the prior dirt road had been saturated with throughout its unlevel, meandering trek. He accelerated, eager to resume his course, and quickly was up to his normal four miles over the speed limit that was his standby. He had always felt that it was the maximum allowance he should give himself to travel without inciting undue notice by any local law enforcement, and so far in his life he had been correct, not once ever being pulled over by over zealous state troopers or other fanatical officials at that unassuming but technically unlawful rate. The engine hummed nicely, the satisfying white noise of its throttling seeming content with his choice of velocity as well. Up ahead he saw the path was straight for several miles, with only the slightest curvature in its direct outline veering to the west. It was clear of other vehicles as well, save only for a navy blue truck directly ahead of him, sedately moving in the same direction as he was going. He encroached on it swiftly with his rapid measure of travel.

Coming up closer to the other automobile, he saw it was a fantastic specimen from the fifties, one of the early F1 series. It had been lovingly restored with shining chrome hubcaps and handles, and its paint job was immaculately sprayed on the exquisite frame. He was no great purveyor of classic cars, but this was a beauty, the kind of vehicle that not only received admiring gazes from onlookers but demanded the attention of its viewers. Exactly the sort of thing little boys know they want to own someday when they are grown, and that teenage boys fantasize about just as fiercely as they do about the girls they would gladly convey inside. The license was wrapped in a flowing silver barbed wire border. The plate itself was personalized with the letters DVLHSDU, and he thought hard, trying to unravel the riddle to the print's meaning, but without any reference to go on the phrase's consonants seemed unrelated to one another, an unfathomable secret to him. The notoriously over-sized fenders were unblemished and perfectly proportioned. As he came ever closer he could see the bed was lined with elegantly planed wood decking, spotless and definitely having never known the rough touch of a heavy load on its virgin surface. The windows he could see were blackened with extremely darkened tint, not revealing any glimpse of the driver of the stylish pickup. He wondered if it was a local farmer or rancher engaged in a pleasurable outing in the late spring air, or perhaps a collector on a long journey between classic automobile shows. The median was a staggered yellow line as far as his eye could see. Now on the verge of overtaking the gorgeous classic truck and the way ahead still blissfully free, he turned on his blinker and eased across the links of flickering dashes into the left lane, attempting to quickly pass the slower conveyance.

As soon as he was parallel to the other vehicle the driver of the truck quickly sped up, preventing completion of his pass. Irritated by the blatant disrespect to his motorist rights, he increased his own speed as well, not willing to let the annoyance go unchecked. The pickup continued to keep pace with him, easily matching his velocity. Expressing his resentment and frustration forcefully at the hindering truck he shrilly blared on his horn, but the other driver persisted in the aggravating erratic behavior. He decided to brake and go back to following the truck, knowing that sooner or later a passing zone should appear in the miles ahead and he would be able to get around the upsetting motorist. The midnight-colored pickup slowed its barreling charge as well, remaining infuriatingly alongside his car, not letting him return to the right lane. Soon he was once again blaring on his horn, stealing alternating angry sidelong glances with the other vehicle and the stretch of road as they sped along together as well. He sincerely wished that the oppressive black tint on the vehicle had been a few shades lighter on the driver windows so he could see his transgressor more clearly, to look his persecutor in the eyes as he expressed his displeasure. He was certain the other driver was laughing at his deteriorating composure behind the darkened glass, probably some country hick having a cheap thrill at a presumed city slicker for his own inscrutable purpose.

Well, two could play that game he thought wickedly, deciding to show this redneck just how far he would be willing to take things. He threw all caution to the wind. His temper overrode his normal reserved demeanor, and he mashed the accelerator to the floor with furious determination. His car surged ahead briefly, but just as rapidly the dark blue pickup caught up, maintaining the side by side distance between the two. Incensed beyond all measure now, he kept the relentless pace up, glancing after a moment of the intense racing down to check his speedometer as reason struggled to restore equilibrium in his raging mind. It read over a hundred miles per hour now, and he wondered regardless of its restoration how the truck could have generated such speed. Surely the engine beneath the hood must have been vastly upgraded over the original stock version to obtain such a dramatic improvement over the original factory performance.

The frantic tempo they had set ate away at the remaining straightaway, and the road ahead began to turn gradually to the right, directly into a large woods. The thoroughfare divided the forest into two unequally split sections. Growing steadily more uneasy with their high velocity, he began to ease off of the accelerator. Predictably the other car remained parallel to his vehicle, but began honking discordantly in response to his action. It was as if its driver had taken affront to his unwillingness to continue their madcap competition. He looked over out of instinct, the noise grating against the straining hum of the engines. Quickly he recovered from his lapse in concentration, turning his attention back to the roadway where it belonged, just in time to see a flash of white appear from the concealing trees ahead. Knowing he had but a split second to react as he heard the oncoming horn's blasting cry, its driver reacting to spotting his untenable position on the wrong side of the road, he made the only choice that made any sense to him, hazardous though it may be to his own personage. He slammed on his brakes as hard as possible, and at the same turned sharply into the left shoulder slinging dirt and gravel ferociously in all directions with the car's sudden interruption of movement from the formerly smooth highway to rough, weed-choked ground. The wheel fought fitfully against his grasp as the wheels protested against the violent treatment they were being subjected to by his forceful direction. Dimly he heard the oncoming traffic to his right shrieking at him as he tried vainly to control the wildly careening car. Then a massive pine tree loomed ahead unexpectedly, and he lost all coherent thought to the sinking blackness of unconsciousness.

He awoke later, his gown-clad body bruised and battered, in a hospital bed with a white haired, matronly woman in a nurse's uniform sitting close by him. Her attention was focused on a magazine lying on her lap, but she looked up from her reading upon his restless movement in the bed. Her blue eyes widened in bewilderment at his apparent revival, but quickly she recovered herself, placating him with soothing words before he can utter a sound otherwise.

"Wait, don't move honey, I'll fetch the doctor right quick." She returned a few moments later, with an older man in the traditional white coat of his station in tow, who she introduced cordially as Dr. Airemm, the resident MD in their small town of Brileith. After the familiarities were observed, the doctor informed him that he has been involved in an accident near the town. He asked him several simple questions, such as his name, his address, and other queries while he checked his vitals and responses for any debilitating after-effects from his collision. He performed adequately to the seemingly endless barrage of tests, answering all the questions put forth to him to the doctor's satisfaction. The lone exception was the query of what was the last thing that he could remember before his recent arrival at the hospital. He relayed what scant knowledge he could recall prior to the aftermath, the details of the events after seeing the encroaching tree coming closer and closer shrouded in mystery to him still. The doctor notified him that the local sheriff was waiting outside the room, and was very anxious to speak with him about his disastrous collision. If he was feeling up to it he could send him in, seeing how he seemed in decent enough health, especially considering his ordeal.

He agreed amicably to the suggestion, and the doctor and nurse departed, leaving him in relative secluded privacy for his meeting with the sheriff. The lawman entered, a big man in his forties with an ample gut from too little action and too much time spent sitting in patrol cars waiting for speeders. But the bright look in his eye showed a mind that was still as quick as ever, and he moved with a catlike grace in spite of his ponderous bulk. When he spoke it was in the plain speech typical to Montana's rural accents, with a simple directness that brooked no nonsense, but still made its recipients at ease with its mellow tones.

"I'm Jack Conall, and I'm investigating your accident over on Midir Road. We had one of the boys from the repair shop haul your car into town for you. It's pretty banged up, you must have really been moving to do that kind of damage to it." The brown eyes regarded him with coolly with interest as the information on his vehicle was relayed to him. Conall was obviously looking for any sign of deceitfulness or discomfort at the topic in the injured man's body language. While he had nothing to hide he couldn't help feeling the normal stress that comes from authoritative questioning, and he hoped the sheriff wouldn't hold it against him if he could detect its tremulous presence. The policeman continued on after the slight pause, as if nothing had occurred, drawing a small notepad and accompanying stub of pencil from his breast pocket as he spoke. "The service manager will be along later to ask what you want to do with it. Now, we just need to get some small details out of the way first between you and me. I'm going to be blunt with you, and if you're honest with me we'll get along just fine and this will be the end of it. Would you mind telling me what happened, and how you ended up in the ditch on the wrong side of the road facing the wrong way?"

He explained the entire proceeding happenings in meticulous detail, exactly as the distressing events had transpired. He held nothing back from his harrowing description, not even his complicit role in recklessly breaking the speed limit to attempt to pass the antagonizing pickup. The sheriff listened closely to his entire story without interrupting, except for the occasional clarification or explanation when needed during the protracted tale. He saw that while the officer had started taking small annotations on his pad at the beginning of his account he soon thereafter refrained from his note taking, simply listening to his description until he at last finished. There was a long pregnant pause before the sheriff spoke, as he evidently contemplated the other man's narrative. When he finally spoke, it was not in the slightest how the bedridden man had envisioned their conversation would have taken place.

"And you're sure it was a midnight blue F-1?" The sheriff asked him slowly, double checking him on the details. "Cherried out, with tinted windows darker than night?" He nodded once, seeing the other man's frank discomfiture at the positive affirmation. The lawman sighed, and put away his writing utensils. The unexpected melancholy emotion took the man in the bed by surprise, and he vocalized that astonishment.

"What is this? You have my details of the accident, the man is a menace. He deserves to be locked up, acting like that on the highways. Is this some kind of cronyism, or some relative you're protecting?" His rising temper at the perceived injustice made his voice rise in pitch and volume accordingly, but the policeman seemed unaffected be his tirade, merely waiting for him to finish before responding.

The Apparition of Midir Road

"You don't understand. I would happily lock up the driver of that truck, he has been a thorn in my side since I first came to this town back twenty years ago, when I was just a raw recruit fresh out of the academy. He has harassed and harmed countless innocent drivers on Midir Highway. He sure as hell ain't related to me, and he ain't no friend of mine neither."

"Then what is it? Why can't you arrest him? Is it other people in the town, the mayor or someone on the city council? Why won't you do your job?" The last question struck the sheriff like a slap, visibly wincing from the comment, then he retorted back with the fury of a thunderclap.

"I can't because he's dead! He's been dead for sixty years now! He's a ghost!" The revelation stunned the wounded man. If he hadn't seen the dead serious look on the other man's face he would scarcely have believed his ears. He struggled to say something, but it was like a torrent had been released within the sheriff, details cascading forth from him that could not be stopped.

"Now, I heard most of all this secondhand from ol' Connor McNess right before he died. Seems like he couldn't go to grave without telling someone, it weighin' on him so much. Other stuff I got from asking around, not that many wanted to talk about it. What's true or not I'll let you decide after you hear it all." The sheriff saw the astonishment in his eyes, and paused for a moment at the reaction, but the injured man's interest was piqued now, and quietly murmured his assent to continue to the big man.

The Apparition of Midir Road

"So back in the fifties there was a man named Don Macridim, a real mean sonuvabitch by all accounts, the kind of fellar that would cut you soon as look at you, or sell his mother for a nickel if it suited his purposes. If there was something illegal going on in town he was in on it, and folks were so scared of him and his crazy ways they tended to give him a wide berth. Hell, even the law left him alone most of the time, especially after one of my predecessors went missing shortly after saying real proud-like about how he was going to take Don down, send him up to Deerlodge. There was even talk Don was into some kind of Satanist worship out there in them Castle mountains where he lived, praying and sacrificing to beings that don't reside in no church of God's. I don't know about all that, but when a man is that evil anything they say could be true." He paused thoughtfully, as if he was pondering his own words, but soon carried on with his tale.

"Yea, evidently Don didn't care for nothing or nobody but a dark blue F-1 pickup, and he loved that thing like a mother loves her child. He lavished all kinds of money on that truck, bought ever imaginable thing to make it purr like a kitten and shine just like a diamond. Even got a fancy plate made for it special and that weren't cheap back then, put his favorite saying on there for the world to see, short for "give the devil his due". And that pickup weren't just some looker either, it was the fastest thing for miles around, nothing could hold a candle to it in a race. And race it he did, out on Midir Road, on that long stretch of straight highway you recently got acquainted with. He'd drive up and down that line, challenging anybody who drove out there, whether they wanted to or not, didn't matter to Don. He would pull that dirty trick of his, going real slow like, waiting for someone to try to pass, then he'd gun it and not let them back over, even if the other fellar slowed down. Caused more than a couple of wrecks out there, some real bad ones too, a few people died and one lady got paralyzed from the neck down, couldn't walk ever again from her injuries."

"Seems that might have been the straw that broke the camel's back there, 'cause the townsfolk decided to get together and go vigilante on him, just like the Virginia City folks did to Henry Plummer over in Bannack back some ninety years earlier. 'Bout twenty pillars of the community got together to form a party, and went out to his cabin over in them mountains. Now, things get sketchy here for what happened that night depending on who you talk with, but I do know it's true that about six of those men didn't make it back home to see their families again. Evidently Don put up a helluva of a fight, all holed up in that cabin before they set fire to it to flush him out. He came out finally, guns blazing through the billowing smoke, but they managed to wound him enough to get close and club him senseless. The good men of Brileith took him out back of his place, looking for a tall tree to finish the job on him. I've talked to some of those folks who were there and most disagree about it, but ol' Connor swore that there was bones hung up in those trees they were fixin' to hang him from, and some of them didn't look like bear or elk neither, something a little more closer to home. There was rocks too, big ones, with some kind carvings on them he said that made him feel real nasty inside, like just looking at them made him nauseous, just like the treatments he had to take later when they found out he had the big C." He paused again, as if remembering the dead man's words, and the injured man patiently waited for him to carry on, rapturously caught up in the strange story. He did after a moment longer, his voice an octave lower as he continued speaking in hushed tones.

"So then they got the rope ready, and set it around Don's neck and up over the branch. Some of the elders asked him if he had any thing to say before he paid for his crimes, but he just laughed at them, said that this wouldn't be the last they'd see of him, his god would see to it that he'd come back and plague their town for eternity. Well, they had enough of his talk then, and hoisted him high in the air, with him choking and trying to breath until he died instead of trying to do it clean with a neck snap. I think they wanted revenge for their buddies he killed. The fire was spreading by then Connor said, so they left him up in the tree to be burned up, along with whatever dark business he had been doin' up there."

"Now, that should have been the end of it. But it weren't. People started complainin' several years later about seeing a dark blue truck out on Midir road again, and those that remembered said it was Don Macridim's old pickup, sure as shooting. Now Don's truck should have been left up there to burn with him, but one of those men who went up there, Lloyd I think he name was, felt that would have been a shame on account of it being such a fancy thing. So he drove it back to town. Now nobody in the whole county cared to see that particular vehicle again, so after a bit Lloyd sold it to a fellar over in Billings, got a pretty penny by all accounts as well. Well when the law went to talk to the Billings man about the going-ons out on Midir they found out he had reported it stolen a couple years earlier, some kids had taken it out on a joyride and wrecked it. Now, the junkyard he sold it to said they had it out back, but when they went to show the officer it was missing. They searched all over that yard, but someone must liked it real good, and made off with it."

"There kept being sightings of that damn truck anyhow out on Midir, a few here and there, but no officer was ever able to catch whoever it was having their practical joke in the act, nor found out where the pickup was being kept. Then Sheriff Fergus, he caught sight of that truck moseying along that damned road, and he got real excited, sped up and got behind, lights flashing, siren blaring, trying to get whoever it was to pull over. They wouldn't so he pulled along side, yelling and screaming to get'em to stop, and he said the pickup just sped up, lickity spit, so fast he had to floor it to keep pace with'em, kept tryin' to get them to pull over till they got to the tree line. Then he figured it was time for more drastic measures, so he went to bash that truck right off the roadway there. Fergus was tellin' me this story right after I arrived in new in town, and I thought he was joshin' me, try to mess with the new guy. But then he looked me dead in the eye while he was talkin,' serious as a heart attack, and said that truck must have had wings, because it had *vanished* as soon as he cranked the wheel to the right, *right into thin air.*"

He fell silent again, this time so long that the man in the bed felt compelled to say something. "Have you ever seen it?" he asked softly.

The sheriff looked at him long and hard. "Yea, I've seen it too. I didn't believe all the spooky ghost crap, thought people were just feeding off each other's fears, and maybe saw what they wanted to see. And it wasn't like it was all the time that people reported seeing it, sometimes years would go by with no new incidents, like it was taking a break or somethin'. But I was out on Midir in the late fall of '92, coming back from a call out near the lake. I was cruising', anxious to get back to town 'cause the Cats-Griz game was that day, and the wife had taped it for me with some cold brews waiting for comfort as well. I hit that stretch of straight-away just like you described, and opened her up, then I noticed that ol' flashy truck toolin' along without a care in the world. Now, I've had a lot of time to think about this later, and now I swear that midnight blue pickup wasn't there earlier, it just appeared. At the time though I thought I'd just missed it, but I recognized it for what it was the second I got close, exactly like the old sheriff had said, down to the plates reading DVLHSDU. Now, I was full of piss and vinegar then, and out to make a name for myself. I did just like ol' Fergus had done, went behind it with lights and siren going full bore, even got on the loudspeaker and told him to give it up, his jokin' days were over. He just kept goin' pretty as you please, so I pulled alongside him and he lit'em up and I followed suit, staying right beside him. I wasn't about to lose him, so I figured it was time to ram him off the road. Now this was before the PIT maneuver became widespread, so normally we did it by pulling alongside and ba-shin' them old school, so I'd better have a damn good reason for banging up my car like that. This had to qualify though, so I yanked it hard to knock him into the ditch.

It was the craziest thing I've ever experienced that hap-pened next, and I'll never forget it long as I live. For a few sec-onds *I was inside the other car, like my car had passed through the other one, and was superimposed on top of the pickup.* Since I was looking to the right side at the time to see how that bump was gonna go down, I got myself a front row ticket to see the inside of that car, and you better believe me it was not something I'd wished I'd seen. It was dark, the inside dimly lit by a ghostly green coming from the instrument pan-el, and it was instantly cold, the kind of cold that only comes every few winters, that even we Montanans decide to stay in-side until it warms back up. It smelled too, like the time we found Charlie Gardener after he'd set rotting in his house dead for the better part of a year, of decaying and putrefying foulness but something else too, something much worse I couldn't place. Then I saw the driver of that accursed truck, right next to me, and just about had a stroke, it was a corpse, flesh peeling and skull and bone showin' through in patches, tattered clothes dirty and ripped, with a noose hangin' around its neck like a some kind of perverted necklace. Then it looked at me, and I still have nightmares from that damned look, it spoke of things men shouldn't know, places where mankind should fear to tread. Then it laughed, a dry rattle that mocked human mirth, and that was it, the pickup and the occupant vanished suddenly, and I was left driving in the sunshine, like nothing had ever happened at all." He did not speak again until cajoled into doing so by the occupant of the room, and when he did his voice was tired, like the story had physically worn him out.

"I don't go out on Midir Road past the trees anymore if I can help it, and the county doesn't do road maintenance out there unless we have to by the state, everyone is pretty much in agreement on that even over in the bureaucrat offices. I'd close that road if I could, but if I told them why I wanted to I'd be locked up in the looney bin for sure. I'm sorry you got caught up in this mess, and I'll do what I can to make sure your insurance company knows it wasn't your fault. I've already spoke with the doctor and you don't need to worry about your visit here. Now, the choice is yours what you want to do or who you want to tell about this, but sometimes it is best to leave things alone." He left his card on the nightstand, and left the room, leaving the other man to his private thoughts. He had been silent while the other man spoke of his experience, but he had remembered something before his crash he had dismissed as nonsense earlier, a sound that he thought he had hallucinated or misheard. A dry, rattling laugh that had mocked him loudly before his car had struck the tree, a laugh that had lost any trace of its humanity all together.

Old Grampa

"**W**ho were you talking to in there, Sean?" His mother questioned him idly when he came back in the living room after returning from his little bedroom down the hall.

"That old grampa again. He told me a story and I asked him stuff," Sean said. He had been talking to the old man about ships, and how he wanted to go on one some day. The old grampa had told him earlier about when he was in the Navy during the war, and all the interesting things he had done there on his ship, the USS Belthrop. The old man always told such amazing tales, about all kinds of different things, some good like seeing the first silent movies and beginning airplanes, and some bad, like the Panic and when the president McKinley was shot. It made Sean feel like a grownup, the way he wouldn't sugar-coat things to him. Sean loved to hear his war stories most of all, typical of boys his age, and the old grampa would tell him about all the different wars, like the Spanish-American War and the Great War. Sean was four years old, almost five and he couldn't read yet, but the grampa could tell him all kinds of details from the different histories he had read about or had asked his great granddaddy about, like the Civil War, or the Pony Express.

His mother was looking at him strangely again, like she did every time he talked about the old grampa. His gramma did too, but mostly she just looked sad when he brought it up, rather than puzzled. His mother, him, and his father had been living with her and Grandad in their big white house out on the farm for the past couple months, and he and the old grampa had started talking soon afterward. They usually chatted in the tiny spare bedroom he was using now, but every once and while he would speak to Sean in the hallway when the little boy was running around the house.

"Sean, why don't you go play outside, it's nice out," his mother said quietly.

"OK, Mama." His mother turned and went back into the kitchen. He went out on the porch and sat down on the weather-beaten swing, swaying silently back and forth languidly. The sound of the screen banging on the garden entrance reached his ears, which meant his gramma had came back into the kitchen after finishing hanging the clean laundry on the clothesline outside. He heard his mother and her exchange greetings, and then his mama began speaking to his gramma in a worried tone. He realized presently that they were talking about him.

"It ain't right, him thinking he's talking to people that ain't there," his mother said.

"Sean's a good boy and he's got a good soul. Ain't no harm

gonna come to the boy. I know your college-educated husband thinks this is all of bunch of nonsense, and it's just as well he thinks that. Sean will grow out of it eventually."

"But Sean *knows things*, Mama. Things a boy shouldn't know about, like what his great grampa did in his life, the people he used to know, things we never said in front of him and he's too young to know. He even knew Grampa Lightsey's pet name for me and I never told him that, not ever. I think he is talking to a *ghost*."

"Land's sake child, is it so bad if he is? I'd love to be able to talk to Daddy again. Maybe he's just more fortunate than the rest of us. Daddy would have loved him had he lived to see him born, and maybe this is God's way of letting Sean get to know his kin. He's a good boy, and he ain't doing no harm."

"Maybe so Mama, but people shouldn't be able to talk to the dead," his mother said quietly, and then the two of then fell silent for a short while. Then Sean could hear her and his gramma change the subject to what they were fixing for dinner, and after finding out it was chicken and dumplings, one of his favorites, he ceased his eavesdropping. He quietly ran to the tire swing hanging on the old pine tree out by the dirt road that ran past the big white house. They called it the big white house because the old grampa had said his house had been white too, but only half the size, so to tell the difference between the two homes his had been called the little white house and his son-in-law's the big white house. He could see from the swing the huge rows of tobacco fields his grandad owned and worked everyday on. His father had been helping him out to earn money during the summer, since he was a teacher and the school he worked at wasn't open again until September.

Sean wondered about what his mother and gramma had said while he was swinging in the big round tire. He had already discovered that no one else could see the old grampa but him, but the news that he was dead was a little bit of a shock. He knew from church that you go to heaven after you die, but maybe the old grampa was allowed to visit. He liked to spend time with him, and he answered all Sean's questions, unlike his Daddy and Grandad. They were usually so tired from working in the fields that after supper they watched a little television and then after the news they both soon went to bed, not in the mood for listening to childish prattle or answering the never-ending questions. Gramma and Mama stayed up usually a little later, and if he was quiet he could stay up with them. He resolved to go to bed early himself tonight though, so he could ask the old grampa about being dead.

Later on in the house, after his daddy and grandad came home they all sat down and had dinner like usual. The chicken and dumplings his mama and gramma made were very good of course, and he was allowed to have seconds of it after he finished eating his whole plate, even the vegetables. He watched television with the two men afterwards for a while, but he was still anxious to speak with the old grampa so he snuck off to the bedroom. He got his pajamas on, turned off the light and shut the door almost all the way, just a little open so the hall light could shine in. He wasn't afraid of the dark, but a little light was nice just in case. He got underneath the covers, snuggling cozily in the big doubled-sized bed. He whispered to the darkened room, "Old grampa? You there? It's me, Sean."

"Hey there Sean. You going to bed so soon?" The old man was in the room with him now, sitting on the old rocking chair in the corner, slowly tilting back and forth, like he had been there the whole time.

"I didn't want to go to bed, I needed to talk to you."

"Oh, what did you want to talk about tonight? Ships? Armies? Maybe about the first cars?" The old grampa continued to rock as Sean told him about what he had heard his gramma and mama say about him being dead, and about it not being natural for Sean to be talking to him. The old man listened, and then ceased his gentle to and fro movements, placing both feet on the floor and leaning forward.

"That would explain some things, Sean my boy. To be honest, I haven't really thought about it. I seem to be sleeping most of the time, having dreams about the old days, good dreams of the good times, like picnics with your great gramma Mildred or when the children were still young and played at my knees. When I wake up I get to spend time with you and I love that just as much, making new memories with my great grandson. Let me tell you boy ain't nothing better than time with your kin. You remember that now." He started rocking again in the slow, rhythmic cadence, deep in thought.

"I didn't know I was dead till you told me just now, and I guess I must not be moved on to the afterlife. Well, if this is dead I don't think I mind it too much, getting to spend time with you." Sean liked that, and it made good sense to him too. They changed the subject and talked awhile, the old grampa telling him stories he had heard when he was a boy about the Indians that used live nearby and their myths and legends. There was the giant deer god Slanting Eyes, who owned all the game animals, and their thunder god and his two sons, the thunder boys whose job it was to bring the rain and thunder. He spoke to him about the Indians' great mounds that they had built, the purpose for which no one living knows for certain. He told him also the story of the king of rattlesnakes, who had a great jewel. Many warriors wanted the jewel, but the serpent king sent his snake minions against them, and they died horribly of venomous bites. One warrior finally won the jewel and took it back to his tribe, defeating the snake king by wearing leather armor the snakes couldn't bite through, and cutting off the rattlesnake lord's head. Sean heard these and other wondrous tales, finally succumbing to drowsiness and comfort in the warm bed. Seeing the boy fast falling asleep, he quieted his tone, letting his voice lull the lad to blissful dreams. Seeing him quieted for the night and breathing deeply and evenly in slumber, he stopped rocking again, and stared at the sleeping boy, quietly talking to him even though he knew he could not hear him.

"I love you, little boy, but you got me thinking about how I miss seeing my Mildred and the other people in my life. I wonder why they aren't here? Why am I here, am I just too latched on to this life? They always said I was too stubborn to die. Maybe they were righter than they knew." He chuckled to himself quietly, and then stood up out of the chair carefully, going to the window overlooking the garden. He could see the crescent moon softly illuminating the plants and shrubs outside, the peaceful scene fading into the darkness where the trees began out back. He watched idly, thoughts in his mind occupying more of his attention than the sights before him, when he noticed with a start that someone was standing in the garden, a woman in a white gown. He squinted, not sure if his eyes were playing tricks on him, and suddenly he was no longer in the room at all, but out in the garden as well, standing among rows of tomato plants. He saw the female figure coming towards him, and he realized that it was his Millie, looking young and fresh again like when they were first married, so many long years ago. He looked down at his hands, and they too were young again, then glancing up again he saw Millie smiling, the special smile she used just for him that said I love you, and she was beckoning him forward to join her. He walked then, ran towards her, grabbing ahold of her in a jubilant embrace, tears of joy streaming down his cheeks.

"I found you, I found you," he cried, hugging her tightly. She responded in kind, head pressed against his chest, arms encircling him. They stayed there several minutes, happy just to be together again. Then they drew apart, and she told him she had been waiting for him, but he had to be ready to go, she couldn't just take him, he had to be the one to make the choice. He told her about little Sean, and what he had said and had got him thinking. She smiled and said he was a godsend, then took his hand, both of them turning towards the trees, vanishing into the night air slowly as they walked away together.

****

Sean woke up, a strange feeling of loneliness in his heart though he didn't know why he felt that way. He called out to the old grampa to tell him about it, but the old man must have been still sleeping, he didn't respond back like he usually did. He got dressed and went downstairs, seeing his gramma and forgetting about the feeling while he chatted to her while she started the morning meal. His mama, daddy, and grandad came in, and they talked and laughed until the two men had to go to work. His daddy asked him if he wanted to come, and he agreed to do so, spending the day riding in the tractor with his daddy and helping the best he could. They came back late in the evening, and after a delicious dinner and a little television he went to bed. He called out to the old grampa again once he was under the covers, mostly just to say goodnight, but he still didn't come. He lay there, alone, and started thinking of the previous night's conversation, about letting the old grampa know that he was dead, and he started crying, thinking he had done something wrong and now the old grampa was mad at him and wouldn't come back. His mama heard him bawling in the little bedroom, and came inside, asking him what was wrong while holding him close. He told her what he had done through hot tears, and she hugged him tight and told him he was a good boy, that he hadn't done anything wrong. He fell asleep in her embrace, cradled in loving arms that didn't need to understand to care and support him.

He tried calling out to the old grampa several times more the rest of that summer, but he never answered despite his pleas. Eventually the season ended and he and his little immediate family moved back to the big city so his daddy could teach again, leaving the farm and the old folks. During the school year his daddy got a job offer in a faraway state, and they moved away from the city near the old farm and his grandparents. His mother got pregnant almost immediately after, and he soon had a new baby sister to play with and contend with. They weren't able to visit like they used to now, only briefly coming back to the farm fewer and fewer times as time and responsibilities permitted. Once was when sadly his gramma had died of the cancer, that happened only a short couple years after the big move. He was forgetting about the old grampa by now, school learning, new friends and experiences taking the place of the older memories. His grandad wasn't long for the world after his gramma died, and after that they had no reason to go back hardly at all. One of his uncles had tried to make a living farming, but when the recession came he lost the farm to the bank and that was that, no more visits any more to the old property that had held such tender memories. Sean grew up and became a man, putting away his childhold memories and escapades in return for the hopes and dreams of adulthood. He graduated high school, joined the Navy, and later met a nice girl he liked so much that he married her after he got out of the military. They had children of their own, three little boys. Sean started a business of his own, and did well, providing for his wife and children amply. Life continued with its ups and downs, some things were good, some things were sad, and some things were bad. Before he even knew it his children had grown up and now had wives, he lost his parents and other people he cared for to time's relentless passage, grand babies came joyously, people moved away, new friendships were made, and all the other little and big things that make up a person's experiences in the course of their lifetime.

Sean was now an old man. He sold his business and retired, played with grandchildren, buried his wife, and eventually, like which happens to everyone in this world, died himself. He never got to see his great grandson, who was born shortly after his death, a beautiful boy his parents named Michael. But the little boy's mother, Sean's granddaughter Clare, has been noticing some peculiar things of late, starting as soon as he turned about four years old. Michael sometimes talks to someone who isn't there, someone named Old Grampa, and he *knows things, things little boys shouldn't know, things that only her grampa Sean knew.*

The Price of Fame

In the fast-paced glitz and glamour of the music industry, it is said that who you know is just as important as how good you are. Sometimes the paramount ear that hears an act leads to the fortunate break to the big time, sometimes it leads down a dead end road with no hope of future absolution for a lifetime spent in vain. Many talented acts have been left by the wayside simply because they are at the wrong place at the right time, or even at the right place at the wrong time. The happenstances of the chaotic life of the traveling musician are variable as they are multiple, causing even greater perturbation in an already aggravated situation. But why does one artist succeed when another fails when both are equally talented and given the same opportunities, is it merely random luck as to which is the more successful? Or is some other force at work, shaping some destinies and denying others with magnanimous power? Such queries are not easily answered when dealing with these quandaries, but it stands to reason there must be solutions to the questions, ones that stretch the boundaries of man's limited scope. Fate is a fickle mistress, perhaps more so than most realize.

Tommy Blaine was one of the fortunate few to be a success, a literal virtuoso of the rock genre. In fact since his rise to stardom he had become one of the mainstays of the rock n' roll world, proving to be not just some one hit wonder. A true artist that delivered original, consistent recordings that could not only entertain and titillate but also awe and inspire. His songs ranged from simple frolicsome tunes for the everyday radio stations to great euphoric scores that could melt even the most cynical critic's icy heart with their fascinating crescendos and choruses. His chords and arpeggios were on par with such esteemed peers as Hendrix or Bolan, while his rhythm and harmony were comparable even to Presley and Holly for their resourcefulness and creativity. In his inventive songwriting, his ability to capture emotion and to weave atmosphere was closely likened to such greats as Young or Bowie for their ingenious talent. His aptitude did not only lend itself to the composition and arrangement, but to his showmanship and stage presence. It has been said that his live shows are as astonishing and impressive as those done by Cooper, Osbourne, or Pop in their heydays. In short he is a consummate performer, complete in every way imaginable in his chosen field.

Anne Carrols knew all this, however. In her profession as a freelance writer for magazines and tabloids it was her business to be as knowledgeable and informed as possible on such stars as Tommy Blaine and others. Nor was that was her only field of expertise, but her talent for being a virtual font of intelligence on the checkered past of modern musical history and similar information definitely was an edge while in pursuit of her stories. Currently she had her determined sights set on a Holy Grail of sorts, an interview with the prestigious Tommy Blaine. To attract an interview was no small feat, she knew, especially since in his entire career he had deftly avoided such meetings, or had foisted the discussions on agents or other band members. He gave only the most rudimentary of conferences when compelled to do so. Her incessant phone calls, letters, and emails had gone unanswered, politely at first but more aggressively as time went by. The story was always the same: Tommy Blaine does not give unsolicited interviews. When she pointed out he did not seem to solicit them either to the last agent she spoke with that did not particularly help her predicament, but it did give her a brief measure of pleasure from the witty retort. She was at his last show in his tour now in order to achieve her insistent purpose, literally being reduced to waylaying the man backstage in one final, desperate attempt to curry his favor. She had even suited up appropriately for the occasion, willing even to use her not unsubstantial feminine charms as a last ditch effort if necessary. While she was not promiscuous or utterly shameless by any means, she was, however, no stranger to old adage of quid pro quo or its uses. If that is what it took to accomplish her goal tonight so be it; she could live the shame and self-disgust in the morning.

Tommy finished his set to the admiring audience, and thanked them profusely for their support. He was all class, in watching him even Anne's jaded reporter instincts were satiated by his artful acknowledgment of the crowd's approval. He had a mannerism that was regal and majestic while still being surprisingly genuine and humble at the same time. She could see instantly why his hordes of fans showered him with their adulation as he strode from the stage like a great Greek god of mythical proportions, larger than life, flawless. A light perspiration gleamed on his bronzed features from the hot stage lights above, making Anne's half-forgotten girlish idolization of rock stars spring headily anew with each passing step he took. As he headed her direction off-stage, she almost forgot her purpose in waiting for him as he swaggered towards her, so mesmerizing his form was to her paralyzed sensibilities. Then, fortunately for her overpowered senses, Tommy returned to a more mundane aspect back in the normal lighting and atmosphere of the backstage lamps. The bustling attendants attempted to shower him with comforts and praises for another successful show, but he casually waved off such considerations, accepting only a simple bottle of water. She steeled herself for the inevitable showdown about to occur, and after taking a deep breath, began walking with serious purpose towards the modern day troubadour.

"Tommy? Tommy Blaine?" she questioned in a pleasing, carrying tone she had artfully rehearsed for years.

The din of the crowded backstage made it difficult to

make sense of specific sounds, but he heard her above the roar and controlled confusion of the packed area. He turned her direction in slow, sublime way that seemed to defy the laws of nature and then their eyes locked as he found the source of the call. She almost looked away nervously, but caught herself and returned his unintentionally ardent gaze. He looked older to her now than he had before under the bright concert lights, but still he was an attractive man in his prime, far from the ravages and decay of old age. He had almost a timeless quality to him she felt, like a photograph of a person caught in time, when you know the individual in the picture has aged but still looks exactly the same forever. He met her in mid stride, closing the distance between the two of them until they were face to face. He spoke to her in a quiet tone that surprisingly took no strain on her part to decipher despite the deafening background noise.

"Yes, I'm Tommy and who are you?"

"I'm Anne Carrols. Big fan. Wonderful show, I enjoyed the view from here immensely."

"It was a good one. But it's Los Angeles, everybody's always great here." He shrugged in a carefree manner, as if downplaying his involvement in the concert. They made small talk, chatting about the stage, the lighting, his song selection for the show among other trivial matters. Her knowledge of the back side of the music industry seemed to intrigue him, and even when offered ways to leave the conversation by the barrage of various roadies, band members, and other assorted personnel who sought a piece of his time he refused, continuing to chat with her. Interestingly it turned out to be him who steered the discussion back towards her true purpose, not her.

"So what brings you here tonight? Pardon me for saying, but you don't seem like a typical fan," his demeanor turned almost apologetic at the next words, "or groupie."

"You saw through me, I'm not," she confided to him. Heart in her throat, she described the weeks of ceaseless correspondence that only received curt dismissals and dejected notices. His eyes widened at the revelation, but he politely let her continue.

"And this is it, my final recourse. So Mr. Blaine, will you consent to a one on one interview from me?"

He seemed to contemplate the idea for an exorbitant amount of time, so long that she feared the only answer would be no. But he surprised her with his reply, giving the dearly hoped assent that she craved.

"Any other night, company not withstanding, I would say no. But you picked tonight of all nights, so yes, I will speak with you," he said, cryptically acquiescing to her desire. He made arrangements for the two of them to hold the interview at his hotel, but first graciously insisted on taking her to dinner beforehand. Her inner warning flags frantically magnified to the possible repercussions of such an act, but her increased fascination with him might prove that to be less undesirable as she previously had thought beforehand. She was attracted to him, and the attraction headily grew with each moment she spent in his company.

Tommy made his intentions known to the one of his entourage, who secured a vehicle for their conveyance, a long black limousine. Upon their arrival at the restaurant he was of course instantly recognized by the maitre d', who immediately whisked them to a private table to enjoy their repast. She noticed that while he accepted a glass of the complementary wine when proffered by the manager at dinner, he did not take a single sip from the offering. When she asked him about it, he professed to having quit drinking years early. She made a mental note to press a little harder on that particular subject later.

As they left the restaurant he was accosted by a trio of women out on a girl's night who recognized him. He warmly received their praise and patiently answered their frivolous questions before thanking them for their interest. Just as before when in front of the crowd at the concert, she detected no hint of egotism or presumptuousness in his character, just an admirable lack of vanity and honest amiability she found refreshing after dealing with so much self absorption and arrogance in her chosen field. She was finding herself even more fascinated with him despite her generalized narrow view of the opposite sex, finding their preoccupation with the here and now attitude of physicality to be the unbecoming norm rather than the exception. But in her rapidly growing infatuation with Tommy she felt he was fundamentally different in a hitherto unknown manner.

The Price of Fame

The ride in the limousine was an affirmation of that newly found desirability, from the touch of his hand as he helped her inside the spacious interior, to the gentle brushing of her legs against his by more design than chance, and at last the pressure of his firm lips on hers. The ride itself seemed to last years and seconds in a contradiction of logical thought, as their ardor seemed to transcend time itself with its passionate embrace. Their arrival at the hotel temporarily ended their intense intimacy, but their rapid ascent to his luxurious suite revealed its consuming aggressiveness. After entering the hotel room, in seconds they were passionately kissing again, her innate desires aching for his masculine touch in needs that neither knew they had earlier but still had to be fulfilled. Their clothes began to vanish as they made their way to the king-sized bed, affording a sneak preview of what each offered the other. Gazing with frank adoration upon his highly toned body she could tell he must exercise and often, noting the exquisite definition in his impressively built frame. He looked at her with unabashed longing and desire, making her blush with its lustful emphasis as well as bringing her pleasure at its implied suggestion. And then he was exploring her body with his firm yet gentle hands, seductively teasing her with his calloused touch while still tasting her lips. Their earnest lovemaking was sustained and fulfilling, leaving both of them breathless from their passionate intimacy.

He turned towards her after they had recovered form their frenzied exertions, carefully stroking her cheek with newfound affinity. She looked deep into his luminous eyes, where the reflection within them formed twin impressions of herself. She felt safe and secure in his arms, not a feeling she had felt in a long while.

"This is not what I meant this evening to be like," he growled apologetically.

She laughed affectionately. "Nor did I. But I'm glad we did, even if you think less of me now," she teased playfully.

"Oh, I definitely do," he replied in mock seriousness. Catching his jesting tone, she threw a pillow at him in feigned anger, which he batted away. He grabbed her offending arms before she could fling another projectile his way, pushing her down to the bed and showering her with kisses which she delightfully returned. They remained in wanton embrace for several blissful minutes, before she wiggled away to sit up. He followed suit, but left his hand stroking subtly on her soft thigh.

Breaking the euphoric mood in reluctant necessity she spoke. "You, Mr. Tommy Blaine, still owe me an interview." Arching one eye in pretended obligation, "And I do believe that I've earned it."

He chuckled and withdrew his hand lightly, laying back against the headboard. "A deal's a deal," he said with affirmation. "How would you like to proceed?"

With elfin grace she departed from the bed, retrieving her panties before producing a recorder and stylus from her oversized purse. He watched her unintentionally erotic movements with open lechery she could feel on her nude form more than glimpse as she gathered her things. She sat down topless in a conveniently located chair to the tangled bed, prepared for the eminent conversation. "I thought an informal conference would do, considering the circumstances," she quipped merrily.

He laughed at her brazen joviality. "I do believe I will enjoy this actually," then dissolved into further merriment. Seeing her puzzled expression, he shared his humorous thoughts between chuckles. "Could you imagine Barbara Walters giving an interview like this?" She quickly shared his laughter, both of them joining together in peals of shaking mirth. After their hysterics ebbed they began the interview, her asking him questions and him providing answers to the best of his ability. She was in her area of expertise, rooting out answers to questions she knew would be of interest to the fans, as well as new tangents as they were exposed in the conversation. He himself was an excellent subject, responding with his naturalness and honest charm that made the task simplistic in progression. She idly wondered why he had been so stringent in avoiding meetings of this nature, and questioned him on the subject, not expecting the seriousness of his reply.

"Because I'm no good at lying, or omitting the truth. I've tried, and I'm no good at it. I know, a weird inhibition for someone in my situation. I have had things that have happened in my life that I can't explain and people would not understand nor believe. I didn't even believe them myself in the beginning. It's easier to avoid talking about such things than it is to face them. Inevitably the conversation would turn down that path, and I'm not ready to speak of it. That's why I don't give interviews, it's a shameful and contemptible reason. You can call me a coward if you wish-"

"You, Tommy, are no coward," she interrupted with earnest vigorousness. Her long concealed gentle instincts welled forth from his candid peeling back of his soul, revealing a sensitive crack in his manly armor that made her heart ache in sympathy. Anne knew what she needed to do for this tender-hearted man. There was a time to be a reporter, and a time to just be a compassionate listener. She turned off the recording and laid down her stylus.

"It's just you and me now Tommy. I won't write about what we discuss, but I want you to talk about it. I can't promise I won't judge, but I will try my hardest not to for you. But why now have you agreed if this is so bad? I'd like to flatter myself and say it was all me, but I seriously doubt that is the case."

He sighed with a mixture of resignation and relief. "Your timing has a lot to do with it. I had something happen to me twenty years ago to the day, a choice I made back then that I've lived with for so long and have never told a soul. It's difficult to even tell you why now after all this time. I'll start at the beginning and tell you the whole sordid thing, for once I start I know I won't be able to stop." She nodded to him in encouragement and assurance to continue, which he did with all the gusto of a dam that had just burst, flowing in a furious outburst, but still clearly so she could easily understand.

"First we have to go back to the spring of seventy-seven. I was in the New York music scene at the time, me and my friend Johnny had taught ourselves to play guitar and sing, and we met Mack who questionably played bass, and then Rocko joined on with us after we took out an ad for a drummer. We weren't very good in the beginning, but we were literally in Johnny's dad's garage daily hammering out our sound, and we even managed to land a few gigs as we gradually improved. We were young and dumb and full of ourselves. Batshit crazy you know? Sex, drugs, and rock n' roll, it wasn't just a slogan- it was the dream. We just knew we would succeed. I mean what band doesn't right?" He laughed sardonically at his own foolhardiness, then continued. "I mean we saw all these guys like the Ramones, the Dictators, hell even the really crazy ones like the Dead Boys getting grabbed by the labels, so we figured it was just a matter of time for us too."

"But it didn't. We played and practiced for two years and had squat to show for it. My dad kicked me out of the house, said I was a lazy bum and he didn't want to see me no more. Our manager Bart would tell us an exec was out in the bar or the hall we'd be at and we'd come up to him after the show and be like "What did you think? Pretty awesome right?" and he'd say apologetic stuff like "Keep at it kids, you'll get there someday." Or even worse he'd get us all excited, saying "Oh yeah, you guys got it. I'll call your manager. Let's do this." We'd ask Bart what was going on and he'd explain that it fell through, the label had too many bands out right then, but hey chin up, we're top of the list now. But nothing would develop; it was like they forgot about us, like we didn't even exist. No break, no future, and no contract. Finally Mack got fed up and left, said it wasn't happening so he was done. We tried to talk him out of it but he wasn't having none. Then Rocko split too, said we sucked and we were never going to make it. That pissed me off something fierce, so after we replaced the two of them me and Johnny kept going and I went kind of nutty, wanting to practice all the time. Figured we'd show them when we were big stars. Johnny stuck it out for a few more months, but when he knocked up Jenny and his dad died, that was it, he was done too. Said he had to get a real job, couldn't afford to screw around with this pipe dream shit anymore. I'll admit I didn't take that as well as I could have. We had a big fight, said some shit to each other you just can't take back, you know real personal stuff you shouldn't say to your friend, especially if he's going through a hard time like Johnny was going through." He closed his eyes briefly, remembering the hurt he caused, and she saw true regret for what he had done when he reopened them, the pain of the recollection lingering on even after all these years. She gave him the time he needed to recover, staying quiet until he resumed his account of the past events.

"So now it's just me and these new guys. They're still hungry and full of dreams, so they want it at least half as bad as I do. We practice, and we play, and we go nowhere. I'm finally starting to lose hope. We go to a gig to open for someone bigger, hoping to catch that break, and have to listen to a crowd telling us to get off the stage, where's the headliner? Like we're nothing, nobody. And the sad thing is they're right. We're losers and nobody loves a loser, and lord if it ain't truest when you trying to come up from nothing."

"So now I'm desperate. I'd do anything to make it, anything to get up there in those bright lights, to see my name on the signs, to get a record deal cut. I'm at an all-time low. I'm really thinking maybe now it's not happening. I've wasted my time, my energy, my money. I've thrown away my friends, my family, my life. For what? Nothing, that's the worst part. I've got nothing to show for it. Then I found out my mom had died and my dad didn't even try to find me for the funeral. So I start drinking, serious drinking. I'm even getting messed up before shows now, screwing up constantly at the gigs. The other guys are getting pissed and I know it's a matter of time till they throw me out of the band. But I've given up, so who cares, right?"

He took a deep breath and was quiet for a moment. She patiently gave him the time he needed to compose himself again. She knew of some of the things he had spoken of from various other band members' interviews she had familiarized herself with, and she had delved as deeply as possible into such historical evidence. His talk of depression and drinking had been unheard of, nor had she known of the family and friend issues he discussed from any of the sources. She found that she had been unconsciously leaning forward with tremulous anticipation on his every word, thrilled and fascinated by the autobiographical story. He did not make her wait very long, continuing his tale onward in his quiet but clear tone.

"Then I'm at a gig in this crappy biker bar, I don't even think we were getting free drinks let alone being paid. Not that it stopped me, I got pretty tuned up before the show. So I'm up there and we're finishing our set and I notice this woman staring at me. Not like she's looking at me, but different, like she's staring within me, very intimately. She looks beautiful, with black hair and very pale white skin in a revealing red dress, but it's real out of place for the scene, so I'm checking her out real close. Figure she's just some crazy chick who gets off on band guys, so I'm pretty anxious to meet her. We get done, and I rush getting stuff put away so I can catch her before she leaves. I go up front and I don't see her anywhere and then when I've just about given up bam! She's right behind me when I turn around. She's even more beautiful up close and personal, and heck, I'm all of twenty-two, young, dumb, and full of.....you know. I ask her name and she says it's Morigan. I figure it's not her real name but if she wants to be mysterious, I'm game. I'm half drunk anyway and I'm about to start hitting on her to see how far she'll take this, but she's already saying she wants to leave here with me." He grimaced ruefully before continuing. "If only I had not gone. Things might have been different." He was momentarily silent again, lost in the memories of yesteryear.

Anne decided some slight coaxing was in order, so she questioned him delicately, "How would it have been different, Tommy?"

He looked back up from his reverie, returning to the present. "Oh I'm sorry, I'm getting ahead of myself. So I left with her, stepping outside and she gets into a black limousine with a chauffeur in the driver's seat. He's decked out in the full garb, hat and everything, and he even opens the door for her. She gets in and then just looks at me like to say are you coming or not? My mind is blown, here I was thinking she was some kind of chick with a groupie fetish, but my only thoughts now are: record exec at last! I can't believe my luck. I get in, and the chauffeur closes the door and gets in the front. I'm sitting next to her, but now I'm on my best behavior and my lingering buzz is straight gone. She's looking very deep in my eyes, kinda like the way she was at the show. She doesn't say anything, but I can tell she's weighing my worth. I stare right back, but it's strange. Usually you see some kind of reflection of light staring back at you, like when I was looking at yours earlier, even in the dark. But with her it is like two black wells, nothing shining back, almost like they were so dark they could suck the life out of you with their inky blackness. And I begin thinking crazy thoughts, stuff I don't know, unbidden images of warriors of past ages brought down in battle, great leaders dying to disease and pestilence, and actors and playwrights poisoned and murdered. I begin to get uncomfortable staring in those soulless eyes and I'm forced to look away, and immediately the images end, swept away like the vestiges of dreams before dawn. I hear her speaking to the driver and she's giving him directions to an address whose name I'm not familiar with. I'm still trying to clear my head and figure out if what I saw was just in my head when I feel her touch me on the shoulder and then pull me close. She lightly kisses me on the cheek, and it's cold, ice cold. I look up at her and she looks at me and says, "Tommy, you want to be famous, right?"

"Now when she says that I snap back in focus. Have you ever wanted something so bad you could feel it deep within you like a worm eating you from the inside out? Like you just couldn't live without it? Like you wouldn't want to live without it? That's how I felt all the time then. It was the one thing I wanted, no, needed in my life to be whole. And she had just said it. I was in, and I didn't care what it took to get me there. "More than anything," I say, and she just grins at me, and then the car stops. We're at some deserted old vaudeville theater, you know the ones that got boarded up after tastes started changing. She motions for me to get out, so I comply and she follows me. I'm like "We're going to sign contracts here?" Pretty incredulously thinking, maybe now this is some kind of joke. She gives me a look, and I shut up instantly. She just so regal and commanding, like if the queen of England told you to be quiet so you better do it. She heads into the structure and I tag along behind her, figuring that if this is some kind of initiation I better play along. We get inside and it's an entryway, like where you bought your tickets for the shows back in the day. I see there's this incredibly tall guy in these long crimson robes and a white mask. He's pretty creepy looking, but she tells me to go with him. He leads me into a small room where he has me change into a robe as well, but mine is all pure white. He gives me an old fashioned drinking horn, motioning for me to ingest whatever he put inside it. It is some sort of bone and has tiny figures carved on it, similar to the ones in my earlier visions but all of them are resplendent in the glory of their life instead of dying. I ask "What's in the cup?" He smiles and says it is the stuff that dreams are made of. So I sip it at first, then figure if it's LSD or something. I've had much worse things at parties before, so I gulp it down, no regrets. It makes me feel a little lightheaded at first, but then I start feeling more in focus, like sharper somehow. It's hard to explain, I never felt anything like it again. It was like when you have a cup of coffee in the morning after a particularly rough night, but amplified like a hundred times. It felt like my life so far had been a dream and I was waking up from it, and was ready to start again." He paused, not so much for a response she could tell but more to gather his thoughts. This encounter between himself and the mysterious woman must have been so much more than a simple meeting to sign a record deal, and she let him consolidate his thoughts and conflicting emotions to express himself properly. He continued his strange recantation after a moment longer, but his eyes were far away and his voice was soft and faded, as if seeing the past occurrence again and dictating the event as it unfolded in his mind.

"The tall man leads me out to the entryway again, then takes me through these antique double doors to what was the old theater proper. There's the stage down at the rear of the massive room and the curtains are down on it. There are seats where we entered, from wall to wall, all the way down to front of the stage, those old gilt fold-down chairs and in every seat there's a person in a crimson robe with a mask on like my guide. But the strangest part I notice is the crows. Lined on the catwalks and light strings they watch silently, without a single squawk or cry. Almost in a haze mentally from the insane scene in front of me, I follow my guide down the aisle to the stage and mount it, and then turn to face the crowd. It's nuts, all these people out there and I can feel their eyes one me, like they are going to witness something, something special that will happen to me tonight. The tall man begins to speak to the delegation in some strange dialect, like he's reciting an ancient prayer. I can't place the language but it seemed familiar, like something primal my ancestors would know. Then the crowd replies back to the tall man in unison, roaring an unholy litany in blasphemous supplication. I can feel the hairs on the back of my neck standing up, and it is more than just terror at the scene before me. I could feel something malevolent calling back, feeding on their adulation, and I turned slowly around because I can feel that presence *behind me.* The curtain starts rising on the stage and I can see that Morigan is there, but she is changed now as well. She is sitting on a great throne naked, and the presence I feel is emanating *from her.*"

"She majestically rises, and I become breathless at the sight of her, so great and maligned is the power coming from her I drop to my knees in sheer adoration. I must close my eyes, her feminine magnificence is so overwhelming and breathtaking. Eyes shut, I feel as much as hear her steps towards me, and then her touch is on me, lightly brushing my head and face in pure ecstatic stokes. I can hear her speak, but not with my ears, it is as if she is in my mind with silken tones. She tells me she will make me famous, more famous than I dreamed possible, all the glory and power I want she will provide for me. But there is a price, she says, and I must accept to gain my dearest wish. She would not name the price, or even speak of it, but I would be bound if I swore to her."

"And bathed in her baleful radiance I knew I must accept, for all that my heart had so desired would be granted unfailingly by her. The idea that it would not come to pass or that I would regret it later never crossed my mind; it was unthinkable that it could be. So I swore to her that I agreed, opening my eyes once more to gaze upon her gorgeous form. She smiled and took me in her arms, and I did unspeakable idolization upon her willing form to consummate our sacrilegious bargain, until I passed out from my exertions. But before I sank into slumber my mind echoed with a final message, that she would see me two more times, and on the final time she would collect the price I had taken an oath to uphold."

"Then I woke up the next day, naked and shivering, alone in the deserted theater. There was no sign of anything I had witnessed the night before, the entire place looked like a mockery of its former self, with smashed and destroyed finery from vandalism and age and neglect everywhere. I found my cast off clothing in a foul puddle, cleaned them off the best I could, got dressed, and departed, returning to my crappy little apartment on the east side. I found myself thinking that it had been a weird dream, that I should quit drinking and partying if this is what my degenerated mind would do. In fact I was angry at myself, thinking that Morigan and the weird tall man had involved me in some sick game and when making me drink the unknown liquid had drugged me into unknowingly revealing my innermost secret wants, and in some perverse fashion fed upon them for their own kicks. Then there was a knock at the door and it was my agent. He has just got off the phone with Kutner Records, they were interested in signing a multi-album deal with me and the band. Today, if possible, we had to go now!"

"The next decade was a blur of studios, tours, and fans. You know that part, but what you don't know is the writing. I had always been pretty decent at coming up with lyrics and hooks, but my skills magnified whenever I sat down to compose. It was like it just flowed out of me ceaselessly, like a steady stream that never ended, easy as that. I've never had any droughts or 'just paying the bills' moments. Which is crazy because everyone must have some block from time to time, but I don't. And the hits that came out! Stuff I didn't even think should go that far took off with a life of their own."

"So everything's going great, just like I hoped. I'm famous, got women all over me, and millions of people listening to my records. So I'm start thinking it's me, especially now that the old band mates have fallen in line with the Tommy show or shipped out. I created this, I'm the one who's name is screamed by the fans, I'm the reason that all these people have jobs via my talent. So I'm getting a big head, and I've forgotten all about Morigan and the promise. It was just some stupid stuff that happened back when I got messed up, right?"

"So I'm at this huge show in Cleveland in the late eighties, last in the tour, and I'm out there really stirring up the crowd, we were tearing it up just like always, and it's going great. I'm singing the a cappella piece in "The Inmost Light," and looking off into the crowd, not really looking for anyone, I mean after all I'm the great Tommy Blaine. If you know me you won't be in the crowd." He wryly smiles at his own stupid pompousness of his youthful self.

"Then all of a sudden it's like the lights and sounds have lowered, like a fog that is making everything surreal and phantom-like. Then I hear the flapping of wings, and I look up and see hundreds of crows freewheeling above the crowd. In my dreamlike state I lower my eyes again to the people down below and then I see her. It's Morigan, and even though she's pretty far off and it's been years I know it's her. She hasn't aged a day that I can tell and she's in that same red dress again, and then I can see she's staring at me as well. Staring through me and into me again. I'm looking at her and I get a feeling I haven't felt since that night, that feeling of a dark aura surrounding her that pulses perniciously right into my mind. Then she speaks to me, telepathically again, and says "Don't forget Tommy. Enjoy yourself, but you're mine. Next time I come for what's owed." Then she vanishes and the lights and sounds come back on in full force, and the rest of the band is looking at me like what the hell because I've missed the cue. So I bolt off the stage."

She speaks up, "I remember reading about that. It's the only time you ever left a show. The magazines said you were sick and couldn't continue. You took a hiatus after that for a while."

He looked at her with admiration. "You really know this stuff don't you? Well, everyone always had my back in those days. My agent put good spin on it, saying I was pushing myself to hard with the new album coming out and the relentless touring. The great Tommy Blaine giving it his all for the fans. Said I needed a break, so I actually took him up on it. I knew now I hadn't been dreaming that night, and I had made a pact with some kind of witch, possibly with my very soul as the price of that foolish liaison. I dived into unearthing the secret of the bargain I had struck, looking for a way out of the hellish accord. I hired unwitting researchers to find out about Morigan and the red-robed cult members, and they supplied boundless historical facts and a wealth of information for me to delve and extrapolate knowledge from to form a hypothesis of her intentions.

I discovered her true name was Morrigan, goddess of fate and death. The ancient druids had worshiped her in old Ireland and other Celtic strongholds until the Romans and Christianity had destroyed them with fire and battle, driving the remnants into hiding. But still she persevered despite the persecution. Many instances of her forays into the mortal realm were simple to see if one could interpret the signs. Appearing in the Ulster cycle of Irish mythology, specifically the *Tain Bo Regamna* and *Cuailnge,* she attempts to deceive the hero Cuchulaninn multiple times and finally succeeds. In *Lebor Gabala Erenn* I learned of her penchant for crows, then later in the *Cath Mage Tuired,* her dark prophecies rang true for the Irish folk heroes who beseeched her, the supplicants discovering the dire fates in store for them were unalterable. And in the Arthurian legends her power as the sorceress Morgan Le Fay as she engaged in manipulative acts against King Arthur and his knights to unfathomable ends was a beginning to an ageless pattern. Her impact was not only in earlier times, shrouded and nearly lost to history. Instances of more modern encounters were in abundance as well. I found many times she was mentioned by great, *famous* men like Nelson, Mac Colla, and Custer in their memoirs and from accounts of their fighting men. Nor were her visits limited merely to men of war; she seems to have taken an interest in poets, writers, and artists such as Van Gogh, Howard, and Poe, outlined as such in their writings and paintings of torturous dark forces. But the most interesting to me, of course, was Morrigan's interest in such music legends as Williams, Morrison, and Lynott, visions of her perfidious beauty and dark magnificence subtly implanted in their poetry and lyrics. I began to notice a disturbing trend among the men she had influenced, a tendency towards an unnatural death before their time should have been due. I began to despair of the short-sighted alliance I had made with this monster, for I knew now what I faced was no simple conjurer of the black arts but omnipotent being with all the accoutrements of a primordial goddess."

"I searched in vain for some sort of salvation, but there was no respite from my Faustian bargain. In all of history I could find no one that had escaped the dark pact they had forged with her unforgiving power. But, as time passed on I realized that since there was really nothing I could do to repudiate my dilemma, life must go on. I began writing and composing again, and going back out on tour. I've tried to live a much better life now, being generous to people and appreciating what time I have left. I'm happier now, and I try to bring some of the happiness to folks back the only way I can, through my music. You're the first person I've been able to talk to about this, and I'm glad we've shared this together. If only we had met sooner..." His voice trailed off, as if contemplating the future they could have shared before stoically continuing his strange tale.

"But that is not meant to be. Tonight while I was out on

that stage I could feel her presence again, and I know she comes for me soon. I saw the crows, lined up like all those years before, waiting and watching with their beady black eyes, foreshadowing her reappearance."

Anne too had noticed the birds earlier, but just figured it was a normal occurrence for an outdoor stage in this area. Her mind rebelled at the seemingly impossible story he had chronicled for her. Her cold, no nonsense reporter side screamed that it was a hoax, a lie conjured for some meaningless reasoning. But her gut feelings and empathetic bond with the man had a different opinion, however unbelievable it may be. She was torn between her opposing halves, between steely science and undeniable logic versus whimsical fantasy and the love of the human heart, and that rent is what caused her momentary mental shutdown, unable to form coherent thoughts to communicate with him. At the height of her mental disarray, the room's lights seemed to flicker and the welcome little background noises of the suite seemed to fade into inaudibility. The sounds of hundreds of wing beats filled the room, quietly at first and building up to a crescendo in the enclosed space, causing her to look outside the window despite her preoccupation. Birds, specifically crows, were apparent in the hundreds, if not thousands, flying, gliding, and alighting on the nearby architecture. She saw Tommy in a dream-like state, slowly rising from the bed, and walking towards the door. She heard a light, hollow knock, and saw him close his hand on the knob. She wanted to scream, to warn him, not to open that door, but it was as if she were paralyzed. No sound could be uttered from her frozen vocal cords, and her incapacitated limbs refused to obey even the most basic of commands. Anne knew she must try, for she could feel a pagan intensity radiating though the door, and she knew despite her previous doubts that *she* had come for him.

Tommy opened the door slowly, revealing a pale, raven-haired figure in a diaphanous crimson dress. Anne tried again to scream, but only a sharp exhalation of air was the best she could manage. That small sound almost seemed enough to accomplish her intended purpose, as he turned back towards her and took one step back towards her motionless form. Then he seemed to blanch, his face going slack, and then turned again towards the now advancing goddess as if he were a puppet on a string, no longer in control of his very limbs. Anne saw with horror-filled eyes as the deity enfolded him in her black embrace, then passionately kissed him on his silently screaming mouth. Anne began to pass out, but did not succumb to oblivion until she saw Tommy's body sag and fall to the carpet.

She awoke some time later, groggily awakening with half remembered nightmares of horror and anguish still haunting her mind. She found herself in the bed, with the covers nestled around her shoulders and a slumbering form next to her. She thought wearily, ah, it was just a dream, nothing to worry about. But the sleeping shape seemed to lie too still for her liking, so she frantically turned on the light and then looked over at the motionless body. It was Tommy, lying on his side, un-blinking eyes wide open, staring at her with his countenance twisted in terror. He was dead before his time should have been, having ultimately paid the final price for his fame.

No Man's Land

"There it is again, Paul." Richard was looking into the evening gloom, towards the tortured swathe of disputed land that stretched between the German and British positions. He had been intently staring at the section of contested territory for some time now, and sporadically he would report his findings to his disinterested fellow soldiers. Most of the men were focused on their own private tribulations, such as the ever present sickness caused by the damp climate and ill-afforded protection from the disastrous elements in the trench, or the incessant lice and rats. Problems of the more psychological nature filled their thoughts as well, ranging from simple homesickness to trauma brought on by the ceaseless repetition of enemy attacks and their own counterattacks. They paid Richard's contemplations little heed as a result. However, Paul Winford was much closer than the others to the firestep Richard was standing on to peer out over the parapet, and so he received the full brunt of the observations from the big Welsh man. Paul personally thought that it was a needless risk on the other man's part, a veritable open invitation for a

Jerry sniper to identify his location and end his obtuse peeping.

Their unit had been diverted to a section of line that used to be a primeval forest near the town of Bras for reinforcement of the wavering Allied line there. Most everything left standing in the wood had long since been destroyed. The timber itself had been blasted and shattered, with only a few hardy survivors to be seen in random areas unaffected by the prolonged shelling from the countless artillery batteries on either side, most leafless, rising out of the blasted landscape like skeletal fingers clawing at the sky. The soldiers had been in the frontline trench now for the past two days, and the long lines of armament and men had been relatively quiet from both the Allied and Central sides. Only the occasional report of a rifle sounded from either an overzealous defender firing at ghosts in the murky fog that incessantly covered the ground, or more ominously from a sniper picking off a choice target. The tormented land between the two sides had seen plenty of action before their arrival with craters and holes torn open from the raw earth. The reminders of past aborted raids were evident with the bodies of both comrades and enemies strewn haphazardly around like carnal chattel. The abysmal carcasses were left to rot by the stationary armies for two reasons. Firstly, the glaringly abundant reason of extreme possible danger to the would-be undertaker of being killed themselves as they recovered the bodies. Secondly was that once retrieved they had no appropriate method to dispose of them properly. Every so often one of the officers would have a conniption over the lack of respect to the dead, and would stage a recovery operation to boost the flagging morale. A simple pauper's grave was the site of most of the dead men's end, buried in the distant land they had fought for with no marker to even remind the world they had been there at all. On occasion, even as new tunnels were being dug, the soldiers would find the area had already been used as a gravesite beforehand, either singly or much more likely as a mass grave. The occupants would be putrefying in the moist earth, pungent with the smell of decomposing flesh and spoilage. Rats would arrive en masse shortly afterward, drawn to the offal scent as their fictional brethren had to Hamelin's storied pied piper of yore.

Rumor had it from the French populace that a prosperous town had once existed in the area, deserted well before the war during the mid eighteenth century, shortly before their Revolution. The indigenous farmers and craftsmen said that the settlement had been struck by a mysterious lethal plague and anyone who had not died from its debilitating effects had decided to give up on a continued existence in the area, leaving for safer parts of the country. The area was still shunned nowadays by all the locals, citing strange disappearances to those foolish enough to stray into its confines. There was almost no sign of any buildings or relics from the period. Any surviving ramshackle structures no doubt had been further obliterated by the complete and thorough destruction caused by the opposing forces currently situated there. The only evidence that humans had ever existed in the area prior to the war's arrival was the decimated town's graveyard. The buried granite tombstones and Gothic crosses of the dead were uncovered periodically by the artillery's churning assaults, and they lay scattered about the field of battle like broken teeth smashed from the earth's maw.

Richard was a new arrival to the front, not yet tested in the crucible of battle. He therefore took unnecessary chances in his naïve curiosity. Paul had been like him once, full of wonder at the older men's tales of the Boer War and the Zulu uprisings in his borough. He had been more than ready to do his part for king and country when the war broke out. His first time in the forward positions had coincided with a surprise German offensive. The enormous barrage of explosive shells had caught the entire line off guard, and he had seen firsthand the destructive power of the modern armament and artilleries. His friend Jasper Elms, who had signed up with him and was assigned to the same unit, had been in the blast radius of one of detonations. His legs were torn from his body and scattered several yards away. Paul had been forced to watch him die, with no way to staunch the profuse bleeding coming from the stumps of his severed extremities, his lifeblood mixing with the brackish rainwater collecting on the muddy ground, adding a slight rosy tint to the dirty grey water. Jasper's grisly death was not the only one to suffer such a horrid fate. Paul was to see much more bloodshed and carnage in his relatively short tenure in the trenches. Others lost limbs or were horribly damaged by shrapnel, or died painfully in wheezing and coughing fits caused by phosgene and chlorine gases unleashed indiscriminately by both sides. Fear of the chemical bombardments was almost as deadly as their deployment. Men frantically climbed out of the dugouts to escape the lung-searing fate only to be mowed down by machine gun fire or cut down with well-placed rifle shots by the enemy waiting above.

So it was that when Richard started his commentary of something strange in the "alleyway," as the soldiers called the disputed territory between the armies, Paul had not cared one fig for his remarks on the subject, and had indeed been actively discouraging the man from his errant behavior earlier. However, little by little the red-headed man's insistent comments began to intrigue the callous listener, and Paul began to pay a hairsbreadth more attention, gathering from the stream of connotations that one of the Fritz's bodies had been moving. After a final moment's reflection of the dismal surroundings in the clay canal, Paul eventually questioned him on the matter, albeit not without a certain tone of reproach in his speech.

"What Richard, is so bloody interesting out there? You said one of the enemy bodies is moving, perhaps the poor chap is wounded and just trying to get to cover. Nothing fascinating in that."

The Welsh giant looked out again over the parapet,

squinting his eyes as he did so. "No, he's very dead. His eyes are open, and he's got a gray pallor about him. He's got bullet wounds as well, looks like five or six, no, there's another, seven." He paused his talking as he recounted, then resumed. "That's all of them I think. There might be even more on him that I can't see from this angle. No, he's definitely dead alright. But every once in a while he quivers and moves slightly, like something is jerking into that hole to his right. But nobody's been out there right? There's been no sorties from the Germans for days now, that's what the fellows we replaced said that first night. How could someone stay out there for all that time? And why give away your position just to pull a dead body in with you if you were caught out there?"

"Maybe he's got a canteen or something else he needs," Paul countered. "Maybe his superior sent him out there to retrieve the body. Who knows? Could be rats. Willie in C Company said he saw one the size of a terrier when he was over in Ypres, and I've seen 'em almost as big. One of those could be dragging it down to feast on, I'll bet that's it, sure as anything."

"Maybe so." Richard looked doubtful, and continued his pointless surveillance. The night was fast approaching, and it wouldn't be long before the lieutenant would be calling the evening's Stand-To-Arms. They performed the ritual twice daily, once when the officers roused them at the crack of dawn, and once again at night, each man firing three shots into the shrouded mists towards the German lines, hoping to catch an enemy offensive sneaking towards them unawares. Someone had poetically named the early light's action "Morning Hate," but Paul had always found it strange that the twilight proceedings did not receive the same picturesque treatment. Perhaps everyone had been too tired by that time to care, or perhaps nothing had seemed suitable or catchy enough to invoke widespread usage.

Suddenly Richard made a loud exclamation of distress. He hopped hastily down from the firestep, landing clumsily in the puddle of dank water below the wooden structure, splashing its foul liquid all over Paul. He protested the intrusion immediately, but the look of undisguised horror on the big man's face reined in his complaints quickly.

"What is it Richard? Are the Germans attacking?" He grabbed his rifle forcibly by reflex, whirling towards the opposing trench wall. It was evident that Richard had seen something that had visibly disturbed him, and he felt compelled to act as a result. Paul shook the troubled man, trying to return him from the nightmare trapping him in his own mind. Richard's eyes cleared of their glazed state from the not so gentle ministrations as he recovered from his alarm sufficiently enough to be able to speak of what he witnessed.

"No, it's not Germans. I was watching that dead Jerry again, because he kept shifting every so often, moving in odd jerks and shakes, and then that's when I saw it." He stared directly at Paul, his eyes still haunted from recent event. "It was an arm, no, more like a claw or talon. It grabbed him and pulled him down into the crater. It was pale, like the corpse it-self but with black veins all through it, and long, too long, and bent at all the wrong places. It stabbed him with its talons, and yanked real hard, like you would a trout when bringing it in. I don't know what it was that grabbed that corpse, but it wasn't a man," his voice lowered almost conspiratorially at the ghastly revelation, *"It wasn't human at all."*

Paul stood aghast at the far-fetched disclosure. It wasn't at all what he had expected the man to say, having anticipated word of a forthcoming German assault, and it seemed so ludi-crous a description that he waited a moment to see if perhaps Richard had been fooling with him or playing a joke to break the tedious monotony of watching and waiting. The big man just stared at him after the dire pronouncement. He saw no trace of duplicity or merriment in his demeanor, only a strange look of dismay and repulsion. Something else was there too, something Paul had been in contact with himself more regularly as of late than he would ever care to admit, and that something was *fear*. Richard was genuinely afraid of what he had seen out there, and that gave his implausible story more credence than any stack of bibles he could swear on to prove the validity of his alarm.

"You men, what are you doing there?" The lieutenant's voice rang clearly behind them, cutting through their previous isolation. They turned to face him, and Paul could not say he was entirely pleased to see the smug officer. He was younger than most of the soldiers that fell under his charge, and word had been that he had only received the commission due to his family connections, the youngest son of some earl or duke. Paul could forgive all that, not really his place to question who the top brass chose to lead, but the man seemed to go out of his way to make life in the trenches even more unbearable than all the encumbrances of lice, rats, and dampness combined. Insisting on unnecessary procedures and draconian punishments for the slightest infraction, his ruthlessness and lack of regard for human life was cause for dismay and alarm for the entire unit. He seemed to be out to prove himself worthy of the posting as well, aspiring to look both valuable and noteworthy to his superiors in spite of his shortcomings. That kind of ludicrous and self-serving thinking was dangerous not only for everyone under his modest command but to the very integrity of the unit itself.

"Well, I'm waiting." He glowered at the two men, impatiently expecting their response. Richard was still too out of sorts to answer, so Paul piped up, not wishing to infuriate the self-important totalitarian further with sluggishness.

"Richard said he saw something out in the alleyway, sir, but it's gone now, must've been the Jerries playing peek-a-boo out there." The lie came easily to his lips, and he ardently hoped Richard would use what little brains he had to back him up.

The officer turned to Richard. "Well, what did you see soldier? Speak up now, I haven't all day." He fairly radiated his disdain for the two enlisted men, his haughtiness and elitism only barely contained in his speech. Richard looked blankly back at him, seeming to have forgotten how to properly form his thoughts. Then finally he was able to pull his mind back together in articulate enough fashion to respond, albeit with much incoherent babbling.

"Th-Th-There's something out there sir, something that took a German body. It's not right sir, it wasn't one of the Germans or another man at all. It was like some kind of animal, but it looked monstrous what I saw, I only saw the arm, but it was all wrong, not normal. It was like a monster. It took him, I don't why, but it took him down into one of the holes."

The lieutenant's face flushed bright red at the preposterous tale, and for a moment Paul thought he might strike Richard so great was his apoplexy. Paul knew the story sounded so absurd that the officer surely thought they were lying, manufacturing a fictional story to make him look the fool in front of the increasing number of onlookers. Paul knew they were done for surely now as Richard just had to open his foolish mouth about monsters. They would be without a doubt pulling guard duty tonight and Paul fervently hoped the penance they would be forced to pay would be so minor a cost.

However, instead of exploding on the hapless Welsh man, the lieutenant's lips hardened into a straight, thin line before retorting in turn. "Well, it looks like we have a true mystery on our hands. Command has already asked for a patrol tonight to see why the Germans are being so quiet. We can investigate this monster of yours as well while we're out there, private. The two of you will accompany me, as well as you and you there," he said, pointing over their heads to another pair of soldiers unfortunate enough to be caught in the cross-hairs of his ire. "We'll just see if this story of yours has any truth to it, gentlemen. Be ready at twenty-four hours at the front sap." He gave them one final menacing stare before taking his leave, swaggering away to harass other members of the unit.

They ate a hasty meal before equipping themselves for the impeding patrol. Close combat weapons such as knives, brass knuckles, and bayonets were the norm, with even shovels and clubs as more fitting arms than the typical rifles and grenades. The standard armament would still accompany them in their mission as well, on the off chance of a firefight. The goal in a successful patrol was stealth, to avoid the nests of machine guns and vigilant sentries who would respond to loud noises such as the crack of a pistol with overwhelmingly superior firepower, a hail of ordinance that would annihilate any luckless soldier caught out in the open ground. Paul had even heard of artillery being called in during extreme circumstances, the guards fearing the unfamiliar racket as a nocturnal full-on attack hell bent on taking over their trench. But orders were orders and while the men may distrust their leader's intentions, the command had been clear. When the appointed time came all four men hunkered patiently down in the shallow channel that led to the furthest extent of the British line into no man's land.

The lieutenant was late, to which he gave no courtesy of

apology to the cramped men waiting for his arrival. He merely made a simple nod of acknowledgment to the waiting soldiers, and then they set off. Their progress was painstakingly slow, crawling out of the trench on their hands and bellies, trying to avoid being seen in transit across the uneven ground. The darkness of night was only thinly fractured by the crescent moon above and while it aided their advance, one could only wish that it did not illuminate them to possible spotters, both on the enemy side and their own. Not many patrols had been decimated by friendly fire, but enough had been the victim of that sad fate that the chance was still regrettably high of occurring. They moved from torn crater to earthen mound, using whatever alternating cover there was as meticulously as possible in their exploration. Every once in a while one of the members of their patrol would unfortunately make an undesirable clatter or scrape and they would all freeze, in the hope that any sentries would miss the clamor of their mistake. Slowly they would begin anew, after a stern look from their neighbor as well as the lieutenant. Paul had been surprised that the lieutenant took the lead in their endeavor, the boldness of the selfless action not fitting into his preconceived notions of the man. The minuscule progress they made slowly but surely added up and as the minutes turned closer to an hour they were able to traverse into the disputed territory closer to the German position.

It was the lieutenant that found the tunnel, a small crack in the bottom of one of the numerous craters. It was barely wide enough for a man to clamber into but a cool breeze of fetid air wafted from its mouth, proof of the depths it concealed with its diminutive nature. The scent from the tunnel was foul, like something that had died long ago and was well into the natural entropy of decomposition, rotting down in the bowels of the earth. It reminded Paul of when one of the Miller's sheep had fallen into a crevasse unnoticed. The odor had so permeated the surrounding area that they had investigated the site to discover the source of the stench's origin. Finding the sheep covered in maggots and worms, with no way to extricate it from the site of its demise they had ultimately decided to leave it to the carrion eaters. The fissure became both the sheep's tomb and a table for its devourers' unsavory banquet.

The young officer was understandably excited at the extraordinary discovery of the warren of subterranean passages. Even Paul and the others knew that this could be a fortuitous find indeed for their side. Then the lieutenant pointed a long index finger downwards, indicating his intent, and began to crawl into the hole's meager opening. Bloody hell Paul thought anxiously, he means for us to go down there in the dark! The prospect of the tight confines of the tunnel's walls did not excite him in the least. The fact that this could be an enemy foothold, packed with Fritz troops did not endear the idea to him either. Again it was not his place to decide their course, so he followed dutifully behind the others down into the obscurity of the cleft, gripping his knife tightly. A few of the men ahead had produced their trench lighters, a cobbled-together affair made from spent .303 casings and petrol for fuel, providing a scanty light to see by. The lieutenant used his more traditional Wonderliter to illuminate his way ahead. The floor sloped downwards at an almost forty-five degree angle. The walls were slick, covered with moisture, and were irregular shaped with varying thicknesses. They came so close together at some points that the men had to wriggle sideways through the tight enclosures. The ceiling and floor were not uniform in height and depth, forcing the men to crawl on their hands and knees at certain spots, with the foul mud composing the floor oozing through their fingers as they did so. The earth around them seemed to press and constrict their bodies, with chunks of dirt and debris falling sporadically with their laborious passage, a terrifying portent of possible collapse. Paul wondered just how far the subterranean tunnel extended and he seriously doubted the veracity of the Germans' involvement in its manufacture. It seemed more like something a wild animal would make. The jagged earth was unevenly ripped and torn out, having more in common with instinctual clawing and burrowing than with the straight lines and consistent edges associated with human engineering.

Eventually the winding tunnel came to an end leading into an enlarged cavern. Gentle moonlight filtered in a gaping hole exposing nighttime sky at the top of the cave making the area seem strangely tranquil and reassuring. More than half of the area was occupied by a great stone mausoleum covered in soil and filth, but still intact except where its roof had caved in, coinciding with the hole at the cavern's ceiling. The bottom section was submerged in the ever-present mud at an almost impossible angle, giving the appearance that the entire structure was sinking into the earth. Two bent and battered metal doors were lying on the ground in front of the crypt, with the hinges on their sides rent and shredded. To Paul the violent destruction of the doors seemed like the wanton act of a powerful creature, rather than the systematic demolishing that a man would execute in their removal. Human hands would have been more methodical and less inclined to harm the structure. Curiously, the doors' fallen positions and the twisted fixtures gave the impression that the vandal came bursting from *inside the tomb*. The exposed damage on the metal pivots themselves was still bright and shiny, like the occurrence had recently taken place. In a low voice, the lieutenant ordered Paul and Richard to investigate the crypt, giving them his light to help accomplish the task.

Stooping down to enter the mausoleum, they found the inside floor was scattered with fractured and splintered wood, from the tiniest of fragments to large, almost whole sections. Richard picked up one of the bigger pieces, and almost immediately dropped it, wiping his hands hastily on his pants. Paul eyed him questionably.

"It's rotten, spongy," the big man replied sheepishly, "Felt gross."

Paul tried to hide his smile, and studied the wood components scattered around. He tried to visualize what they could have been before their devastation. When he finally realized their purpose he felt a little discomfited himself, as obviously the shattered parts when together had comprised a coffin. He searched through the wreckage and found broken bits of chain mixed together with the wooden splinters, the links burst and ruined. Now that's strange, he thought to himself. He looked at his companion, and debated on whether to tell him of his discovery. He ultimately decided against it, remembering the Welsh man's previous troubled state. Last thing they needed was one of their own people cracking under the pressure in this precarious situation, he reasoned. Going slightly further into the recesses at the rear of the crypt, he went directly below the hole in the roof. He saw evidence there that an artillery or mortar shell had been the source of the opening. There was damage to the walls and floor as well, but to a lesser degree, the blast leaving fallen rubble and shattered stone scattered in the vicinity. Some of the rubble seemed to be made of a different material than the grey stone of the mausoleum. He bent down to retrieve a sample, and held it up to the light for examination. It was of a more yellowish color and had been painstakingly inscribed with bizarre symbols and strange shapes. He did not recognize any of the figures, but it seemed to be a very old runic writing style, and he idly speculated as to the meaning of the message that had been etched so laboriously in the solid rock. Finishing their search of the crypt, they returned to the others, and reported that there was nothing of importance in the burial chamber. He decided to withhold the mystery of the broken links and cryptic writing from the officer, feeling that the information would not be appreciated by the other man especially given his reaction to Richard's story earlier.

Leaving the tomb behind, the squad continued onwards through another irregularly built passageway until they reached another cavern, even larger than the first one they had previously encountered. As they entered into the cave's voluminous span, they heard a crunching sound, as if they were walking on eggshells or broken glass, crushing the fragile unseen items beneath their boots. Peering down at the ground, they were horrified to discover a multitude of bones littering the floor and strewn the length of the cave. The flesh had been wholly stripped away, leaving only the white remnants behind. There were bones of all shapes and sizes, hundreds if not thousands of them, and they all had one disturbing characteristic in common, that they appeared to be of human derivation. Some were noticeably aged and dirty, as if they had been there an extremely long time. There were more recent additions as well, identifiable by their glaring pale color. However, all the bones regardless of age were marred with scrapes and scratches. The men spoke in low tones uneasily to one another, the macabre scene unsettling the normally stolid soldiers. The horrors of war were one thing, but this was something else, something unholy and primal, and *unknown*. It seethed with unnatural perversion and pure evil. While they could adapt and deal mentally with the constant attacks and endless barrages in the trenches, the enemy perpetrating those acts were human as well, with human intentions and reasoning. This had been caused by an entirely different being, one that was inhuman and alien, devoid of such considerations and taboos that normal man possessed, something evidently consumed by a relentless hunger for the flesh of man.

In a darkened corner they found torn and shredded clothing lying in discarded heaps like over-sized shucked corn husks. These were obviously removed by the cannibalistic epicurean to facilitate more efficient consumption of the human corpses. That would have been bad enough on its own, but the most disturbing part of viewing the garments was the recognizable remnants of materials from German and British uniforms, and the undeniable horrific realization of whose bones they had unknowingly trodden upon. Paul felt ill at the thought but maintained his composure in spite of the dreadful revelation. The growing horror of what they were dealing with was slowly insinuating itself within him. Looking at the other men's faces he knew they too felt the terrible tension of its ghastly insistence, and that Richard had been right all along, that something not man nor beast had caused the loathsome spectacle before them.

But then Paul turned his eyes to the lieutenant, and he saw instead of fear or revulsion something different displayed across his youthful features, an excited craving and enthusiasm. It was a look he had seen before, the fervor of the chase.

Men wore it when indulging in hunting and fishing, the exhilaration and thrill of tracking down prey and flushing them out of their hiding spots. He knew that the lieutenant would not rest now until they found the creature that had committed these atrocities, until the monster was as dead as its victims lying ignominiously all around them. The resolved look frightened him, and the officer whispered words in the preternatural dark that confirmed his fears.

"Richard, looks like you were right old chap. There is something down here, no denying it. What we've seen it's terrible, that's for certain, but it is our duty, nay, our very purpose to destroy this creature. We came here for the war gentleman, but this is something neither God nor man can abide."

He outlined his plan, that two of them would stay behind in case the monster was coming back to its lair from the direction they had came. He and the other men would continue ahead, scouting for the creature's presence and rendezvousing back later if they found no sign in the next hour. He selected the two other soldiers to accompany him and left Paul and Richard to guard the rear. The steady tramping of their footfalls died away quickly, and the two men were left alone in the darkness, relying on their hearing to warn them of impeding danger, needing to conserve what little fuel they had left.

The obscurity of the gloom was almost welcome at first, hiding from their sight the disturbing imagery of the gnawed bones and ragged clothing. But the darkness brings with it its own terrors and suspicions, and every creak and rumble brought with it nervousness and trepidation to the two men. The imagination runs wild in the dark, and the need for silence meant they could not even find solace in the distraction of prattle between themselves. Paul could feel the earth closing in on him, its moist breath seeming to be panting with anticipation, *salivating for him*. He could hear Richard as the man exhaled near him, his breath as restless and as ragged as his own. The endless waiting was unbearable. He felt trapped and apprehensive, wondering if the very creature they were lying in wait for had stolen on them unawares, silently climbing through the passageways, and was now stalking them amongst the dispersed remains of its countless casualties. Then came distant shots coming from the direction the lieutenant had gone with the others, and he breathed an involuntary selfish sigh of relief, which he was instantly ashamed of, but drove him to action.

"They need our help Richard," he said quietly but clearly, jumping to his feet at the same time. "We can't leave them to fight that thing alone." Richard concurred, and Paul relit his lighter, leading the way ahead down the tunnel. The passageway seemed wider than the previous ones they had traveled, and the going was much less rough than it had been before. There were smaller side tunnels that led off from the path they were on, but they stayed on the larger course, figuring this to be main transit and it being unlikely that the lieutenant would have explored the additional corridors before securing the main branch. Their logic was morbidly rewarded upon finding the two soldiers lying on the floor ahead, one dead with his throat slashed so deeply it exposed bone, and the other horrendously wounded, his chest and abdomen lacerated and punctured. Paul bent down to assist him, and the fading man pulled him close, gurgling and spitting blood on his already frothing lips, as he tried to speak.

"Don't say anything, save your strength," Paul tried to reassure him, but the man fought to make himself heard nevertheless, striving against the death that was swiftly overtaking him.

"I-it t-took him, it t-took h-him d-down there." He gestured feebly in the opposite direction from which they had came, and then gasped sharply one last final time and expired. Paul laid him gently down and closed his staring eyes, before standing again to face Richard.

"Let's go, we need to find where it took the lieutenant." They swiftly scooped up the fallen men's trench lighters off the ground, knowing the dead men no longer needed them. Setting off, they hurried as quickly as the terrain would allow, stumbling over roots and clods of dirt in their haste to catch up to their target. They saw the tunnel's roof ahead of them soon giving way to unblocked full sky, still thankfully black except for the sliver of moonlight and a few stars bright enough to be seen. Slowing down, they doused their lights and cautiously crouched down, creeping to the end of the burrow. They could make out blood smears and disturbed ground leading from the edge of the excavation down to a shallow gul-ly to their right. They followed the trail down warily, intent on finding their captive officer and offering what assistance they could. What disagreements they had had earlier with the lieu-tenant and his methods were gone. Now was not the time for their previous petty and inconsequential problems. A fellow human being needed their help and they would not leave him to whatever appalling atrocities the monster had in store for him.

Rounding a sharp bend in the ravine, they saw their quarry ahead, a hunched figure dragging the limp man by his shoulders. It was hideous, a malformed revolting thing that not even the most imaginative nightmare could have created, with a corpse-like cast to its skin. Grotesque black veins and arteries spider-webbed over its taut, bulging musculature. Its legs and arms were bent at odd angles, like it had more joints in them than those of normal limbs, more like an arachnid than any mammal's conforming shape. The head itself was de-void of hair, but lumpy and scarred, covering the top and fore-head completely, even down to the tops of its eyes. The orbs were soulless black pits, rudely almond-shaped and set at highly irregular slants. There was no nose apparent, just two vertical slits that expanded and contracted as it breathed loud-ly. The sound of its exhalations were wet and nauseating, like it respired through a vile slime or mucus. But its mouth was its truly most horrifying feature, with no lips to speak of but rows of needle-like teeth, impossibly razor sharp and glistening with saliva. It gave the appearance of grimacing with unintentional menace and repugnance. The creature's hands were as Richard had described earlier, and the cruel talons were digging into the lieutenant's shoulders, in what assuredly must be excruciating agony for the sufferer. But the man himself made no sound, and Paul saw that he must have been rendered unconscious, either by the creature or his wounds. Seeing the vile abomination not more than several yards away in all its sickening glory was mesmerizing to Paul, causing him to hesitate from his previously thought out actions.

But not Richard. With a bellow of fury and rage that would have made his Celtic ancestors proud he charged forward, rifle in hand, firing shot after shot recklessly towards the monstrous being as he ran. Paul saw some of the bullets reach their target, and the creature howled in wrath and pain at the assault, then cast the unconscious body of the lieutenant forcefully aside like it was a mere toy. It surged angrily forward, misshapen limbs contorting and rippling with deadly purpose. Paul could see the danger coming directly towards his companion, and that finally cracked his frozen reverie. Then he too screamed and fired at the stampeding monstrosity hurtling towards them. He heard a steady stream of machine gun fire erupt from a neighboring region from one of the trenches, then quickly followed by other locations. The massive hail of bullets narrowly whistled above the two men's heads as the forward emplacements on either side of them opened up at the disturbance caused by their firing and yelling.

The monster itself seemed disoriented at first by the new sounds, but then quickly corrected itself, zeroing in on the big form of Richard. Paul was still a few steps behind him, and pulled back the bolt on his rifle feverishly, reloading and firing over and over at the hated countenance as fast as he could, praying for the inhuman fiend to fall down and die. Richard had run out of ammunition and had discarded his weapon, pulling from his side the big trench knife he had brought for close fighting. The demonic shape loomed colossally closer and closer, seeming to shrug off Paul's rounds like nothing more than gnats, a mere inconvenience to its powerful frame as it sprinted with impossible speed. It had not seemed so large crouched over the lieutenant, but now fully extended he could see it easily dwarfed even the big Welsh man, and he was forced to watch as the two collided, unable to shoot now for fear of striking his friend. He fumbled for his own melee weapon, the sharpened shovel he carried on his back. As he did Paul saw the red-headed giant plunge his blade mightily in the creature's abdomen, the steel glinting wickedly in the moonlight seconds before being covered by dark ichors pouring from the wound. The monster roared again and stabbed Richard mercilessly with both its clawed appendages, piercing his chest before savagely biting his unprotected neck with its razor sharp teeth. The big man screamed in pain and the hopelessness of his position, unquestionably innately knowing that he would be dead soon from the grievous injuries.

Paul finally pulled his shovel free and ran toward what surely would be his own demise, choosing to die fighting rather than be cut down from behind by the scything talons in a cowardly retreat.

Then all hell literally broke loose all around them, artillery shells exploding blindly without clemency or even discrimination of their target. The previously slumbering large cannons and howitzers had awoken now, and were roaring their displeasure at the nighttime intrusion. Paul watched as the creature howled at the new development, trying to disengage itself from the dying man it was connected to by its own extremities. He saw Richard pull his arms around its waist, trapping it in his final embrace. The ghoulish thing fought to escape, biting and clawing in desperation. Then a shell struck the entwined pair, enveloping them in fiery destruction, and the resulting shockwave knocked Paul aside like he was mere kindling. He hit the ground hard and lost consciousness, sliding into the depths of carefree slumber.

****

Paul awoke in a field hospital later, uncertain of how he had come to his present location. A nurse saw his awakening, and ran to inform the doctor of his miraculous resuscitation. The doctor informed him that the lieutenant, wounded himself, had dragged him back to the British line after the shelling and firing had stopped. Paul had been asleep for several days now, the blow to his head and devastating injury to his right arm no doubt accounting for his long slumber. He looked at the aforementioned extremity, seeing the entire arm wrapped in white bandages. The doctor gently told him that he had been struck by shrapnel, and it was possible he might never use the arm fully again. He would be going home; his part in the war was done now.

The lieutenant came to see him before he was released from the hospital, bandaged from his hardships but already back in service. Paul thanked him for saving his life, which he modestly accepted, saying that Paul would have done the same had the roles been reversed. They tried to make small talk, but the horrific ordeal they had gone through was like the proverbial white elephant, forcing itself to be noticed, and eventually their talk turned to the ghoulish creature. It was Paul who brought it up first, asking if indeed it was dead. The lieutenant closed his eyes and nodded curtly in affirmation before speaking.

"When I came to the dawn was just turning to light, so I didn't have much time to survey what was left, but chunks of that foul, rotted flesh was in abundance all over, intermixed with poor Richard's remains. Then I saw you lying there, barely breathing but alive. It had cut me good earlier, and my shoulders were pierced where it dragged me, but I knew I had to get you out of there. It should be I thanking you. If you and Richard hadn't come for me, the things it would have done....." His voice trailed off, and they both thought of the mounds of stripped bones they had discovered deposited in the large cavern. "Richard was a good man and so are you, doing what you did especially after how I treated you." He stood and saluted the prone man, then turned to leave.

"Wait," Paul said quietly, and the lieutenant turned back to hear his words. "What do we say? What did you tell the command?"

"I told them the truth. My men acted courageously and without hesitation, giving their lives to discover what the Germans were planning. I let them know about the maze running under the no man's land, and we used that knowledge to launch an attack yesterday evening, opening up with a barrage while our men hid underground. Some of the side tunnels led almost to the German line, and we popped out before they had recovered from the strike, taking both the frontline and reserve trenches before they retaliated back and secured their line. It wasn't enough to win the war, but it was the morale boost we needed. You'll be hailed as a hero when you get back home."

"But the creature, what of it? What did you tell them of it?"

"I saw that thing just as you did. We believe it is real because of what we saw, but no one else would ever believe us. It's too fantastical. They would declare us mad and lock us up. Let it go, go back to England and forget about this." He left, leaving Paul to ponder his advice.

****

He finished convalescing in the hospital, and eventually the doctors cleared him to return home. The injury to his arm never fully recovered, but he managed, finding work as a bartender in the local pub to make ends meet. The Great War ended, but the specter of what had happened in the distant no man's land never really left him. He spent his free time researching what the creature could have been, and why it had been lurking in the forgotten graveyard. His studies took him years, but he persevered, almost obsessed with learning the truth of what had occurred, delving into accounts and histories of the area with furious gusto and absolute abandon. He learned more than the most scholarly historian knew of that particular spot in the French countryside, and finally was able to piece together from the multiple sources a hypothesis of the strange monster's origins.

The abandoned village he discovered had been named Paivant, and it had been fairly prosperous, being an important source of fennel as well as other agricultural products. The folk living there had led a simple, pious existence, and its early history was uneventful until the middle of the seventeenth century. At the time the previous lord of the area had perished, leaving no heirs. The current monarch, King Louis XVI, appointed a new overseer for the area, a distant relative of the queen's by the name of Sigismund. It was an unpopular move by the sovereign, the appointee being from Austria, but time overwhelmingly showed it would hardly be his kingship's last error in judgment. At first however, all seemed well and the new lord instituted several accommodating changes in crop rotation and food storage, ingratiating himself with the local populace. He married a French girl from another noble family, and their union produced two offspring, a boy and a girl, further increasing his stature in the eyes of the residents. He was reported to be fair and honest in his dealings as well, and soon he was treated by subjects as well as any natural resident of the area.

However, an unfortunate tragedy soon struck the now beloved ruler's life, and that of his happy household. An outbreak of plague reared its ugly head at Sigismund's home. It claimed the lives of both his children quickly. He and his wife turned despondent, hardly leaving the manor anymore to wallow in their all encompassing sorrow. Others in the surrounding lands caught the dreadful sickness as well, and many died as the disease spread like wildfire throughout the region. At last Sigismund's wife herself caught the plague. He was desperate to stop the death of the last living member of his family, and he invited numerous doctors to visit in an attempt to find a cure. Nothing the physicians tried had any effect, and Sigismund began trying more esoteric remedies and methods of healing. Rumors of strange visitors to the manor emerged, witches and warlocks from distant lands performing dark ceremonies, Black Masses, and much worse at the lord's insistence. The area began to be beleaguered by disappearances to add to its troubles. At first it was only a few, mostly children. But then more and more people went missing as time went by, making the untenable situation come to a head.

The remaining populace, scared for their lives, formed a

mob and marched on the now hated manor. Armed with farm implements and torches, they set fire to the house, driving the inhabitants out with smoke and flame. Three women ran outside to avoid the blaze, and the villagers quickly arrested them, taking note of their strange dress and curious speech. They found Sigismund attempting to escape in the back, struggling to pull the burning corpse of his dead wife out of the fire. They quickly surrounded him, and he screamed at the men, telling them she was still alive, not to let her burn. He was raving madly, she obviously had been dead for some time. They left her to be consumed by the now towering inferno, letting it become her funeral pyre. He wept as he watched, in his madness cursing them for killing her, saying the flesh he and the women had harvested had healed her, she had only needed to rest to complete her remedy. He babbled of unholy rituals and unspeakable acts, performed with the power of the three witches, and of his own horrific deeds in kidnapping the victims and reaping the required parts for the unholy sacraments. They listened to his confession, horrified, and knew what must be done. His own lips had condemned him, and they lined up the evil perpetrators, to punish them for their crimes one by one. As they did so the women began to chant nightmarish litanies, and they hurried to slay them, to stop the evil words of power before they could take effect. But appallingly the witches still continued to chant even after the mob struck them down. They decapitated the witches as well, but even that did not still the nightmare chanting; their severed heads mouthed the mystic words from beyond the grave. Distracted by the ghoulish spectacle, the captors guarding Sigismund let their defenses lapse and the fanatical lord attacked, assaulting them and wresting one of their member's crude knives away. Instead of attempting to escape however, he plunged the dagger into his own chest, ending his own life. They buried the bodies in a hastily dug mass grave, presuming it would be the end of the horrific plight they had been forced to endure.

So they had thought. Three nights later, a farmer and his son, returning home after plying their wares in the village, were attacked by a demonic beast. It rushed from the nearby woods, savagely injuring the father, and carrying off the son, for purposes only it knew in its infernal contemplations. A passing traveler found the farmer wailing inconsolably at the loss of his child, trying to follow the animal even in his wounded state. He was raving after the encounter, speaking of impossibly shaped limbs and narrow, filed teeth. The local healers were able to restore his body, but there was nothing they could do for his loss or resultant madness. It seemed too coincidental in lieu of the recent activities performed by their former master, and the village elders visited the gravesite they had left Sigismund and the witches to molder in. There were signs of violently disturbed earth, so they prudently exhumed the grave, finding to their dismay the lord's body was gone.

Peasant gossip began to circulate that Sigismund's witches had resurrected him, and that he wanted vengeance on the populace that had foiled his satanic plans. Other villagers soon began to go missing as well, always in the dead of night or early evening, never in the full light of day, giving credence to the outlandish rumors. Even families, barring their doors against the malevolent intrusions and seemingly fortified in the safety of their homes, were brutalized by the nightmarish creature, the neighbors the next day finding only smashed windows and broken doors when checking in on their nearby fellows. Occasionally they found witnesses to the atrocious carnage, hidden in such a way the rampaging fiend had not found the survivors. However, the victims were almost always catatonic or delirious, their minds shattered by the horrors of what had transpired before them.

When the local priest went absent, the godly trappings in his home rent and smashed, that is when the true measure of the doom that had fallen upon Paivant became clear to the townsfolk and its outlying citizens. God himself, it seemed, had shunned them, leaving them to their grim fate. An industrious people not given to despair, they organized hunting parties, seeking to catch the monster unawares in the daylight hours. However, the creature was cunning, secreting itself in such a way that made detection impossible. As more and more victims fell to its inexorable onslaught, the village elders made the difficult choice to fall back on ancient magics and rites that their ancestors had turned their backs on long ago, seeing finally no recourse by conventional means. They sought out an old witch, living in the depths of the vast forest alone. She was one who still knew the ancient ways of the Carnac stones and menhirs, and how to perform the forgotten liturgies and observances. Shunned for years, fearful legends and the forest's supernatural air kept the curious as well as the maligned against her breed distant. Out of options and in fear for not just their lives but their families, the villagers visited her crude hut, telling her of the monster's attacks and unearthly origins.

She acquiesced to their advances, agreeing to help them in their quandary. At her orders they requisitioned the massive stone edifice in the graveyard that housed the desiccated cadavers of the previous lords of Paivant. They built within it a large oaken coffin, and laid strong chains of iron underneath it. She worked with the local mason as well, having him carve runic symbols and mysterious ciphers at her exacting specifications into a circular piece of limestone. The trap was set, and now all they needed was the bait. The farmer who had lost his only son to the monster agreed to be the enticement they needed, waiting alone for the diabolical creature outside the mausoleum while the witch and several strong volunteers hid inside. The rest of the villagers hid in cellars, barricaded forcefully against the demonic menace, leaving no option to satiate its ravenous hunger other than the man waiting in the graveyard.

The plan worked perfectly, the monster chasing the farmer into the structure, where it was surrounded by angry men with pitchforks and crude spears. They heroically held the malefic giant at bay while the witch intoned ancient incantations, forcing it with her help to lie in the prepared receptacle. They fastened the heavy chains across the coffin even as it howled and beat at the lid, and at her direction the men placed the round stone on top of the vessel. Its strange runes glowed with a bright blue radiance, and the thrashing and fighting inside the tomb ceased immediately. They sealed the metal doors, and returned to their homes, content in their labors. The next day the witch told them that the land would be cursed there for many years, and only time and nature's embrace could truly rid the world of the evil that was sealed in the crypt. Aghast at being forced to leave their homes, they nevertheless obeyed, razing their structures to the ground, salting the area and its surrounding fields to make them infertile and uninhabitable for others. The villagers buried the titanic sepulcher so no one would ever disturb the grotesque horror that slumbered within. They spread stories that a malignant plague had struck, and that anyone who ventured there would be struck down by its virulent corruption.

The piecemeal tale was one of fabulous fancy, and most men would discard its telling as simple folklore, nothing more. But Paul had seen things with his own eyes, impossible things that made him believe the authenticity of what he had discovered in the forgotten annuals and histories. He conjectured that an errant shell, smashing through the thin layer of earth above, had damaged the subterranean tomb below. The blast had somehow caused the rune stone locking the fell beast away to break, releasing it to begin its gruesome practices anew. The timely explosion that destroyed both the monster and Richard had seemed to finally end its eternal evil, but he wondered still if such mundane means could ever stop such a being. The thought was an unsettling one, and it made his blood run cold at its insistent pervasiveness. What if, instead of obliteration, it had merely been wounded badly? What if it merely secreted itself away in the underground labyrinth of graves until it could grow strong again, powerful enough to resume its endless terror anew?

And The Meek Shall...

There is an imbecile named Jacques Soveneau. This may be an uncouth way to say he is mentally challenged, or retarded, or "special" when he is not in fact special, but the people who live around him call him much worse than even these unflattering terms. They refer to him as the moron or the idiot mostly, or even as the buffoon by a few of the more literate yet still heavily prejudiced against those of his sort. He lives in the large city of New Bayeux in the south eastern section of Louisiana, a massive metropolis sprouting from the dismal swampland like an anthill on a green lawn. It is in the essence of most large cities, where one no longer cares or even bothers to meet their fellow neighbors, and when interest is shown it is generally of the unwelcome or even villainous nature, best avoided by the more dutiful of the populace. The city had grown in the usual way in that region of the southernmost states, first explored by the Spanish conquistadors searching for mythical cities of gold, as well Ponce de Leon's unsuccessful quest for the storied Fountain of Youth. Colonization came later, starting as a small backwater village in the late sixteenth century until enough demand of the expanding influx of commerce from its large port had promoted rapid economic and urban development to take place. This led to the annexation of its neighboring suburbs and towns, and eventually even several of the bordering local parishes (as counties are colloquially known in Louisiana) fell to its mighty expansion. It has spread in many directions since its inception, but mostly to the east through the old bayous and primordial swamps. This exponential expansion had required the tremendous knowledge, the great industriousness, and the persistent doggedness of the American worker of past bygone centuries, before they were absorbed by their decadence and hedonism of modern life in the present-day world. In fact the municipality had consumed many of the local holdings and plantations of that area as well, slowly transforming them to houses and small shops, and eventually they too changed into apartments, malls, and large shopping centers. The last transformation is always the most hideous, when the inevitable decay sets in and the area becomes a shadow of its former self, where slums, vacant lots, and boarded up buildings become the norm instead of the vibrant, thriving community of before.

In one of these rundown sections of the city is where Jacques Soveneau lives, in a quaint, old fashioned house from bygone times with no electricity, plumbing, running water, phone, or literally any of the amenities deemed necessary by the civilized world nowadays. But he has no need of such things, living as he has for years just as his mother and father had before him. He has a stout wooden fence that runs the length and breadth of his property, enclosing both the front and back yards with a well-made front gate for egress and entrance. Various aging graffiti is scrawled on the fence, belying the sturdiness of the home within, and the defacing scrawls serve as a small deterrent against unsolicited visits to its unassuming nature. Large, nut bearing trees provide pecans and walnuts for his collection, and a small, functional garden in the backyard grows food for his continued consumption and as a source of income for him as well. Indeed his wares are highly sought after for their flavorful taste and exquisite appeal when he takes them to the massive farmer's market in Clydesdale Park, located several miles distant from the squalor of his abode. It is one of the only times he leaves his home. He does so to make money to pay for the ever decreasing taxes on his property, as well as for what few items he requires that he cannot provide for himself. Afterwards he walks home with his empty burlap sack wearing his quaint, homemade clothes, that sometimes get jeers from ne'er-do-wells with nothing better to do, but he gives them a wide berth. Jacques in fact will not go anywhere near the nefarious delinquents that make up the majority of the population of his neighborhood, choosing longer, safer routes over a quicker, less secure methods. His father used to say trouble is easier avoided than dealt with, and Jacques follows the advice soundly.

Once home Jacques locks his front gate, then goes inside

his house and locks his front door. He never leaves them unlocked, his parents had taught him long ago to never trust the outside world. If it is too late when he gets back from his errands he goes to bed, but he always makes sure to tend his garden first, lighting his old lantern if necessary to light his way. He waters his plants carefully from the old well in the yard, his sole source of water. He then checks for aphids and other pests, and does all the other necessary duties of garden work. Whatever is required of him he performs without complaint. He has a multitude of vegetables and fruits in his garden, and he takes care of them the same way his father and mother showed him years earlier, before they had left and never returned. Jacques still misses them terribly, but even in his limited intellect he knows that they will not return after all this time. He follows their wishes fervently even now, by working dutifully, praying frequently, and never talking to strangers about his life or the well.

Jacques is a very industrious individual. In addition to his gardening and clothes making, he also pickles and cans food to see him through the winter months. He cooks and cleans, performs maintenance on the old house, and any of the other odd jobs his solitary lifestyle requires. His father used to say idle hands are the devil's work, so he stays busy as to not fall into sinful habits. Occasionally, however, he has free time, which he spends in different ways as it suits him. He looks at the pictures in the books his parents had owned and the new additions he purchases at the market or finds in his travels.

Sometimes he tries to read the accompanying words. Some words he can make out, being of the simple vernacular, other of the more challenging variety he can only guess at their hidden meanings to ascertain the gist of the writings. His mother had taught him to read very simple words and phrases, but his mental deficiency hinders him from performing the more advanced skills necessary to master the craft. He has fared better with numbers and figures, grasping the rudimentary concepts of addition and subtraction and even some multiplication with stolid accuracy albeit somewhat slowly in comparison to the ordinary person.

However, there is one thing that Jacques Soveneau excels at and that is painting. His skills are not only beyond that of the normal layperson, but quite possibly even acclaimed masters of the craft such as Rubens or Vermeer. Even Rembrandt would have been hard pressed to have matched his degree of dexterity and technique. In his mind, great vistas, sweeping landscapes, and other picturesque settings are given a life unto their own, astonishingly lifelike, precise, and intense of bountiful emotion in both subject and backdrop. Whether natural or artificial environs, mobile or static poses, bright or subdued lighting his capture of realism is uncanny with his amazing talent. While not able to match the relentless speed of Teniers or other prolific artists, his end result negates the handicap of an extended time span required to finish his masterpieces. His medium is oil painting, favored more of the Baroque period than in this more modernistic age, having been disposed by more pliable technological advances. Indeed even his style would be more reminiscent of such an archaic era, to the point of wonderment on the part of an observer. Some of his paintings decorate his humble abode, like the large landscape of New Bayeux during midsummer curiously done with buildings and vehicles from the 1920s, creating a veritable snapshot of the city during that time period. Another piece is of a small wooden church, seen with parishioners of the mid 1800s in their horse and buggy. The hallway boasts of three works, one a view of a market of Revolutionary War times, secondly the Lacq River, clear and languorously beautiful before the city's pollution had taken its toil during the early 19th century, and lastly of a picnic by the Tangres Lake, the picnickers dressed in the formal attire of the colonies. In his bedroom is a portrait of his father and mother, interestingly done with clothing more suitable of the early 1600s, with the stern countenance of the hardy folk from that era.

In a large study he has a massive collection of paintings covering every available space from wall to wall, floor to ceiling, except for a small space on the northern wall. This is the residence of the vast bulk of his prodigious efforts, an impressive display of his talented exertions. Here too he is able to capture amazing encapsulations of time and place, fascinatingly accurate in their depictions of era. An observer can see a farm of the sixteenth century, a bus on a busy street from the fifties, a group of young children from the 1980s, a riverboat from the mid eighteenth century, Confederate soldiers on the march from the Civil War era, a baseball game from the early nineteenth century, and many more. Interestingly as well is that the physical age of the paintings seems to match the time period depicted, the twentieth century renditions looking the newest and the colonial pieces looking aged and antique.

But the most curious painting is in the center of the southern wall, and it is the oldest painting in the home. The painting is done in a similar, but yet different style, not done with the adept hand of a seasoned practitioner but a seemingly earlier incarnation of that prodigy. It is a simple portrayal of the old well in the back of the house. The well itself is not as interesting as the figure drawing water from it and the date inscribed on the back. The figure is a self portrait of Jacques Soveneau himself, and the date *is of 1612!*

Phantom Pain

Gavin Taliesan's accident had been completely unexpected, as most mishaps generally are to their unsuspecting victims. He had been employed part-time at the local juice stand, making smoothies and shakes for any interested passers-by in the glorious summer heat whenever they chanced upon his station. Watching the multitude of patrons meandering along the boardwalk, he could tell most were lazily walking along with no clear direction or purpose, content to merely enjoy the unsullied air coming from the nearby pounding surf, the ocean's waves cooling the breeze to a refreshing temperature. He had been at the job since he was seventeen, two years earlier. While the pay was meager and the hours trivial at best in their unreliability, the view is what truly kept him coming to work on a daily basis.

Endless feminine sights were constantly paraded before his eyes, sauntering tantalizingly without even the thought they were being so provocative, seductive in their supple, natural strides. Young girls, barely twenty, with their firmness of figure that only the newness that fresh flesh can provide, so overtly seductive in their scanty bikinis and trim tank tops worn for relief from the relentless summer sun, ambled back and forth beneath his lecherous gaze. Gavin was not a man of singular taste however, paying the proper amount of lewd attention to the more mature ones as well, bodies voluptuously padded in all the proper places, aged like a fine vintage of unequaled taste. They tended to have more concealing clothing, but the more chaste coverings served only to accent their appetizing, refined flavor.

Two youthful girls close to his age had engaged him into making their orange smoothies, shyly flirting with him as he worked blending fruit and milk together in delectable harmony. He had been playing it cool, pretending to not be interested in their simple games, but secretly thinking he could maybe hook up with one of them later that evening. Then he saw *her*, and they were instantaneously forgotten, nothing seemed to exist but the wondrous creature moving like a poised panther through the crowds towards him. Her blonde hair was darkened in layers by the sun's caress, and her slightly tanned flesh free any imperfection or mark. She had a high but ample bosom, along with impeccably proportioned matching hips, and a slight build that was not overly muscular to the point of excess vulgarity, or so undefined to have no resistance upon a man's tender stroke. Her age was unknowable, the harsh embrace of time's passage leaving no scars on her perfect frame, but it was not youth's gift that caused her body's flawlessness so much as her aura, her very essence that radiated raw sexual longing in every man that saw her. He formed an instant attraction to her, but her very being screamed to him she was entirely out of his grasp, a marvelous thing that no man could ever hope to obtain, least of all a simple one such as himself. When she stared coolly in his direction and made her way enticingly towards him he could not believe his phenomenal luck, knowing that if only for a few minor seconds in her company he could bask in the glory that was *her*, and that would almost be enough to satiate his growing hunger. Finishing her graceful sway to the counter, she finally stood directly across the bar from him, wanting his attention, needing his attention-

That was when he stuck his hand in the blender's twirling blades, and how Gavin Taliesan permanently lost his right hand that fateful day. He had not been using the proper tools, preferring to use the simple plastic rod to mash the fruits down in the machine, and in his daydreaming state he had not noticed the dire predicament of his situation. His tight grip slipped on its smooth surface, allowing his tender flesh and bone to pass through to the waiting vortex of spinning teeth, to be mangled and shredded. The captivating woman's sexy mouth, half parted with the anticipation of the words she was about to say, opened wide hysterically instead, a horrifying shrill scream issuing forth as she was given a front row seat to his gory catastrophe. Not that she was alone in her view of his poor hand's demise, the two girls sitting at the counter, who also observed his disastrous injury and mutilated flesh, added their voices to the squealing chorus. Soon it was joined by more horrified shrieks, including his own, but it was not pain that caused his outburst so much as the terror created from the image of seeing what exactingly was happening to his disfigured body part. He fought to activate the emergency shutoff, but the blood spurting from his wounds like a fountain had covered everything, and had made the button slippery, causing him to fail to trigger the safeguard. Struggling to yank his lacerated appendage free instead, he was appalled to discover his shattered digits and shredded tendons had cruelly wrapped around the still spinning blades, not only disallowing his exodus from the terrifying trap, but sucking his hand further inside it as well, winding the maimed strings of meat around and around like a reel. He yanked harder, the desperation of the situation giving him renewed strength, and with a last powerful tug his arm finally came free, flying out of the container and slinging blood over all the observers of the graphic scene, including the trio of women screaming madly nearby.

The rampant blood loss at last began to catch up to him, and the final images before he shut his eyes was of the perfectly gorgeous woman, entirely covered in his blood and tissue, her delicate mouth still open wide in mid scream. Time seemed to move slower, and he zeroed in on her right front tooth. Something about it didn't seem quite right, and it dawned on him that the incisor was set slightly in front of its fellow teeth, causing her to be ever so faintly snaggle-toothed.

Oh, she wasn't so perfect after all, hardly worth the distraction and effort, he thought to himself with dark humor, the irony of his situation seeming to amuse him in his delirious state. Then he blacked out, oblivion mercifully alleviating his horrendous suffering.

When Gavin awoke in the hospital later it was to the life-changing realization that his hand, wrist, and part of his lower right arm were forever gone. The throbbing pain was what broke his unconsciousness, drawing him back to his unfortunate reality. He looked over at his wounded body part from his reclining position on the pillow his head rested on, and he was horrified to discover what the unstoppable machine had not destroyed with its horrendous severity the doctors had been forced to amputate to properly attend to his injury. They had been thoroughly complete in their work, shortening it easily by another inch. The white bandaged end of his extremity seemed entirely too stunted for the amount of pain issuing forth, even with knowing what hellish atrocity had happened to him. Reflexively he leaned forward and tried to open and close his hand to alleviate the soreness, of course seeing no response from the inanimate stump but a slight quiver. The effort and accompanying disappointment weakened him, and he lay back again, worn out by the mental and physical exertion. Seeing a call button nearby, he used his good hand to summon a nurse from her station. After a short visit from an available doctor as well as a veritable battery of questions and well-meaning assistance from all the medical staff present, they gave him more medication for the constant pain, and he drifted to sleep again, finally able to relax.

His time in the hospital passed quickly, mostly consisting of rest and empty, thoughtless television watching. His friends, caught up in their own lives and affairs, came to see him frequently at first, but the visits were more and more seldom as time went by, the young people being naturally more interested in their own narcissistic day to day lives than the plight of another human being. His mother visited him multiple times however, she crying and lamenting over his crippling injury while he tried to keep up a brave face for her. It was hard on him to do so, especially with the perpetual and severe agony in his hand driving all other thoughts out of his mind. It was strange, the limb was gone but the uninterrupted ache issuing from the missing area was real, continuing on like a broken water tap, flowing and flowing with a dogged persistence. The doctors told him that he had a form of phantom limb syndrome, that the sensations in the removed limb were continuing to be sent by his brain. They explained that even though the hand was no longer there, his nerves still recalled the sensory input from before his accident, and were caught in a loop. Most people in his situation, they informed him, did not feel such agonizing pain, only a sense of the appendage still being there, but in his case, apparently his senses were more in tune with his pain receptors. Lucky me, he thought grimly, and then asked for more pain medication. After a few weeks he was able to leave the hospital, the doctors declaring that there was nothing wrong with him physically anymore. Except he was missing his right hand, he thought darkly to himself. His outlook on life had changed, the constant pain making him bitter and sarcastic, as well as unable to function in normal day to day life. He moved in with his mother, his disloyal roommates having already replaced him during his stint in the infirmary. He was outfitted at that time with a prosthetic limb, a metal and plastic monstrosity featuring a hook at the end he could activate with certain arm twitches and spasms, like some kind of robotic nightmare.

The doctors, seeing his dependence on pain relievers as a crutch, began to try to wean him off the drugs, which he of course resisted strenuously. They did not understand the excruciating torture that regularly plagued him during his conscious hours, telling him over and over that it was psychosomatic in nature, a mere symptom of his impairment, created by his own mind. He was given a deluge of psychiatric appointments, but all gave their educated opinions that he was just another junkie, not willing to give up his fix and attempt real treatment. Even his own mother tried to intervene, repeating the same words of the uncaring doctors, and adding her own dash of guilt and shame as well. Her constant harassing merely added to his misery, the well-meaning words just cycling repetitiously over and over with no real concept of his endless suffering. Eventually he grew tired of it and left, choosing homelessness over the steady flood of continuous nagging. His disability check wasn't enough to afford a place to live, but it was enough to buy a regular stream of different street drugs to supplement his meager supply from the prescriptions the doctors could be still persuaded to write for him. Oxycodone, fentanyl, hydrocodone, methadone, morphine, butorphanol, even heroin, he didn't care what it was as long as whatever it was made the incessant pain go away for a while, nor did he care for improving his vagrant lifestyle, just as fine being a bum as he had been working when he had two hands. He lived for euphoria, and nothing else mattered whatsoever in his dismal life. He had sank almost as low as a man could sink in his situation, and was having an excellent time doing it.

Every junkie needs a dealer, and Gavin was no exception, forming a relationship with a local pusher with the colloquial name of Big Ludd. Big Ludd, true to his namesake, was a massive man of fairly preposterous bulk, nearly seven feet tall and almost comical in girth, with an incredible appetite to match his bulky form, whether it be food, women, or drugs. He had set up shop in the Tara Meath housing complex, a ghetto home to countless low-income destitutes and fellow criminals. Living there with his ever increasing brood, his illegal organization was a regular family affair, which included help from his numerous sons and daughters, stretching in age from two years old to their late twenties, who seemed to match their father's everlasting cravings while not in proportion but most equivalently in spirit. His Irish girlfriend of the past quarter century and the mother of most of the children in the household, Irnan, who put up with his dalliances and unlawful behavior for her own unfathomable reasons, maintained the squalid living quarter's upkeep. She was the only semi-temperate member of the lot, and while she left the face of the business to Ludd, rumor had it that she was the one who dealt with the periodical "problems" that occurred in their line of work. People spoke of her alleged connections with forces that were of a dark, mystical nature, performing supernatural rites brought with her from the land of her origin. While she could never be connected to the inordinate amount of disappearances or accidents that seemed to take place in the neighborhood, no one could easily deny the correlation between the victims and their embittered relationships with her obese lover.

Gavin, being less debauched than their normal sort of junkie, always paid in cash and upfront, therefore having no problems at all with the fat drug dealer or his Celtic woman. This continued for almost a year, until one day when he called on Big Ludd's home for his usual cocktails and remedies, the enormous man had said that Irnan wished to see him in one of the back rooms. This was not something Gavin wished to do in the slightest, but seeing one of the older boys slowly fingering a machete at his side he choose to accept the singular honor, following a dirty little girl all of eight years old back to the proper area. She left him in front of a closed door, which he timidly knocked upon for admittance.

"Come in, hook-man," said a female voice that he could

only presume was Irnan's, the rich accent carrying easily through the thin entrance. He did as he was bade, not particularly enjoying the reminder of his deformity, but not really in any sort of position to complain. One takes a few steps down after you become crippled, he supposed, and especially after you decide to spend most of your days in a drug-induced coma. His hand throbbed as a reminder of his true purpose for being here, and he hoped whatever she had to say would not interfere with that plan, or take very long. The interior was dark, with the windows and walls covered over by various objects and decorations, most haphazardly placed or hanging without a particular rhyme or reason to their arrangement. The area was devoid of normal furnishings for the most part, only having a large blanket on the floor that the woman was seated upon lotus style, her long legs crossed in front of her. Her eyes were closed, and she was surrounded by small weaved baskets, the room too dark to make out the contents held within. The only source of illumination was a single brazier in the middle of the room, copper in color, its small flame flickering back and forth in random shapes and intervals, creating matching dancing shadows on the dingy grey walls. Opening her eyes, she stared unabashed at him, seeming to size him up, then motioned with a fluid gesture to sit across from her on the blanket. Only once he was comfortably seated did she speak.

"You have been coming here a long time now, hook-man. I see you, you are in pain all the time, yes?" He didn't feel it was a question so much as a statement, but he nodded curtly anyway. "You come to Ludd, you give him lots of money, you cause no trouble. You are a good customer. Now you wonder why I want to talk with you." She laughed, not unkindly, but not exactly in a soothing fashion either. "I want to help you, hook-man." Her offer to help him seemed surreal, especially given the surroundings. She seemed to sense his misgivings, and she leaned closer, her hot breath wafting across the fire. It smelled sweet, and vaguely spicy, like cinnamon, but something else lay at the bottom of the scent, something cloying and not at all as fragrant.

"You wish the pain to go away? I can help you do that. I can make it all go away, forever." Her eyes reflected the quivering light, twin flames radiating out from the dark liquid pools that seemed to hypnotize and devour him. He knew she was waiting for his response, but he did not know how to reply. He would like nothing better than to no longer feel the unendurable, never-ending anguish, but there was something not quite right with her suggestion, something just, well, *wrong* about it, something felt more than seen. Then his missing extremity flared again, and then he knew how he would respond, that nothing and anything would never be too high of a price to rid himself of the mounting torment that overwhelmed him daily. He nodded once to accept, the pain and anguish causing a single tear to roll down his face at first, and then like an avalanche the flood of pent-up emotion and distress erupted from within him, and he pleaded for her to help make it stop, anything to make it stop, if only it could *stop*. She watched him without any indication of offering comfort or even sympathy, seeming unmoved by his dramatic outburst. He subsided after a short while, able to pull his shattered disposition back together to mere stifled heaving. She pulled a wisp of some threadlike material from one of the many baskets surrounding her, throwing it with a practiced hand into the fire. An acrid smell filled the small room, the odor so pungent he could taste it on his tongue, a bitter flavor similar to black coffee.

"Look into the fire, hook-man. Look deep." Her voice was quiet but so clear, mesmerizing him with its rhythmic cadence. He did as he was told, staring into the flame, seeing nothing but the bright blaze waving as it consumed the substance. She added more ingredients, each making a different aroma, some pleasant in their agreeable bouquets and others almost choking in their pungency and spiciness. She continued to have him watch the blaze, her voice lulling him to the point of drowsiness. He wasn't sure when it started to begin, but he began to see shapes in the fire, simple at first but then coalescing into frightfully detailed images. He saw his accident again, the horrific damage done to his body seen from a third person point of view this time. He saw the EMTs loading his unconscious body onto the ambulance, but that was in the background of the scene, the view stayed strangely locked on the blender with his severed hand. It was loaded at the same time as he was, carefully lashed down to avoid spillage and packed with ice, riding like a grisly gift to a party. He saw the ambulance stop, and the item was whisked away by a hospital staff member, the contents dumped unceremoniously out and studied by a doctor, poked and prodded until at last she declared them unfit for reattachment. It was then loaded into plastic bags with bio-hazard logos on the front and disposed of, shoved down a long chute ending at an incinerator.

But it never reached the waiting flames, a short man in an orderly uniform catching the bag before it fell inside. He looked harder, as the view did not change and he saw with chagrin that the man stuck the medical bag with *his hand* inside a black duffel bag and left the room. He placed it in a locker, and then the scene seemed to increase in activity, centered only on the locker as figures whizzed back and forth at a rapid rate, time being evidently sped up for him. The orderly returned, and the view slowed to normal progression again. The man changed from his hospital attire to street clothes and then took the duffel bag with him. Gavin saw the man was *stealing* his lacerated hand. As the hospital worker left he waved and cheerfully replied to the goodbyes of coworkers, all of them clueless as to his macabre keepsake lying in the sack. He boarded a bus, and a short ride departed, walking to a local park. Once there he met up with a tall tattooed man, who he exchanged the duffel bag with for a small wad of money. The tattoo itself was of multiple circles, all intersected by two "I" letters crossing each other and the circles exactly at their middles. The tattooed man was now the sole focus of the viewing. He left the park, walking for several blocks, and then once in the privacy of what Gavin was sure was his home he opened the bag and withdrew the hand, placing it on a brazier curiously similar to the one the maimed man was staring into now.

Uttering mystic phrases and pouring some sort of liquid on the mangled body part, he lit the brazier, roasting Gavin's hand in the enveloping fire. He could see the flesh curl and blacken, the skin shrinking and cracking, exposing the charring muscle underneath, while bodily juices rose to the surface, frying and making a nauseous sizzling sound as they made contact with the metallic surface. Still continuing to chant in the unholy language, the unknown ritual's executor, revealing a wicked blade, slicing deeply into the cooked meat of his palm. Removing a sizable amount of the whitish muscle, Gavin was horrified to see that he then brought to his lips, closing his eyes as he did so in either reverence or ecstasy as he ate the flesh that the consumption of both God and man equally forbade. It was gruesome sight no man would ever want to see, his own parts being roasted and eaten for some eldritch purpose. It sickened him to his core, but still he watched, unable to tear his disbelieving eyes from the horrifically tantalizing scene. He was thankful to see that after the initial bite the cannibal did not follow it with further ingestion of his being, the one taste seeming enough for his palate. Extinguishing the small fire and anointing the scorched flesh with additional powders and tinctures, the tattooed man then placed the tortured extremity on a small, carved altar, covering the entire desecration with a pale blue cloth when he had finished. Then time sped up again, and he saw the malefactor return to the altar, praying and casting spells before the sacrilegious shrine in regular intervals, using his beleaguered hand to assist him in his demonic worship. The scenes mercifully came to an end, and the fire in Irnan's quarters became a simple normal flame again, the strange portal now closed to his gaze.

"You see now, hook-man, Goll took your hand, and has been casting black magic with it, that is why you can not find peace, why the pain follows you everywhere. The dark forces are angry at his control, and the demons, since they cannot attack him for his sacrilege, constantly rip at your soul, finding you through the hand's nearness to their depraved realm. It is as Goll wants it, you paying the price for his misuse of the sacred Druidic spells. But I will help you hook-man, help you free yourself from his control, and shatter the connection between the netherworld and your stricken limb." Numbed by the terrible vision, he could only nod his assent. She smiled at his affirmation, much like the cat that caught the canary, but he ignored the warnings in his heart, only wishing to rid himself of the dreadful, enduring pain. Informing him of her plan, she told him that she needed three things in order to cast the spell to break the gossamer chains that held him captive, and if he helped her gain them she could put an end to Goll's foul meddling.

The first one was simple, a small piece of his own flesh to bind her to the spell, and could be arranged at the proper moment when needed. The erstwhile hand was the second, necessary to be reclaimed from Goll's control so she could destroy it, breaking the bond between the shadow realm and the physical world. The third would perhaps be the hardest to procure, a piece of Goll himself was essential to prevent him from overriding her influence, and salvaging control of the devious liaison he had created that they so eagerly sought to sever. She needed him clear-headed for such work, and his protests of the pain preventing his completion of the tasks fell on deaf ears, her like so many others not caring for his plight. If he truly wanted to be free, she said righteously, he could bear the agony for the short time required. He finally acquiesced to her wishes, trying to dull the writhing misery with the salve of promised liberation.

Big Ludd provided Goll's whereabouts, and he studied the comings and goings of the warlock furtively, trying his best to remain hidden and unnoticed by the tattooed man. The spellcaster's abode was located in a slightly more upscale section of town, but the rampant poverty of the city had its dismal touch here as well, and the area was overrun with penniless unfortunates swarming around, begging for a handout on every available corner and lying in their own filth and offal in the dank alleyways. Gavin's general lapse in hygiene and worn, careless attire aided him in his evasiveness, the trappings of his own homelessness and vagrancy allowing him to blend seamlessly into the mob of beggars, just another impoverished soul in the crowd. He hid his artificial right hand in the sleeves of a large overcoat, the hook being too noticeable and easy to remember to allow it to be seen by the subject of his study. The marked diviner kept odd hours, coming and going at strange times almost random to Gavin in their spontaneity, and he always went alone, no one else accompanying him on his trips. Rarely also did he have any visitors, only once having anyone come by at all, a woman in her thirties, that he took to be perhaps a paramour of some kind at first, but she then only stayed briefly, leaving after less than an hour. He began to quickly notice a pattern during his surveillance, however, that the sorcerer would leave almost exactly at half-past three in the afternoon daily, and would not return for a least an hour each time. He resolved to see if he could reclaim his erstwhile body part and fulfill the need of Goll's parts in the same interval, thus accomplishing his tasks by the recognizable axiom of two birds with one stone.

The constant shadowing and activity was wearing on him, especially without the numbing doses he had grown accustomed to relying on, and the corresponding withdrawals besieging him from his forced abstinence were remorseless. But it was the unendurable pain that was truly his bane, always there to remind him of what he had lost, a ghostly memento built of wretchedness and suffering. Breaking into the sorcerer's home at the appointed time was straightforward enough, finding a small back window he was able to pry open with minimal fuss that allowed his smooth entry. The interior was cool and dark, and he wasted no time beginning his search, desperately looking for what he had came for. The dismembered hand was easy enough to find, the grisly trophy lying under the azure fabric just as he had seen in the fiery vision. Secreted the hand away on his person, he next looked for any sign of the tattooed man's essence. Stringently he explored, hunting high and low for any indication or chance find, but there was nothing physical of the warlock's body available for him to abscond with.

He was running out of time, and his throbbing stump reminded him of the price of failure. What he evidently could not find by subterfuge he knew he must take by force, so he covered all traces of his ransacking and rummaging as best he could, and then hid out of view behind the front door, waiting for the spell-caster's return. The knife he had stolen from the mage's kitchen felt unwieldy in his left hand, the extremity still woefully unused to handling objects with its lack of skill and training even after all the time he had spent of late using it. His thought was to force the sorcerer to comply to his request, to make him give what Gavin so desperately needed through intimidation and brute force. The minutes stretched like hours with the long period of inactivity, him unwilling to jeopardize his hiding spot by moving about, knowing that the man could come back at any time. When he finally heard a key turning in the lock, he felt a strange mixture of emotion, blissful relief from the end of the suspenseful waiting and the raw terror of knowing what was soon to transpire.

The door opened, and he saw the sorcerer's head and shoulders emerge first from behind the open doorway, but he waited until the tattooed man moved the rest of the way inside, not wanting their impending struggle to be intervened upon by well-intentioned outsiders. As though through some unnatural clairvoyance or sixth sense the warlock turned towards him, and he heard the other man's sharp intake of air upon seeing an intruder in his home. Taken aback by the unexpected glimpsing of his person, all thoughts of threatening the mage for his essence disappeared from his mind, fear instinctively taking over in that split second. He lunged forward with the knife outstretched, hoping the shock of indecision would give him the edge in the conflict, but the sorcerer had already recovered, jumping back and bring his arm down like a mace, knocking the knife from Gavin's grasp. Instead of seizing the initiate himself however, the tattooed man began to chant in a strange tongue, evidently intent on casting some nefarious spell upon his attacker. Gavin knew he could not let him finish his diabolical incantation, and sprang forward with the only weapon he had available left to him. Bringing his prosthetic arm up as he charged and then slashing downward with the sharp hook, he cut a cruel line across the warlock's face, the almost hissing of the magical words replaced with a scream of pain at the viciousness of the assault. Not waiting for a response to his brutal act of violence, he bludgeoned the other man over and over until he slumped to the floor, his face lacerated with cuts and stabs where the metal implement had gouged and gashed him unmercifully.

Retrieving the knife from its fallen resting place, he set to his ghastly work, slicing a long strip of flesh from the man's forearm, carving deeply into the muscle as well as the skin and fat for a substantial sample. He heard the sorcerer moan in response to his hideous labors, but he struck him heavily a few more times and the lamentations subsided, letting him continue working in peace. After finishing, he thought for a moment, and then took the other man's thumb for good measure, not sure how much of the man's person the witch required for her incantation, and not willing to take any chances on coming up short of the necessary bloody tissue. The mage was much quieter this time around during his ministrations, and after a quick search of the kitchen he found a suitable receptacle for the transport of his gruesome prizes. He left through the front door this time, careful to shut it behind him as he went.

He walked quickly through the crowded streets, trying to avoid unwanted notice, making his way directly back to Big Ludd's abode with his macabre plunder. Returning to the witch's house, he was immediately ushered in, and was led to the now familiar darkened room. Irnan was waiting for him inside, and as he revealed the bloody trophies her face changed from its normal emotionless banality briefly, and the look he saw was one of undisguised hunger and salivation, before it was masked again by her usual reserved expression. It was so quick he was not entirely certain he had seen it, and his aching hand further compounded the issue, swiftly distracting him from the event and driving out all other thoughts but the promise of salvation from its tyrannical grip from his mind. She readied the promised spell, lighting the metal brazier and throwing a mixture of ingredients from her baskets into the flames, one constituent at a time. The witch bade him to sit across from her and to place his arms on either side of the instrument's base, almost like he was cradling the item, but without making any contact. She began to chant in an unknown language, but it was clearly reminiscent of what he had heard Goll vocalize when the warlock was performing his incantations. It was extremely hypnotic, and lulled him into a complacent half-dozed state, the smells coming from the assortment of burning components aiding in that endeavor as well.

He saw her place the mutilated parts he had taken from Goll into the brazier, and the fire briefly shot up, with the flames turning a florid red as she did so. This was followed shortly thereafter by his newly recaptured hand, and the flames changed yet again, this time to a sickly green color accompanied by a nauseous odor, that reminded him of gangrene and putrefaction. The smell of it churned his stomach, but the vile stench did nothing to alleviate his strange drowsiness. He heard a sharp intake of breath from the spell-caster suddenly, breaking her continuous chanting, and sleepily he tried to see the source of her exclamation. Fighting against the

reverie that was swiftly overtaking him, he saw she was staring into the flames, and the look on her face was clouded and
angry, as if she was seeing something she did not like within
the depths of the blaze. Finishing her scrying in the fire's aug-
uries, she stood abruptly and walked to the wall behind her,
retrieving a large object he could not make out in the poorly
lit condition of the room. She ducked her head down low and
fiddled with the undetermined article, before raising her head
again and returning to the fire.

He could see she had a wooden mask on now, the brown
material shiny from a varnish or lacquer, with jade symbols
painted in an oval gathering, the largest at the forehead in the
form of a spider-web. It had no face to speak of drawn or
carved on its surface, just a pair of rudimentary eye-holes allowing vision. She sat down again on the blanket, tossing a
feather-like whitish material into the flames, and a biting
scent wafted through his sinuses at the new element's diffu-
sion into the smoky air. It produced an immediate effect in
him, an even more pronounced languorous sluggishness so intense that he did not think he could move from his spot on the
blanket even if he had wanted to do so. As she did so she began her intonations anew, but this time there was a different
edge to sounds, a harsher, more keening timbre. Even so his
weariness only intensified, and he barely had enough strength
left to keep his eyelids open. But the increasingly lethargic effect of the chanting's rhythmic cadence coupled with the para-
lyzing smell finally won its relentless assault on his senses,

and eventually he closed his eyes. He slipped into a mysteri-ous state of limbo, not quite asleep and not quite awake, where he felt as if he was resting but could still hear the dron-ing from the witch's incantations clearly. It was a beautiful song he felt now, an unearthly mantra that calmed and paci-fied him. None of the constant pain that had been plaguing him for so long was even remotely evident, and he felt like he was far away from himself, very much like some of his more intense drug-induced stupors, but more completely than any of the myriad of medications had every done. Presently he felt an insistent tugging on his left hand, and he wondered briefly of its cause, that perhaps the witch was trying to wake him. He could not rouse himself, or even voice his concerns, the ef-fort seeming to great for him in his weakened daze. Even the thought to do such a thing was extraordinarily difficult for him, and soon he let the unknown action pass unhindered, the will to do anything but listen to the fanciful music non-existent. After a short while the persistent chanting stopped, and he heard Irnan speak to him, her voice low and slightly malicious.

"It is sad for you, hook-man, that you killed Goll in order to steal his essence. That was not to be. If you had left him alive he could have been the surrogate for the spell I am cast-ing. He would have been a much better choice, his flesh was trained in the old magics and Druidic ways." He could sense the vitriolic fury barely restrained in her speech, but the dan-ger in the tone and even the meaning of her discourse still seemed far away, though he could understand the words through his euphoria. As she spoke her voice seemed to grow even more distant, as if she was far away on a mountaintop, and he could barely hear her final words before he slipped into a deep, dreamless sleep.

"But I will make do with what we have available."

****

He awoke much later, the glare of a fluorescent light shining unmercifully into his eyes from its crooked fixture directly above him. Looking around at his newfound environment, he shortly comprehended he was lying in a hospital bed, surrounded by the familiar presence of medical equipment and apparatus he had grown accustomed to in his previous lengthy stays in such settings. Then he felt the familiar throbbing pain, and his heart sank, knowing then that the arduous spell had been unsuccessful. He closed his eyes as tears of frustration and injustice swept over him, rolling down his tremulous cheeks in waves. He moved to wipe them away with his left hand, but something seemed wrong, he could not brush his hand across his face. Then he opened his eyes, and saw in horrified disbelief a bandaged stump where his only remaining hand should have been. The full extent of the Irnan's final words struck home for him then, and he tried to scream in horror at the sight of the severed appendage. But that too was denied to him, only a strange, discordant screeching issuing forth from his mouth, an inhuman sound that seemed too unrecognizable to be his own. The strangeness of it gave him a momentary pause, but then the terrifying realization that *the witch had taken so much more than just his last hand* fell on him like an avalanche, and he shrieked in his new voice over and over.

The Culvert

Luke Kramer was a detective, and one of the rare people who was exactly where he wanted to be in life. He had worked his way up through the precinct's ranks, starting as a simple beat cop. However, through his hard work and perseverance he had been able to achieve a coveted position, that of becoming one of the permanent full-time detectives working at the Ashcroft police department. He had five years experience under his belt now serving in that capacity, in fact making him, while not as venerable as Greg Farincourt, the senior detective, no longer the lowest man on the proverbial totem pole. He was now masterfully on his way to an accomplished career. He was quite trusted by his fellow officers in spite of being known as a bit aloof, if not a bit unfriendly, but he had a reputation for a single-minded intensity for solving the cases assigned him by the department and was a good man to count on for fulfillment of his duties. The work he had done in the Lewis case had been exemplary, resulting in the return of the boy to his family in good health after he had gone missing from a local supermarket. In the Plover case, where a young girl having newly acquired her license, hit and ran over two homeless men and then had attempted to cover up the unfortunate accident, his attention to detail and logic led to the conviction of the hapless student. Detective Kramer was a hometown hero who had done well, both for himself and for his principality.

Tonight he was working late at the small office he shared with his fellow peers, as was his usual custom. The other detectives had gone home hours earlier to spend time with their waiting families. Detective Kramer's life is a solitary existence, he hadn't had much of a reason to go home early in a very long time. The time was put to good use instead finishing up the seemingly inexhaustible paperwork that his chosen profession generated. While he toiled through the mounds of reports he was interrupted by Officer Tom Burnham from the front desk, who rang him on the office line and asked if he could come downstairs to speak with a visitor to the station. He acquiesced, knowing the recent budgetary restraints had stretched the staff officers to the limit and another hand at the helm was always appreciated. Shelving the files he had been working on in the tall filing cabinet, he hastened downstairs to the front lobby. Officer Burnham was engaged in a heated discussion with a large woman who Detective Kramer immediately recognized as the longtime widow Mrs. Vera Rundise. She was a frequent visitor to the precinct, on account of her ongoing feud with her neighbor Mr. Brady Sheridan. In a few short moments he could gather the gist of her problem, naturally concerning Mr. Sheridan's hound of ill-repute. Officer Burnham caught sight of him, and waved him over to large desk. He came over warily, fearing he would soon be dealing with the fearsome widow, and wishing intently that his good deed would go unpunished. Fortunately for him Officer Burnham directed him to an unassuming man waiting patiently in the lobby instead, and resumed his disparate conversation with Mrs. Rundise. The man was in his early forties, with an average height, slightly obese, with graying brown hair and green eyes. He had a mustache and matching beard, and was dressed in a plain gray t-shirt and blue jeans, worn but not shabbily.

After a brief conference with the man he took him upstairs to his office, and settled him at the chair across from his desk, then seated himself. Pouring himself a cup of coffee from the convenient pot located nearby, he inquired of his guest if he wished the same or any other kind of refreshment. The man declined politely, but waited patiently for the detective to savor a taste of the brown liquid. He seemed troubled, like a man with too much on his mind, but his behavior was reserved, leaving Detective Kramer to open the dialogue between the two.

"How can I help you, Mr....?

"Milron, James Milron."

"Well Mr. Milron, the officer downstairs said you wished to speak with someone. He did not give a reason for your visit at this late time, and if it was urgent you could have called the emergency line. So how can I help you this evening?"

"Well it is not urgent, but it is time I confessed."

"Confessed? For what?"

"An accident, a mistake. I made a terrible choice years ago and now I would like to rectify that mistake and come clean about its terrible lie I have participated in over the years."

"Perhaps you should start from the beginning so I can understand clearly what you are saying."

"It happened almost 30 years ago......."

****

James Milron was 13 years old and typical of boys that age, did not have many cares in the world. Not enjoying the decorum of his formal appellation, he choose instead to go by the moniker of "Jimmy" instead. His parents were decent, hardworking people, and while not overly rich, they were not exceedingly poor either. He had a dog named Lady, an affectionate black lab that was unfortunately none to bright, and an orange cat named Harold who most definitely was in the extreme. His best friend in the world was Billy Winters, and the two of them had been inseparable since the third grade. Billy had covered for him when Sarah Smith had told Mrs. Schaff that Jimmy had pulled her hair in the classroom, and their friendship had blossomed from there. They had shared many escapades and adventures together since then, and in fact he was looking forward to doing so today as well.

The two met up at the playground at the elementary school near Billy's house. It was a Saturday, so normally Billy had his kid brother following around them, but he had deserted him early on so he couldn't ruin their fun. They had made big plans for the day, involving the rain overflow culverts that ran underneath the town. They had found an unobserved entrance by the drainage swamp behind the local K-mart, and naturally wanted to explore them, the insistent call of adventure overriding any reservations they may have had about possible mishaps or recriminations. Jimmy had watched a special on television about cave exploration, and this seemed to be the next best thing, a grand adventure for the two best friends to share together.

"Did you bring the stuff?" Jimmy asked.

"Yea, you got yours?" replied Billy.

"Yea, sure do." Jimmy patted the backpack slung across his bike's handlebars. "I've got some chips, the flashlight, and check this out!" He looked around furtively like they were being watched, then not seeing anyone noticing their clandestine behavior, unzipped the backpack and opened it a crack so Billy could catch a glimpse within its inner compartment.

"Whatcha got in there Jimmy?" Billy tried to inspect through the minuscule opening, but was unable to do so successfully.

"My dad's .38," he said proudly in a hushed voice. "I nicked it when he wasn't looking. Just in case, you know."

"Oh, cool," said Billy. "I brought the rope, the flashlight, some cookies and a couple spare batteries."

"Good thinking, we might need those. I didn't bring any

extras."

"You ready?" Billy nodded in the affirmative, and they started pedaling down in the general direction of K-mart.

It was a pleasant day, warm for May, but had a light breeze to keep the heat off. Far off some clouds were beginning to accumulate, but the two explorers weren't about to let a little rain ruin their planned expedition. The K-mart wasn't too far from the school, only a couple miles. They used the back streets and alleys to speed up their journey, only once going out of their way to avoid the Myers' dog. Holt was a big black rottweiler, and he was as mean as he was big. He barked ferociously anytime someone passed the peeling wood fence that barely contained his animalistic fury, and you just knew that he eventually would break through the meager enclosure and absolutely murder whoever was unfortunate enough to be caught on the other side. Mr. Myers seemed to find it funny when passersby were shocked from their daydreaming by the huge monstrosity, the beast suddenly appearing as if by magic, straining across the flimsy wooden structure to attack, snarling and barking with horrific savageness and rage. His jerk son Colin would join him in the merriment as well, the two ruthlessly heckling the individual walking by on their natural reactions of self preservation from the terrifying canine. Little Betty Miller had actually soiled herself when caught unawares one time, running back home crying to the two's merciless mirth echoing in her ears, a tell-tale stain marring the rear of her pink dress. Colin had come to school the next day and told everyone about it, which had resulted in her new nickname Betty Poop. Both Jimmy and Billy knew enough to avoid that street, it just wasn't worth going down there no matter your hurry.

The K-mart parking lot was packed with Saturday shoppers, but the two managed to avoid detection as they pedaled past. Rounding the building, they looked anxiously for some sign of further unwanted attention, but the area was deserted, only abandoned shopping carts and discarded pallets laying careless strewn at the edifice's rear. They headed towards the break in the chain link fence they had spotted earlier that week, dismounting from their bicycles and dragging them down the steep embankment to the swampy drainage below. The abundant bushes and trees formed perfect cover to hide their bikes, laying them down carefully in the high grass behind one especially thick and bushy specimen. They crouched down as they walked through the swamp, casting clandestine eyes upon the edge of the embankment to see if anyone was spying on their stealthy progress to the great mouth of the culvert. A large pool of water formed at the edge of the drain, filled by a rivulet of water flowing from the pipe, submerging the surrounding grasses and shrubs. They headed to the left side of it, where they could climb sideways across the embankment face to avoid getting wet as much as possible. The ground was soft and grassy, quickly giving way to the concrete that formed the boundary of the culvert. They easily swung inside, using the edges for balance. The pipe measured roughly six feet high, and the front was covered with a heavy steel gate that opened vertically from the ground. It was almost too heavy for them to lift, and they took turns holding the gate open for each other, both straining against the weight of the enormous entrance. The plentiful daylight was already vanishing within the gloom inside the giant pipe, so they pulled out their flashlights to view the way ahead.

Jimmy took point and shined his light down the dark tunnel. It went on for as far as he could see, wide and round walls continuing in a straight line until they vanished into inky blackness. "Oh this is so cool," he exclaimed.

"For sure," his buddy agreed.

There was a rivulet of brackish water running down the center of the pipe to contend with, so they straddled it as they walked to avoid the filthy wetness flowing beneath them. The sides began as the light gray of smooth concrete, but quickly turned darker with mildew and organic growth on them as they progressed. They walked for a few minutes without incident, quietly moving within the large tunnel, neither one choosing to speak. It was strangely spooky, the absence of the glaring brightness of daylight they had traveled in earlier making a sharp contrast with the gloomy interior they now traversed. It felt otherworldly, like they were the only ones who had every been in its dark confines, and while it did not feel claustrophobic or restricting, it did create an almost hallowed air, like the ambiance of a deserted church or cathedral, empty but still full of something. The temperature quickly fell in the shaded, subterranean passage, and both boys felt its cool embrace, further amplifying their preternatural feelings of sacrosanctness. Then Jimmy spotted something small and dark on the left side of the culvert floor up ahead, and the mesmerizing spell passed, lost to the curiousness of youth.

"Hey what's that?" said Jimmy, shining his light on the dark mass up ahead.

"Dunno, maybe clothes or something," Billy replied.

"Clothes? Who would get naked down here? Nah, it looks different than that, maybe it's a.....oh it's a rat!" he exclaimed as the subject came into full view. The rodent in question was about fourteen inches long from its nose to the tip of its pink tail, with blackish brown fur. It wasn't moving and appeared to be not to breathing as well, its eyes shut peacefully.

"You think it's dead, Jimmy?" Billy asked..

"Yea, it looks dead Billy," Jimmy answered with authority. He walked up to it and nudged it with his shoe, to which it hissed angrily in the way that dead things shouldn't do and attempted to bite Jimmy's offending sneaker. Jimmy froze in astonishment a second before reacting to rat's violent rise from the dead.

"HOLY SHIT BILLY IT'S ALIVE!" Jimmy nearly knocked Billy over in his earnestness to escape the vengeful rat, who now was in seemingly hot pursuit of the boy. It darted to and fro between the two boys, who both screamed hysterically, beat, and kicked in their horror of the raging rodent. It ran quickly up Billy's leg and then just as quick ran back down before he could react, then darted off in the direction of the gate.

It took a moment or so before the two had regained their shattered composure and were able to continue down the pipe, Billy taking the lead this time. They walked on, banally poking fun of each other for their previous unheroic behavior before reaching a junction ahead that went to the right with a much smaller pipeline. The main culvert continued straight ahead, and they began to notice an intermittent rumbling sound ahead from that direction. As they listened more closely it became clear it was not steady noise, seeming to have no rhyme or reason to it whatsoever. They decided to investigate it, leaving off the small pipe for now. The sound grew louder and louder, becoming apparent to its source, a manhole cover in the ceiling. Then they realized what it was.

"Cars....that's Cedar Street up above!" Billy yelled.

"Yea, that's crazy, they're driving right over the top of us!"

The sound was deafening at its source so they walked further down the culvert to escape it, spotting a speck of daylight far up ahead. They walked towards it without incident, still avoiding the runoff in the middle of the pipe as best they could. Reaching the light, they saw it was shining through a grate in a street gutter up above, and Jimmy climbed Billy's back to look outside. He could see it was a residential area now they were past the main street, and he could see outside the various houses and trees. Then he heard talking, distant but coming closer.

"Whadda you see Jimmy?" Billy said from below.

"Shhh, there's some kids coming," he said, noticing the voices seemed younger than himself and Billy. Then he had an idea.

"OOOOOhhhhhh, we're trapped down here," he said as ghostly as he could. He could hear one the kids exclaiming, "Where's that coming from?"

"Dooowwwnnn heerrre, Dooowwnn heerre." He could feel Billy laughing silently to his joke. Above the sound of the kids walking was coming closer to the grate. *"Weee allll floooat doowwn heeerre,"* mimicking a horror movie he and Billy had watched late one night clandestinely during a sleepover.

This was too much for poor Billy, his body so quaking with suppressed laughter that Jimmy had no choice but to jump down off his back, or risk falling off. Both of them took off further down the tunnel, laughing loudly the entire time.

"Oh man those kids had to have been freaked!"

"I know, that was awesome!"

In a little while their mirth subsided as they continued their journey. They came to a large four way junction, and they decided to try going left for a change. They found a wider section where they stopped to eat, Jimmy sharing his chips and Billy sharing his cookies in typical friendly fashion. After they had finished they noticed that the water in the center of the pipe was getting wider now, and at the next grate they could see water was pouring in. Billy jumped up on Jimmy's back and reported that it was raining outside now, the warnings of the impeding storm having come forth to deliver on its promise.

"Well, do you want to head back?" Jimmy asked.

Billy shrugged and said, "I don't know, whadda ya think?"

Jimmy thought on it. "Well, it's not like we can get rained on down here, right? And if it looks too bad we can always head back then." Billy agreed, so they walked further down the pipe until they came to what looked like a large square room. As they shined their flashlights in it they noticed the ceiling and sides were made of brick instead of concrete, and looked much older than the previous sections they had been in. The ceiling was much higher as well, and the floor was completely submerged. Jimmy shined his flashlight on the water and noticed he could not see the bottom. Billy rolled his sleeve up past his shoulder and reached into the black water.

"I can feel the bottom," he said. "We might be able the cross it."

"OK, sounds good, my feet have already got wet anyway, not like it matters anymore." They rolled up their pant legs up and began to ford the inky waters, Billy in front and Jimmy following behind. The floor felt solid, but bumpy, like it was made of the same bricks that lined the walls and ceiling. The water had some kind of oily film on it, causing a dark rainbow to be reflected back from their flashlights. Then Billy stood stock still.

"Did you see that?" Billy asked softly.

"Dude, knock that off, that's not cool." Jimmy knew his

friend's sense of humor, but was not finding it particularly funny at the moment. The black waters were already a bit freaky to him, and he did not want to ponder what denizens could exist in such dismal surroundings.

"No, I'm not joking I heard something splash."

"Dude, you better be joking." The hair on the back of Jimmy's neck began to rise, and he swallowed hard to stamp down his growing apprehension.

"Maybe it was just a frog that got lost." Billy said doubtfully. He seemed to be trying to convince himself as well as Jimmy as to the origin of the disturbance. He began moving forward again however, a little faster than before, evidently having enough of the opaque water's mystery and wanting to cross as quickly as possible.

"Yeah, I saw some of those outside in the pond, must be one of 'em." Jimmy was speaking now to agree with Billy to avoid the intolerable silence that would lead to him imagining things, things about what was down in the water he could not see, and most certainly he did not want to feel. He shined his flashlight anxiously around the water, vainly attempting to pierce the inky blackness to no avail. He picked up his pace, moving closer to Billy, almost overtaking him. Then he felt his foot push down on something soft and unfamiliar, and he shrieked with pent up nervousness as he ran straight forward right into Billy, causing the other boy to pitch forward. Billy struck the water hard, causing an enormous splash in the dirty water.

Jimmy expected Billy to come up out of the water immediately, but when several agonizing seconds passed and he didn't do so, Jimmy knew something was very wrong. He reached into the water and felt around until he grabbed the back of Billy's shirt and tried to haul him up out of the blackness. Billy was unresponsive in his grasp, and when he pulled at him he was unmovable, like he was stuck on something. Jimmy pulled harder, then he came free with a sickening slurping sound. Jimmy turned Billy over in his arms, trying to ascertain what was wrong with his friend. Then, as he pulled Billy's head back he saw with horror a gaping black hole where his left eye had been.

"No, no, no, no, oh, no, Billy, please be OK," he softly whispered, on the verge of hysteria. But he knew Billy was not OK, he was never going to be OK. He tried to feel for a pulse but there was nothing, so then he put his ear to Billy's chest and listened for a heartbeat, finding no response there as well. Billy was dead.

****

"And there I left him," the man said to Detective Kramer. "He must have struck something sharp that was just under the water when he fell. I was so out of my mind I just left him in that old square culvert section. I honestly don't even remember heading back out of the tunnel. I just remember struggling with the gate and all the water pouring down the culvert nearly drowning me before I was able to open it. I went home and my parents were still not home yet. I went up to my room and I recall thinking that I should call the police and tell them what happened. But then I remembered that I was the one that pushed him, so I was the one that murdered him. It was an accident but in my young mind I was thinking about the fact that we shouldn't have been down there in the tunnels, I shouldn't have pushed him, I shouldn't have left him there alone. So many wrongs that I was responsible for. So I didn't tell anyone. Even when the police were searching for him and questioning everyone about when they saw him last I lied and said I hadn't seen him that day, that we were supposed to meet at the school playground but he never showed up. They were already suspecting an old bum that all the parents had been complaining about, the one that had been bothering their kids on the playground earlier that week, so they really weren't looking very hard at anyone else. The police never found his body, it must have got stuck somewhere in that maze of tunnels. Then my dad lost his job when they closed the plant and a few months later we moved away, not real far just to over to Harding, and I kind of put it out of my mind. They say life goes on after someone dies and I guess it does, I grew up and just let it lie, buried from my day to day thoughts. Thirty years went by like that. It had been so surreal that even on the few occasions I thought about it I had almost convinced myself that it hadn't happened, that it was just a story I'd heard or read. That was until I saw on the state news they found his body. Evidently there was a big storm, the biggest the town had ever seen, and it washed all kinds of things from their resting spots, collecting at the mouth of the culvert for everyone to see."

"Then came the nightmares. Every night I dreamed of that tunnel, and of us being down there, and him falling. Every time it would end the same way, with me pulling him out of that dark water with his face all bloody and then I would stare down at the damn black hole where his eye should have been. Then, right before I'd wake in a cold sweat he'd whisper, *"Why'd you leave me Jimmy? Why? We were friends."* I tried sleeping pills, meditation, drinking, you name it but that damn dream keeps coming to me every night, giving me no peace for months. Not that I deserve it for what I've done, but now I know I have to confess to hopefully stop these nightmares. And Billy deserves some closure. I need to give Billy that at least."

James fell silent, apparently lost in his own thoughts. Detective Kramer thought for a short moment himself, then said, "I would like you to show me where it happened, so you can walk me through everything."

James looked up, as if just remembering the detective was there, and in a quiet, detached voice gave his consent to do so. Detective Kramer went to a pegboard that held several different keys, selected a large silver-colored key, putting it in his pocket. He then grabbed his jacket and motioned James out of the office back down the stairs. Officer Burnham was off-shift now, and his replacement buzzed the two men out with little care or fanfare. Detective Kramer noticed the night air was still overly warm from the summer heat of the daytime. They walked across the street together to the station parking lot, and got inside Detective Kramer's waiting unmarked car. They drove in silence, neither man interested in making small talk in light of the horrific confession. They went down past the dark middle school, then passed a crumbling deserted house with an old broken down wood fence that was missing one large section on the right side. They drove past the moving company that had bought the old K-mart building after the company went bankrupt. Finishing their journey, they parking above the embankment on a small, nondescript dead-end dirt road. Both men exited the vehicle, and Detective Kramer removed a pair of leather gloves from the trunk which he donned before grabbing a grey duffel bag and a large black flashlight. They walked down the embankment through the trees and bushes into the swampy wetland, and presently maneuvered their way onto the grey concrete culvert entrance. Detective Kramer produced the large silver key from earlier and unlocked a large padlock fastening the gate shut.

He spoke as if sensing James's unspoken question, "After we found the body the mayor and the city council decided that maybe leaving these areas open for kids to get into wasn't the best idea. So they outfitted locks on all the entrances and gave keys to the police and fire stations so we could get inside in an emergency situation. I think this is the first time it's been used, wasn't sure if it would work." James nodded his affirmation in understanding, still unwilling to speak. They made their way inside, avoiding the center where debris and silt had collected after the last runoff had dried up. James led, with Detective Kramer following close behind to provide light. They walked without talking for the most part still, only when taking a different direction would any of them make any sort of rudimentary conversation. Even to grown men the silence and darkness was like a living thing, encroaching on their minds, adding to the disquiet caused by the purpose of their visit. After long last they arrived at the older brick section of drainage.

"It looks exactly like it did back then," James said, finally breaking the quiet between them. "It is exactly like in my dreams except for being dried up." The floor was indeed visible now, showing the same bricks that had been used in the manufacture of the walls, with the exception of where the floor bricks had caved in from sinkholes undermining them, leaving several large holes in its surface. The summer's drought had baked any abundant water out of the subterranean cache. There was garbage here and there on the floor, strewn in haphazard fashion from the absent rainwater, left to rot after being trapped in the room's restrictive boundaries. They stepped into the large chamber and James went on ahead again, walking forward as Detective Kramer lighted the way. "We were crossing here when it happened. I must have stepped on one of these garbage piles and then I ran forward and struck him....this is what he must have been what he was impaled on...." His voice trailed off as he saw the large piece of reinforced concrete lodged in one of the sinkholes. It had a wicked piece of rebar sticking almost straight up out of it, and it gave no reflection on its black surface, coated with a residue that was dried but obvious as of its origin. "Billy...I'm sorry, I'm so sorry..." James sobbed, collapsing to his knees and covering his face in his hands. He stayed there a moment, lost in his grief and guilt over his childhood friend.

When he looked up he saw Detective Kramer standing in front of him now, but the detective's face was twisted with rage instead of the placid demeanor that James had seen from him in the brief time they had spent together. It was quite a change, and he did not understand the metamorphosis of the man's features, or the cause of his anger. He did not have to wait very long to find out however, Detective Kramer spitting words at him like venom.

"You...you're sorry? You led my brother down here to die and you left him here to rot alone! To be eaten by the rats and worms! We searched for months! We tried everything to find him! My dad and mom split up because of you! She left him and remarried a prick that beat her, you bastard! She would have left him except my dad let him adopt me because he couldn't look at me without seeing Billy! After I left she finally committed suicide because of her guilt over it and you're sorry??!! You killed my brother! You killed my mother!"

Detective Kramer raised the big black flashlight and brought it crashing down on James's upturned face. "Sorry?!" he said over and over as he rained blows in tandem to his manic cries, striking indiscriminately all over the other man's quickly battered body. Only after the flashlight started blinking from his furious assault did he relent, standing over his now comatose victim. "I'll show you sorry! You're going to stay down here like you left him, but you're never coming up again!" He placed the flashlight down with the light pointing at the ceiling, where it cast a blood red glow over the chamber. He went to over to James's motionless body, and grabbing him by his hair hauled him to the broken concrete slab with the sharp rebar sticking out like a blackened lance. Grasping James's head firmly he rammed his face forward into the waiting black steel, eye first, feeling the soft resistance as the metal punctured up into the spongy brain matter. Then walking over to the discarded duffel bag, he removed an entrenching tool and proceeded to start digging in one the depressions, leaving his still victim to slowly bleed over the uneven floor. He removed the bricks and carefully set them down to the side of his excavation, one on top of another, making a neat pile. He then dug down into the mixture of soil and gravel until he had reached what he felt was an appropriate depth, then dragged James's unmoving form to his new home in the culvert's floor. He replaced the displaced earth and then carefully restacked the red blocks on top, before putting away the shovel and reclaiming the flashlight. Glancing around for anything amiss, he gazed one final time at the wet piece of rebar before heading back down the culvert. Once back at the entrance he locked the padlock and turned off his flashlight. He waited for his eyes to adjust to the darkness and then made his way back by starlight to the remnants of the shrunken pool, stooping down and washing off the flashlight before then tossing it in the center of the pond. He had others, and it was unlikely that a connection of its significance would ever be made even if found. He peeled off his dirty gloves and placed them in a small plastic bag he carried on his person, then secreted the bag away for future disposal. He made his way back up to his car and before he left he gazed one final time at the direction he had come from. It really was a pretty spot, he decided. He might need to start taking his lunch here.

The Dreadful Call

The forgotten path was massively overgrown, hardly noticeable with all the wild greenery crowding throughout its edges, with even a few hardy plants attempting to make their way onto the trail proper. However, the dense terrain seemed inconsequential to the Indian guide Tey he had hired in the village. He was as knowledgeable of the remote landscape as he was surefooted, finding the scant signs of the hidden pathway with ease as he deftly moved through its thick underbrush. Professor Rhodes was having trouble following him through the forest's abundant foliage, but neither his pride as a man nor his impatience to arrive at the fabled ruins would have ever let him ask the lithe native to ease up on his rapid pace. The llamas they were using as pack animals seemed to have no trouble with the tempo or terrain, placidly following behind the men with the casual aloofness typical of their breed. The professor had come to this far-flung corner of the globe after copious research and diligent study, poring over forgotten parchments in neglected museums and tomes of yore in musty libraries and dank repositories, finding bygone secrets lost to mankind and even time itself for countless centuries. He had uncovered a great revelation of academic interest and knowledge rivaling that of the recent discoveries of Tutankhamen's tomb and the ruins of Machu Picchu, or even the earlier deciphering of the Rosetta Stone, and he knew that its significant unearthing would catapult him, Professor Howard Rhodes, to heights of professional accolades and possibly even that of the public's eye as well. Finding unequivocal evidence of a vast and improbable worship of eldritch beings, under the guise of gods and goddesses to many different ancient peoples, whose absolute devotion required up to and including monstrous practices such as horrific human sacrifice, riotous orgies, and disturbing mutilations of their own bodies and possibly even the minds of the supplicants. Reading the ancient texts the primitive Sumerians had made in their first written records as well as the enigmatic hieroglyphics of the early Egyptian priests and rulers had given him the first glimpses into a linked past that was shared across multiple bygone cultures and prehistoric peoples. Searching further, he realized that even the illegible proto-historical records of the baffling Indus script, the classical Vinca Signs, and laborious Jiahu symbols had enigmatic images that correlated to the same connections of veneration and adulation of these dark elder gods. Paradoxically within the Celtic druids of the British Isles and Germanic tribes of Western Europe of more contemporary times, even here he found evidence that supported his hypothesis into this grand association of an all-encompassing religion.

In all of the histories however, he discovered the same apocalyptic result, that of the destruction and eradication of the temples and shrines of the worshipers, even their baleful priests themselves slaughtered. The carnage was done either by antagonistic empires and tribes offended by their debaucheries and malicious customs, or by their own people aligned against them, who were jealous of the malignant power and sinister sway held over the unseeing populace, or simply wishing to end their nefarious, unholy practices. Finally, after perusing though countless volumes of esoteric enlightenment he made a startling disclosure, found in the puzzling Nahuatl glyphs of the Aztec peoples, and also in the previously indecipherable Incan knotted strings known as the Quipu, that of one final temple untouched by the ravages of the conquistadors or the deprecations of the indigenous populations. Local legends told that the creators had held a considerable empire, until an uprising within obliterated their grand city and the surrounding regions. The victors of this massive revolt reportedly had terribly murdered anyone venturing into their forbidden territory, in strange and horrible ways. The remote area itself was shunned by the local tribes even after such significant time had elapsed.

His theory and the empirical answer to its solution had been summarily dismissed by the small-mindedness of his contemporaries and peers. Even the university where he held his position had been unsympathetic to his needs of funding for the expedition. He had been forced to finance the journey with his own meager resources, scrimping and saving, and even ultimately selling several valuable items from his own collection of artifacts to come up with the monies necessary for such an excursion. The further investigation had required a great deal of intense fieldwork and countless interviews with the local populace, many of whom had been unwilling to speak to him of the forgotten shrine, fearing even now the shrouded forces that had been its dark undoing. It had taken persistent badgering, laborious mingling, and especially extensive bribery to overcome the natives' superstitious trepidation to ascertain even the most rudimentary clues to the whereabouts of the mysterious temple. The subsequent journey to the rumored edifice had already proved long and arduous in the extreme, but the sweet taste of victory loomed closer than ever before in Professor Rhodes's mind.

Tey, stopping his brisk stride momentarily, motioned for him to follow suit, and he obeyed without question, relying on the guide's expertise in the situation to have considerable merit especially given the rough terrain and unpredictable nature of their immediate journey. In Lima his contacts had all been unanimous in their agreement on the tracker's credentials, and thus far his conduct had been exemplary. He had proven to be a boon companion as well, a spirited conversationalist in spite of their language gap, loyal and intelligent, and a decent cook to boot. The steadfast Indian stared momentarily down the direction they had been moving towards, and then silently motioned the professor forward. He quickly complied, moving as quietly as possible to the tracker's position. The guide pointed to a shaded spot in the trail and whispered "Jach'a titi" in his native language. After scanning the impenetrable area he was gesturing towards, Rhodes finally spotted the glaring reason for which they had stopped their hectic pace. A majestic jaguar was cleverly concealed in the lush foliage of a leafy tree, his spots intermixing with the shadows of the plants while his tawny coat blended perfectly with the yellow grasses he was lying in so placidly. Rhodes could have very well walked right past him and remained clueless to the predator's presence, unless of course it had chosen that particular moment to pounce on him. He studied the feline creature intently, feeling it was too rare an opportunity to be passed up. The leonine beast he estimated to be roughly a yard and half long, and probably weighed close to two hundred pounds, with a short muzzle and large, powerful jaws. The limbs looked much more stocky and muscular than most big cats he had seen, with the fur mostly yellow working up to a darker red on the back and top of the head, while the belly and throat was off-white in color. The leopard-like markings themselves had an interesting "eye' look to them in some places, like a spot within a circle as opposed to the more normal splotch or dot pattern in other locations on its supple body. It was an amazingly beautiful animal, able to look fierce and noble yet completely relaxed while lazing in the tree's ample shade. Rhodes was about to turn back to his comrade to see what he thought of the magnificent creature, but then seeing movement from the big cat again he redirected his attention back to it. The languid jaguar, seemingly tired of being the spectacle of their scrutiny, had stood up and was now leaving the vicinity of the path. He watched it slowly stalk away, marveling at the sheer grace that such a large beast could have and at the same time the tiny idiosyncrasies it shared with its tiny cousin, the common house cat in both temperate and attitude.

His guide, speaking in a low voice, told him that jach'a titi normally do not come this far into the mountains, but to see one here was considered to be good luck. Rhodes said he certainly hoped so, which seemed to amuse the usually solemn tracker, his face splitting into a large grin before resuming his place at point. They continued on, slowly making progress through the increasingly difficult landscape, the countryside swallowing the path entirely to Rhodes's inexperienced eye, leaving him to rely wholly on the guide's expertise. The two men kept up the strong pace until late evening, stopping to camp in a relatively clear area, staking out the llamas on long tethers to give them rein to choose their own beds. They put up their tents quickly with practiced hands, and then after starting a roaring fire, Tey prepared dinner while Rhodes attempted to ascertain their location from one of his maps. After finding solid confirmation of their position he believed they should reach their destination within the next few weeks, as long as the weather and their luck both held out. Night fell, and after they enjoyed the repast Tey had prepared, the two of them made idle conversation before the fire as the flames slowly died down. They spoke of the trip ahead, and then the conversation turned to other areas the guide had explored in the mountains and surrounding countryside. The professor shared some of his stories of expeditions in the Sahara, as well as excavations he had done in the El Tur mountain range. Rhodes had always been fond of the world outdoors, and while the jungle trek and hard lodging that they had been doing for the last week was arduous and extreme compared to other trips he had taken, at times it reminded him of pleasant memories spent camping when he was younger in the Scottish highlands and the Canadian wilderness with his brother and father. He had asked Tey about his family, and had learned that the man had come from a "small" family in his village, only having five brothers and four sisters. It had led Rhodes to wonder just how big a large family was, but when he was about to ask, a rustle from somewhere outside of the fire's perimeter made both men instantly cease talking and listen closely to the disturbance. The Andes were not without their share of dangers, and they were deep within their majestic confines, in an unforgiving place where the indigenous peoples and wildlife was not as respectful of mankind as it is in the more populous and less savage places in the civilized world.

Tey, spooked by the out of place noise, slowly reached for his machete lying on a nearby log, and Rhodes unbuttoned the strap on top of his holster, pulling the Colt 1911 he carried just for such emergencies from its resting place on his thigh. They both scanned the darkness, their eyes adjusting from the low light of the fire to the moonless night as they peered out into the blackness for some sign of movement or other disquieting intent of malevolence from the possible danger. Even the llamas seemed to sense something amiss, cowering down on the ground, perhaps attempting to hide in their instinctual fear of whatever predator awaited in the dark night. Rhodes could feel unseen eyes watching them, in a manner he could not explain but was absolutely certain of, and by state of Tey's noticeable apprehension it was evident that he felt it as well. After several tense seconds the feeling of concealed examination ceased, and Rhodes could have swore he heard a repetitive booming sound dwindling in the distance, so low in tone even as it started to be almost outside the range of human hearing. He strained his ears, attempting to place the unfamiliar noise. He softly asked Tey if he had heard any such sound, but the man said he had not heard anything except the first disruption. He seemed very interested in what Rhodes had thought he had discerned however, and after hearing the learned man's explanation of the event his eyes went wide with terror.

"Jaxsa jamach'i," he said faintly. "This is a bad omen, Mr. Rhodes. Very bad. My people say those who hear the jaxsa jamach'i will be not be long in this world. I fear for you, my friend. Perhaps we should turn back tomorrow."

"Turn back? Are you daft, man? We've come so far, and

we'll be reaching the temple any day now. This is the entire purpose for my visit, my academic future, my very life. We can't turn back now. Now I understand you have your superstitions, but I've paid you well and if it is my life that is in danger, well, I for one choose to keep going. For all we know turning back could be what kills me." He further exhorted the guide, listing various reasons for the plausible noise from natural occurrences to simple tricks of the mind. He finally finished with saying he was not interested in hearing anything more of the jaxsa jamach'i or any other supernatural old wives' tales the man wished to relate. Tey listened to his lectures gravely and soberly, even taking the criticisms of his beliefs with stoicism and grace, but still shook his head at the professor's insistence of continuation of the excursion, finally saying, "It is your life, masi." The tracker left for his tent, and after staring into the darkness for a short time, Rhodes retired to his abode as well, pondering whether he had actually heard the sound and Tey's strange reaction to his disclosing of it to him.

The next day was heavily overcast, the chill of the mountain air as foreboding as the strange premonition Tey had made the night before. They broke camp quickly, with a smooth routine they had practically down to a science now. Starting back out on the trail again warmed their freezing blood, and before long the vigorous pace Tey once again set for them ate up the miles as they ascended higher into the vast mountains, coaxing the animals to cross meandering streams, and passing thick jungle swathes of cedar, quina, and greenbriers. The next four days passed relatively uneventfully, with only timid alpaca, wild llama, and the occasion fox to be seen for fauna, with the inclement weather thankfully holding despite the increasing threat of rain. The barely discernible path they had been following began to lead off into an unwanted direction, leaving them to venture their best guess instead of concrete validation of the proper route. Using Rhodes's steadfast findings from his studies and laborious calculations of probable sites as well as Tey's apparently limitless knowledge of the Andes and its encompassing areas as their tools of navigation, they trail-blazed across virgin landscapes that had not been trod by explorers in years or centuries, perhaps even ever before in human history. Finding a picturesque waterfall cascading from a rocky precipice after several more days of travel, they discovered ancient stone steps carved into the steep cliff side, providing definite proof at last that they were still on the proper course to their final destination. Rhodes called a halt to their progress so he could study his maps and notes on references to the lost temple, recalling citations of the waterfall after consultation in his log jogged his memory. The mention of the waterfall and accompanying steps he had found in an account penned by Joseph Pentland, the famed Irish explorer of the early eighteenth century, calling it the "Terrible God's Climb" in his oft overlooked historical records. He now remembered a colorful if not altogether ghastly description of the religious purpose of the falls that the prominent geographer had learned from a local Indian tribe, the stories passed down in their oral traditions. He had described in his memoirs ancient worshipers of a forgotten religion who would bind those supplicants chosen by the high priest for their unwavering dedication to the sect, taking sets of them to the top of the waterfall's apex twice daily, once in the morning and again in the evening. Generally seven members were selected per outing, but on feast days and certain important holidays as many as fifty could be taken to the towering heights. The faithful devotees then would chant litanies to their dark gods while the high priest would slit each of their throats in turn, before hurling their dying bodies to the pool below, staining it red with their blood. Even now as Rhodes stared into the waters below the fall they seemed to have a reddish tinge to their turbulent depths, and he was not altogether sure the effect was a trick of the light, his imagination, or something far more sinister left over from the atrocious history.

They climbed the timeworn staircase, the neglected steps still serviceable in spite of the centuries of disuse and entropic decay from nature's relentless aggression of wind, weather, and water upon their stony surfaces. The ridge at the top proved to be an excellent campsite, and they prepared their temporary accommodations with the same usual efficiency as in the many evenings before. Tey prepared the evening meal, simmering and spicing the simple fare of ocas and papas for their consumption with practiced culinary skill. After dinner, the professor studied the ever-ascending tangled vegetation that lay ahead of them in the sun's last rays, the dying light creating eerie shadows in the rising topography of the massive, jagged peaks. Tomorrow's climb would be the most difficult yet, with the purported temple's location said to be found somewhere high on the mountains spread out before him. Try as he might, he could not ascertain any sign of man-made impression upon this untamed countryside, leaving him only to hope that Tey's impressive pathfinder skills would carry them to the final end of their long trek.

They made little conversation after dinner, both men consumed with their own thoughts of the coming ascension on the morrow until it was time to rest. Rhodes lay unsettled in his tent, trying to will elusive sleep to come and bring its relief from the constant worries and anticipations his mind endlessly churned through. When slumber finally came however, it was sullied by dark and disturbed images, of disembodied shapes chasing him through twisting, dank hallways in what he knew must be the temple. The floor was a quagmire of loathsome, fetid matter, sucking at his boots, impeding his progress so his tormentors could come ever closer. He heard the same booming sound he had tried to pretend was his mind's folly, coming closer and closer until he could feel the power of it resounding off the walls and resonating in his bones. Too terrified to turn and look at his foes, he ran on, stumbling and slipping in the dark halls as the relentless horrors closed in on him. He felt a powerful thrust of an unseen assault into his unprotected back, and then he awoke, drenched in sweat, but grateful to have his rest disrupted, free of the disquieting reverie. As he stared at the ceiling, trying to slow the rapid pace of his beating heart, the noise of it pounding in his ears like waves on a broken surf, he began to notice a low reverberation ever so quietly somewhere outside of his bodily concerns. He tried to dismiss it as a carryover from his recent nightmare, but the incessant sound continued in its aggravating factuality, causing him to rise and dress to inspect outside the tent's narrow confines. He brought the pistol as well, the cool metal providing a comforting feeling of security in his hands. Opening the tent flap, he crept silently out into the humid night air, scanning the surrounding area as he did. Tey was still sleeping soundly in his dwelling, the steady light snoring issuing from within like clockwork. Glancing at the llamas, they too appeared to be unperturbed by the differing beats, the gentle rise and fall of their sleeping forms the only motion he could detect. He choose not to the disturb the man, feeling his late night investigation did not warrant the guide's presence. The discordant bass sound was louder outside without the walls of the tent to muffle it, and he recognized it now as the soft booming he had heard the night before, only slightly increased in volume, and more numerous in repetition, creating an almost eerie cadence to the modulation. Searching for the source of the infernal sound, and by now having eliminated the nearby environment of having any origin of it, he scanned the tree line for anything amiss. At first he saw nothing in the blackness of the foliage, but then his ears, having become hyper sensitive due to the sustained effort of narrowing down the location of the monotone vibrations, lent his eyes the needed support and he found the root of the constant sonorous tones.

The low illumination in the thick trees masked the presence of the intruder almost flawlessly, but subtle differences in the shades of black within their dark clusters betrayed the mysterious prowler's form. Rhodes squinted, trying to see as much detail in the camouflaged tree line as he possibly could, and then miraculously the source of the uncanny noises stepped forward out of the shadowy vegetation and into the relatively brightened clearing, making its outline plain to visibility. The stranger was large, slightly taller than a normal-sized man, but its shape was unlike any bipedal primate, with a body much wider than its legs, a thick, powerful neck, and an over-sized head. It was devoid of fur, but not naked, instead having an abundant feathery plumage that was a rich brown in color with streaks of a reddish tinge as well. There were no arms to speak of, but instead it had vestigial wings that fluttered seemingly of an instinctual accord, twitching aimlessly with an irregular timing. The creature's most prominent feature however, was not immediately apparent until the shimmer from the stars above struck it in just the most consummate lighting, revealing a large, cruel beak, almost a foot and a half in length and dark grey in hue. The angular proboscis was thickest at its base, with the top mandible overlapping the bottom one, with both curving sharply towards the end, but the former finishing with a wide, hooked tip, similar of that of a bird of prey. Every so often the long bills would open, and the inharmonious booming noise would issue forth from its cavernous maw, the ponderous tones traveling through the warm air to the professor's location easily. He watched the creature from his vantage point near his tent, wondering at its inscrutable purpose in the peculiar serenade and why it seemed to be surreptitiously following him on his exploration into the mountains. Could it be some sort of mating call or perhaps a warning to rivals or enemies? Zoology was by no means one of his stronger suits, but the creature seemed of a prehistoric nature, like some relic from a past age that may have belonged to such primitive surroundings before the advent of man and his hereto dominance of the planet. Rhodes was fairly certain he had heard of such large flightless raptors before, a carnivorous predator known as the terror bird, but it had been his assumption that such creatures had been extinct for tens of thousands of years, if not a million. To see a magnificent fossil of such antiquity living and breathing in front of him, literally right before his eyes, the exhilaration of such a significant occurrence was overwhelming and enthralling.

If sensing his quiet observation, the creature suddenly stood stock still, and he caught his breath, trying to will his racing heartbeat to slow as to avoid detection. He dimly remembered hearing somewhere that some predators could only detect movement in their ocular capacities, but he could not recall if that particular tidbit applied to present circumstances, or to some other branch of the animal kingdom. The monstrous bird of prey took a few ginger steps in his direction, and he decided to bring his pistol to bear on it just in case the abnormal beast was inclined to charge him, but he did so as slowly and quietly as he possibly could to avoid provoking that specific unwanted response. The freakish avian, seemingly unnoticing of his defensive posturing, made a few more of its unnatural booming croaks, and then ran off back into the darkened woods, its heavy footfalls diminishing as it moved further and further away. Rhodes let go a deep exhale, not realizing until then that he had been holding his breath in suspended thrall during the captivating moment, and then eased from his combative stance into a more relaxed pose. The creature was truly an unexpected marvel, and he was half tempted to wake his sleeping companion and share the stupendous experience with him. But then, remembering the reactions of the superstitious Indian man when he had merely mentioned the strange sounds before to him, made Rhodes think the better of such a decision and he decided to keep the incident to himself for now. After contemplating the nature of the mysterious beast a few more moments beneath the starlit skies, he decided the best course of action would be to return to his tent for now, and perhaps in the morning question the guide on anything further he know of the primeval birds, albeit in a roundabout fashion to dissuade any irrational actions from the other man.

The Dreadful Call

The next day dawned much as the day before, with the clouds hovering maliciously above their heads threatening rainfall at any given moment. As they broke camp he questioned Tey on whether anyone in his tribe had every seen the jaxsa jamach'i in the flesh before. Tey, his eyes narrowing at the mention of previously taboo topic between the two, studied the white man intently before replying.

"No one has every seen the jaxsa jamach'i and lived to tell of it, Professor Rhodes." He returned to the packing, seeming to be deliberately avoiding further discussion of the subject. Rhodes, thinking of the doomful words and change in his heretofore candid guide's demeanor, decided to leave the matter alone for now. While study of the bizarre creature could be rewarding in its own right, and might end up being a great academic find, he was an archaeologist at heart and the knowledge that he was so close to the focal point of his quest for the validation of his theories overshadowed any compunction he may have for instead attempting to track down the mythical animal. That, and the almost surety of losing his only guide in the unfamiliar mountains and forests due to his mistaken ignorance of local prohibitions and customs.

They finished the task at hand with little conversation, and continued on their course for the fabled temple. The trek was strenuous and difficult, more so than any of the hiking they had encountered thus far, and even with Rhodes's iron-willed determination to see the object of his search the progress they made was maddeningly slow and belabored, each step a struggle between man and nature. Even Tey was forced to backtrack constantly as time and time again they came to yet another dead end in the unexplored terrain, the scant sign of mankind's mark lost in possibly hundreds of years of overgrown vegetation, hiding its secrets from even his seasoned expertise and competence. At last late in the afternoon they came to crumbled wall, the remains of a once magnificent structure now destroyed and devoured by age, time, and the ever-encroaching jungle foliage. Rhodes called a stop to their trek, searching among the ruins for some kind of sign or record that the broken enclosure was part of the temple he sought so diligently, perhaps some sort of outer palisade or outlying checkpoint. Unfortunately any identifying marks or connections to a shared past between the shrine they sought and it had long since been erased and eradicated, if they had even existed at all, so they proceeded past the decayed stones further up the increasingly mountainous countryside.

Pushing on through tumultuous terrain and congested undergrowth, Tey was able to finally locate a substantial clue, a shattered road with its flagstones erupting from the uneven ground at jagged, rutted intervals, hoary plants spreading and shoving it apart in a chaotic fashion, slowly reclaiming the man-made contrivance for a return to nature's earthly possession. Following the disorderly thoroughfare as it wound up and around the richly verdurous mountainside, climbing higher and higher until it reached a broad, relatively flat section, massively forested at all sides with enormous cedars and other deciduous trees. As the overgrown route continued into the luxurious woods, they took a moment to stop for a rest and explore the immediate area. Rhodes found ancient stones and blocks scattered around either side of the roadway, perhaps used for permanent residences and administration purposes. The vine-covered ruins had fallen into disarray, but their significance to the expedition still undisputable. At last they found a faded runic symbol, the impression nearly washed away by the passage of time and nature's aggressive touch, but undeniably still imprinted on a fallen arch's keystone. Lightly brushing the debris and soil caked liberally on the mark, the professor gave a soft exclaim as he recognized its design, five small stars in a semicircle showing plainly up from the characters that remained. Under the stars seemed to have at one time bore more to the diminished pattern, but nothing discernible remained for identification of its source. However, the rudimentary hieroglyph's partial arrangement was well known to him, as the recurring motif from the surviving evidence featured in other civilizations that formed the basis to his theory, at least those in which the hated sign had not been obliterated by vengeful adversaries or destructive upheavals. This amazing mark provided the needed irrefutable evidence that the professor's thesis of unified worship was true. The staggering fact was that a matching icon between two cultures separated by not only by very distinctly different time periods but also the Atlantic ocean itself, a vast geographic barrier not known to have been crossed before the fifteenth century by any seafaring peoples except the Vikings, and even then only in the more northern waters near Greenland. After recording it in his notes, he called Tey over to share in his excitement over his discovery, who unfortunately did not share his enthusiasm at all, viewing the symbol with visible trepidation and discomfort. Seeing the negative reaction, Rhodes asked him the meaning of his surprising response.

"I do not like it, masi. It reminds me of stories my awicha used to tell us children when I was young, legends of bad people who kidnapped and murdered my tribe long ago. They would come in the night time, and take the people who had darkness in their hearts back to their mountain stronghold. She said they especially wanted the boys and girls that didn't obey their parents, and they would raise them up to be as evil as they were. I thought she was trying to scare us into being good, now I'm not so sure that's why she told us these things. She could have been warning us. This is a cursed place, Mr. Rhodes. We should not have come here." He turned and walked away, clearly still perturbed by the strange sign and in no further frame of mind to talk. His doomful mood however, did nothing to dissuade the doctor from eagerly advancing further up the demolished road into the heavily shrouded forest, gallivanting boldly over obstacles with a renewed second wind, scanning the terrain for further evidence that supported his theories and suppositions. Occasionally he would find another hieroglyph or symbol, some similar to one he found from before, others that even his abundant knowledge could not place. He would pull his log from his backpack and make a short description of the new mark, where its placement had occurred, and a small, quick illustration of it. Tey followed behind, dragging his feet after the professor in a seething, sullen fashion, but staying close enough to not be left alone in the gloomy woods. Even the llamas seemed to balk intermittently, strangely ill at ease under the canopied cedars. Eventually as the early evening progressed the shadows grew longer, and with the feeble light filtering down through the broad trees no longer providing enough illumination to reasonably see by, Rhodes decided to call a stop to their day's journey. However, upon informing Tey that they would make their camp right there in the forest, the Indian pathfinder vehemently protested against the action, and would not acquiesce to the professor's wishes otherwise. Finally Rhodes was required to agree with him to backtrack to a clearing they had seen set off a small ways from the roadway. Rhodes was not so small-minded to have tried to force the issue with him, knowing that while he found the guide's superstitious attitude tiresome and a general waste of their time, the fact of the matter was that without Tey's help he would be hopelessly lost in the Andes, with little chance of making it back to civilization let alone accomplishing his academic goal. He would just have to tolerate these primitive objections with as much courtesy and manners as he could fairly muster under the circumstances.

After making camp, they silently consumed their supper,

neither man in the mood for conversation with the other. Tey sat staring into the fire, absorbed in his morose thoughts while Rhodes contently wrote in his journal, expounding further on the day's events and his erstwhile findings. Looking to gain an early start on what he hoped would be a fruitful day of discovery as well as bone tired after the hard climbing and drained from the ceaseless activity, the professor wisely decided to turn in early. The night was hot and muggy despite the higher elevation they were at, and it interfered with the rest he so eagerly sought, causing him to toss and turn repeatedly, unable to get comfortable enough for sleep to come. When he finally succumbed to reverie the terrible nightmare came again to haunt his dreams, drawing him deep within its voracious clutch. He was once more in the dank and dismal hallways, trying to outdistance the unseen hunters who were chasing him ceaselessly while engulfing mire pulled doggedly at his boots. The raw terror coursed through his veins like ice water as he ran blindly down the dark corridors, and finally when the crushing blow came crashing behind him as before he had the foreshadowing knowledge it was going to happen, and that expectation somehow made it seem infinitely worse this time. Blissfully he awoke immediately as the staggering strike collided into him just like in the previous incarnation of the dream, and he lay drenched in a cold sweat that came more from the slowly ebbing fear caused by the horrifying vision rather than the humid climate trapped in his tent.

Inexplicably he noticed the hushed booming had returned, penetrating the thin walls of his enclosure. He dressed quickly to surveil the mysterious intruder a second time, but forswore his socks and shoes in his haste, hoping to ascertain why the strange terrible bird had such interest in their ongoing trek, to such lengths that it seemed to be incredibly stalking them through the miles of jungles and mountains. It had not attacked before, so it seemed that it was not interested in them for food, nor had it attempted to drive them off in a territorial dispute. It just appeared to be fascinated in them for some unaccountable reason, and Rhodes wondered the import of the puzzling nighttime serenade. He did, however, bring his pistol with him as well, not trusting that a wild animal would continue its strangely benevolent behavior with his life possibly at stake if he was wrong.

Opening the flap and stepping outside, he glanced to and fro about the unkempt clearing, sweeping the area thoroughly for his nocturnal visitor. It did not take long to spot the towering raptor, semi-hidden on the edge of the clearing, the dark plumage camouflaging with the thick bushes as the unmistakable shape of the bulging neck and long, swept beak silhouetted itself against the night sky. The brilliant stars gleamed with an ineffable light that provided much more detail than in his last experience, highlighting the immense crown and shades of color within the creature, and he could see now it had a strange sense of beauty to it he had not noticed before, a noble presence that was almost awing in its paramount existence. Looking at the magnificent animal it had a certain familiarity to him, and he was fairly certain that his surmise of it being the same creature from his previous encounter was correct. Even now he could see it was watching him as he watched it, the dark eyes like pools of pitch, reflecting pinpricks of the starry sky ever so often in their inky blackness. Opening its mouth, the thick mandibles separating wide apart slowly like a man would in a satisfying yawn, the glorious beast let loose one of its soft booms, almost if it was questioning him. His analytical mind wondered if this was perhaps their way of communicating, a basic language of sorts shared among the species, maybe even done by a series of long and short calls with different meanings in combination, like in birdsong used by its more common cousins of the air. The theory seemed sound, and he thought briefly of attempting to call back to the inquisitive raptor, but thought the better of it, knowing that with no reference to the rudimentary emanations he would be conveying gibberish at best, or at worst could provoke the animal with an unintentional faux pas.

The terror bird, ceasing its undulations for the moment, took a few tentative steps from the brush towards him, and he tensed unconsciously, the instinctual urge reacting uncontrollably to the possible threat. But then the sublime avian began its preternatural call again, this time bobbing its head up and down in a steady rhythm while fluttering its atrophied wings at its side, the powerful legs stamping the hard earth in place in a continuous beat. It almost looked like a prehistoric dance to Rhodes, similar to the savage gyrations performed by the primitive cave men and Neanderthals around their campfires in their arcane rituals of belief and ancient rites of worship. The booming noise increased in volume steadily as the creature pranced, and as it did one of the llamas, disturbed by the deep reverberations, drowsily raised its head to view the boisterous interference to its slumber. Spotting the savagely cavorting raptor in the midst of its riotous throes, the bewildered creature responded with its characteristic high-pitching braying, the shrieking cry splitting the night with its resounding uproar. The shrill clamor immediately caught the attention of the feral bird, who ceased its unfathomable dance and cocked a cold eye towards the strident noise maker, a split second before charging full bore directly at the hapless llama, its quickness surprising for such a large creature. Rhodes, shocked at first into frozen indecision by the llama's piercing bray and the deadly reaction by the frightening terror bird he had so recently witnessed, composed himself quickly and leapt into action upon seeing the rushing terror bird hurtling pell-mell towards his person as well as that of the unfortunate beast of burden. He raised his Colt in a rapid motion, firing several deafening shots in quick succession towards the appalling monstrosity as it charged heedlessly forward. Whether or not any of the bullets struck home was unknown to Rhodes, but the stampeding terror bird veered off from its cataclysmic course, darting instead back into the foliage of the abundant jungle greenery. Moments later Tey appeared, the ruckus of the blaring intrusion waking him with its raucous tumult. He was clad only in his drawstring pants and barefoot, but was brandishing the naked machete with lethal intention. He stared at the pistol in Rhodes's grasp, now lowered at his side instead of trained on a target.

"Masi, what has happened? What were you shooting at?"

Rhodes almost reflexively responded with the truth, but remembering the nervous apprehension of the native man to any mention of the creature his people had dubbed the jaxsa jamach'i, decided against telling him the real story of what had transpired seconds before his arrival. The anxious guide was already on the brink of mutiny, and if he discovered the actuality of events that had just occurred it may serve to push him over the precipice that his superstitious mind teetered on so precariously. Instead Rhodes decided to feign ignorance of the identity of his target, in order to placate the man's curiosity yet avoid any unwanted repercussions from the recent encounter.

"It was either a jaguar or some other big cat. Possibly even a bear," he answered smoothly. A little sincerity never hurts to convince another person of a lie, he thought darkly, then continued with more truthful words. "One of the llama were braying in distress, so I went outside to check on it. I saw something large charging towards it, and opened fire. Whatever it was it ran off into the woods, I don't know if I hit it or not, it was so dark and far away." He glanced away from his companion, sorry that he was compelled to take such dishonorable action, but turning back was relieved to see innocent acceptance of the lie in his compatriot's eyes. After Tey retrieved a lantern from their supplies, they proceeded to the spot where he indicated he had shot the enraged animal, and after careful scrutiny of the area, they found several splotches of dark, red blood glistening wetly on the crushed grass.

"You hit it masi!" the guide exclaimed jubilantly. "Just grazed it I think though, not too much blood here. It probably will survive, but good job Mr. Rhodes!" The Indian happily squatted down to examine the substantiation of the professor's true aim more closely, the light from his lantern reflecting wickedly off the damp gore as he lowered it. Rhodes happened to glance to his right with a passing look, and with alarm he spotted a long, chestnut feather lying innocently in the trampled grass, obviously fallen from the belated creature in its frantic exodus. He casually paced around Tey, pretending to examine the various flora for further clues before nonchalantly wandering over to the area of the incriminating evidence he wish to hide from the other man's view. Rhodes watched Tey circumspectly, trying to avoid having the tracker witness his secret concealment of the auburn plume, waiting until just the most choice moment to lightly place his right foot on top of the offending trace. Then he silently grinded the feather into the ground, mashing it into the earth thoroughly, hiding it from passing observation. As he waited for Tey to finish his investigation, he stared off into the unknown blackness of the jungle landscape, wondering again at the portent of the avian behemoth's curious behavior. What was the meaning of the relentless shadowing, the strange utterances, and now the bizarre dancing? Was he merely reading too much into the situation, seeing connections where there was none? Tey stood, his inspection of the blood-soaked ground finished.

"There could be tracks elsewhere, masi. Perhaps closer to the forest's edge." He began to walk away from the site of the professor's recent deception, and Rhodes gave an inward sigh of relief, his secret safe from the other man's purview for now. However, it would not do to have the dogged Indian find some other sign of the momentous bird waiting in the underbrush, and from what Rhodes had seen of his well-deserved reputation for tracking that was a very real possibility under the circumstances.

"Leave it be Tey. We have a full day tomorrow, and I doubt the beast will return tonight, no matter what it was, especially after being wounded by my shot. Let's return to camp and try to get some rest before tomorrow." He tried to make it sound as authoritarian as possible without seeming too tyrannical, and thankfully Tey acquiesced to his wishes with no complaints on the subject, agreeing it was an acceptable idea to abandon the search. Walking back together from the edges of the clearing, they said their good nights to each other and then returned to their tents. Slumber came quickly to Rhodes after their late night's activities, and his sleep this time was blissfully absent of any dreams or nightmares to haunt him.

The next day they were off to a fairly strong start in spite of the previous early hours' excitement, packing up the llamas quickly and retracing their steps into the cedar forest they had abandoned for the lower clearing the night before. The willful pack beasts still did not care for the gloomy interior of the tightly packed woods, and stubbornly resisted the men's progress, fighting them implacably the entire duration of the stringent climb farther into forest's shadowy depths. After much prodding and pulling, they were finally able to navigate the intractable beasts further up the devastated roadway past the tumbled down masonry of various plant-covered buildings and walls, making their way into sites of large, somewhat undisturbed sections of structure. Rhodes paused to inspect the ruins they encountered periodically along the way, and Tey took a more involved role in the search this time as well, calling over the professor whenever he spotted a particular piece of possible historical note, such as the occasional hieroglyph or artistic design that he deemed worthy of Rhodes's study. Rhodes found the change in the guide's demeanor refreshing, with the haunted expression that had been plaguing the man's features missing, and he seemed wholly devoted to the professor's cause just as he had been before the troubling incidents had occurred that separated the two men. He wondered if the transformation in attitude was a result of the preceding night's encounter.

They progressed through the devastated rubble at a leisurely pace, and after several miles of deliberate exploration through the vestiges of former civilization he realized that the area must have been an ancient city of considerable size, a veritable metropolis for its early time period. He secretly hoped that perhaps it had cropped up around the temple he so eagerly sought, a bygone testament to the mesmerizing influence and vast economic wealth the cabalistic religion had spawned in the region throughout the ages until its cryptic demise. Several smaller avenues were visibly connected to the giant roadway they traveled upon so laboriously, but Rhodes kept their focus confined to the remains of buildings and enclosures along its wide locality. He studied each new revelation they found carefully, trying to ascertain from the mystifying signs and runic texts if they were headed in the proper direction to find the enigmatic shrine.

Rounding a deep bend in the derelict thoroughfare, they were greeted by a momentous finding, that of a wide-ranging ring of tremendous monolithic statues, spaciously spread apart and facing inwards towards each other, seventeen in number. The roadway they had been following so diligently met four other thoroughfares here at an intersection, with the figures solemnly posing like sentries around the center. The virulent jungle creepers and ivy lay covering the effigies, clothing them in a green and white finery, but on Rhodes's insistence he and Tey removed the centuries of growth from the largest of the statues, revealing a miraculously well-preserved male form sitting down on a throne carved from a raw umber limestone. An arresting blemish on the figure's forehead caught Tey's eye as they cleared the head of debris and he rubbed the area deftly, and after the vigorous scrubbing he revealed a runic symbol carved deeply into the reddish stone. The crude hieroglyph was of five stars on top of a horizontal sword, the blade made to look dripping while the hilt curiously has open lips framing sharp, little teeth in the cross guard. It was a symbol that Rhodes knew all too well, one of the many hieroglyphs associated with the Celtic druids incantation stones and other ancient culture's mystical implements of worship, used by all of the linked peoples in lost, hideous rituals and pagan fertility rites, yet more evidence to support his unified worship theory. The ancient, carved face stared straight ahead unwaveringly into what would be its opposite's eyes, and while the sculpture conveyed an aloof, powerful countenance that some would consider attractive, Rhodes couldn't help but feel there was an onerous look to its chiseled features the longer he gazed at it, buffeting him in a feeling of malefic evil that emanated from its frozen expression in a continuous stream of uncanny watchfulness. Looking over Tey, he could see the Indian's expression of disgust and revulsion mirrored his own aversion to the statue's recoiling visage, and he for once concurred with the native's superstitious thoughts. He made some perfunctory remarks about a lack of interest in the sculpture, and walked away from the site of the uncomfortable aura. Tey gladly departed as well, and Rhodes couldn't help but notice the relief plainly spelling out over the pathfinder's taciturn features as they left the disagreeable figure's presence. Though he would be loathe to admit it even the professor himself was eager to be leaving the cursed artwork for other, hopefully more benign, relics from the past.

Lacking the interest to uncover the other, less imposing sculptures after their recent shared experience they opted to continue down the largest of the roads, which rose gradually further up the mountainside, the flagstones buckled and collapsed from possible seismic disturbances in the past. Rhodes presumed that the storied temple would be at the greatest height of the formerly grand city, most likely the focal point of the entire metropolis, a beacon for the devout as well as a constant reminder of the power and influence of the unhallowed priesthood to the populous. Here they saw more signs of decoration and pomp than ever before, with the ruins of fountains, artificial ponds, and stonework for gardens intermixed with single walls bearing the remains of mighty frescoes and highly skilled engravings. The archaic pictographs were too badly damaged from time, weather, and other forces of nature to ascertain what the depictions had been, but their very existence was almost proof enough of the importance of the prodigious roadway. This boded well for the professor's theory that they had chosen the proper path to the sanctum, and he found himself constantly scanning the side of the mountain at their forefront, hoping to spot the fabled foundations of his journey's focus. As they traversed the jagged route however, he began to feel the disquieting notion of being watched, by whom or what he was unsure, having no evidence to support the groundless suspicion but the nagging notion doggedly remained stuck in his mind. He looked over at Tey to see if he noticed anything amiss, but the tracker seemed blissfully unaware of the hidden watcher's presence. Convinced he was imagining the entire affair, Rhodes tried to put the apprehensive feeling from his awareness, and tried to concentrate instead on the artworks and carvings as they climbed. But just barely out of his peripheral vision he would see a flicker of movement or slight change of shadow, and the doubtful belief would return in spite of his insistence that it was a natural occurrence, caused by the wind or his nerves.

Tey excitedly called out to Rhodes, informing him of his latest discovery, thankfully disrupting the professor's worried thoughts. He had located a pictograph of some note, and when the professor joined him he was pleased to see the art was not as savaged by the elements as the others they had passed earlier on the climb, and still had most of its design thankfully intact. The scene was of a great battle, with crude figures maiming and killing one another with abandon, some normal-sized and others giants in comparison, clad in armor, casting spears and hewing at each with swords. The bloody field they fought on was obviously an island, etched with a rough, uneven outline complete with bays and inlets, with the easily recognizable shapes of crashing waves surrounding the land here and there. The irregular coast had several long boats with square sails anchored along its edge, and some of the attackers issued forth from their confines, weapons held at high, ready for battle. Further inland broad hills, small lakes, and gushing rivers along with patches of green forest became the norm, and intermixed between were concentrations of rudimentary buildings and simple walled fortifications, all defended by miniature men wielding spears. Curiously there were farms and animal pens in abundance as well, with one such steading enclosing a gigantic brown cow, who was seemingly the luckless target of plundering by axe-wielding raiders. It was strange, but the armored characters and scene of the encompassing island warfare did not seem to fit with what he knew of any local history, or even that of the South American continent. Trying to take in the picture as a whole, Rhodes noticed one powerful giant figure seemed more predominantly featured than the rest, with an almost handsome, proud profile and arrayed in splendor, rallying a sizable band of warriors in a desperate attack on one of the beleaguered fortifications. His facial expression seemed eerily familiar as well as his outstretched sword, and looking closely at the blade Rhodes could see the strange mouth and teeth motif emblazoned on the hilt as the colossus held it aloft. He was fairly certain this was the same personage as the hideous statue they had found earlier depicted, and the longer he stared at the minute representation the more he was put at unease again, the same feelings of baneful scrutiny pouring forth from its cruel aspect, crashing into him like tidal waves. Turning away from the unsettling scene, he mumbled some terse words to the effect of needing to keep moving, and the professor was grateful that Tey did not question his worrisome judgment in the situation, or see the puzzled expression from the growing mystique they had delved upon so plainly evident on his face.

They passed more of the destroyed murals and dilapidated finery as the day progressed languorously into late afternoon, and Rhodes began to wonder just how large the ancient city was in scope. The sloped thoroughfare seemed to go on and on, winding through the mountainside, linking peaks together with its coiling embrace. Looking down into the valleys below him off the edge of the road to his right, he could see signs of devastated man-made creations spread throughout the area, but inspecting the high side of the mountain to his left he could detect no signs of habitation at all. Perhaps this was a high road of sorts, one only used for the processions of the priests and their inscrutable purposes. The idea had some merit, and while he pondered the thought he casually glanced at Tey leading the way ahead of them. The guide had stopped his rapid pace and was standing stock still, staring farther down the roadway. Rhodes followed his intense gaze and immediately froze himself, the object of their shared scrutiny overwhelming both of them with its awe and importance.

There, at the end of the twisting path they had followed for so long, was the enigmatic temple they had sought so eagerly. The sun's golden rays illuminated a massive grey structure, fallen down in some places and in foul disrepute from centuries of neglect, but to Rhodes it was just as beautiful as the Taj Mahal or as majestic as the Vatican. Thick, voluminous bushes and tall, leafy trees grew around the derelict temple, pushing at the ample walls and encroaching on the cavernous roof in places, creating countless crevices where jungle denizens no doubt called home now that man's past dominance had disappeared. Here and there, however former signs of majesty could still be seen, ornate etchings and numerous sculptures peaking through the debris and overgrowth. A band of running scroll-work ran along the top of the walls near the edge of rooftop. Although it was cracked and broken from the passing years, it still showed the consummate skill that only a race of master craftsmen could have possessed. However, the true signal that this was indeed the cryptic shrine they had quested for was found blatantly out in the open for all to see, untarnished and seemingly untouched by the ravages of time. There at the apex of temple front facing was a large overhang with the massive sword hieroglyph and a bas-relief of a figure all to familiar to him from their previous discoveries and his laborious studies, the visage of the cruel warrior giant from the murals and frescoes, triumphantly made to stare down coldly at all who climbed the immense steps to gain access to the inner sanctum. Seeing the immense gargantuan now in this context, the professor was willing to make a small leap of logical thought, that the frequently pictured titan was the very god the ancient worshipers had been praying and worshiping to so very long ago, and that this temple was indeed his shrine.

Rhodes walked slowly towards the gigantic stone edifice, brushing past Tey in a fog of academic wonder. The exuberant

Indian was congratulating him, but he barely heard the words, so lost he was in his awestruck veneration and amazement on finally seeing the pinnacle of his lengthy quest. Only when the tracker lightly seized his shoulder did he break from his reverie, and fully listen to what the man had to say.

"You did it, masi, you found it," Tey exclaimed. Rhodes protested the praise, insisting that it was both of them that had discovered the fabled shrine, but Tey refused any such accolades or praise, unwilling to usurp the professor's moment of glory. "No, Mr. Rhodes, this is your temple. No one would have ever found such a thing without your yatxatawi, but we need to be watchful now, no time to be careless or sloppy. You never know what kind of animal is using such places like this for its uta. I've seen jukumari as well as asirus use old buildings like this as caves to live in. I had a cousin who died in a Spanish pukara because he thought it was safe and nothing lived in it. He was wrong. This whole place looks very unstable as well and could fall on top of us at any time. We have several hours before the sun sets, let us set up camp and water the llamas, then we can explore your temple, but we do it right. We still have several days of supplies left, we have all time we need now."

Rhodes agreed to his suggestion, for while he did not understand every word of the man's bewildering mixture of Aymara and English his intent was clear, and he knew that the advice coming from the experienced tracker was as firm as the ground they stood upon. He was truly grateful for the man's help, knowing that without the guide's expertise he could never have gotten this far in such a formidable expedition. The sudden change in Tey's attitude from pessimistic unhappiness to encouraging cooperation had been an unexpected boon, and the professor considered the drastic metamorphosis a favor of the utmost contribution to his cause. It was not a gift he was inclined to squander needlessly due to either his impatience for exploring or a selfish need to control the situation. So in spite of his fervor for examination he helped Tey secure the still reluctant animals, who queerly rebelled at the restraints placed on them before settling down almost resignedly to their fate. They set up their temporary lodgings for the next few days hurriedly before arming themselves with the gear necessary for delving into the uncharted shrine, bringing rope, tools, weapons, and their canteens. Walking down the road towards the temple, Rhodes was again struck by the sheer enormity of the monstrous bulk that comprised the obscure building. The size was truly momentous, on par with the Theatre of Marcellus of Caesarean Rome or the Sanchi Stupa of storied India past, a true marvel of ancient architectural genius. As they climbed the cracked and scarred steps, the stony eyes of the haughty giant watched them with an eerie malevolence that belied its nonliving form, and Rhodes felt once again the pulses of strange alertness directed at his person. He dismissed the unwanted feeling once again as his imagination. Once they were out of the giant's sight line beneath the overhang it was as if the event had never happened, like a fragment from a forgotten dream rather than an incident in the flesh and blood world of reality.

The portico was as long as the entire front of the building, with the colonnade supporting its roof rising with gigantic pillars, the bases subtly wider at the bottom than at the tops. The inner walls were adorned with hieroglyphs encompassing nearly every scrap of available space on their textured surfaces, masterfully worked with such precision and deepness that the drawings were still amazingly preserved in spite of the years of neglect. The ornate structure itself was made from huge slabs of limestone, long darkened from their original whitish color to the dingy grey that they now saw before them. Rhodes studied the masses of antiquated writing as Tey fastidiously checked the structural integrity of the entrance and its accompanying accoutrements, looking for any sign of imminent danger from the decaying materials of their time-worn construction.

The glyphs were artistically done in striking horizontal rows, with solid black borders separating the differentiating lines of prehistoric text. Trying to piece together what commonality the incomprehensible script before him shared with the various picture writing languages known throughout history, Rhodes drew upon his substantial knowledge of bygone characters from his extended studies into the esoteric subject. He knew that most hieroglyphs consist of three parts, firstly the representation of the subject or action displayed, secondly the pronunciation of a syllable, and thirdly clarification for subsequent glyphs. True translation was an extremely long and laborious process however, requiring years of aggressive study and dedication, and he had no illusions that he could miraculously decipher the riddle of the hieroglyphs' meaning with a few scant moments of cursory examination. What he was looking for in the unintelligible scripts was not the interpretation but rather which symbols that shared a prevalent occurrence between themselves and the runes and pictographs corresponding to his unified theory of worship. He found several instances of exactly the sort of imagery he sought hidden in the lines of pictorial text, and while the reference was unknown, the symbolism itself was not. Here was a sign he knew to be associated with ancient Egyptian burial rituals; here another that the early Harappan people of Bronze Age India used in their indecipherable inscriptions on faience amulets; and yet another that was an exact match to marks chiseled onto the massive Celtic stones found in glades known to be utilized in the past for rituals involving barbaric human sacrifice.

A lifetime's worth of noteworthy analysis and research could be constructed from the overwhelming display of illustrated characters, but looking behind him at the quickly descending sun Rhodes knew he did not have the time to lavish on the massive frontage if he was to explore the undetermined interior of the towering building. He rejoined Tey, who was finishing his inspection of the condition of the elephantine entrance, which consisted of enormous double portals made of a tarnished bronzed metal, warped and discolored from the rampant buildup of oxidation, time, and disuse. Here too were fanciful embellishments, but instead of the continual writing displayed on the walls there was a relatively simple pattern, that of the sword emblem they had seen repeated earlier, imprinted carefully on each titanic door. The tracker reported that the entry to the temple was tightly shut, but did not appear to have any sort of locking mechanism to impede their progress. It took both men's efforts, shoving and prying the stubborn doorway open, to force the doors apart. It revealed an interior too dark to see properly within except for the crack of light coming from the evening sun their endeavors had created. Cold air with a stale and fetid smell wafted through the small opening, its concentrated presence so dense and vile it seemed that it should have a visible or physical form to behold. Choking back the urge to retch from the nauseating stench, they wrenched the obstinate opening further apart to admit entry, metallic screams of protest issuing from the strained materials, unaccustomed to such use in recent times. The two men shrank back from the uncovered interior, letting the repugnant odor from within dissipate into the air outside before they continued inside to its shadowy depths.

The widely open doors had revealed a spacious antechamber, rectangular in shape with another set of double doors directly opposite the ones they had previously passed through, and sets of hefty stone benches set up alongside both of the longer walls, running the entire length of the span. This seemed to be a sort of waiting chamber, and Rhodes would have passed it by without further notice, had he not seen gigantic murals set above the rock seats, so heavily layered with dust and grime that it almost camouflaged the megalithic artworks from casual notice, one of the compositions on each wall. Stepping near one of the gigantic portraits with Tey close by for support, he tested one of the stone wrought benches vigorously before standing atop of it. Upon closer inspection he could see that the painting was a relief as well, the border of the piece as well as details carved into the walls creating a three dimensional pattern. He removed two of his large brushes from his knapsack, handing one to Tey and keeping the other for himself while instructing the other man on his intent, and then both of them began lightly brushing the dirt from the ancient slab. The dusty filth, while abundantly prevalent on the surface, was not hardened from moisture or mold fortunately, and came off easily at their hurried yet careful ministrations.

When they were done the picture revealed a scene of the cruel titan, this time shown sleeping in an iron wrought high backed throne to the right side of painting, while an oval portal of sorts stood on the left side. Small human figures bowed in supplication on the other side of the threshold, some chanting litanies and others prostrated themselves before the dreaming god. The figures on the far side seemed pale and shimmering, as though he was looking at them through water or another liquid. The gateway itself was ringed in an elaborate obsidian frame, almost giving the impression of a portrait within a portrait. Despite the worshipful activity, the intricate appearance of the ornate chassis seemed to Rhodes that when he took in the portal as a whole that he could not liken it to anything other than that of a mirror, like one of the large formal ones displayed in certain parlors of Victorian homes. The art's format itself was of unusual and extraordinary quality, with the different pigments used artfully to good purpose as well as the layered technique carved into the stone face creating a fascinating light and shadow effect, skill far beyond what he considered normal for the rudimentary time period. He and Tey cleared off the next artwork, this one displaying a massive feast, with both young and old natives united in hearty fellowship, drinking and eating contently while engaged in laughter and conversation. The scene was shown in a clearing, with the ominous temple standing like an unyielding observer in the background, stern witness to the celebration and camaraderie. Wooden tables were piled high with various tubers, beans, and corn as well as different kinds of meat, some blackened from roasting, others a pale, whitish color perhaps from boiling. Taken altogether, this seemed to be a holiday feast, one the entire community would take part in, a thanksgiving or remembrance meal.

Turning to the third in the series, they finished the cleaning quickly, unveiling a picturesque panorama of what was most obviously the construction of the very temple they now stood in. The subject matter was interesting enough, a normal scene of ancient fabrication and erection along with its various labors, but two observations in the antiquated picture quickly caught the professor's attention, causing him to momentarily start with their surprising appearance in the scene. One such portrayal was yet again the recurrence of the fair-featured giant, this time overseeing the construction of the temple with his merciless aloofness as the workers went about their back-breaking tasks. While still eerily disturbing in its own right, the reappearance of the giant was not altogether unexpected to Rhodes, who was beginning to harbor a very unexplainable and unscientific deep resentment to the figure in question. The other bewildering instance in the portrait was infinitely much more provoking to him, that of seeing several of the terror birds helping the native workers in their tasks, being used as beasts of burden. This was the more shocking of the revelations to him, and while he was not altogether pleased at seeing the incongruent avians, knowing their unwelcome effect on his superstitious helper, the excitement of seeing that the animals were not just an evolutionary throwback peculiarly still living in the area but were used in the everyday life by the very aboriginal people he was investigating was of extreme scientific fascination to him. The scenes seemed to be telling a linked story, and he was certain that he was viewing the artwork out of sync. It seemed that logically the crafting of the enormous edifice had came before the communal feasting, whereas which segment of the timeline the sleeping giant featured in he was not certain, with no point of reference to facilitate its joining to the others.

Stealing a furtive glance at his generally indomitable companion, he saw to his dismay that the artful representations of the beast the tracker had called "jaxsa jamach'i" had not gone unnoticed by the guide. While the guide's thinly concealed reaction may fool another man, Rhodes had spent too much time with Tey to not know the source of the emotion he could see written plainly on the other man's face, and that source was fear, plain and simple. He went to steer their exploration in a different direction, hoping to avoid another outbreak of hysteria from the man's groundless panic concerning the antediluvian artwork, but a shrill, undulating scream shattered the still air, followed by more shrieks and high-pitched braying.

"The llamas!" Tey bolted for the entrance, and a split second later Rhodes was hot on his heels, both men rushing pell-mell towards the horrifying cries of pain. Tey jumped the stairs lightly, bounding from step to step with an effortless grace while Rhodes scrabbled down with grueling uncertainty, trying to keep pace with the younger man while still being as careful with his footing as he possibly could be. Tey jumped off the last of the stairs in a gigantic, flying leap, and then drawing his machete in a fluid motion, he raced towards the still screaming llamas in a dead run. The tracker rounded the curve swiftly, and soon disappeared from Rhodes's view, leaving the professor to frantically try and catch up to him. He followed as best he could, noticing an ominous silence that was more sinister in the finality of its hush than the bloodcurdling shrieking had been before in their ear-splitting clamor.

Exerted and breathing heavily, he eventually reached the site of their camp, seeing Tey crouched behind a low, partially collapsed wall as he arrived. Catching sight of the professor as well, the guide motioned him down, and Rhodes followed his silent signal, dropping down and clambering close beside him at the rear of the ruins. Tey brought a single finger up to his lips, the universal sign for silence, and then brought up his hand, pointing over the wall. Rhodes raised his head barely above the stone structure, just enough to see what lay over the other side. There he beheld a disturbing and terrible sight, that of a formidable pack of six terror birds, savagely ripping and devouring chunks of llama flesh with primeval brutality and satisfaction. The men had left them tied up, not wanting the animals to wander off in the unfamiliar territory, and in being so restrained as the poor creatures had been they had stood no chance whatsoever to escape their grim fate. One of the beleaguered animals was barely alive, bleeding profusely from dozens of wounds, but still its tattered chest was rising and falling strenuously with death-defying will. The injured llama opened its wearied eyes for a brief moment, its orbs rolling around wildly in half-crazed pain and anguish before centering directly on Rhodes. He fancied that it had an almost human expression of betrayal on its features, as if it was blaming the man for the dolorous atrocities it had been made to endure so unreasonably. Then the ravenous birds closed in on it, gouging more angry red furrows into its already lacerated hide and tearing out strips of abused muscle, turning them into snippets of delicacy until they mercifully ended what little life remained in the dying creature.

There was nothing more the two men could do for the expired animals, and now their very lives were in a very striking and real danger by their close proximity to the prehistoric killers. Rhodes had his pistol, and Tey his machete; however an open conflict between themselves and the abhorrent monsters seemed foolhardy, especially with six of the foul beasts present currently and an undetermined number perhaps nearby. Modern day animals may have learned respect for mankind and his accompanying weapons of destruction, but these relics from a bygone age had surely never known that innate fear of firearms so bitterly learned by their kin. Their only recourse would be to retire back to the temple, at least there with its thick, solid walls and defensible entrance they could make a stand or wait out the terrifying creatures. Knowing that any stray sound could mean the end of them, he quickly gestured to Tey his intent, and the native man nodded his head in assent, evidently already arriving at the same conclusion Rhodes had come to recently. They began to back away from the ruined wall, staying crouched and trying carefully to avoid making any excess noise as they retreated. The sounds of the bird's nauseating feast provided cover for their escape, the disgusting sounds of shredding and swallowing filling the air with their clamorous activity. As their slow but steady progress put more and more distance between themselves and the avian menace, a stray dry branch, unnoticed by the professor in his limited pathfinder skills, snapped under his weight with a resounding crack, causing him to instinctively wince from its implied doom. The men froze, as an uncertain stillness came from the other side of the wall. The look of horror on the tracker's face matched his own sickening feeling in his stomach, and for though he wanted to believe that the sound had been lost in the terror bird's frantic commotion earlier, he knew it could not be true, however much he wanted it to be. Then a raptorial head loomed above the broken wall, eyeing them with bestial menace, and that was enough to goad the guide into spurious action.

"Run, masi, run!" Tey cried out, taking his own advice as well, bolting back in the direction of the temple. Rhodes had needed no such exhortations to action however, as his feet already springing into action almost of their own volition with his haste to flee the dangerous area. Though the Indian was younger and faster, and had already proven to be the superior runner of the two, this time the raw, undiluted fear of the predators' merciless attacks he had just witnessed was enough for the professor to keep pace with his junior partner. Whether real or imagined he could hear a shuddering pounding behind him as he raced, like a multitude of great footfalls, and he ran like he had never ran before, never bothering to look back even once behind him to see whether the horrifying creatures were gaining on them or had even bothered to follow them. Only when they had reached the top of massive stairs did he dare to give a brief glance back in the direction they had came, and that one look was enough for him to redouble his efforts to gain the safety of the temple's thick walls. The grotesque pack of terror birds, while still a good twenty feet away from the crumbling steps, were closing with malicious intent on acquiring prey of the two-legged variety. The two men bolted past the ancient entrance, and each man quickly positioned himself behind one of the tarnished metal doors, shoving with all of their might to close the aperture. With screeches of protest the gates closed slowly, firmly sealing the egress, and then they braced themselves against the doors for the assault they knew assuredly would come.

Scant seconds later it manifested alarmingly, the monstrous birds colliding off the doors with such force that they would briefly open a few inches inward in spite of the men vigorously reinforcing them, both Tey and Rhodes striving desperately to have them back in place before the start of the next attack. While the strikes were mercifully over in just a few moments after they had first started, to the men valiantly holding the doors it seemed an eternity, as with each powerful impact they could feel the warped framework shuddering under the pounding pressure, and Rhodes wondered if the archaic structure could hold out against such naked aggression. Fortunately for them it did, and after a few more resounding bangs and bashes, less frenzied than before but nonetheless equally terrifying, the animals seemed to give up on their futile onslaught.

They waited a few fear-stricken moments longer, before

softly conferring in hushed tones on their next plan of action. Needing light to accomplish their tasks, Tey held the bronze doors closed forcibly, as Rhodes retrieved his flashlight from his backpack and switched it on, the cold illumination making eerie elongated shadows dance as it played over the sparse furnishings as he shined it about the room. Placing the torch towards the ceiling to allow free use of his hands, he fetched one of the heavy stone benches, bracing it against the doorway. They built a makeshift barricade with more of the primitive seating, making sure the entryway was secure against further depredations by the hostile creatures before wearily resting on the cold stone floor.

"Never did I think I would be unfortunate enough to see the jaxsa jamach'i in this lifetime, masi, let alone be forced to run from a pack of them," Tey said wryly. "We are in big trouble Mr. Rhodes. They have killed our llamas and have cornered us in this place. This may be our amaya." Rhodes was unfamiliar with the native word, and while in most instances he could decipher the tracker's meaning from the context the man used, this time he was ignorant of the translation, compelling him to ask the man what the strange word meant.

"Grave, Mr. Rhodes. It means grave," the tired guide wearily informed him and then lapsed into a broody silence, keeping his dark thoughts to himself. Rhodes had no wish for further communication as well, and instead chose to examine the rock paintings they had abandoned earlier. He had noticed unsynchronized character to the art earlier before the disturbance, and now with more time he was fairly certain he understood the order to the images, believing they ran in a cardinal direction pattern, with north being the painting they had yet to uncover, east being the construction of the temple with the now hated jaxsa jamach'i, south being the generous banquet attended by the devout worshipers, and in the west was the dreaming god in his iron throne. Rhodes, his curiosity peaked now, retrieved one of the brushes from the cold stone floor, and set himself upon the task of clearing the final picture. Tey stayed silently sedentary during the professor's work, evidently choosing not to help the other man in his inquisitive endeavor, glumly staring at the barricaded entrance instead. Finishing his hurried cleaning of the mysterious artwork, he stood back to admire his handiwork and discover the prequel picture's substance.

It was plain to see that the elaborate scene had a similar style to all the other paintings in the antechamber, and Rhodes surmised that all four had been created by the same skilled craftsman. The subject matter itself was particularly fascinating, that of the haughty giant god meeting Indians on the pure white sands of a coastal seashore. The look on the natives' upturned faces was of awe and worship, with some figures in various acts of veneration, either carrying gifts, singing praises, or kneeling down in servitude, while their leader prostrated himself before the massive deity. A tremendous darkened ship could be seen in the background, scaled accordingly with the giant, with square black sails and serpentine, raised sides, coiling around the gigantic hull like a sleeping asp nestled around a pillar. It conformed to no such vessel he had ever heard of, and was well beyond what he knew of the technical knowledge of the time period. Issuing forth from the colossal transport were smaller boats equipped with rowing oars for conveyance. They were carrying what he presumed was the giant's retinue, a small, dark-haired race with Caucasian features, some in armor similar to what he had seen on the fresco Tey had found on their ascent. Comparing the two distinctly different art styles now, he was unsure which of the two was older, for while the scenes in the temple showed much greater skill to his puerile perspective, logic dictated that they would have occurred before the colorful mosaic pictures lining the temple's thoroughfare. It was his view that generally art ran in similar veins to technological advancement, that is that the more detailed creations should be younger in chronological age to the older, more unsophisticated works of art, but that seemed counter-intuitive to what he saw before him. Perhaps, he mused, the talented artist of the temple was a veritable virtuoso, a prehistoric Rembrandt or Michelangelo of his day.

"Masi, we must decide what to do." Tey interrupted his conceptual deliberations, bringing the grim matter of their menacing predicament back to the forefront of his mental focus. They discussed the situation and their limited options, along with the ramifications and repercussions of each scenario presented. Leaving the safety of the titanic shrine seemed out of the question, with both men agreeing that with the unknown number of antagonists and their meager armament available that fanciful cowboy antics of attack would only end in their injury and almost certain death. Having fired three shots at the rampaging terror bird during the previous night he had but four bullets left in his Colt, and he cursed his lackadaisical thoughtlessness in not reloading the weapon from his paltry store before setting out earlier this morning. There was the fact that the creature had not fallen to his assault as well, and the thought of close combat with the evolutionary refined predators did not hold much appeal with either man. Rhodes broached the subject of further exploration into the temple's depths, and while Tey was not enamored of the idea, the crucial point that they did not have many options available to them was not lost on the tracker. They agreed that a slow and cautious search of the temple's confines could avail them of the solution to their dilemma they so desperately needed, that there could perhaps be an alternate egress hidden somewhere within the building, only waiting to be discovered.

The crumbling interior doors had fared much worse in the centuries' passage than the outer set had, being made from a wood that may have been inlaid cedar at one time but now was only a decayed, dilapidated remnant of its former glory. The withered entrance parted easily at Rhodes's touch, well nigh disintegrating upon his contact with the process of opening of it. The spoiled, foul odor that they had noticed earlier reemerged vengefully with the unsealing of the doorway, and was even more potent this time around, causing them to return to the vestibule, retching and gagging. The two men hurriedly cut swatches of material from a disused cloth Rhodes retrieved from his pack, and managed to create makeshift bandannas to protect their noses and mouths from the offending vapors. Satisfactorily refurnished, they were able to return to the secondary chamber, the improvised masks bringing the unendurable stench to a more tolerable level.

The room in question was itself enormous in scope, the majority of the voluminous space open with only dust-covered decorations breaking up the smooth monotony on the walls and floor. Diffused light streamed in from skylights cut high above in the roof, and after considering the nature of their construction he realized that the fixtures were made from some sort of translucent crystal, thick enough to prevent shattering but thin enough to allow light to pass through, albeit at a much reduced effect. The illumination added a ghostly parlor to everything it spread upon, adding an almost ethereal look to all the meager contents of the room. Rhodes looked over at Tey to see its reaction on organic matter, and was appalled by the cadaver-like cast to the tanned man's face, causing him to quickly look away from the disturbing visage and resume his examination. A striking auburn-colored dais rose majestically upwards at the opposite end of where they stood, with a forbidding black stone nearly twelve feet tall standing alone atop of the platform. After surveying the gigantic chamber and its contents from his vantage point near the entrance it was Rhodes's hypothesis that its apparent purpose was that of devotion and worship, and in all likelihood that this was the very location where the faithful congregated together for their unwholesome debaucheries and black rituals in ages past. There were no benches or seating of any kind on the terrace or around it, and given that depictions of prostrate followers numerously appeared in the scenes he had viewed earlier throughout the temple's displays, he imagined that in distant times waves of thronged worshipers filled the cavernous hall in droves, humbly paying homage to their dark god by bowing in supplication on their hands and knees.

Tey skirted the outside perimeter of the dark sanctuary, checking for exits in the empty room as he went. His archaeological interest piqued, Rhodes moved towards the dais, wanting to study the solitary stone more closely. The trip took more than a little time even with his less than leisurely pace, and he estimated the room must be at least three hundred feet in length.

Arriving at the steps finally, he realized that there was much more to the rising structure than he had first surmised. There was a round semi-circular pool at the base, with a deep channel leading from it up to the top of the dais. The pool itself was a perfect half sphere inlaid into the floor, and while it was empty from disuse and the lengthy time that had passed, its surface was still heavily stained at its bottom and throughout the nourishing channel, in the way that fluids would have naturally made by cascading from up above and then collecting at the lowest point within. Rhodes climbed up the steps alongside the carved passage, reaching the top of the peculiar edifice. The cloying odor that had plagued him earlier was at its strongest here, its pungent smell cutting through his meager facial covering. A section had been hollowed out directly above the carved pathway, roughly oval and vaguely man-shaped, with the crescent-shaped front sharpened to razor thinness along its edge. This too was equally stained with the darkened ichors. After inspecting the curious timeworn construction his eyes widened in shocked comprehension, as he suddenly realized exactly what kind of horrific liquid had flowed through the dais's channels in centuries past. He shuddered to think about what kind of diabolic sacrifices had been perpetrated by uncaring priests of the reticent order in this very spot, and just how many of their pitiful victims had been slaughtered in its horrid confines as well.

Turning his attention from the disturbingly stained pool for now, he studied the large rock looming foreboding above the sacrificial altar, which reminded him greatly in size and presence of the unexplainable boulders of Stonehenge with its tall, elongated shape and general impressive structure. The block's composition seemed to be made of sarsen, a type of sandstone that could only be found in England, mostly on the Salisbury plains and in the Marlborough Downs. He could see now that he was closer that the monolithic menhir had a multitude of runic symbols carved into its rough surface, wrapping around the stone in a myriad of onerous shapes and figures. The ancient writing's origin was known to him very well, as he recognized the strange hieroglyphs from his travels in Ireland and northern France, that of the prehistoric Celtic glyphs carved by the druids into their unhallowed places of mystic veneration. How the metaphysical signs from a wholly different continent's religious sect could be inscribed in such detail in a rock that was not known be native to the New World was a monumental mystery that would bore serious investigation in the future, he thought to himself with unabashed delight over the prospect. Returning to his observation, he noticed that one sign was visibly larger than the rest, and had been placed in the most prominent position on the black rock, directly facing outwards in the direction of the sacrilegious altar. The representation was ominously again the five stars on top of the horizontal animated sword, the nefarious emblem that represented the lord of the temple he had walked into so readily, the callous giant god. He reached out and touched the enigmatic mark, feeling an uncanny coldness radiating its defined features, and a wave of nausea and revulsion washed over him as he held contact. The whole of the dais he stood on seemed removed from time itself, as if the perpetrators of the villainous rituals could return through the massive double doors at any moment and begin their deadly offerings anew, slaughtering innocents in the unknown name of their cruel god. So great was Rhodes's contemplation on this distracting daydream that when Tey called out to him excitedly with news of alternate exits, he was startled to hear the other man's voice, the unexpected action forcibly calling him back to their present state of affairs.

"There are two ways out of here, Mr. Rhodes," the guide happily reported back to him. "Hopefully we may find a rear entrance up ahead, one that the jaxsa jamach'i do not know about, somewhere that will lead us away from this cursed place."

Rhodes assented, knowing while he was anxious to explore the monstrous temple and discover all the scientific curiosities it offered within its shadowy depths, the hostile quandary they had found themselves in brooked no time for such dalliances. Surviving the unexpected ferocious assault from the predatory avians was of the utmost importance now, for while he had unearthed the very evidence he had sought, the somber thought of not being able to return to civilization to laud his empirical find seemed almost a worse fate to him than the horrific one the birds seemed to have in store for him. After the two men made their way back to society he could return later on a more organized, well-funded expedition, complete with a contingent of armed mercenaries for protection, and whatever threat the prehistoric birds posed would be swiftly dealt with by man's superior technology and cunning.

Tey was standing beside the remains of a shattered doorway, waiting for the other man's attendance before further continuing his delving into the temple's depths. The door itself lay fallen inside the accompanying room, and both the frame and the visible front of the broad entryway had marks of violence, long scratches and torn, broken mounts bearing witness to the savagery of long ago. The room was dark, the light of the sanctum barely revealing the first few steps within. Turning his electric light on again, the two men were horrified to see a desiccated corpse lying outstretched on the red limestone floor, fortunately face down so they could not see its visage, but nonetheless bloodcurdling by its very existence. Peering closer at the mummified cadaver, a large, fracturing wound was plain to see on the back of the skull, as if struck by a heavy, sharp implement with considerable force. Nor was that the only sign of trauma, with the shoulder and spine showing the same cataclysmic damage in several areas, and its overall body position was in such way the hapless recipient seemed to have been trying to escape its woeful fortune in a vain effort of crawling away from its tormentor, before the final, almost merciful blow had came to end its agonizing suffering. The figure was wearing the vestiges of an antiquated costume that seemed reticent of the Mayan and Aztec temple priests, with a long skirt and headdress made of what he hoped was animal bone, even though in his heart he knew it to be made from something much closer on the evolutionary chain. Tey moved nearer to the inert form, studying the body for his own inscrutable purposes while Rhodes appraised the other contents of the enclosed space, leaving his light on a nearby bench to provide illumination for the two of them.

The dust covered room itself, while still of an impressive

size was nowhere near the ostentatious magnitude of the previous chamber, and as Rhodes wandered around his surroundings it soon became apparent that the site was a staging
area for the priests and their entourage so they could prepare
themselves before performing the exaltations and rites necessary to their faith. Large wooden wardrobes, in some places
rotted and barely standing, while in other sections hardened
to a brittle shell that cracked and splintered at the slightest
touch, contained within their enclosures amazingly preserved
garments and accouterments, in a variety of styles and designs. Rhodes wondered idly if the different garbs would be
used in various ceremonies and festivals, with each celebration requiring its own customary attire. The room also
boasted several large tables that held strange implements of
unknown designs as well as various weaved baskets containing now dried or decomposed residue, the open air having destroyed the majority of the materials. On another rounded
work surface several lidded clay jars were lined up in an ascending order, and after a spurious opening of one of the
closed containers he lost further interest into unsealing the
contents of the other canisters, the vile stench of whatever in-
habited the vessel he had chosen permuting the air so thoroughly that even Tey ceased his examination long enough to
deliver a reproachful look to the professor at the disruption.
He instead choose the wiser option of seeing what lay in the
room's only darkened exit, which lay open at the far side of
the room. A stone staircase descended down into the bowels

of the earth, with a damp and mildewed smell wafting on a chill breeze from the depths.

"Masi, I believe this man died from an attack from the jaxsa jamach'i. Look at the shape of his wounds, and how they match what we saw earlier happen to the llamas. This is bad, Mr. Rhodes. If the jaxsa jamach'i can get inside the temple from some other area we are in bigger trouble than we thought." The thought was a sobering one, with possible life-threatening consequences if the presumed safety of their sanctuary was merely an illusion that the dreadful terror birds could dispel at any moment. Forgoing descent into the subterranean regions under the building, the men agreed instead to investigate the other egress they had seen on the other end of the tremendous sanctum. The most likely way out should be on the upper floor they reasoned, and it could be the knowledge of an alternative exit may have been lost to the carnivorous beasts after so many centuries had elapsed since their savage atrocity in the staging room.

Returning to the unhallowed sanctuary, they both noticed the light coming from the ingenious skylights had greatly diminished from their initial exploration, the stark implication being that the night would soon be falling only adding to their growing list of insurmountable problems. The doorway to the rearmost entryway was in the same state of decomposing disrepute as the original one they had passed through from the antechamber earlier, the double doors slowly moldering into oblivion and scarcely functional any more. Alert now to the possible presence of the ghastly terror birds, they employed countermeasures against such a contingency, having Rhodes cover the entrance with his pistol while Tey stood with his back against the wall to the side of the doorway, who then slowly pushed the crumbling door open while maintaining a firm grip on his raised machete. This room had been equipped with the quartz skylights as well, at least making visibility not an issue for their inspection. Both breathed concerted sighs of relief on not spotting any sign of the dreaded creatures, but stayed vigilant in case appearances were not quite as they seemed.

The rectangular room was cluttered with bronze cages and stone tables loaded down a wide variety of items, such as large earthen pots, styled bulbous jars, sharp flint knives and strange implements that upon closer inspection seemed to have veritable multitude of bizarre uses, none that he was even remotely familiar with. Seeing the large cages and various tools as well as knowing what inhumane crimes had been performed within the temple, he speculated that this was some sort of torture chamber, a terrible place where blasphemers and enemies of the order learned the price of their disenfranchisement from the powerful priests. It was Tey that finally ascertained the inexplicable room's true purpose, after discovering three massive fireplaces along the western wall, two equipped with humongous cauldrons and the other with an empty, forked spit cunning devised with a short handle for rotating the meat. This was a vast kitchen, most likely used for preparing communal meals or perhaps for feeding the faithful during feast days, explaining the strange tools he had seen obviously being of a culinary nature. On a whim the professor shined his light within one of the blackened cauldrons, not truly expecting anything to be left inside the voluminous pot, and while the contents were mostly gone, telltale bones lay in a small cluster at the bottom. He looked more closely at the macabre heap, and was horrified to discover a human jaw intermixed between other bones he quickly recognized as tibias and femurs, as well as various other familiar body parts of man's derivation. His mind recoiled at the awful implication of the grim remains, that not only had the malevolent worshipers engaged in blood-soaked rituals of human sacrifice, but had been involved in cannibalistic banquets of such frequency that they had actually built a room wholly devoted to the preparation of their unwholesome delicacies.

His curiosity more than slaked with the morbid discovery, he moved to the rear of the kitchen, towards the closest egress from the morbid chamber of horrors. Tey soon rejoined him, having explored a small room on the eastern wall with its door halfway ajar. He reported that it had simply been a larder, but his haunted eyes spoke of seeing things in its stockpile he would rather had not seen. Rhodes did not press him for additional information on the subject, instead focusing on the task at hand. They operated the same as before, one man on alert while the other opened the decayed door, revealing a comparatively tiny chamber. The air was visibly warmer in this area, perhaps as much by as ten to fifteen degrees. It was free of obstruction, being empty of anything except for the prevalent dust coating the interior. A single exit led out of the room, and excitedly but in hushed tones Tey pointed to the pinpricks of pale light poking around the wooden door. They resolved to open it in their now routine fashion, and was rewarded by natural sunlight shining in from the outdoors, the familiar scene of the jungle's thick vegetation several yards away a joyous sight to both men.

While the hot, humid air and fading sunshine of the quickly vanishing evening was a relief after being trapped within the murky temple and its ominous dark past, they were wary to the possibility of the monstrous terror birds presence, studying the giant, overturned blocks of stone and foliage several yards away intently for any sign of the menacing creatures. Camouflaged predators could be lying in wait of the men, poised between the dappled patterns of leaves and shadows before delivering a savage offensive, so they scanned each possible hiding place with proper deliberation and diligence, leaving no potential danger to chance's fickle fortunes. Finding no indications of the avian threat, they quietly crept from the dubious safety of the entryway. The two men hunched over as they made their way forward, the relatively clear area nearest to the walls they needed to move past forcing them to almost crawl to take advantage of the limited cover it had to offer. Rhodes followed behind Tey, letting the more experienced man lead the direction of their exodus from the hellish sanctum. The tracker choose a northeastern route, making for the thinly wooded area that led farther away from the concealing boulders and blocks that might hold a devastating ambush of the terrifying monsters. They moved silently forward, and had crossed roughly half of the distance when Tey ceased his progress in front of the professor, his muscles tensing with trepidation as he spotted something amiss ahead. Rhodes looked around him to spot the source of the man's halted advance, and his heart leapt into his throat, seeing one of the dread birds peering back at him not even twenty yards distant, its black eyes filled with vicious intent on seeing its cringing quarry.

In situations such as this the prey have but two options: fight their way free from their tormentors or flee as quickly as possible from the scene of their possible demise. Tey made the choice for the two of them, rising to his feet and yelling to the professor to do the same, his normal broken English even more pronounced with his fear and terror.

"Masi, he has seen us! Sarana! Run!" The man exploded into a sprint towards the lightly forested section that had been their target. The terror bird squawked at the change in events, then began its own charge towards the men. Rhodes had but a split second to formulate his own response to the impending doom hurtling towards him, and he was unfortunately secure in the knowledge that the younger man could easily outdistance him on foot, with the probable outcome being that the pathfinder would, however unintentionally, leave the slower man behind for the bird to devour. He chose instead the quasi-safer choice of retreating back to the temple depths, turning around and bolting towards the doorway they had left open. Running as fast as he could, knowing that his very life depended on it, he reached the opening in seconds and continued on without stopping to check on the bird's decision of which morsel it wanted more, him or Tey. He shot into the gruesome kitchen, only slowing enough to avoid running into any of the grisly tables or malicious cages, not bothering to shut any of the doors behind him in his haste. Then the telltale sounds of the heavy footfalls of pursuit ringing on the stone floors reached his ears, and though he would have not thought it possible before, his alarm and anxiety reached an even greater pitch of fear-induced panic.

He ran with the burning fervor of self-preservation, the will to survive giving him an incredible endurance fueled by pure adrenaline and nightmarish fright, straight out of the kitchen and into the mammoth sanctuary, heading directly towards the unexplored cellar steps. The choice was one born of pure desperation, for he knew that he would not have enough time with the beast's uncanny speed to remove the barricades from the front doors to escape, and the decayed condition of the various other wooden doors in the building making them dubious at best in their assistance in impeding the horrifying creature's charge. As he barreled into the staging room he leapt over the dead priest's remains nimbly, then ripping his pack from his back in mid-stride, hunted feverishly for the flashlight he so urgently needed to find as quickly as possible. His hand felt various unwanted objects, then with huge relief he felt it close on the desired item. He threw the unnecessary pack behind him with an uncaring toss, thankfully lightening his load as he switched on the light. Rhodes bolted down into the darkness, the stone steps echoing hollowly from his frantic pace. He thought he heard the bird behind him in the previous room, and that was enough to continue his pell-mell descent in spite of the danger imposed by falling down the cold, hard steps. The air was sour with mildew and dankness, but he sucked in mouthful after mouthful without hesitation, trying to fuel his gasping lungs and pounding heart for more speed. Spotting the end of the long staircase ahead, he saw two arched wooden doors and outstretching his arms, shoved as he rushed forward, praying that the entry was not locked.

Mercifully open, he staggered through the opening, using the last reservoirs of his fading strength to slam the doors shut and brace himself against them, expecting the heart-stopping assault to come crashing at any moment behind him. But strangely it did not, not even after almost a full two minutes of tense waiting. The unexpected time allowed him to catch his breath and calm his elevated heart rate, and while he was not willing to take any chances with prematurely relinquishing his hold on the only thing between him and a monster from the mists of time that was intent on his demise, he knew he could not stay in this tentative position forever. Turning around and placing his back against the doors, he shined his flashlight around the dark surroundings, looking for anything to use as a barricade. Regrettably there was nothing at hand to fulfill that particular need anywhere in sight, seeing that the area was a vacant entryway, with the far side having a hallway that ran in both directions from it. That left him with a perilous choice, on whether to continue holding the doors against a threat that might not even be there anymore, or leave the entry unguarded while trying to find another egress. Both options seemed equally terrible, the literal definition of the proverbial rock and hard place. He chose the latter, but not before placing an ear against the wooden surface, listening carefully for any sign of stirring on the opposite side.

Once he was sufficiently certain nothing was amiss, he began slowly stepping backwards from the entrance, keeping his eyes riveted on the double doors, half-expecting them to burst open at any moment. As he continued to retreat, he noticed the ground beneath him began to be more unstable, tugging at his boots in a mire-like fashion. He took his eyes off the possible danger at the doorway momentarily, to glance downwards at grasping ground beneath his feet. He saw that it had indeed become a boggy mess, his footsteps leaving plainly visible tracks in the earthen floor, the hollows filling with a murky, brown water with each step. Looking back up at the doors for any sign of opening by the abhorrent threat he faced, he was thankful to see that it had remained closed during his small lapse of attention. He continued his escape, the corner of the wall to his right appearing in his peripheral vision as he walked backwards, and he slowly edged around it, until the doorway vanished from his sight. Turning sharply around then, he broke into a full-fledged run, tearing down the dark hallway, the mud fighting against his progress as he sought to find a safe haven from his unknown pursuers. Shut, rotted doorways, some reduced to merely openings appeared on the sides of the hallway, but he continued his fear-stricken blind running, not wanting to be caught by the ferocious creatures in the suffocating darkness under the temple, trapped in a room with no escape. Seeing an intersection, he briefly slowed, then turned right down it, before coming to another a minute later, choosing the leftmost route this time around, trying to confuse anything that may be following him. His pounding heart and labored breathing was drowning out any attempted warning he would be able to make out if the swift creature was indeed pursuing him, so he forced himself to slow his pace, trying to move more silently in the process through the slippery quagmire of a floor. After rounding yet another corner, he stopped his necessitated flight, straining his hearing, intent now to detect any audible sign of the fearsome animal tracking him down through the subterranean corridors. The only sound he could hear now was his own faint inhalations and exhalations, now returned to a more normal pattern from the brief respite from the exertion, so after a few more moments of observant rest, he resumed moving again, this time at a more unhurried, quiet walk.

As he walked he noticed the continuation of corroded

doors and the rotted remains of other such erections on either side of the long hallways, and he took time now to inspect the ruined interiors of the open rooms as he passed, looking for any solution to the current dilemma that was occupying his thoughts. Most rooms seemed to be devoted to sleeping and quartering, the remnants of beds and other domestic structures in moldy shambles and deserted spoilage. Some of the cots had blankets covering lumpy masses, and he did not stare too long at the unknown shapes, guessing perhaps too correctly at their explanation. Occasionally the odd storage room would appear as he delved deeper within the underground labyrinth, its space occupied with shelves, jars and vats, the contents no doubt having turned putrid and unusable in the centuries of languishment in their clay tombs. The subterranean complex was much bigger than he had thought possible earlier, so large that he was beginning to have difficulty remembering the way from where he had came from, the stony walls the same dark gray dinginess in every direction he looked, and the ground the same sludge-like mass at every step he took. Time seemed to have no meaning in the surreal surroundings, and he moved from hall to hall in a dreamlike state, with everything becoming increasingly harder to see clearly as he journeyed further into the abyssal depths. He wondered briefly if the unrelenting darkness was playing tricks on his mind, or if he was inhaling some sort of hazardous gas filling the moisture-laden passages. Finally he realized that his electric light was growing dimmer and dimmer as the last remainders of its power supply gradually dwindled away. His searching for an exit became more frantic, and as he wandered down the dark corridors, he finally succumbed to its disconcerting maze of long tunnels and directionless rooms, becoming wholly lost within its deep embrace. When the flashlight finally died, leaving him sightless in the tangled labyrinth, he bitterly cursed his lack of foresight in tossing away his pack with the spare batteries so callously. He was reduced to groping the darkness like a blind man, the claustrophobic walls pressing down on him at all sides, crushing him with their unseen weight.

Using only his sense of touch as a guide, he felt around the clammy walls, and made his way around a particularly sharp corner. There, like the first ray of dawn that cuts the night's gloom, he saw a sliver of light ahead, splitting a bright vertical line in the dark directly ahead. Elation soared through his tattered nerves, and he shuffled forward, struggling against the clinging mud, but the welcoming radiance guided him forward, until he was at last directly in front of the entrance. He reached out and fumblingly touched the doors, noticing they were cold and hard, with a smooth finish more reticent of metal than wood, before eventually finding embellished handles located on either side of the glowing stripe bisecting the doorway. He turned them together, and the doors parted easily, revealing a gargantuan cavern, immense beyond his wildest conceptions. There were steps hewn from the rock itself leading from his vantage point at the entryway down the middle of its length, with large landings interposed between sections of the long stairs. The voluminous sides to the staircase were open, but leveled off in descending segments parallel to the landings, each area continuing downwards to the rear of the cave. The ceiling and walls had been sanded down and decorated with a multitude of impressive paintings, all representing a common theme of dominance and fealty to the cruel god of the temple. Damage must have occurred in the subterranean hall at some point in its long history, for the glorious ceiling was cracked and even detached in several damaged patches, littering the once magnificent floors below with its strewn rubble. It represented nothing closer than an ancient amphitheater, such as the Theatre of Delphi used by the Greeks in their Apollon worship he had seen while researching there, or the early Minoan structure he had visited once in Phaistos.

All that paled in comparison, however, to the focal point to the enormous room, a gigantic mirror standing at the end of the colossal chamber. He could see now that the light that had guided him to the doorway and even now was illuminating the cavern was emanating from the mirror itself. As strangely as though it seemed it was calling to him, an irresistible pull that caused him to descend the stone staircase towards its large frame. As he drew closer he could see more detail in the mysterious object, and realized that there were large cracks in its surface, spider-webbing in random directions all over its reflective facade. The closer he came the stronger the unnatural attraction became, and with a start he knew that he had seen the portal before, in the cardinal drawings that Tey and himself had first discovered in the temple's antechamber what seemed a lifetime ago now. Pondering the relationship between the painting and the real-life article before him as he walked farther down the staircase, he made a startling connection, *that the view in the image had been from within the mirror looking out,* instead of the more natural reverse. Visualizing now that the large level sections to either side of him containing a vast number of parishioners praying and worshiping the enigmatic mirror, it was a prefect fit for what he had seen in the cardinal pictures.

He reached the bottom of the flight of steps, and hoisted himself up on to the platform cradling the extraordinary mirror. He could not explain it, but he was possessed with an innate need to feel the object, to have a physical connection between himself and its essence. Sidestepping the large hunks of fallen rock as he drew near to its shining surface, he raised his arms, palms outward facing, making contact with its glossy exterior lightly when the two touched. He had expected it to be warm to his caress, with the mysterious light pouring from its depths, but instead it was cold, almost to the point of being uncomfortable. He closed his eyes without even knowing he was doing so, his body taking actions now before his mind could comprehend the changes, and then he was no longer alone in his mind, feeling another presence touch him through the vast gulfs between each other. His soul seemed to burn with an unquenchable, icy fire as he melded with the otherworldly being, as if more power was being conducted through him than his insignificant mentality could absorb. The other entity, seeming to notice its undue effect on him, reined in its unchecked power to a more manageable level.

It showed more than it spoke, utilizing mental pictures to translate its thoughts to him, but it was more than that, he could relive the very memories of the individual he was connected to, and he learned its history and origin through the unusual linkage between them. He knew the name of the strange being was Bres, and he had been the ruler god of all of Ireland in the bygone ages of that country's cloaked past. But he had lost his kingdom, and after a final great battle between the Tuatha De Danann, his former subjects who had turned against him, and his supporters the Fomorians, twisted powerful giants that cared for nothing but pillage and slaughter, he failed in the attempt to reclaim his throne, and was driven from the island. He sailed far to the west, to a new land where the usurpers would never follow, and there found a new race of people to lead, the Nuktaw tribe. He taught them the ancient Celtic ways of worship, and accepted their gifts of devotion graciously, rewarding them with his knowledge of craftsmanship and warfare. They took eagerly to their new skills and new deity, enslaving their neighboring rivals, domesticating the jaxsa jamach'i, and building the great city to live in for perpetuity. They fashioned the magnificent temple complex in honor to their benefactor, using it for the sacred feasts and a center for conducting their holy rituals. When the time came for his great sleep that he needed to rejuvenate his weary, aged yet immortal body, they constructed the mystical portal to his specifications and vowed to protect it from harm while he slept. The preternatural glass allowed him to pass through the veil that separated the parallel universes between the normal earthly domain and the ageless Otherworld, a shadowy dimension where time and its endless entropy no longer existed, where Bres could gather his strength again before returning again to rule the Nuktaw and lead them to even greater heights of dominion. He rested in his silver throne, lulled by the faithful chanting and hallowed litanies of his fanatical followers, nevertheless still able in his solitary slumber to help his chosen people by exuding his strength and influence through the portal's facet.

But then the unthinkable happened, an earthquake of such magnitude it toppled buildings in the great city, shattered the laborious network of roads, and killed many of his followers with its deadly tremors. Much worse than that, however, it cracked the enchanted mirror's face in the process, and the portal turned to a cage, imprisoning him within, its fractures becoming solid bars to his power and reentry into the mortal world. He was forced to do nothing but watch as his people prayed to him for deliverance, needing his guidance more than ever in their darkest hour while he was helpless to intervene. They tried on their own to rebuild the broken city, and maintain their hold on their fallen empire, tire-lessly pushing themselves and the jaxsa jamach'i to the utmost limits of endurance. The lethal creatures rebelled against the tyrannical treatment, no longer having their training reinforced by the god's charming power to stop them from rising against their rulers. The terrible raptors ran rampant, slaughtering their former masters and their ilk, until nothing that was human survived within miles of the ruined capital. They claimed the region as their own, the territory so hotly contested by the beasts that even other tribes left the close vicinity, not willing to live anywhere near the formidable monsters and the ruins left by their insurrection. Bres was left alone in his never-changing prison, and while time and its entropic effects had no sway over the other world, he could see through the portal the change of the world he longed to return to. With nothing to do but wait for his release he began probing the walls of his confinement relentlessly, learning after years passed in the mortal realm more and more ways to circumvent the damaged threshold. He began to exercise his power in the smallest increments to descendants of the jaxsa jamach'i, slowly influencing their actions over time. The changes were in small ways at first, a nudge in an unfavorable direction, or a simple adjustment while the beasts made their uncanny calls. Unfortunately he discovered that his control was incontrovertibly linked to his target's proximity to the shattered mirror, therefore being limited to only the closest of the creatures at first, but later his range increased, little by little adding to his influence's distance. He had found each succeeding generation to more susceptible than the previous one, the will to resist being eroded slowly by his constant efforts to tame the atrocious monsters.

The jungle claimed the beautiful city with the passing centuries, but the jaxsa jamach'i stayed on, becoming his eyes and ears in the earthly plane. He could command the creatures miles from the temple's epicenter now, using them to scout the surrounding areas for the key to ending his solitary confinement. He had all the time in the cosmos to find the answer to his dilemma, but the solution was compounded by the very source of his voyeuristic escape from his enduring prison. He could control one terror bird at a time, no more, and while he could easily leave one animal and move to another quickly, the fiercely territorial creatures were highly efficient killing machines, and trying to quell their bloodlust was well-nigh impossible at times. For what the trapped god needed was help from a more intellectual source, the only being in the earthly sphere that could reason, create, and implement the remedy to his quandary, the fabrication of a new mirror, *but the accursed birds murdered or drove away every single human that crossed into their chosen province!* The extremely competent predators had built such a reputation for themselves that soon the indigenous peoples had seldom strayed into the jaxsa jamach'i's selected boundaries, and when they did as soon as they heard the animal's peculiar call it gave them ample reason to depart once again. In such remote surroundings even when the conquistadors and other explorers, unfamiliar with the blighted area's storied history, had penetrated into the region's inner nucleus, they were either persuaded by their native guides or the rampant attacks of the terror birds to leave. Indeed the last time any traveler had crossed the neighboring lands it had been almost a century earlier, before Rhodes had specifically come looking for Bres's forgotten temple.

Bres showed Rhodes his unique view of the professor's journey, captured in breathtaking detail by the large female bird that the god had found the easiest of all his subjects to manage, a fortunate accident perhaps caused by his endless manipulation. The creature was the dominant matriarch of one of the largest packs, and in being so made Bres the true ruler of the jaxsa jamach'i roost. Rhodes saw everything the animal saw, from the first captivating night Rhodes had heard the creature's soft booming to the hectic chase down the stairs to where the mysterious portal lay. It was strange looking at his own events and actions through the eyes of another, and his mind fairly swam with the fantastic imagery he was being subjected too, almost overpowering with its insidious nervous tension. He could feel the god's need for escape as hotly as if it was his own, and then furthermore the deity made offerings to him, of every worldly pleasure and vice that he would bestow if Rhodes was only willing to be its advocate, showing him riches, women, and glory beyond measure within the mental bond between the two. The man saw everything he could want or aspire to being freely given in exchange for his help, but within the depths of his keen scientific mind came a simple question, one that he could feel the divine being's helpless rage and frustration over his very asking. Why couldn't the exiled god, with all his amazing powers, simply force Rhodes to do his bidding? The venom at the plain query coming through the connection was shocking in its intensity, and while the answer was not altogether clear in its picturesque translation, the root of it was. The divinity could not usurp the mortal man's mind because it was almost impossible for him to do so, the human brain being far too complex for the god to contort and manipulate directly in spite of his repeated success with other lesser creatures' more simplistic, more basic intellects.

This led the professor to several further queries, his scientific curiosity piqued, unbidden thoughts that the link shared whether he wanted to or not, and he could feel the other being's anger growing even more blistering at their unintentional blasphemy. What was the other realm like? Why did Bres need to sleep to recharge his immortal body? Why the nauseating rituals of sacrifice and cannibalism? What purpose did they serve? Dozens of questions peppered the god from the learned man's inquisitive mind, and Bres did not understanding the endless questioning and interrogation from the scholarly researcher, for he had grown complacent and unpracticed from his years of dealing with dumb animals and before that his own uneducated, fanatical followers. He was ill-equipped to deal with what he believed to be disobedience and contempt, for in his one-dimensional viewpoint it was the god's place to rule mankind and theirs to be rewarded to doing so. That was the way it had always been with the mortals, easily manipulated with the promise of fulfilling their base desires, but the human before him was strangely different from any mortal Bres had encountered in his long lifetime, seemingly uninterested in any reward that he had to offer, and heretically treating him as an equal, demanding to know the hidden answers to cosmos that the gods themselves should only know. Each mounting expression from Rhodes he considered a further challenge to his authority, a personal affront of the highest magnitude, and his rage burned hotter and hotter at what he perceived to be the professor's insolence, until at last he could take it no longer. Devoured by his own towering inferno of wrath and indignation, he attempted the endeavor that he had told the man could not be easily done, to forcibly compel him to do his bidding. He sent coiled psychic tendrils into the man's awareness, looking for cracks in his psychological resistance, trying to tear away his ego, to replace him with a more compliant, accommodating version of himself.

Rhodes could feel the mental assault attacking the very fibers of his cohesive thoughts, seeking to warp and change the formulated arrangements in his mind into more susceptible patterns. He rebelled against the forced intrusion into his psyche, refusing to submit to the monstrous god's dominating will, trying to force himself to awake from the telepathic link. He pushed back, thought versus thought, but the deity's strength was like iron, and he felt like a child trying to wrestle a grown man, ineffectual and laughable in his efforts. The invasion of his mind hurt physically, and he could feel synapses severing as the god ran rampant through his battered brain. His head felt as if it was in a vice, being crushed and strained into uncompromising forms. Frantically differing tactics, he struggled with an uncompromising resolve, attempting in other ways to vanquish the being from his mind. He tried counterattacking, to probe the aggressive mind even as it battered his, but quickly desisted that line of resistance when there was no perceptible reprieve from the inexorable psychological violence. In his despair he tried multiple avenues of escape, including reciting passages of memorized literature, quoting lines from Tennyson's poems and snatches of Hawthorne's *The Minister's Black Veil.* He switched to performing mathematical catechisms, computing the arrangements of column heights in the Temple of Delphi and the years elapsed between the Egyptian dynasties. Finally Rhodes even projected positive thoughts of goodwill and compassion to no avail.

Fighting back as hard as he could, he tried a different approach, conjuring visions of disrespect and loss in his mind, sending derisory pictures of the god shrunk to the size of a bug and being squashed beneath Rhodes's boot, then another representation of Bres perpetually locked in the Otherworld, never to return to man's world as he so dearly wished. The god howled at the impertinence of the images, and Rhodes began to feel his overpowering grip weakening, his hold on the man's consciousness shrinking away as he was distracted by the agony and aversion of the loathsome portrayals. Rhodes pushed harder, going on the offensive, sending every contemptuous concept he could think of like daggers at the intruding mind until at last he was released of the deity's control. Finally he was able to yank his hands free from their contact on the fractured mirror and step back from its malefic persuasion. As he stumbled backwards from the shock of what had transpired he stepped on one of the collapsed ceiling stones scattered across the floor, and his fear and ire at the scathing indignity, the horrific distress at what had almost occurred, the very near loss of his free will surged forth in cascading torrent of emotion. Snatching up one of the heavy rocks he screamed at the glowing portal, his voice rising in pitch as he vented his pent-up rage at the affront.

"You wish to control me? Me, who has made it his life's work to find you! I am a human being, not some dog to play fetch, nor some ignorant savage to bow down before the likes of you at some pretty words! I am a scientist, not an animal, *a man, and I can destroy you!*" He heaved the stone with deadly accuracy into the mirror's face, finishing the job the earthquake had begun centuries earlier. The missile shattered the already splintered glass, and a million cracks spider-webbed out from its damaging radius, the harsh tinkle of fallen shards hitting the ground below. He fetched more projectiles, lobbing them without letting up at the smashed, otherworldly threshold until most of it lay on the floor, the pieces losing their incandescent radiance, slowly plummeting the room in darkness as they did so. Turning around quickly, he ran back up the staircase, scrabbling on his hands and knees in some places in his haste to exit the depraved chamber. Finding the doors, he struggled with them momentarily until they opened at last, allowing him to flee into the darkened hallway.

He slogged through the mucky passageways, feeling his way painstakingly through the desolate halls as he went. He longed for lighting, a torch, anything to pierce the shrouded blackness, but he knew even if such an opportunity presented itself he had nothing on his person to create fire, the boon would be useless in his ill-equipped state. His only thoughts now needed to be of survival, but the traumatizing recent events coupled with his wearied body quickly deteriorated his rational thinking, and he stumbled around the warren of burrows with in a fruitless stupor, unable to realize in his blindness and delirium if he was going in circles or following the proper course. After what seemed like hours of futile, painstaking searching for a way out of the underground labyrinth, and now thoroughly exhausted by his ordeals, he was forced to succumb to rest, thankfully finding a small, fairly dry storage room with its decayed door mostly intact to shut behind him as he slept. When he awoke he felt it was but a short time later, but he felt vastly refreshed by the quick nap, and anxious to continue on his journey, now able to function at a higher capacity. He attacked the relentless plodding with a newly inspired vigor, refusing to give in to the crushing weight of despair. Several times he was forced to backtrack while he traveled, once retreating when the water level reached his thighs before he thought the better of that particular chosen direction, as well as a few mistakes in judgment that had led him erroneously to large rooms instead of the corridor spaces he sought. The abysmal darkness was absolute in its midnight cover, and with not even the tiniest of light sources present there was no way for his eyes to adjust to its ever present, overpowering gloom. The silence of the dead temple was equally oppressive, the quietness so complete that his mind began to play tricks on him with its lack of noise, making him hear make-believe half-whispers and faint footfalls around him as he struggled through the mire. Twice he stopped his never ending progress, so convinced by the auditory hallucinations that he waited with stilled breathing, anxious to discover if he was in fact being followed or possibly walking into an ambush. The only sound in the shadowed realm was his own thudding heartbeat in both anti-climatic episodes, and he sheepishly returned to his task at hand after the pointless distractions.

He noticed the unexpected warm breeze immediately when it came softly billowing down the hall, the humid air a relief after the cold, dead atmosphere of the waterlogged passages below. Excited by the possible escape from the black depths, he hurried forward, and was rewarded by the ever so small lifting of the preternatural gloom, the tiniest of light filtering into his eagerly receptive eyes with all the satisfaction of a dying man in a desert finding an oasis. Soon he could continue forward unaided by his groping hands, with the illumination providing his vision just enough light to walk independently of his other senses. The tunnel grew brighter and brighter, until finally he could see the brilliant moonlight pouring into the hallway ahead, the way miraculously clear of obstruction. Quickening his already rapid rate even more so, he ran down the corridor, all thought focused on the sweet release from the temple's tomb-like ambiance he had been trapped in for so long.

Then he heard it. A familiar sound, the soft booming of a terror bird's haunting call, and his heart sank at its horrific tidings, knowing now that his exodus from the subterranean depths would be compounded by this additional threat. He paused his movement, hoping against hope that the animal would leave off from its present course, but the infernal sound regrettably came closer and closer, until an inquisitive plumed head appeared in what was supposed to be his salvation, cocking back and forth as it investigated the tunnel. He tried to will his heart to slow, to stop its thunderous beating within his chest, but the traitorous organ refused, seeming to cry out in sickening alacrity to the bird as it stepped fully into the passage. Then he saw another avian, and then another, and even though he knew it was most likely pointless, he raised the Colt one final time and squeezed off the last four shots, trying to make them count, placing two of his shots at the most forward of the advancing creatures, and then the other two at the one right behind the his first target. The roar of the gun was resounding in the cramped confines, and while the monstrous beasts seemed ruffled by the unexpected noise and stinging projectiles, it did nothing to deter their momentum, indeed accelerating as they ran towards him, eager to devour his succulent flesh.

Unarmed and helpless now before their superior evolutionary prowess, he turned and fled from the prehistoric menace, running back down the mud-filled hallway he had already came. His mind was nearly racing as quickly as his feet, wondering at the untimely appearance of the animals. Had they been waiting, perhaps at the final command of their vanquished master? Or had it simply been coincidence, a pack of the predators that had been merely wandering by and happened to find him? As he attempted to escape with his life, forgotten things were remembered, that his dreams of the previous nights had been haunted by this very situation, and the seemingly predestined assuredness of his plight shattered his last vestiges of sanity. When the hammering blow on his unprotected back struck, he did not know whether to laugh at his ironic predicament or cry out at his misfortunate luck.

****

Tey looked back one final time from his viewpoint atop of the mountain pass overshadowing the valley leading to the falls. It had been a grueling escape, one that had even tasked his substantial skills. He had genuinely liked the professor, but after the two had split up following the deadly creature's attack he had noticed the jaxsa jamach'i had pursued Rhodes persistently, and while the man had paid well for Tey's services, it was not good enough for the tracker to risk life and limb in a disastrous rescue attempt. He had thought briefly about looping around to their campsite to retrieve some of the provisions and perhaps seeing what could be done, but quickly discarded the foolhardy notion, not worth the possible jeopardy involved with the inane proposition. It had seemed almost as if the creatures were ignoring him as long as he was leaving the vicinity, some even passing him by at one point in his escape only a scant few hundred yards away from his location, seemingly focused on congregating around the sacrilegious temple. The professor was doomed, and it was as Tey had warned him, he should have listened to the guide's dire explanations of the meaning of the jaxsa jamach'i and the portent it had held for the man. He would be alive now if he had, Tey pensively reflected, or perhaps it had been his damned fate all along, only the gods knew for certain. Bringing his thoughts back to more immediate concerns, he knew the journey back home would not be pleasant, and would force him to use all his survivorship expertise to its fullest extent. But he would be alive, and when he returned if any foolish man ever sought to find the unhallowed sanctum again he would not do it with Tey's help. There are places in this world better left undisturbed, lost for all time.

About the Author: Jon Ring lives in Helena, Montana with his wife Honey, his three sons Jack, Henry, and Wyatt, along with various pets his family forces him to abide with. He is owner of the White Knight Games & Hobbies with his brother Joel Ring and can be found regularly there even in his off time, rolling dice and recreating historical battles with miniature armies. And he reads, alot.

About the Illustrator: Vinessa Sanford lives in Helena, Montana with her service dog Jack at her family's equestrian center, working as an artist and illustrator. She is currently studying at the Helena College of Technology to further herself and her art career.